BLAKEWELL MAGES BOOK TWO

GHOST CURSE

BRITTANY ARDEN

Veritas University
Airport
NEW TOWN
McDara's apartment
Motel
The Obsidian Quill
OLD TOWN
Police Station
The Black House
BLAKEWELL

Contents

For the readers who fall for the bad boy
and don't mind heroines who make questionable decisions about him.

1

The cold always found its way in.

Not in the literal sense—though the Black House, for all its sleek, mirrored grandeur, carried the chill of a mausoleum. But deeper. Beneath skin. Beneath memory. In the brittle quiet between footfalls. In the breath I held walking past curtain-shadowed glass, wondering how many watched from behind.

Two weeks since McDara had collapsed.

Two weeks since I'd seen his face inside a hospital ward.

Two weeks of silence.

He didn't want visitors. Not even me.

I'd begged off starting my training because of him. Told the Matron I needed time. That McDara needed me. I'd believed—stupidly—that if I just waited, if I stayed still long enough, things would right themselves.

It hadn't gone the way I planned.

And now I couldn't stall anymore.

Not that I needed to.

Two weeks was enough time to sit with the truth of it. Enough time to feel the weight of the curse settle into my bones. Enough time to understand that wanting things to stop didn't make them stop—and wanting to save someone else didn't mean I could ignore myself.

If I was going to survive this, I needed to act. But gods, was it hard to drag myself out of his apartment today. I wanted so badly to call the hospital and tell him that my training was starting today but Dom was clear. He didn't want visitors from anyone.

I told myself he just needed time. Healing. Space to breathe. That it wasn't personal. That the way he'd looked at me—right before everything broke—hadn't changed.

But I was starting to feel like maybe *I* had changed. Or maybe the space we'd carved together couldn't hold its shape now that real magic and real curses and real deaths had started to squeeze around the edges.

McDara's sister had been consumed by dark magic. Not just a victim—*the* Malifax Mage. The one who'd crossed a line so sharp it carved her apart from the inside out. I still remember the way he'd looked that night in the hospital, when he finally let himself fall apart in front of me—like he was drowning in guilt, in grief, in a thousand things he couldn't put words to.

And I had left. Not out of cruelty. Not because I didn't care.

But because I'd just learned I was cursed. That on my twenty-fifth birthday—if the Black House legends were true—I would die. Just like every other Whisperer in my family born before me.

It was all too much.

Too much death. Too many impossible choices.

And I hadn't known how to help him grieve when I was breaking open from the inside myself.

Still, a part of me kept wondering if I should have done more.

Stayed. Sat beside him. Offered something, *anything*, even if I was breaking open.

He'd just lost his sister—to the kind of dark magic that didn't just kill, but devoured. And McDara had watched her unravel from the inside out.

And I had left him. I told myself I needed space. That learning about the bloodline curse was too much. That I couldn't breathe, let alone help someone else grieve.

But maybe if I'd held on just a little longer.

Maybe if I'd waited to fall apart—until *after* I'd helped him hold his pieces together—

Maybe he wouldn't have told the hospital he didn't want visitors.

Maybe he wouldn't have shut me out.

I didn't know if I'd failed him or just confirmed something he already believed:

That people leave.

That even the ones who say they care won't stay when it matters most.

And gods, what if he was right?

The Black House loomed before me—tall and gleaming, all razor-glass angles and reflections that fractured the street into jagged shards. I hated that I could see myself in its walls. That I looked like someone pretending not to be afraid.

A soft shhhkt came as the front doors opened without touch.

The air inside was still, tinted slightly lavender from the curtains draped like funeral veils over the outer glass. Somewhere behind them, New Town buzzed on in its clean, ordered chaos—but here, in the belly of the House, sound dropped dead.

And still, I walked in.

Matron Black met me near the stairwell without so much as a nod of greeting. Her hair, silver-white and twisted into a crown of braids, gleamed under the hallway sconces. She turned without a word and began walking.

No small talk. No welcome. Just the soft sound of her heels on the marble-tiled floor and the weight of her presence in the air, like frost spreading over glass.

"I assume you know what today will entail," she said, not looking back.

"To begin training," I answered, matching her clipped pace. "Basic Magecraft."

She hummed—a sound that might've meant agreement, might've meant doubt. I couldn't tell.

We passed two closed doors and a mirrored hallway that reflected our movement like ghost doubles. I didn't ask questions. Not about where we were going. Not about what exactly basic Magecraft *was*. Not about how many people in this House already knew I was cursed.

I didn't know who was safe to ask anymore.

Calypso had always seemed...kind. Guarded, sure, but in the way that said *I've learned to be careful*, not *I'm hiding something from you*. But her twin?

Pandora's smiles cut like blades.

Some days she looked at me like she was curious.

Other days like she was just waiting for me to crack.

If Calypso was the storm wrapped in velvet, Pandora was the lull before lightning struck. I couldn't tell if she wanted me here. Or wanted me gone.

And McDara—

No. I wasn't going to think about him. Not here. Not now.

Being in Matron Black's presence meant I had to be on my guard. Any weakness, even thinking about his dark, brooding stare, would be too much of a risk.

This was a house of wolves, and I was a sheep desperately looking for a weapon.

We turned down a staircase of sleek concrete and steel. The air grew colder, sharper, as we descended. I counted the steps without meaning to—twelve, twenty-two, thirty-six—until the walls turned white and the glass was gone entirely.

This was the underbelly.

It reminded me of the hospital.

Too clean. Too still.

Like they'd scrubbed the humanity out of it.

The hallway ended in a matte white door with no visible handle. The Matron placed her palm against a panel beside it, and the wall whispered open.

Inside: bright lights, seamless walls, sigil pulsing faintly over a mirrored floor. A few others were already here, dressed in dark training uniforms marked with the House sigil—obsidian flame on silver thread. They turned to look at me as I stepped in.

None of them smiled.

One boy—tall, freckled, hair like spun copper—whispered something to the girl beside him. She smirked. A third Mage, standing near the mirrored wall, openly assessed me with flat eyes and folded arms.

I didn't recognize any of them.

And clearly, they knew who *I* was.

Matron Black didn't address them. She just turned to me and said, "You'll begin here. Even though today is foundational, I do hope, Sonia, that you pay attention. If you build your skills on unsteady ground, we will both be disappointed. You'll be observed."

Then she left.

No warning. No instructions. Just the sound of the door closing like a verdict behind her.

I was alone. In a House that wanted something unknown from me. With a curse I still didn't understand. And a name I wasn't sure I wanted—Ghost Whisperer.

The others watched. Waiting.

I stepped forward anyway.

The shadows didn't whisper here. They waited.

The room was too white. Too clean. A place where magic was supposed to be ordered, not felt. Like a laboratory of secrets that hadn't been uncovered yet.

I stood near the back as the other novices settled into a loose semi-circle. Most looked to be between fourteen and sixteen, still soft around the edges, skin flushed with the stubborn kind of youth that thought magic made them powerful instead of vulnerable. No one spoke to me.

The trainer entered from a side door—tall, sharp-lined, with storm-gray eyes and the expression of someone who expected to be disappointed.

"Form up."

The others straightened. I followed late, earning a flicker of annoyance in the trainer's eyes.

"I'm Elion. You will address me as Instructor Elion. You're here because you've been accepted into the Black House training program. That means you will learn to wield your magic the Black House way. If that is unacceptable to you, you're welcome to walk into the street and try to join up with another Mage House, but be assured they are lesser. Any training you will receive will allow you the ability to wield a quarter of your power."

A few of the younger ones stiffened. The redhead beside me snorted quietly.

Most of the others were holding something in their hands—strings of stone or bone beads etched with sigils, like a rosary reimagined for magic. Each student seemed to move their thumb along a specific bead in rhythm, almost unconsciously, like they'd done it a hundred times before.

I didn't have one.

I leaned toward the redhead beside me. "Where do I get one of those?" I kept my voice low, almost a whisper.

Her eyes flicked to mine, then to Elion, sharp with warning. "Don't talk right now," she muttered. "Just...trust me."

The heat of embarrassment crawled up my neck. I straightened, wishing I hadn't asked.

Elion's gaze snapped to me.

"Well, that didn't take long," he said. "Your first Black House class and you can't even stay quiet long enough to hear the rules."

A few of the students shifted uncomfortably.

Elion didn't pause. "I don't know why the Matron would waste her time—or mine—on a ticking clock."

The words hit harder than I expected. Not because they weren't true. But because they were delivered like I was a defective weapon someone had dragged into a war. And the fact that my apparent teacher knew about my curse and was commenting on it in front of the whole freaking class.

"Don't be a disappointment," he said, voice cold. "Take your training seriously. An untrained Ghost Whisperer is dangerous to everyone in this room."

The silence that followed cracked like frost across my skin.

I kept my expression still, even as my fingers curled against my thighs. I didn't know what to say. What *could* I say? He wasn't wrong—not exactly.

But how did he know about the curse?

Had Matron Black told him? Had she told *everyone*?

Or was the fate of Ghost Whisperers common knowledge in the Mage world? Some dark bedtime story passed around Houses like a warning: we always die at twenty-five. Did that happen to all Ghost Whisperers or just my family line?

Was that the fate of every single one of us?

I clenched my jaw tighter. I wasn't going to fall apart in front of them. Not here. Not now.

But bless the Wood, I wanted to show him what dangerous *really* meant.

He stepped toward the center of the mirrored floor and motioned for us to sit in a circle.

"Lesson one. Every Mage has a core. Your thread. Your source. It exists below the sternum and above the navel—where your life force anchors your magic. Today, we begin by finding it."

I knelt slowly, crossing my legs. The floor was cold beneath me.

"Close your eyes."

I did.

"Breathe in through your nose. Out through your mouth. Let the rhythm settle. Slow. Controlled."

In. Out.

The words felt familiar. The cadence of them, too.

McDara had walked me through something like this once—weeks ago, when the world had still felt like something we might survive together. He sat beside me, voice low and steady, guiding me as I tried to find the place where my magic lived. I'd been terrified then, too. But not like this. Not alone in a glass cage under judgment.

I missed him. The quiet steadiness. The way he'd said my name like it meant something.

My mind wandered. I let it.

I followed the thread of memory like a current and landed back in the Deathscape.

The red sand. The silver sky. The river of black fire.

Him.

Death had stood before me like a secret I wasn't meant to find. Ancient. Cold. Beautiful in a way that made no sense.

My entire body flushed.

The air around me changed—just slightly. Like something pulsed beneath my skin.

My magic stirred.

Not the thread Elion wanted.

Not the steady line of a well-trained Mage.

But something older. Wilder. Bound to grief. To longing.

I drew in a sharp breath.

And felt the moment it slipped away.

Something else took its place.

The atmosphere shifted. Subtle but suffocating. Like the light dimmed—though the overheads hadn't changed.

I kept my eyes closed. But I wasn't alone anymore.

A cool breath slid just behind my ear.

"Did you call for me, Little Bird?"

My eyes flew open.

Elion's voice cut the air. "Focus, Whisperer."

I jerked, looking just over my shoulder, breath tight in my throat.

Standing behind me—where no one else looked—was *him.*

Death.

He didn't touch me. Couldn't, not here. Not in the Living Lands.

But his presence coiled through mine like smoke curling into lungs. Every hair on my arms lifted. My heart kicked against my ribs.

He leaned forward again, close enough that I swore I felt the brush of his voice against my cheek.

"I'll find you after you're done playing Mage."

"Sonia." Elion's tone had sharpened. "You will *not* bring your distractions into this space. If you cannot control your focus, you will be removed."

I didn't answer. I was still staring at Death.

He flicked a look toward Elion—razor-edged, pitiless.

Then he turned back to me, and smiled. "Fragile minds pretending to be masters. And they look at *you* like you're the monster."

"Sonia," someone whispered. I turned—slowly—to see a younger novice watching me, wariness in her eyes. "Are you...are you seeing a ghost?"

Every gaze in the circle was on me now. Like they were waiting for me to explode.

Like I was already the punchline to a tragedy they hadn't finished writing.

And maybe I was.

But I still had teeth.

I smiled—slow, sweet, sharp at the edges.

"I see Death," I said. "He says hi."

Death's low laugh bloomed across my spine like a hand made of silk and ash.

The air still felt scorched by his presence, even as he disappeared.

But no one else reacted. Only me.

The others just watched, waiting to see what I would do next.

Waiting to see if I would break.

Elion's voice snapped like a blade through glass. "Enough."

He clapped his hands once—sharply—and the energy in the room shifted again. The others turned away, murmuring quietly as they returned to their seats. I followed, slow, like moving through water. Death was gone.

But my skin still felt the echo of him.

We spent the next half hour repeating the centering exercises. Breathing. Visualizing. Controlling. I did what I could to mimic the others, to fake stillness where I felt nothing but static and pressure. I didn't find a core. I didn't find anything that felt like what Elion had described. Only a vague hum that built with each attempt to suppress what wanted to rise.

The hum grew louder.

Then came the pull.

It wasn't the sharp, hungering tether of the Deathscape—not the windless drop that tried to suck me under every time I got too close to that realm. This was something else. Cooler. Familiar.

Ghosts.

The connection unfurled before I could stop it. I reached for stability. Tried so hard to stay away from the dark, twisting thread of the Deathscape that I plucked at the only other one my magic had found. And it was frozen.

A blast of cold roared through the room.

The lights overhead flickered once—then again, stuttering like a dying breath before plunging the room into sudden darkness.

Someone gasped. Another swore.

Then came the chill.

A biting cold rolled through the room, unnatural and immediate, sinking into bone. Frost skittered across the floor in veins of silver-blue, webbing out from my feet like a spider's web catching fire in reverse.

Screams rose. A chair clattered over.

"S-something touched me—"

"I can't see!"

"Why does the air feel like—"

I was standing now. Couldn't remember rising.

Ghosts swarmed the chamber. Some were no more than blurs of motion and cold. Others hovered in jagged outlines—soldiers, students, figures cloaked in shadow or fire or ash. A figure stepped out of the haze—slow, halting, her gait wrong in a way that prickled beneath my skin. Each step dragged, as if her bones didn't quite remember how to belong to her body. Her dress hung in tatters, colorless in the dim light.

When she lifted her head, my breath caught.

There was no face.

Where eyes, mouth, and nose should have been was only a pale smear, as though someone had reached into her skin and *wiped her clean of herself.* The edges of that absence shimmered faintly, bleeding light like the surface of disturbed water.

The woman tilted her head as if trying to *see* me, but there were no eyes to find me with. Her hands trembled in front of her, reaching, fumbling, the motion jerky and desperate.

A low, broken sound escaped her—part moan, part breath—the echo of a voice that had been erased.

And though she was terrifying, I couldn't look away. Because beneath the horror, there was something heartbreakingly human in the way the faceless woman kept reaching forward—like she still remembered what it meant to *want* to be seen.

I tried to breathe, to reel it back. To will the door shut.

Nothing.

"Elion—" someone shouted.

But Elion was already there, in front of me, grabbing my shoulders so hard it sent pain lancing down my arms. "Snap out of it, Byrd!"

I blinked. The ghosts flickered. The cold burned deeper.

"Now."

I closed my eyes. Pushed—not toward the Deathscape, not toward that hungry dark—but toward that frozen thread. My own magic.

Go.

The word wasn't said aloud. It was shaped in thought, in feeling, in command.

The ghosts obeyed.

They vanished with a hiss and a crack, like glass snapping under pressure.

The lights surged back on. The frost remained, glittering on the floor and clinging to the walls like veins of ice. Every student stared at me.

Elion's hands dropped away.

My breath sawed in and out of my lungs. My body trembled. But I was still standing.

Barely.

Elion dismissed the group with a flat, "You're done for the day."

Then he looked at me. "Stay."

The others filed out. One girl cast a glance over her shoulder, eyes wild and steps hurried.

When the room was empty, Elion gestured toward the hall. "With me."

I followed him up the stairs, past the violet-curtained glass and into the colder, older bones of the House. The floors creaked in places. And then we reached the door at the end of the hall—the one I'd been inside before—when Matron Black accused me of murder and McDara had to drag me out.

He knocked. Waited, looking like a man about to make a foolish decision. In this case, it would be throwing open the office door and storming inside.

Seconds ticked by, and then the door cracked open on its own.

Matron Black was waiting at her desk, fingers steepled, back lit by pale Magelight on the wall behind her.

"She's undisciplined," Elion said without preamble. "She undermined the lesson. Refused to follow direction. She deliberately scared the other students. She called ghosts into the damn class!"

Matron Black didn't blink. "She's new at using her magic."

"She's unstable."

"She's also the only Ghost Whisperer we've had access to in a generation." Her voice stayed calm. Cold. "If you can't handle that, Elion, I'll find someone who can."

He stiffened but didn't argue. After a beat, he gave a shallow bow and left.

The door clicked softly shut behind him.

The room went silent.

I stood in it.

Alone.

I really wished I'd let Phontine come with me today. She'd begged to come. I'd said no, thinking it would be safer for her to stay away, that I'd be fine.

I wasn't fine.

Matron Black finally looked at me. Her gaze was colder than Elion's ever could be.

She didn't need to shout. She was the kind of person who *unraveled* you with a whisper.

"You made a spectacle today," she said.

"I didn't mean—"

"No. You didn't. And that's precisely the problem."

I swallowed the words I wanted to say. That I hadn't asked for this. That I was trying. That maybe the reason my magic didn't respond like theirs was because it wasn't like theirs. Sometimes it felt like I wasn't a Mage at all.

But I said none of it. I needed the training she had promised me. If there was any hope of me finding a way not to succumb to the bloodline curse unraveling my very life, then I needed to understand my magic and be able to *use* it.

Matron Black rose from her chair, crossing the room slowly.

"You want advanced training," she said. "Ghost Whisperer specific training. Do you think that comes without cost?"

My hands tightened at my sides.

"You will comply," she continued. "With the instructors. With the methods. With the rules. Or you won't get what you need, Sonia."

I nodded. Because there was nothing else to do.

Because I was desperate.

Because I didn't know how to survive what was coming without it.

"Good," she said, turning away.

Dismissed. Like I was just another lesson that hadn't stuck.

I left the room with my jaw locked and my pulse echoing in my ears.

2

Somewhere behind me, the House was still watching.

I didn't hear footsteps. Didn't hear voices. But I could feel it. That weight pressing behind the glass walls—the press of polished floors and unsaid judgments, held together by spells, spite, and perfect posture.

I took the long way out.

There were too many Mages in the front hall murmuring behind mirrored cups and judgment-thin smiles. I didn't want to pass through them. Didn't want to see who would whisper or who would pretend not to see me at all.

So, I doubled back. Through the narrow corridor that led toward the back of the House. The hallway walls were ordinary here—no glass, no shine. Just white paint and dull sconces and the ghost of footsteps that had walked this same route for decades.

The moment I stepped into the back courtyard, the air shifted.

Cooler. Quieter. Sharp with the faint scent of lavender and ozone.

Training grounds stretched beyond the exit—flat, slate-tiled space cut with ward circles and impact pits, the kind of terrain meant for Mages who didn't need to be coddled. Beyond that, a massive greenhouse rose like a crystal lung breathing in the afternoon light.

It glowed faintly. Not just from the sun.

Something inside pulsed—slow and living and wrong.

I didn't know what they were growing in there, but the plants leaned too perfectly toward the glass. Too aware.

Even the shadows around it didn't fall quite right.

A faint rustle of footsteps behind me broke the trance.

"Sneaking out through the back?" Calypso's voice was light, but not unkind.

I turned. She wore her usual soft layers—flowing cream sleeves, gold thread catching the light. Her black, curly hair was half up, a pen stabbed through the knot like she'd gotten bored halfway through fixing it.

"Not sneaking," I said. "Just...avoiding."

She didn't ask who. She just fell into step beside me as we walked past the greenhouse, down toward the edge of the property. The glass fence shimmered ahead—ten feet tall, seamless, humming faintly with protective sigils. Beyond it: more of New Town's perfect rows and antiseptic skies.

"So?" Calypso asked, glancing at me sideways. "How was your first day?"

I exhaled. "About as fun as you'd expect from being publicly called a curse risk and then failing to feel my magic while surrounded by teenagers who already hate me."

"Oof." She winced. "Elion teaching?"

I nodded.

She frowned, twisting a gold bracelet around her wrist. "He's a good instructor. Terrible human."

My breath stuck for a beat before I asked, "How did he know?"

She blinked. "Know what?"

"About the curse," I said, remembering the desperate way I had texted her the night McDara told me of the bloodline curse just to see if others knew about what happened to Grace. What would happen to me. "He said I wouldn't live long enough to be trained. That there wasn't time before the curse took me." I looked at her then, really looked. "Is that something everyone knows?"

Calypso was quiet for a second too long.

Then, "Everyone in the House...mostly knows. Our parents' generation especially. They all grew up with Grace."

My stomach twisted.

"Most of the younger ones just know the rumors. They whisper about it on the top floor of the House. Our dorm halls. They also have been whispering about it in training circles like it's a ghost story. They don't say your name out loud, but they know you're the reason the Matron keeps the wards up tight."

Not tight enough to keep a swarm of ghosts or Death out...Unless they weren't meant for things like him, but then what did Matron Black need wards for?

"And outside the House?" I asked. "Other Mages? Other Ghost Whisperers?"

Her lips pressed together. "I don't know," she said. "I've never met another Ghost Whisperer. You're the first one since Grace."

She was watching me now. Not with pity—*assessment*. Like she was weighing how I'd take it. How much of it I already knew. How much I could handle before cracking.

I tried not to show anything.

But the truth bloomed cold behind my ribs anyway.

Maybe it wasn't just my family.

Maybe this was how *all* Ghost Whisperers died.

Twenty-five. Marked. Doomed.

And if that was true...then I wasn't cursed by chance. I was born to die.

Before I could respond, another figure broke off from the training circles behind us—moving fast, black braid swinging like a blade down her spine.

Pandora.

She joined us with a little smile that didn't quite reach her eyes.

"Look at this," she said, voice honey-coated steel. "The girl who survived her first Black House training. And here I thought Elion would've turned you into powder on day one."

"Guess I'm sturdier than I look," I said, keeping my tone even.

She tilted her head. "Mm. Must be all that practice playing nursemaid. Builds resilience. You've been staying at McDara's place, haven't you? Must be *so* cozy, tucking him in at night while he recovers."

My jaw flexed.

I didn't answer.

Pandora's smile deepened. "Nothing to say? No sweet nothings to defend your honor?"

Before I could open my mouth, Calypso swooped in, voice bright. "Leave her alone, Pan. Sonia's had a long day."

"It's always a long day here," Pandora muttered, but she dropped it. She tugged at her fitted, black tracksuit's collar. The gold from her bracelet shined in the afternoon light. It was the only jewelry on her, and she wore it like it should be grateful she let *it* grace her body.

Calypso touched my arm lightly. "Listen...if you ever get tired of dealing with Elion or if McDara needs space to recover, our apartment has a spare room. We're on the east side, near the arboretum dome. It's quiet. Private."

I blinked. "You're offering me a place to stay?"

She nodded, brushing hair from her cheek. "Only if you want. But it might...ease some tension with the Matron. She doesn't love that you're so tied to McDara. Politics and all."

And family drama since McDara was her *nephew*. Not that Calypso would come out and say such a thing.

Pandora rolled her eyes. "You mean she wants Sonia somewhere she can *watch* her."

"I mean," Calypso said smoothly, "that Sonia deserves to feel like she belongs here. Without extra pressure."

The way she said it...made it hard to tell if she was offering kindness or strategy.

Maybe both.

And maybe that was the most dangerous thing of all.

The bus ride back to Old Town was a blur of glass reflections and half-heard whispers. I didn't realize how tightly I'd been holding my breath until the door hissed open and I stepped out into the cobblestone streets near McDara's building.

Twilight clung to the city like it didn't want to let go. The air was sharp, tinged with exhaust and old magic. My legs ached from sitting too long, from standing too long, from *pretending* too long.

I pulled my leather jacket tighter around me and started walking, keeping my head down as the sidewalk thinned and the scent of char and caramelized oil hit the back of my throat.

Old Town pulsed with life in a way New Town never could. The buildings were close, like they'd grown up tangled together—grime-smudged brick and steel bones stitched with copper piping and pulsing spell-veins that glowed faintly when you looked too long.

Signs flickered with glyphs only Fae could read, and the hum of magic threaded through the air like a second city living beneath the one everyone could see.

Here, Magicals didn't bother hiding.

A Goblin with a mechanical hand argued with a Vampire over a broken enchantment stone outside a pawn shop. A Shifter kid—barely older than ten—darted across the street on all fours, his limbs fluid, his eyes golden. No one flinched. No one stared.

And then I saw it.

Across the street, a man with sigils inked along his arms tossed sparks into the air, juggling fire that twisted into the shape of leaping foxes. He had a small crowd gathered—mostly tourists, by the look of them. Bright-eyed. Distracted. He had to be a Mage. Only Mages could use sigils.

I almost didn't notice the other Magical—the one drifting close behind a woman in a long, green coat. He moved like smoke. One flick of his fingers, and her bag unlatched. A spell pulsed. Her wallet floated out.

It was a performance. One stole the eyes. One stole the rest.

Then—something shifted.

A shimmer rolled across the world like heat off pavement. The light went flat. Color dulled. A pressure lifted, and suddenly—

Silence.

True silence. The kind that makes you realize you'd been listening to something your whole life, and it had just...stopped.

The woman in the green coat blinked. Looked down.

Her wallet hovered in the air beside her.

"What the—?"

She turned. Saw the man who'd tried to take it. Her face twisted—shock, fear, anger blooming behind her eyes all at once.

Then the shimmer dropped again—like a curtain falling between worlds.

The sound of footsteps returned. Magic buzzed faintly. The lights seemed brighter. Louder.

The woman blinked, shook her head. Looked at her phone like it had distracted her. The thief was already gone. She walked off, dazed. Unbothered.

And I—

I swayed on my feet.

My stomach flipped, and I pressed a hand to the wall of a building to steady myself. Something cold and soft pressed against my cheek.

"Hey, hey," Phontine's voice chirped beside my ear. "You okay, Spooky?"

Gods, she hadn't called me that since I was a kid. Actually, why was she pulling out old nicknames? Why did my eyes burn like they were too dry and blurred like water clouded them?

I turned, blinking fast. My mouth tasted like static. I couldn't quite remember what I'd been doing.

"Yeah," I said, though it came out like a question. "Yeah. Just...lightheaded all of a sudden."

"Hm." Phontine landed on my shoulder, wings fluttering once before settling. "You ever get that weird feeling like...something just happened? But you're not sure what?"

Her voice sounded careful, more thoughtful than I knew my Pixie friend to be on our regular walk back to McDara's apartment.

I looked at her. "Why?"

Phontine tilted her head. "No reason. Just...Old Town's got its quirks."

We kept walking. But the cold lingered. And deep in my bones, something whispered that I had forgotten something important.

I turned down the narrow street that led to the apartment. *His* apartment.

And froze.

Death was leaning against a lamp post like he'd been waiting for hours. Or maybe like he'd only just decided to appear, now that the sky had bruised into something that looked almost like his realm.

He looked impossibly at ease. Hands in his pockets. Shadows curled around him like they belonged there.

"You walked out of that lesson like someone had stolen your spark, Little Bird," he said, voice velvet and ruin.

I didn't stop walking. "I didn't realize you were auditing my magical education."

"I go where you go," he replied, easily falling into step beside me. "It's part of the bond, remember? Or did you forget that along with how to channel Mage magic?"

I glared at him. "It was my first day."

"Oh, dear," Phontine sighed dramatically. "Is the Lord of Skeletons here again?"

He arched a brow, smoothly ignoring her. "And already the class disappointment. Tsk. I suppose it's not your fault. It's hard to mimic magic you were never meant to wield."

My spine stiffened.

"Somehow, I don't remember asking for your opinion."

"No," he said, drawing the word out like silk across skin. "But I gave it anyway."

"I'll see you in the apartment," Phontine said, and I gave her a tight nod. "Don't let the crypt keeper talk you into anything." Then she was gone in a puff.

We passed under a flickering streetlight. I could feel him watching me even when I didn't turn. That steady presence, quiet but overwhelming. Like gravity. Like drowning slowly in the softest darkness.

"Tell me," he said softly. "When will your *real* training begin?"

I hesitated.

Because I didn't know.

Whenever Matron Black decided I was worthy. Whenever I passed enough tests. Whenever I stopped being a threat and started being something they could use.

"Soon," I said, but it didn't sound convincing.

He stopped walking. I took two more steps before realizing he wasn't beside me anymore.

When I turned, he was closer than he should've been.

I didn't feel the touch. He *couldn't* touch me here. Not in the Living Lands.

But my breath caught anyway, the ghost of his presence sliding against me like memory.

His eyes burned silver.

"I could train you."

My heart kicked.

"You?"

"Who better?" he said. "I've known Ghost Whisperers longer than the Black House has existed. I've *ended* them. Watched them rise—and thrive. But you...you're needing to learn magic that should have been growing from the moment of your birth. I can help grow your magic."

I snorted, trying to mask how unsteady I suddenly felt. "With you, there's always a price."

His smile curved slow, suggestive.

"Not all prices are a burden to pay."

Heat curled beneath my skin. I hated that he could do this—rattle me with a look, a line, a whisper close enough to steal the breath from my lungs.

I exhaled hard and turned away. "I'm going home."

I stomped up the steps toward McDara's apartment. Behind me, Death muttered something under his breath.

I looked back.

He stood at the edge of the bottom step, glowering like a cat left out in the rain.

"You can't come in," I said, smug. "Wards, remember? McDara was very...thorough."

His scowl deepened. "They're petty."

"They're smart." I grinned. "You're pouting."

His head tilted slightly. That smile returned—but it was the wrong kind of smile. The kind that belonged to monsters under beds and kings in crypts.

"I do not pout," he said, voice low and dark as grave soil. "And I do not forget what is mine, Little Bird."

The air thinned.

"Regardless of how many wards are between us...I have your soul. When I want it near, *nothing* will stop me from having it."

I swallowed.

He didn't move. He didn't *need* to. His presence wrapped around the space like smoke—no fire, no touch, just the *threat* of it. A pull that reached into the part of me I tried not to name.

My neck began to burn in the exact spot where his hand had gripped all those weeks ago. Where he had branded me and created our bond.

Then he vanished. A flicker of shadow and offense.

I keyed into the apartment and stepped inside.

The door shut with a soft click.

And just like that, the world went still.

The scent hit me first. Clean. Familiar. Faint traces of sage, smoke, and something else I couldn't name. Something that lived in McDara's shirts and the way he said my name when he was tired.

I stood there, keys still in my hand, in the hush of his apartment.

And told myself it was fine.

That I wasn't unraveling.

That I didn't want to turn around and see if Death had found a way through the wards after all.

Then—

Zzzzzzzpft!

A sharp flutter zipped past my ear. "*You're alive!*" Phontine's voice crackled with relief and bottled energy like she had been waiting by the window as I'd walked down our street talking to what would have looked like myself. She landed on my shoulder with a wobble, wings still vibrating like she was ready to throw hands with the embodiment of death.

"Okay, I have waited long enough while he-who-must-not-be-named chatted your ear off." She buzzed. "They didn't throw you in a dungeon?"

I blinked at her. Oh, right, first day at the Black House. "It was a training room, not a dungeon."

"Pfft. Close enough. It was probably warded and windowless. Cut off from the world. *They could have stuffed you in a room and no one would have ever found you!*"

I laughed, despite everything. "You would have found me."

She huffed, crossed her arms, and leaned against my jaw like she was prepared to glue herself there permanently. "I don't like you going there alone."

"I didn't think it would be that bad."

"It's the Black House, Sonia. They *eat souls* there."

"They don't eat souls."

"They might *snack* on them."

I shook my head and headed to the kitchen. I pulled leftovers from the fridge—some kind of takeout rice and soup combo I barely remembered ordering the night before—and started reheating it while Phontine hovered beside me, arms still dramatically crossed.

I told her about the training. The awful instructor. The way the other novices looked at me like I was a ticking curse bomb.

And then I said, "Death is upset he can't get past McDara's wards."

Phontine froze mid-flap. "Sonia."

"I didn't invite him in."

"Did he say anything? Like besides the whole '*you are mine, Little Bird,*' crap. You know, something useful."

I tried to keep my voice casual. "He offered to train me."

"Absolutely not."

"I didn't say yes."

"You *thought* about it."

I turned my back to her. "That's not a crime."

"Sonia." Her voice dropped, serious now. "You cannot flirt with an entity who literally drags souls out of bodies for a living."

"I'm not flirting."

"You tease him like he's a guy in a bar, not the personification of eternal darkness."

I dumped the reheated food into bowls. Mine was a normal size, hers came from a custom doll shop online. The only way I could get her to use it was because she could customize the colors. It beat her trying to fly a full-size bowl around the house and dropping it. "Thanks for the vote of confidence."

She grumbled under her breath but accepted the bowl, settling onto the counter with a dramatic sigh. "Anything else happen today?"

"Calypso offered me a place to stay. Said I could move in with her and Pandora if I wanted."

Phontine gave me a flat look. "That doesn't scream 'safety' so much as 'prelude to a controlled magical surveillance situation.'"

"Maybe. But it was...nice of her. I think."

"She's too nice. That's suspicious."

I gave her a look. "You're suspicious of *everyone*."

"Yes, because I'm *smart*."

My phone buzzed. I wiped my hands and checked it, heart kicking a little before I even saw the screen.

It wasn't McDara.

It was my mom.

I answered immediately.

Her voice lit up the moment she heard mine. "Sweetheart! I've been waiting to hear from you."

"I know," I breathed, shoulders sinking. "Sorry. Training started today and it's been...a lot."

Phontine waved enthusiastically at the phone.

"Oh! Phontine's here," I added. "She says hi."

My mom laughed softly. "Tell her to keep you alive and fed."

"I'm trying," Phontine stage-whispered. "But it's like wrangling a lightning storm in a teacup."

Mom chuckled again, then her voice gentled. "How's everything else?"

She didn't say what she meant.

She didn't ask if I'd tried again.

She didn't mention the graveyard, or the rituals, or the way my voice used to shake when I said *his* name out loud.

We didn't talk about my dad.

Not like that.

She worried—about what it would do to me if I failed to call on his ghost. About what it *meant* that I couldn't let go.

But I couldn't stop.

Not when I was this close.

Not when I didn't know if my dad had moved on. It'd been seven months now, what if he'd moved on from the Deathscape already and I lost my chance to see him again. Forever.

So, I told her what I could. "The House is...intense. But I'm okay."

She paused. "Just promise me you'll be careful. Please."

"I promise."

It wasn't a lie. It just wasn't the whole truth.

We talked for ten more minutes—about nothing and everything. She asked if I was eating enough. Told me she found one of my dad's old CDs and cried in the car. Asked if I'd figured out more about my birth parents.

I gave her the same vague answers I always did.

She didn't know about the curse. And until I knew how to break it, I wasn't going to give her something else to lose sleep over.

When we hung up, the apartment was quiet again.

Phontine finished her food with a little sigh and curled up on a coaster, wings tucked like a tired moth.

And that's when it hit me.

Everyone had checked on me.

Calypso. Phontine. My mom.

Gods even Death.

Everyone but *him*.

McDara hadn't called. He hadn't texted. He hadn't even called and left a message in the apartment I was still sleeping in like some forgotten ghost.

I told myself he was still recovering. That he was mourning his sister.

That he was doing what he needed to survive.

But there was a hollow place inside me that pulsed with his absence.

And no amount of logic could fill it.

3

I had been training for a week. Which was a generous way of saying failing.

For a week.

Elion's methods were precise. Measured. Void of anything that resembled instinct or warmth. Every lesson was a drill, every question met with clipped reprimand, and every attempt I made to follow his directions ended the same way—silence. Stillness. At least I didn't summon anymore ghosts, but I knew my tight hold on my magic's threads didn't exactly help me.

The other novices kept their distance.

Which was fine.

It made it easier not to pretend.

Matron Black had started attending the sessions two days ago. She never spoke. She didn't need to. She just stood in the far corner of the training room—like a statue carved from winter and willpower—and watched. Always watching. Always *calculating*.

Then she'd leave. Without a word. Without expression.

I told myself it didn't matter.

That she could stare until her eyes iced over, and it wouldn't change anything.

But gods, it unnerved me.

The only moments I could breathe were the ones I wasn't supposed to want.

When *he* appeared.

Death didn't come every day. But often enough that I had started to expect it. Sometimes in the street, sometimes a shadow in the corner of a café, sometimes perched on a rooftop like some Gothic gargoyle too elegant to admit he was lonely.

He teased. He taunted. He made unsettling promises in that velvet-wrapped voice that knew too much and offered too little.

And I'd started to look forward to it.

He was terrifying. But he didn't lie to me.

And when he was near, I didn't feel so alone.

It was almost worse when he *didn't* show up.

Phontine, of course, hated this. She hated even more that Matron Black looked at her like she was made of ingredients, not wings and wit and loyalty. After that first day she had stubbornly come with me to the Black House. That had only lasted two days, we both agreed she should steer clear of the House entirely.

Instead, we'd started a routine: after training, we met at The Obsidian Quill. It wasn't far from McDara's apartment, and the baristas knew us by name now. Phontine always ordered a lavender syrup iced coffee she never finished, and I just tried not to melt into the booth cushions.

Keyleth usually stopped by on her break to gossip, to bleed sunshine into the very veins of everyone she spoke to like some life-giving force, and to slip me smuggled pastries. She never asked how I was doing. She just knew.

And I loved her for that.

But tonight...tonight the air felt strange.

Phontine was chattering beside me as we turned the corner toward the apartment, her cup bouncing slightly in her hand, another special order to-go cup from the doll shop, wings buzzing gently in the quiet.

Then I saw them.

Two figures at the base of the steps.

One tall and broad—Dom, unmistakably. Sun-kissed hair, open expression, arms full of trouble.

The other—

My heart stopped. Then surged so fast it made my knees go weak.

McDara.

He was leaning on Dom, clearly favoring one side, but upright. Moving. Alive. *Here.*

I froze halfway up the block.

The joy hit me first.

Sharp. Bright. Blinding. He was okay. He was finally okay.

Out of the hospital. Back home.

And then the joy collapsed.

Like a wave pulling back from the shore before it drowned everything in its path.

Because he hadn't called.

Hadn't texted.

Hadn't told me he was being released.

And now I was standing here like a ghost in someone else's story.

His head lifted—slow, like it hurt—and his eyes found mine.

There was a flicker there. Something unreadable. Surprise. Maybe guilt.

Maybe...worry.

And I didn't know if it was *for me,* or *because of me.*

I didn't think—I just moved.

Up the steps. Past the shock pinning my feet to the sidewalk. Past Phontine's startled gasp.

"You're home," I said breathlessly as I reached them. "I didn't know—"

McDara didn't meet my eyes at first.

"Didn't mean to surprise you," he said, voice low and careful.

Dom gave a short grunt and adjusted his grip beneath McDara's arm. "He's still on painkillers," he offered, like that explained the mood pressing into the air between us.

I opened the door and stepped inside, grabbing McDara's worn, black duffle from where it hung off Dom's other shoulder. It was heavier than I expected.

Inside, the apartment felt exactly the same.

Which made everything worse.

Dom guided McDara to the couch with more gentleness than I'd ever seen from him, like even he knew this wasn't just a physical recovery.

I stood awkwardly near the kitchen counter, one hand still curled around the strap of the duffle like I didn't know what to do with it now.

But I couldn't stop looking at McDara.

After more than three weeks of silence, he was right there. Pale. Tired. And yet, something in him felt...far away.

He wasn't looking at me.

He hadn't looked at me *once* since I walked up the steps and came close enough to touch him.

Dom noticed. Of course he did. He looked between us, expression flickering with something that might've been sympathy. "Think I'll let you two...unpack."

Phontine, hovering near the bookshelf, caught the signal immediately. "Oh! I left my—thing—at the Quill," she blurted, wings already buzzing. "Sonia, I'll, um, check in later."

The apartment door clicked shut.

Silence settled like dust.

Heavy. Suffocating.

I turned toward the kitchen before I could think too hard about the ache behind my ribs. "Do you want tea?" I asked, already reaching for the kettle. My voice was too light. Too quick. "I'll make some."

McDara's mouth opened slightly, but he didn't speak. He just looked...lost.

"I'll make tea," I repeated, before he could answer. My hands were already moving, like if I kept them busy enough, I could hold all the pieces of myself—and him—together. "You should have something warm."

I moved through the motions like muscle memory.

Measuring out leaves. Filling the kettle.

It helped. A little.

The focus. The small, ordinary act of caretaking.

Like if I just did something *right,* I could fix this invisible fracture stretching between us.

Like if I made the tea just the way he liked it, we could go back to what we were. Or at least pretend.

By the time I placed the mug in his hands, the tremor in mine had almost stopped.

He took it gently. "Thank you," he murmured.

I sat beside him on the couch—not close enough to touch, but close enough to feel how far away he was.

"How are you feeling?" I asked, eyes on the curl of steam between us. "Do you need to take anything? Medication? I can check the bottle or refill your—"

"Sonia," he said softly, cutting through my flurry of worry. "I'm okay."

"You've been in the hospital for three weeks."

"I'm home now."

"But you still need to rest. Or eat. Or—"

"You don't need to fuss over me."

Not cruel. Not cold.

Just *polite.*

Like I was a well-meaning stranger.

Like he hadn't kissed me like I was the elixir to every hollow, broken edge in him.

Like the touch of my skin hadn't quieted something inside him, something burning and aching.

Like his eyes hadn't lit up when I spoke to him, *argued* with him, like every word I gave him stitched something back together.

His apartment had been empty while he was in the hospital.

But it was the closest I'd felt to *home* since the moment I stepped foot in Blakewell.

I set my cup down. Untouched. My hands curled tightly in my lap.

"Why didn't you want visitors?" I asked quietly.

The question burned in my chest. It had lived there for weeks, twisting tighter each time he didn't reach out.

And now that it was out in the open, I felt like I couldn't breathe.

But the silence that followed was worse.

Because he didn't answer. Not right away.

And in that pause, something in me started to panic.

I thought of Dom.

Of the ease between them. The way Dom had lifted McDara's arm, had *known* what to do.

Had known not to call me.

"Was it just..." My voice cracked before I could stop it. "Was it just me? You didn't want to see me?"

His eyes finally met mine—deep brown, the color of burnt amber in shadow, warm and aching.

And full of something broken.

I was already bracing for the hit.

"I couldn't face anyone," he said at last. "Not after Deidre."

His sister. His only family. The one he couldn't save.

"I thought…I thought if I just rested, I'd get better. That the silence would help. But it didn't. I couldn't think. Couldn't breathe. She's gone, and it's my fault, and I'm still here, and I don't know how to carry that."

His voice frayed. I felt every unraveling edge like a blade under skin.

"I'll help you, Sonia," he said, looking at me again. "I'll do everything in my power to save you. Whatever it takes. I *will* find a way to break the curse."

And for a moment—one breath, one heartbeat—hope flared so hard it almost choked me.

But then—

"I can't love you."

The world dropped out from under me.

His voice broke open, quiet but raw. "I'm already halfway there. And it's killing me."

He shook his head, like the pain was something he could shake off if he just moved fast enough.

"If I let myself fall the rest of the way—if we try and fail and I lose you…" His voice faltered. "I won't survive it. I *can't* lose anyone else. Not again. Not like her."

The silence stretched, echoing with everything he wouldn't say.

And I—

I wanted to scream.

To grab his face, shake him, kiss him, *something*.

Anything to make him see I was right here. That he already had me. That I would've fought through fire for him if he just *asked*.

But I didn't move.

Because what was worse than hearing him say it, was the thought of him seeing me fall apart.

So, I swallowed the pain like glass.

"I understand," I whispered.

He looked away.

"I'm glad you're better," I added. My voice barely held. But I meant it. Even if saying it felt like pulling a knife out of my own chest.

Then I stood. Walked away.

Past the photos I didn't know the stories to.

Past the kitchen where I'd waited for updates.

Past the empty hallway full of rooms I no longer belonged in.

The guest room door clicked shut behind me.

I stood for a moment, stunned by the silence. My body still holding the shape of hope like it hadn't gotten the message yet.

And then I broke.

Not with a scream. Not with rage.

But the kind of quiet collapse that feels final.

I slid down the wall and pressed my face into my hands. My shoulders shook, my chest heaved, and the tears came fast—hot and soundless and cruel.

I had held on through everything.

Through training. Through silence. Through the agony of waiting and not knowing.

And still, in some part of me, I'd hoped.

That when I saw him again, it would matter.

That *I* would matter.

But the truth was colder.

He'd looked at me like I was a risk he couldn't afford to take.

And this time, I wasn't strong enough to pretend it didn't wreck me.

The air stirred.

Phontine appeared in a shimmer of wings and worry, landing softly beside me.

"I didn't go back to the Quill," she whispered. "There was something wrong here. The second he stepped through the door, I felt it. The whole place felt wrong. Like the magic in the walls went still."

Her voice dipped. "I thought it might be Death. He gets pissy when McDara's with you."

I shook my head without lifting it. "He didn't show up today."

Phontine hovered closer, wings flickering low and slow. "I'm sorry," she said softly. "I wasn't trying to spy."

I stared at the floor, tears still clinging to my lashes. "I didn't mean to cry."

My voice cracked, raw and quiet.

"I thought seeing him again would help. That it would make everything feel a little less broken."

I blinked, and the first sob shuddered up my spine before I could stop it.

"I didn't think he'd walk in and *end it.* Not like that. Not so...gently."

She didn't say anything. Just pressed her hand tighter against my arm.

"I thought I mattered more than that."

"Sonia—he's a coward."

"No." My voice broke before I could stop it.

I shook my head, tears falling again. Slower now. Like something was unraveling in me stitch by stitch. "He's grieving."

The words barely made it past my throat.

"And how could I ask anyone to love me when I'm destined to die on my next birthday?"

Saying it aloud cracked something deeper open. A hollow I couldn't fill. A truth too sharp to carry.

"I want him," I whispered. "Gods, I *want* him. I miss the way he made everything feel steady. Like the world wasn't always tilting."

My hand pressed to my chest. Right where the hollow lived.

"But it's not fair, Phontine. Not to him. Not to anyone."

I sat up slowly, like every movement took twice the strength it should. My body ached with something grief couldn't explain.

"But that doesn't mean I have to stay here," I added. Softer now. "Not in this apartment. Not when I'm not wanted."

Phontine didn't try to stop me.

She just hovered there, watching, wings folding back like she was trying to make herself small enough not to break the moment.

I stood and crossed to the closet. Pulled out the suitcase I hadn't touched since the day he was admitted. Shoved my clothes inside. None of them folded. Just movement. Just motion. I tucked my notebook into my bag. My key ring.

I wiped my face with the edge of my sleeve and finger combed my bob into submission with trembling fingers. Told myself this was what strength looked like.

Not staying.

Leaving.

I opened the door.

McDara was still on the couch.

Exactly where I'd left him.

Head in his hands. His whole body hunched, as if grief had pressed him into the shape of a man who couldn't carry any more.

He looked up as I stepped into the room, and the moment his gaze caught on the bags in my hand, his breath caught like it hurt.

He moved to stand. Or as close as he could get with his hunched shoulders. It looked painful when he breathed. Agony laced through every motion. But he tried anyway.

"Sonia—this isn't what I meant—"

I held up a hand. Gentle. Steady. Breaking inside.

"It's okay," I said. "I heard you."

He flinched like the words were a blade.

"You don't have to—"

"I do."

I met his eyes. Brown and bleeding with pain I didn't know how to hold anymore.

"Because if being with me is too much for you..." I exhaled. "Then staying here would be too much for *me*."

His mouth parted. But no words came.

And I didn't wait for them.

I walked past him. Suitcase wheels brushing across the floor. Phontine's glow flickering beside me like a second heartbeat.

The door clicked shut behind us.

No Death waiting on the stoop.

Whatever Phontine had sensed was a flicker—*there* and gone—of a faceless blur at the corner of her vision.

Probably a ghost.

But tonight, I didn't have the bandwidth to give a shit.

The rain started—light at first, then steady. A slow, soaking grief.

We walked in silence to the nearest bus stop, my jacket already damp, Phontine huddling under the collar of my shirt.

I pulled out my phone with half-frozen fingers and hit the contact.

It rang once.

"Calypso?" I said, voice low.

"Hey," she answered. "You okay?"

I closed my eyes. "Does your offer still stand? About the apartment?"

There was no hesitation.

"Always."

4

The lights of New Town blurred behind the bus windows, all too bright and too still—like someone had bottled the glow of a showroom and cast a glamour to keep everything pristine. Too pristine. The kind of place where shadows were scrubbed clean before they had the chance to settle.

It didn't fit how I felt.

Nothing did.

Phontine buzzed beside me, a faint shimmer against the tinted glass. She didn't speak. Didn't need to. I think she knew if she asked how I was doing, I'd either lie or fall apart.

The bus hissed to a stop.

We stepped out into the hush of an evening that had no business being this quiet. No storm overhead. No ghosts. Just the air—cold, still, perfect in the way New Town always was. Even the rain from earlier had vanished, like it'd been politely asked to leave.

The twins' apartment building rose like a glass monolith. Sleek angles. Enchanted lights glowing lavender-blue under every eave. The front doors opened before I touched them.

"Wards," Phontine whispered, wings twitching. "Everything here's spelled to within an inch of its life."

"Yeah." My voice was hoarse. "I know."

The elevator had no buttons. It knew where I was going. Of course it did.

The ride up was too short. The hallway too quiet. And then—

The door opened before I could knock.

Calypso stood there barefoot, hair in a messy braid, holding a wineglass the size of my face.

"Took you long enough," she said, voice warm. Not quite teasing.

I didn't have words. Just a suitcase and a heart that still hadn't figured out how to beat right.

"Come in." She stepped aside and raised her glass in a silent toast. "Welcome to the chaos."

The apartment was...stunning. Modern, geometric, and sleek—but softened with layers of glam. Velvet curtains spilled from ceiling to floor in wine-colored waves. Candles hovered in slow orbits, their flames dancing in an unseen breeze. The art was all sharp angles and impossible geometry, pieces that shimmered when you weren't looking directly at them. Windows glistened with enchantments that shifted the view—sunset over a desert, rainfall in a jungle, a storm rolling in over cliffs. None of it real. All of it beautiful.

A spell for every mood.

Pandora appeared around the corner in leggings, an oversized shirt that said *Witch, Please,* and eyeliner sharp enough to be legally classified as a weapon.

"There she is," she said, and before I could brace myself, I was being hugged. Tightly. Fiercely. Like maybe she *was* okay that I was here. "About damn time."

"Hi," I managed, muffled by her shoulder.

Pandora pulled back and looked me over with sharp, calculating eyes. "You look like shit."

"Thanks."

She snorted. "Wine helps."

Without warning, she snatched the glass from Calypso's hand and thrust it into mine. "Here. Medicinal purposes."

Calypso rolled her eyes. "That was mine."

"I'm rebalancing the universe. Be grateful."

Pandora stepped back—and immediately locked eyes with Phontine, who had dissolved from invisibility and landed lightly on my shoulder.

"Oh." Pandora arched a brow. "So this is the glitter gremlin."

Phontine crossed her arms midair. "This glitter gremlin is her emotional-support Pixie. I stay."

"You bite?"

"Only if provoked."

Calypso sighed, stepping between them. "Phontine, you're welcome here. As long as you don't burn anything or curse the neighbors."

"Deal."

Pandora shrugged. "Cool. Long as you don't shed sparkles in her room or the shared spaces."

I blinked. "You gave me a room?"

Calypso gave me a look. "We *cleared* a room. We figured you'd come around."

She led me down the hall past framed spellwork and floating light fixtures that pulsed in tune with soft, instrumental music. My door was already open.

The room was like something out of a dream I didn't know I needed—velvet throw blankets, constellation charms glowing faintly on the ceiling, a window spell showing soft snowfall over a mountain cabin. There were plants that watered themselves and a crystal-laced diffuser already steaming with something that smelled like calm.

It was too much. Too kind. Too safe.

"I'll let you settle in," Calypso said gently. "Dinner'll be ready soon."

She left. Phontine floated in slow circles around the room.

"They did all this...for me?"

"Looks like it." She landed lightly on the edge of the desk. "Feels weird, huh?"

"Yeah." I dropped my bag by the bed. "I know them. But not...like this."

"And Keyleth—?"

I shook my head. "She's too close to McDara. I needed distance."

Phontine didn't argue. Just hummed. "It smells like moon tea in here. They *really* want you to sleep."

I gave a weak laugh and headed for the door. "Come on. Let's pretend to be functional."

The kitchen was a study in magical efficiency. Cabinet doors opened and shut on their own. Spices floated in midair, measuring themselves. A cutting board chopped onions with a dagger that definitely didn't belong in a kitchen.

Calypso was stirring soup with one hand, levitating a bottle of wine with the other. Pandora was skewering vegetables with a lazy flick of her wrist while her phone hovered at eye level, blasting music only she could hear.

"Dinner in ten," Calypso said, barely looking up. "You okay with something vegetarian and spell free?"

"I'm okay with anything."

"Good," Pandora muttered. "Because I'm not doing a meat run."

Phontine zipped toward the spice rack and made a face. "What in the name of raw aether is *that*?"

The tiniest glass bottle sat on the shelf. It was unremarkable except for the bright cerulean swirls of what looked like churning liquid inside of it.

"Don't ask." Pandora grinned. "It's imported."

I stood in the doorway, arms wrapped around myself.

I felt like a stranger desperately trying to pretend that I belonged.

The room was too quiet.

Too clean.

Too *new*.

I lay curled on the edge of the mattress, hair damp against the back of my neck, the borrowed blanket tucked around me like armor. My skin still felt raw from the too hot shower—and the crying I couldn't stop doing in it.

Across the room, Phontine let out a soft snore from the dresser where she slept in a tiny, wooden bed Calypso had magicked from an old statue. Something from a trip to Greece—a goddess of hearth or wisdom or war, I hadn't caught which. Calypso had said she didn't like it anymore. Said I could use it if I wanted.

I hadn't asked why.

Didn't have the energy to care.

But now, in the stillness, I couldn't stop *feeling*. The tension in my chest. The hollowness in my stomach. The ache that bloomed like a bruise every time I remembered the look in McDara's eyes when he had told me he *couldn't* love me.

He was probably lying on his couch right now, injured and alone. Maybe still in pain. Maybe needing something. And I wasn't there.

I'd left.

Walked out without looking back.

Because I had to. Because I needed space. *Wanted* it, I told myself again. Over and over, like a mantra I needed to believe.

My fingers clenched the blanket tighter.

I was trying to breathe evenly, trying not to cry again, when the air shifted.

No wind. No sound.

Just that cold prickle along the back of my neck.

And then—

"I see you've upgraded your accommodations."

Death's voice slid through the quiet like silk dragged over a blade—smooth, dark, deliberate. He stood near the dresser, half-shrouded in shadow, arms folded, posture lazy. But the sharpness in his eyes betrayed the lie.

I didn't answer.

Didn't even flinch.

The ceiling above me was clean, white, geometrically perfect. The kind of perfection that made you feel small. Like even your grief should fit inside neat, quiet lines.

The silence stretched.

And stretched.

Until it wasn't just silence anymore—it was pressure. A weight. Something *watching*.

He exhaled once through his nose. A breath barely audible. But in the quiet, it scraped like glass.

Then, low and steel-laced:

"Did the Mage kick you out?"

My chest tightened.

The question sliced too cleanly through what little composure I had left. I stared at the ceiling harder, as if I could burn through it with sheer force of will.

He took a step closer.

I heard the shift of the air before the sound. Like the space between us didn't want him moving through it. Like it knew what followed him.

"Sonia."

He said my name like it mattered.

Like it *hurt* him to say it.

Still, I said nothing.

Couldn't.

He moved again. Silent. Near.

The weight of him settled over the room like a second sky—darker, heavier. Even though I knew he wasn't fully *here*, my skin prickled like a storm was brewing just under it.

"I waited," I whispered, not to him. Not really. "I waited in that apartment. For him. For something. Anything. I kept the lights on like an idiot, thinking maybe he'd text. Or call. Or that I would be enough for him to choose me."

I bit the inside of my cheek hard enough to taste blood.

"He didn't even ask me to stay," I said, the words slipping out too fast. "Didn't even *look* at me like...I...I don't even know."

My breath sawed out between my lips and a fierce burn sprung up behind my eyes.

"I wanted to matter so badly. To be enough." I nearly whispered the words. "Nothing is ever enough. I tried so hard to be good at cooking, but that wasn't enough. I tried to be a good daughter so that I could keep the set of parents that wanted me, but that wasn't enough either. Why? *Why?*"

A beat of silence. Then another.

Stillness so profound it felt like the room forgot how to breathe.

"But then he said I meant too much," I went on, voice cracking. "That if he loved me, and—if it didn't work, he wouldn't survive it."

Had I nearly told Death that I was destined to die? Freaking Wood, what was wrong with me? He might already know.

I huffed a breath that could've been a laugh if it didn't taste like ash.

"I guess it was easier to let me go while he still could. While he could convince himself it was mercy. That he was protecting himself. Maybe even protecting *me.*"

My hands were fists in the blankets.

"I feel stupid. For holding on. For hoping. For thinking I was—" My throat locked. "For thinking I was worth staying for."

Another pause.

Longer.

He was quiet. So quiet.

Too quiet.

I forced myself to look.

Death wasn't leaning anymore. He wasn't even breathing, not really. He stood in the middle of the room like something the earth had tried and failed to bury. His eyes had gone hollow and burning, that soft, ember glow of power simmering just beneath the surface.

Not rage, exactly.

But close.

The kind of rage that waited.

Coiled.

Promised.

"You think I'm pathetic," I said hoarsely. "Don't you?"

He blinked once. Slowly.

And then his voice, low and deadly and somehow *aching*, filled the space between us.

"No," he said.

Just that.

One word. But it landed like a thunderclap.

And then, quieter, sharper, "If I ever stand face-to-face with that Mage..." His tone darkened, the syllables roughened by something colder than anger. "He will *regret* the way he made you feel."

My breath caught.

He didn't move.

Didn't raise his voice.

Didn't need to.

The room had already shifted around him—temperature, pressure, gravity bending to something that didn't belong in the Living Lands. Something old. And feral. And *his*.

He looked at me like the very idea of me hurting was an offense to the laws of the universe.

Not romantic.

Not tender.

But *true*.

Frighteningly, ruinously true.

And suddenly I understood—

He wasn't angry *with* me.

He was angry *for* me.

Because someone else had made me feel like I didn't matter.

And that?

That was the *real* sin.

I didn't know what to say.

Didn't know what to *do* with the way he looked at me. Like my pain had become his own. Like the name *Sonia* was a spell, and he was bound to it. To *me*.

But it wasn't the look that undid me.

It was the silence that followed.

He didn't press closer. Didn't reach for me. Death was many things—terrifying, ancient, devastatingly certain—but he wasn't being cruel.

He didn't crowd my grief.

He let it echo. Like, somehow, it wasn't a tainted, shameful thing.

"I'm fine," I said, even though my voice sounded like it had been scraped raw by glass. "You don't have to stay."

He blinked again, slowly, as if time moved differently for him. Maybe it did. Maybe in the Deathscape, seconds stretched into centuries and feelings refused to die.

"Fine," he said at last.

Another truth carved clean.

And then he stepped back.

Shadows curled tighter around him, like the room was trying to take him back. Like it knew the thread of him had unraveled too far into this place already.

"I will leave you to your rest," he said, voice low. Smooth again. But quieter now. Like the edges had dulled, tucked away behind layers of restraint.

But something *rippled* beneath it.

Like the weave of reality had bent for a breath and the space he occupied wasn't entirely his to contain.

His eyes lingered on me for a beat too long.

Then—

The shadows swallowed him whole.

Gone.

No sound. No flash. Just a soft distortion in the air. A disruption.

But I could still feel him.

His presence hung in the room like a phantom heartbeat. Like the ghost of thunder before the storm arrived.

A promise.

A warning.

A *witness* to my ruin.

Phontine stirred softly on the dresser, still sleeping in her carved bed of forgotten gods. A little snore slipped past her lips, fragile and sweet. The only soft thing left in the world.

I turned on my side and pulled the blankets tighter around me. The sheets were clean. Soft. Calypso-scented—warm and elegant, with hints of roses and smoke.

Not *home*.

But safe enough for tonight.

I didn't cry again.

I just lay there, staring at the shadowed ceiling, feeling the cold where Death's presence had been, and the heat of something he hadn't said still burning in my chest.

He hadn't looked at me like I was broken.

He'd looked at me like he'd *burn the world* for letting me believe I was.

And that, more than anything, kept me from falling apart.

Even as sleep never came.

Even as the hours slipped, silent and slow, into the mouth of morning.

5

Two days later I stood in the back courtyard of the Black House. It was drenched in heat and humming with power.

Sigils burned faintly along the border stones, etched deep into the slate like scars. Old ones. Older than this glass house. What did the original Black House look like? Or the original Blakewell, for that matter, before polished perfection became a disease in New Town? The sigils pulsed beneath the surface, barely visible in the daylight, but alive. Watching. Waiting.

Yesterday, I found that if I dug deep enough until I felt like my mind would splinter, I could access a thin tendril of active magic. And if I gritted my teeth and forced the nausea down, I could will my magic toward the shape of a spell. It did not want to take that shape. Anything that wasn't related to the Deathscape or ghosts or, well, death in general I guess, my magic wasn't fond of.

But screw that. Screw the shitty hand of magic I'd been delt. I needed to learn mastery over my magic, or there would be nothing of me left come the end of winter when my birthday arrived.

I dragged in a breath and pulled more magic to my fingertips.

Again.

The spell fizzled on my tongue as I reached for the Veil.

It didn't come easily. But I wasn't going to stop just because it was hard. Just because it *hurt*.

Especially not now.

Especially not after he said he couldn't love me.

My palms trembled, not from fear, but from strain. Magical exertion always felt like it scraped something raw inside me. Like the magic wanted to come out, but the channel was too tight, the passage splintered.

Still, I forced it forward.

The ghost thread ignited—pale and flickering—and my spectral tether wrapped halfway around the training dummy before sputtering out.

Dammit.

Across the court, Elion watched me with his usual, unreadable expression. Polished. Stern. His tailored coat skimmed the stone with the quiet precision of someone who never made mistakes.

"Again," he said, barely loud enough to carry.

I nodded and moved back into position.

The air behind me shimmered. Spellfire cracked somewhere to the right—one of the more advanced Mages was testing shielding sigils. Another group nearby was practicing aerial bursts. The aerial bursts went off in violent blooms of magic, flaring and collapsing in on themselves before they could reach the stone below. The impact rattled my teeth anyway—raw power barely leashed. I watched, just to see what real, trained Mages could do, and caught the sharp flick of a long, black braid that was unmistakably Pandora, and beside her, as he always was, was the tall, broad form of Elias.

Pandora's focus—thankfully, because her focus was akin to being slowly filleted alive—was pinned to a sunken hole one of their classmates was practicing aerial bursts in. Elias's eyes were pinned on me, or well, my group of fledgling Mages. And by the gods, I hoped he wasn't watching my sad attempt at magic.

Too much going on. Too many eyes. And still not enough.

I knew I needed to be *seen*.

To be *taken seriously*.

To be more than the cursed girl with too many ghosts and not enough control.

I needed Matron Black to see someone worth training, but all that pressure just made the channel my thread of active magic traveled through grow tighter and more uneven.

At this moment, though with the eyes of Elion and my Mage "friends" on me, what I wanted—no, what I needed—was for McDara to be wrong.

"You're going to pop a vein," Calypso's voice called behind me, light but edged.

I turned to find her standing near the water fountain, her hair swept up and her bright green eyes narrowed in amusement—and concern.

"You know you can't brute-force magic, right?" she said, crossing her arms. "That's not how controlled casting works. You're pushing too hard."

"I'm fine," I replied, already turning back.

"Sonia—"

"I said I'm *fine*."

The next tether snapped tighter, ghostlight streaking across my vision. I wrapped it faster this time, forcing it to obey.

Across the court, Pandora gave me a slow, approving smile. She was leaning against one of the sigil-etched pillars, arms crossed, wine-dark lipstick unbothered by the unseasonable autumn heat that shimmered from all the active sigils. Outside the protective barrier that kept the air comfortable to practice outdoors, the season was turning crisp and cool—but here, under the charged glow of magic, the air pulsed like midsummer fire. An aerial spell burst behind her, scattering embers of light that drifted down like falling leaves.

"Well, someone's finally getting serious," she called over all the spellcraft sounds. "About time."

Her words felt off. Sweet on the outside, like candy laced with poison.

I turned away.

Just focus.

Just *one more time.*

I inhaled.

Recentered.

The air crackled.

And then—

"DOWN."

The voice was ice. A scream carved in frost.

Not mine. Not Elion's.

Not living.

I hit the dirt hard, my shoulder slamming into the ground just as a blast of spellfire sliced through the space where I'd been standing.

It scorched the air—and the edge of my arm.

Agony bloomed instantly. A searing line of fire licked across my upper bicep, through the cloth, through skin.

A scream rang out—from someone else this time.

I rolled over, coughing, vision white-hot and ears ringing, the scent of burned fabric curling up to choke me.

Calypso was already sprinting across the containment sigils that enclosed our class and had done nothing to protect me.

Elion appeared at my side a heartbeat later, hands raised, scanning the crowd.

"Who cast that?" he barked.

But no one answered.

All the Mages had stopped. Frozen mid-motion, hands lifted or clutching sigils or pressing to their chests in shock.

"I said—who cast that spell?"

Still, no one moved.

No one claimed it.

I sat up slowly, chest still heaving, trying not to jostle my arm. The pain was raw—skin blistered and cloth fused to the wound. I could smell the charred edges of myself. Could *feel* the spell's intent lingering in the air like a warning.

It had been aimed at my heart.

Not a ricochet. Not a misfire.

Targeted.

"I—" Elion looked down at me, composed again, smoothing the panic from his features like he could erase it. "It must've been an accident. A training misfire."

Right.

And I was the goddess of spring.

"You should go see the House Doctor," he added, eyes flicking to the burn. "Get cleaned up."

My fingers shook as I brushed gravel off my legs. I didn't touch the wound. Couldn't.

Stopping next to me, Calypso's eyes took in my arm. Her expression unreadable now.

But I'd seen it.

The moment it happened.

The fear.

The truth.

This hadn't been a mistake.

Someone had just tried to kill me.

And I had a ghost to thank for still breathing.

The hallway felt colder as I walked it alone.

Calypso had offered to come with me—to wait while the House Doctor patched me up—but I told her I needed a minute. Just one.

She didn't argue. Just pressed a hand to my good shoulder and pointed me in the right direction.

I walked the other way.

The locker room was blessedly empty. Cool, tiled, sterile. And silent.

Was it stupid to hide away in a secluded room when someone had just tried to kill me? Probably.

But if someone wanted me dead, they wouldn't make it look this obvious. Not here. Not now. Not after they had failed out in the courtyard and obviously wanted it to look like an accident.

Which only made the question echo louder:

Why?

Why would anyone go after me now—when I was already marked to die?

Which begged the question of who all knew the details of my Ghost Whisperer curse in the Black House. Calypso had said our parents' generation and older knew because they had lived with Grace. But the younger members...would they have been told more than stories meant to spook them? Would they have been told the truth?

Even so, that didn't answer the most pressing question. Why? Why would someone want to kill me...period? What could someone possibly gain from my death? It's not like I had enemies!

I fitted my forefinger and thumb to the bridge of my nose and squeezed viciously, willing any burning tears *not* to fall.

The bloodline curse would claim me on my birthday, at the end of February. I was a ticking clock.

So, what was the point in accelerating the inevitable?

What was going on that made my death worth *rushing?*

The burn throbbed as I peeled off my shirt and stood in a thin camisole. I hissed when the cotton tugged at the edge of the wound—where it had fused, where it had *melted* into my skin. The fabric clung like betrayal.

I gritted my teeth and braced a hand on the bench, struggling to keep from blacking out.

And that's when the air changed.

A shimmer of wrong. A flicker of cold.

Then—

"*Sonia.*"

His voice cracked against the tiles like thunder.

Death stood at the edge of the locker room, shadow-wrapped and half-formed, like he hadn't finished tearing himself into this world before racing to find me. His coat hung from his shoulders like smoke stitched into fabric, and his eyes—those fathomless pits of ancient rage—were wild.

He crossed the space in three strides.

"What the hell happened?" he rasped, the words a gravel-lined edge.

"I'm fine—"

"You are not fine," he snapped. "You were attacked."

"It was probably a misfire—"

"*Do not lie to me.*"

His voice shook the walls.

He looked at the burn.

At the blackened sleeve melted into my skin.

And something *snapped* in him.

Not just his gaze—but something deeper. *Older.*

"Come to the Deathscape," he said. No softness. No seduction. Just command.

"No."

"*Now.*"

"No."

I didn't have time to brace.

His magic detonated.

A raw, guttural *snarl* tore from his throat as the air cracked open, thick with shadows. One of the steel lockers behind me screamed—*screamed*—as it caved in like paper, the metal *slashed* in half by invisible claws.

The entire room trembled.

So did I.

For a breathless second, he changed.

His face twisted, flickering into something monstrous—fanged, hollow-eyed, *not human*. A shadow beast wrapped in the memory of a man. His power surged in black waves, swallowing every corner of the room, bending light to ash.

And then—

He pulled it back.

Barely.

His body flickered, weakened, unspooling at the edges like smoke unraveling in water. He stood there, breathing hard, the whites of his eyes rimmed with silver light, skin too pale even for him.

But when he spoke again, his voice cracked open something raw and ruinous.

"*Someone just tried to kill you!*"

I turned away, breath ragged. "Matron Black will do something. She *has* to—"

"She let you train out there. Surrounded by strangers. Surrounded by magic you have no defense against and no one to guard you."

"She didn't know—"

"She *doesn't care.*"

He moved again, closer. He couldn't touch me, but he came close enough that I could feel the essence of him like a lashing. The grief. The fury. The possessive magic trembling just beneath the surface.

"I will not lose the only creature in the Living Lands I am bonded to."

My heart stopped.

The words slithered through me, sharp and cold and deeply, *deeply* hollow.

So that was it.

I mattered because of the bond.

Because I was his tether. His link.

Not because I was *me*.

My voice came out rough. "So, that's why I matter? Because I'm your possession?"

He stilled.

"Well," I said, swallowing around the heat in my throat, "at least you've always been upfront with me."

I turned away. Started toward the door.

He blurred—vanished—reappeared in front of me. So faint after his outburst of magic.

But his eyes...they still burned.

"Where are you going?"

I stared him down, heart hammering. "Does it matter? You'll just follow me, won't you?"

My voice cracked—as mocking and cruel as I could manage. "Tag along like a good little master watching his pet."

Something inside him twitched. Flickered. A spark of something furious and *wounded.*

"Sonia—"

"*Fuck you,*" I spat, shoving past him. My shoulder cutting through the insubstantial matter of his arm.

I didn't look back.

Didn't wait for another word. Didn't let the thought that he shouldn't be able to use magic in the Living Lands latch onto my mind.

I left the smell of scorched magic and shattered steel behind me, heading straight for the House Doctor.

If I didn't, I was going to scream.

And I wasn't sure if I'd ever stop.

6

The hallways of the Black House were *not* designed for the wounded or emotionally wrecked.

Every corridor looked the same—walls of polished glass lit by flickering, blue sigils that pulsed like they were trying to remember what century it was. Each turn whispered confusion. The layout felt like a spiral slowly winding in on itself.

Like the House wanted me lost.

Fine. I already was.

My arm throbbed, but it was nothing compared to the sick pulse beneath my ribs. Like a bruise I couldn't reach. I moved faster, refusing to limp. Refusing to let even one more part of me fall apart.

Because if I slowed down—if I let myself feel—I might scream.

Or worse.

Cry.

No.

I'd cried enough. In a stranger's shower. In a guest room that still smelled like him. I wasn't falling apart again.

I was just...walking.

Angry. Alone. Haunted by two men who'd broken me in very different ways.

McDara with his silence. His retreat. His soft words that had left jagged wounds.

And Death—gods, *Death*—with his possessive rage and need to own what he couldn't even hold in this world.

I gritted my teeth and kept walking. The glass walls bled into white smooth stone the farther in I went, the deeper my feet led me. One foot in front of the other. Just find the med lab. Get my arm checked. Pretend I wasn't unraveling.

But the silence changed.

So subtle at first, I almost missed it.

No footfalls. No echo.

Just...hush.

Then cold. *Deep* cold.

The kind that sucked the warmth from marrow. My breath curled in front of me, visible in the flickering wardlight.

A single tear escaped down my cheek. Not from pain. Not from fear.

From the ache of missing Phontine. From the soul-deep *loneliness*.

And that was when the void opened.

Not literal, not spatial—but *felt*. The air in the hallway collapsed into something denser. Frozen and wrong.

A shadow peeled itself from the corridor ahead—

No, not a shadow.

A woman.

Or what was left of one.

Her movements were jerky, uncertain, like she couldn't quite remember how to walk. Each step dragged as though she was fighting the air itself, arms trembling, fingers reaching out to feel a world she could no longer see.

When she lifted her head, my stomach turned to ice.

Her face was *gone.*

Not burned. Not hidden. Just...erased.

A smooth, colorless smear where features should have been—like someone had wiped her clean of identity, of existence. The faint shimmer of unspent magic rippled beneath the surface of that emptiness, flickering like disturbed water.

She tilted her head, black hair sliding around her shoulders, searching for me with nothing but that blank expanse. The motion was slow, disjointed, heartbreakingly human in its confusion. A sound escaped her—a low, trembling, keening, the echo of a voice that no longer existed.

I stumbled back, every instinct screaming *wrong, wrong, wrong.* My magic surged to the surface, cold and frantic.

But she didn't move closer.

Didn't reach for me.

She just stood there.

One, trembling hand rose—not in attack, but in warning. A gesture of stillness. *Wait.*

The air shifted, temperature plummeting. Frost spread behind her, climbing the wall in delicate, laced veins until words began to form—scratched in ice like a message written from the grave.

BELOW.

I froze. The letters glimmered faintly before two more words shimmered to life.

NOT SAFE.

My pulse stumbled.

The Faceless Woman tilted her head again, as if desperate to say more—

But there was no mouth to speak with. Only that smooth, terrible void where a face should be.

And then—she was gone.

No flurry. No fade.

Just *gone.*

The frost remained.

So did the dread coiling in my gut like a prophecy.

Below.

Not safe.

The Black House had secrets. And I had just been warned by something no longer alive.

Or maybe something *too* alive to ever find peace.

The frost melted slowly, running down the stone wall like tears.

Below. Not safe.

The words still burned in my mind, even after the ice had faded and left nothing but slick stone behind. I couldn't move—not yet. The air still thrummed with leftover magic, humming under my skin like it was trying to tell me something I didn't want to hear.

My pulse wouldn't settle. Every sound—the tick of cooling wards, the whisper of air through the corridor—felt too loud. Too close.

Did she mean the Black House itself?

That was hardly a revelation. I'd already suspected it—had *felt* it in the way the halls seemed to breathe, the way the wards pulsed like a heartbeat when I walked too far alone. Someone had just tried to kill me in the courtyard not an hour ago. The House wasn't safe. It had never been.

But the Faceless Woman hadn't looked *up*. She'd gestured *down*.

My stomach turned. Beneath the House.

The stories whispered through the teenagers in my beginner's class came back all at once—rumors about sealed rooms, about tunnels that stretched under the grounds where magic had once been bound in blood. The kind of stories people laughed about to keep from wondering if they were true.

I made myself turn away and forced my feet to move deeper into the House. In the direction Calypso had pointed me toward and hopefully to the med lab and not whatever sought blood below.

The infirmary was colder than it should've been. I almost wanted to look around for a ghost, but there was no ice in my bones since leaving the hall, which meant The Faceless Woman hadn't followed me. Probably.

Sterile and still, like even the air knew not to move unless told. Light bled from the sigil-laced sconces in pale, clinical ribbons. It was softer than the wardlight that took a light sigil and placed it into a Fae-enchanted relic to keep the light from ever going out. Cabinets lined the walls, filled with labeled vials, neatly folded cloths, and gleaming, enchanted instruments suspended midair like they were waiting to be used. Waiting to bite.

I stepped just inside the door, my arm cradled close, the charred edge of my sleeve fused to raw skin. Of course, I knew why I was here. Elion had all but ordered it after the blast. But the truth was—I'd have come anyway. Not because I thought the House Doctor could make the pain stop. But because I needed someone—*anyone*—to fix something. Even if it was only the surface of my skin.

The floor creaked softly beneath my step.

He looked up from the counter near the back of the room—an older man dressed in that casual but put together way old men always seemed to manage. The soft sheen of healing sigils danced before him, and with a flick of the wrist, he reordered them before stepping back and studying them. Like he was trying to find a better way to heal something. He looked understated. Precise. Like the calm at the center of a storm. His gray hair curled slightly at the edges, and when his eyes met mine, they were gentle.

Not surprised. Not suspicious or with something lurking beneath a too bright smile. Just...kind.

"I was wondering when you'd show up," he said, voice low and warm. "Elion sent word about the...misfire in the courtyard today."

He studied me a second too long. Something in his gaze flickered—worry maybe. Or knowing.

"I'm Dr. Corwin Fenwick." He said. "You were lucky."

I didn't answer. Didn't correct him. I hadn't been lucky. I'd been *warned*.

Instead, I let the door click shut behind me and crossed the room with my arm curled against my side. The burn had stopped screaming, but a dull ache throbbed beneath my skin, deep and relentless.

"Sit," he murmured, gesturing to the padded bench. "Let me take a look."

He didn't ask for details. Didn't push. Just moved with unhurried care, collecting salves and charmed cloths while the enchanted tools hummed quietly in their glass cabinets.

When he finally peeled the charred sleeve from my arm, I hissed.

His expression didn't change. Only softened further.

"This'll sting," he said.

It did. But not more than the weight in my chest.

I watched him work, eyes tracing the practiced movements of his fingers as he created the healing sigils. His hair was slightly unkempt, like he forgot to smooth it in the mornings. His cardigan had threadbare sleeves, and his shoes looked like they'd seen a few too many potions spilled on them. No glamour. No cold precision like the rest of New Town.

Just quiet care.

He hummed while he worked.

And then, as if the silence had grown too heavy for even him, he spoke.

"You know," he said mildly, wiping away charred residue, "when I was a novice, I used to collect stories. The kind the professors scoffed at. Old folktales. Things scribbled in margins of texts no one's read in a hundred years."

He chuckled, a low, thoughtful sound. "I found something once. An old journal—pre-1870s, long before Mages came from the Woods. Back when magic was still rumor and folklore."

His touch was featherlight as he worked the salve into my skin, but his voice...it carried something heavier. A thread woven tight with intent.

"There was a story in it about people who could see the dead. The writer called them Whisperers. Ghost Whisperers, actually. Said they walked alongside the Veil, spoke with the ones who'd passed on—long before anyone knew what a sigil was. Before magic had a name."

I stilled, just barely.

Not enough to seem startled.

But enough that he noticed.

"They weren't trained," he continued. "Weren't taught. They were *born*. Or maybe *claimed*. The Veil didn't just let them in—it called to them. Chose them."

He paused, dabbing gently where the skin was most blistered. Then, quieter:

"Not because of spellwork. Not because of study. But because something ancient lived inside them. Something not even the Mages could replicate."

My breath stuck.

He glanced at me—not directly. Just a flick of his gaze.

"Their magic was described in this document as instinct." He said. "It was a part of them and learned from the Veil itself."

Was...Was this Black House Doctor trying to tell me that I couldn't learn Mage magic? But...

Another pause.

Short. Measured.

"Based off the logic this author speaks, it would only make sense that a wielder of such magic would need a teacher of similar origins."

Not a Mage? The words felt so visceral on my tongue I swore if I unclenched my jaw they would fly out, but I couldn't let them because what he was saying...There was *no* magic in our world until the Three Great Woods appeared. Ghost Whisperer's *couldn't* have been here before then.

He didn't explain what he meant.

And my sorrow had been polluted by fear.

The Faceless Woman had said danger lies below…Did that mean the med lab? The doctor?

He wrapped the bandage gently, fingers sure but slow, like he wasn't in a hurry to be done with me.

"I made you a blend for the nerves," he said, nodding toward a bag of tea behind him. "You'll bruise. But the worst of it will pass. The healing sigils have repaired any damage beneath the skin or any risk of infection, and the salve will heal the skin barrier."

His voice didn't hold pity. Just quiet truth.

I stood slowly, wincing as the weight shifted across my shoulder.

He didn't ask if I was alright.

Just walked with me to the door.

Before I reached for the handle, his hand rose—not to stop me, just…to pause.

"Be safe, alright?" he said softly. "And smart."

Something about the words—the cadence, the care in them—hit like a bruise under my ribs. Like something Dad would have said as I was rushing out the door to some cursed kitchen job.

The backs of my eyes prickled, and heat made my vision blur. I blinked rapidly. The last thing this guy needed was some weird girl crying because he told her to be safe.

He pressed a small charm into my palm, along with the bag of tea. "My door's open. Always."

I swallowed hard. Nodded once.

Then turned away before I said something stupid. Like how much I missed my dad. Like how the smallest bit of kindness felt like a splint holding the rest of me together.

The hallway outside was empty. But the ache followed.

Warm.

And so damn lonely.

7

By the time I reached the twins' apartment, my arm was throbbing like it had its own pulse—slow, jagged, furious. The Black House's so-called healing salve was still damp under the fresh bandage, and the ache reached bone-deep.

I wanted nothing more than my bed. Phontine. A movie on low and something sugary to distract me from the reality that someone had tried to incinerate me today.

But the second I stepped through the door, I knew I wasn't getting silence.

Pandora was perched on the edge of the couch, legs crossed, fingers drumming on her arm with military precision. Her gaze landed on me like a spell. No smile. Elias was sitting on the couch near her. He was never far from Pandora, I had found.

Calypso, who'd been pretending to rearrange the coffee table books for the third time this week, spun around so fast her white, drape sleeve nearly knocked over a candle.

"There you are," she breathed, eyes raking over me. "Are you alright? Did the salve help? I made a blend—come, sit down, you need something warm."

Before I could respond, she was already guiding me toward the wine-red, velvet armchair, a mug pressed into my uninjured hand. It smelled like honey and mint and something faintly glowing.

"I'm okay," I lied, collapsing more than sitting.

"You're not," Elias said, not unkind but the dark eyes watching me without blinking, the head tilted softly to the side screamed intense, piercing and…something I wasn't sure of. It was like he was evaluating how I was handling almost getting killed and having my arm magicked back together.

The answer, Elias, is that I'm not handling shit but masking it as a sorry excuse of stubbornness.

"She survived," Pandora said flatly, rising from the couch like a storm on legs. "Which means she's officially initiated."

"Into what?" I asked, wary.

She grinned, sharp and glossy. "Into Black House misfire survival. Rite of passage. Congrats."

I blinked. "Do misfires happen often?"

Pandora waved it off like I'd asked if birds flew. "Please. Mages are still human. Sort of. Training is messy. Someone always screws something up."

But I wasn't buying it.

Not when that spell had aimed straight for my heart.

Still, I stayed quiet. My fingers curled tighter around the tea, the warmth grounding me even as my instincts screamed that today hadn't been an accident.

Elais reached into the pocket of his tailored coat and pulled something out. Gold glinted in the low apartment light, catching the shimmer of floating candles and casting it back in sparks.

He handed it to Pandora, who barely had to look to know where his hand would be, and then she extended the object out to me. A bracelet.

Not just any bracelet.

A delicate, gold chain, inscribed with micro-sigils that caught the light just enough to suggest magic—subtle, soft, beautiful. The central charm was an old sigil I didn't recognize. A circle enclosed by interwoven lines, like a braid forming a knot.

"It means strength in numbers," Pandora said. "Weak alone."

She flicked her wrist. An identical bracelet shone on hers. Calypso's peeked out from beneath her sleeve.

My chest twisted.

"We figured it was time," Pandora added, clasping it around my wrist before I could speak. "You've earned your spot in our little band of Mages."

I looked down at the bracelet.

It shimmered faintly. Warm against my skin.

"Everyone deserves to have allies in that House," Elais said, sparing a glance at Calypso's tight expression, before Pandora sat back down next to him. He swung those piercing, invasive eyes to me. "You deserve to belong, Sonia, just as any Mage does in their House."

I nodded because it seemed like he and Pandora were waiting for some acknowledgment from me, then I slid a look to Calypso who was sitting next to me with that unblinking stare. Was...was Calypso unhappy with Pandora all but inviting me into their besties club?

I had never had siblings or anything that felt like that. Not even when I was at the orphanage before my parents adopted me. Well, I had Phontine.

I swallowed. I would not be keen on sharing Phontine with anyone.

"Thank you," I said slowly, unsure if I was touched or unsettled. "It's beautiful."

Calypso hadn't said anything.

She was watching the bracelet. Watching me.

I swallowed again, a prickle running up my spine. "I—I didn't mean to step into something sacred. If you don't want—Just don't feel like you have to—"

Calypso moved then. Leaned close and took my wrist in both her hands, the one now adorned with the gold charm.

"You didn't step into anything," she said, smiling gently. "You're the fourth half of this chaos now. And you'd better be careful with that. We don't want to lose you."

Her touch lingered a moment longer than necessary.

And for the first time since I'd walked through the door, I didn't know whether to feel safe...or bound.

The air tightened as I watched the bracelet glint in the soft lighting of the living room. Then the noise, noise that I hadn't even realized was there, cut off.

Everything seemed to echo. My breathing, my heartbeat. Even Pandora's silk pants as she shifted on the velvet couch.

The feeling intensified until it felt like I could hear the blood slogging between my ears, my vision needling to pinpricks.

Then a muffled shoosh, like cotton placed over a too sensitive ear.

Instant relief.

Dizzy, I gripped the couch, breath sawing in and out of my mouth, but I heard none of it.

A shrill beep shattered the odd silence.

Elais practically tore through his pocket to pull out his phone and snap it to his ear. He didn't say a word before ending the call and looking at the twins.

"Some fucking idiot tampered with a Veil Tower."

"What?" Pandora all but jumped to her feet, a storm brewing behind her dark green eyes. "Do they even realize what they could do to all of us if they take them down?"

"What?" I managed, eyes pinballing between Pandora and Elias, but it was Calypso that took my hand, her thumb brushing my new bracelet.

"We can explain later but right now—"

"We need to go." Elais was already at the door, Pandora on his heels.

"Maybe I should stay with—"

"No," I shook my head with all the emphasis I could manage. "I'm just going to crash. Go. I don't want you to get into trouble with the House."

She watched me for another moment, completely ignoring the impatience rolling off her sister and best friend in waves, before she nodded and the three of them left.

Alone. I turned to the hall that led to my room. Brain fuzzy and—what just happened?

The twins got a call. No, it was Elias. He got a call from the Black House and...but why did they all leave?

Confusion chased me until I came to my bedroom door, but as I gripped the door handle whatever thought I had been trying to piece together was gone and all I cared about was solitude. Well solitude with my favorite Pixie.

My room was quiet when I stepped in, moonlight and soft magic orbs painting silver shadows across the walls. On the nightstand was a scrap of lilac parchment, folded in half.

Gone to the Other Side to recharge

don't wait up

–P

No punctuation. Just that messy, little signature with the loop in the P that Phontine always added like a flourish.

After all these years, I still didn't know what *the Other Side* meant. She never took me. Never explained. Just vanished for a day or two to replenish whatever ancient, elemental magic fueled her tiny bones.

I stared at the note a moment longer before peeling off my bandage and heading to the shower. The water stung where it hit the edge of the burn, and the scent of the salve clung to the steam like lavender-smoked iron. I washed my hair too, even though it didn't need it, just to fill the silence.

I brushed my teeth.

Dried my face.

Stalled as long as I could.

Then I lay down on the bed.

Pulled the covers up. Stared at the ceiling glowing soft with orb light. Tried to remember what quiet used to feel like when it didn't echo.

It was too late to call Mom. Even if I did, she'd hear it in my voice. The crack beneath the calm. The unraveling at the edges. I couldn't do that to her.

So, I lay still, trying to find some hint of sound—cars, wind, life.

But New Town was silent as ever. Silent and peaceful and wrong.

Minutes passed. Maybe more.

And I realized I was waiting.

Waiting for the whoosh of wings, for Phontine's voice to chatter beside my ear and complain about the state of my bedside table.

Waiting for my phone to buzz.

For McDara's name to appear on the screen like he could somehow *know* what happened. Like he might still care.

But beneath it all...the real reason sat deeper. Heavy and sharp and shameful.

I was waiting for Death.

For him to show up in the corner of the room like a shadow uncoiling. To be arrogant. To press. To demand I come to the Deathscape. Or maybe...ask if I was okay.

When the truth hit me, I curled onto my side.

Pulled the covers over my head like that would shield me from the truth of it.

And I whispered into the dark, "Don't you dare show up."

But part of me...hoped he would anyway.

And that was the worst part.

I woke to the sound of parchment crackling in the air.

Not paper.

Magic.

It swept into the room like a breath through unseen cracks—cold, glittering, *aware*. Every hair on my arm rose as the temperature dipped. Something shimmered at the edge of my vision.

A scroll—made of dark vellum, stitched with threads of starlight—unfurled midair above my bed.

Gold ink bloomed across its surface like it was being written in real time.

Sonia Byrd, you are hereby summoned. Black House. Matron's Office. Immediately.

The script glowed briefly, then faded.

The scroll rolled itself shut with a neat snap and vanished in a puff of silver mist, leaving behind the scent of thick, black ink and acid.

For a heartbeat, I lay frozen—blankets bunched in my fists, pulse thundering in my ears.

Then the magic brushed across my skin again.

Not warm.

Not kind.

Like the tap of a finger on a coffin lid.

She knows where I am. Hell no.

I shoved off my blankets, already halfway to the door. The twins were in the kitchen, both still in their pajamas, bickering over the last lemon scone.

"I'm so tired." Pandora complained. "I hate being put on hunting detail—"

"Morning," Calypso said brightly, butter knife in hand. Then her smile faltered. "Wait. Are you okay? You look like you saw a ghost. No pun intended."

"Shit," Pandora glanced around. "Did you see a ghost?"

"No. I got summoned." My voice sounded strange to my own ears. "By the Matron. Her magic came straight into my room."

Pandora raised a brow. "Creepy, right?"

"She can just...do that?"

Calypso hesitated. "She *shouldn't* be able to unless you're on House property. But...well. Mages of the same House have a...connection to each other. So. Yeah."

The unspoken *you live with us now* hung in the air.

I swallowed hard. Not fear exactly—just...unease. Knowing that no matter where I went, the Matron could reach me. Could *find* me.

The Black House loomed as we approached—towering glass columns and modern glass set against the morning mist. It looked more like a luxury fortress than a seat of magical power. But the deeper you went, the more the glamour frayed.

I'd seen the bones underneath.

Calypso touched my shoulder just before I entered. "I'll be here when you're done. Promise."

Something in her voice softened the edge of my dread. She didn't owe me anything. And yet...she stayed.

Maybe my suspicions had been unfair.

Maybe she really *was* on my side. It would be nice if someone in this weird city was.

Matron Black's office was a contradiction made flesh.

The Black House might have been all glass and light beyond these walls, but here, she had sealed herself away from it. Obsidian-stained wood paneling swallowed the room whole, dark enough to drink in sound. No windows. No view outward. The only light came from candle sconces fixed along the walls, their flames steady and smokeless, casting a low amber glow that refused to reach the corners.

Black tapestries hung between the sconces, heavy with age and power, runes stitched into the fabric in thread so dark it only caught the light when you weren't looking directly at it. The air felt thick—private. Intentional. Like this was a place meant for secrets to stay buried.

But her desk...was new.

And *wrong*.

It looked carved from ancient bone. Not bleached white, but gray and grooved, crawling with etched sigils that pulsed with subtle light. The glow moved—like a current beneath skin—illuminating carvings along its base that made my stomach twist. One looked like a creature mid-scream. Another looked like it had *eyes*.

The Matron stood behind it, hands clasped.

Expression unreadable.

"New desk?" I asked, words barely ending before a nervous tremble slipped out. "It's cool, I mean kind of scary. I've never seen magic in a piece of furniture before—"

"Sit."

Clamping my mouth shut against any further anxious rambling, I obeyed.

She didn't waste time.

"I want to be perfectly clear—what happened yesterday was *not* a misfire."

My breath hitched. "You *know* it wasn't—?"

"It was an attempt on your life."

The way she said it—flat, cold—made the floor feel like it tilted. My chair suddenly didn't feel solid beneath me, but something in my gut eased. Relieved that someone else had seen it for what it really was.

"I don't know who cast it," she continued, eyes locked on mine, "or why. Yet."

"*Yet?*" I leaned forward. "How does a House Matron not know who tried to kill someone on her training grounds?"

Silence fell.

Cold. Sharp.

Matron Black didn't move—but the air in the room *changed*.

"You forget yourself, Miss Byrd," she said softly.

And that softness was somehow worse than yelling.

"I am not omniscient," she continued, voice precise as a scalpel. "I will find out who did it. But for now, I will personally oversee your next several trainings. And I strongly suggest you consider formally joining the House."

I blinked. "What does that have to do with—?"

"Safety," she cut in. "You are not protected without my tether. Our bond. That is what grants members access to House security wards. And to the advanced training you are desperate to earn."

I couldn't breathe.

"What happens if I don't join?"

She didn't answer immediately. Just stared. And in that stare, I saw something calculating and merciless.

A warning dressed in elegance.

"You'll no longer be under my protection," she said at last. "And the House's resources will no longer be available to you."

I didn't speak. I *couldn't*.

"You have until the end of the week to give me your answer," she said coolly, already standing. "In the meantime, consider the alternative."

Being Houseless, she meant, and not learning enough about my magic to break my bloodline curse.

Her fingers rested lightly on the carved desk. The sigils beneath them flared once—hungry and aware.

"I will continue investigating the attempt on your life. But if you want to survive, Sonia..."

Her eyes met mine.

"You'd be wise to make a decision soon."

I stumbled out of the office on unsteady feet.

Calypso was right where I left her, standing impossibly still but her fingers twisting around one another, and Elais by her side. He lounged against the wall, fatigue marking him beneath the eyes, but his gaze was as sharp and invasive as ever.

Calypso stepped toward me immediately. "That bad?"

I nodded.

But the truth was worse.

Because for the first time since this whole nightmare began...I didn't feel scared.

I felt *cornered*.

And something inside me had started sharpening its claws.

8

The Obsidian Quill smelled like cinnamon bark and ground espresso, the air thick with enchantments that kept the windows steamed and the music low.

It was the only place in Blakewell that hadn't changed.

Calypso walked beside me, her usual bounce muted to something quieter. She hadn't let me come alone, hadn't even argued when I said I didn't want to go back to the apartment yet. Too many sigils. Too many shadows. Too many eyes that might not be hers.

She'd looped her arm through mine, and said, "Let's go somewhere they can't find us."

"I'll drive," Elias had said, and with no other comment, led us to his car. He didn't even complain when Calypso told him to go to my favorite coffee shop. That was not in New Town. I wasn't sure if Elais had ever stepped foot, willingly, outside of the perfectly curated life New Town offered Mages and Fairies.

We stepped into The Obsidian Quill, and before I could fully register the warmth, I was nearly knocked flat by a whirlwind of white-blonde hair and too tight hugs.

"Sonia Byrd, I have *missed you* so much I could *scream*."

Keyleth.

She clutched me like I might vanish if she let go, arms wrapped tight, bangles chiming against my back.

"I wanted to text you so bad after McDara was being a *total dick*, but Dom convinced me you needed space and would call if you wanted to talk. Which—ugh, terrible advice. I should've known better." She pulled back to look at me and gasped. "Wait. What the hell happened to your *arm*?"

I didn't have time to answer before Calypso stepped in. "There was a misfire during training."

Her voice was calm. Controlled. A little too neutral.

Keyleth's brows shot up as she turned to me again. "A *what*?"

"Spell went wide," I said, shrugging with the uninjured shoulder. "Nothing major."

Keyleth's gaze flicked to Calypso, to the silent Elais, and back to me. She didn't believe it. Not for a second.

She didn't have to say a word.

I looked at her. She looked at me.

We both knew.

Calypso was still in denial. Maybe not all the way, but enough to believe it was safer not to ask too many questions. And I didn't have the heart to tear that comfort away from her.

Instead, I took Keyleth's arm and steered the group to our usual spot by the corner window, hands wrapped around a mug that tasted like cinnamon and ginger, and tried—for a minute—to pretend we were just three friends, and Elais, catching up.

We weren't.

But for a moment, it helped.

As Calypso was sliding into a seat, Elais bent close to her. I could make out the words, "Pandora," and, "almost the anniversary," then, "gift." She gave him a tight nod and then the unsettling experience of being the focal point to Elais' stare landed on me.

"See you around, Sonia, be safe, okay?" Then he was out of the Quill as fast as his designer shoes would take him.

"Not a fan of Old Town?" I asked Calypso.

"Snobbery can be an inherited trait, I've heard." She shrugged. "But at his core Elais is a good guy."

I opened my mouth to ask how she and Pandora had met Elais. How long they'd known him and if he was secretly an evil puppet of Matron Black's, but Calypso seemed to see the floodgate of questions opening and quickly asked me what Matron Black had told me during our meeting.

Sighing, I told her and Keyleth about the ultimatum of joining the Black House or being out on my own.

Keyleth stared at her. "That's not creepy at all," she muttered.

Calypso offered a faint smile but didn't argue. "It's not just about control. Joining a House means structure. Safety. Magical protection wards keyed to your blood signature. Specialized training. Access to spell archives most independent Mages can't even dream of. They cover higher education, living stipends, medical care—including magical burnout recovery. And if you're ever in danger, House loyalty means something. It's the difference between fighting alone and having a battalion at your back."

She didn't say it with pressure. Just facts, laid out like stepping stones.

But I could feel her watching me from the corner of her eye—measuring the weight of her words.

I couldn't say anything.

Because in that moment—any connection to Matron Black, any connection she had to *me*, over me—I knew something with blinding clarity.

I couldn't join the Black House.

I wouldn't.

I'd find another way to learn.

Even if it meant doing something reckless. Dangerous. Stupid.

Even if the next time I messed up, there wouldn't be a ghost to scream at me to *get down.*

The idea hit me like a cold blade.

And I knew—without even speaking it aloud—I'd already made my decision.

The twins had gone quiet hours ago.

The apartment was still. Still enough to feel like something might be listening.

I sat cross-legged on the floor, surrounded by cushions and the soft glow of a warding orb Calypso had placed by my door—its light a little too pure, a little too trusting. My bandaged arm throbbed in time with my pulse. But it wasn't the pain keeping me up.

It was the feeling.

Like eyes on the back of my neck. Like breath I couldn't hear until I was already inhaling it.

Matron Black couldn't be watching me. Not all the time. Not unless she was some kind of monster who never slept and had enough power to burn the Veil in two. No spell could keep surveillance going indefinitely. I knew that.

And yet...

I waited. Waited until I was sure the twins were asleep. Waited until the walls felt less like they were breathing with someone else's magic.

Then I reached inside myself.

Not to *that* place. The tether that led directly to the Deathscape, to the endless, red sand and poison-silver sky where *he* reigned.

Instead of pulling on that thread and letting it drag me to the Deathscape, I tapped it. Like tapping my fingers on someone's shoulder to get their attention. Hopefully there wasn't enough of my essence touching it to drag me under.

Quietly. Carefully. Like tracing a name in fog. Like whispering into a storm and hoping it would whisper back.

I didn't want to see him.

That's what I told myself, anyway.

I didn't want to step into his world and feel the full force of what he could do to me there—not after the locker room. Not after the rage and the crackling darkness and the way his magic had *touched* me when it wasn't supposed to.

But I still called him.

I called because I didn't have another teacher. Because time was running out. Because part of me still wanted to see his face—even if it was only to argue again.

The tether didn't answer at first.

But I kept going. Over and over, like tapping a vein that refused to bleed. And finally, finally—

The shadows pulled inward.

Air warped.

And Death stepped into the room like he'd always been there, silver eyed and scowling.

His voice was a cut-glass whisper. Cold. Sharp.

"If I did not answer the first *hundred* times you called down our bond, Little Bird," he said, "it's safe to assume I did not want to be summoned."

The air thinned.

I stared up at him, heart hammering, pulse bitter.

"Wow," I said, sweet and sharp all at once. "So, the almighty Death needs time to sulk now?"

His expression didn't shift. But something around him did.

The shadows behind his shoulders twisted like serpents made of smoke. Not dangerous. Not yet. But watching. Waiting.

"So, we're pretending *I'm* the one who started that fight?" I snapped.

"You lied to me that you were okay, which is ridiculous because your arm was practically falling off," he said, seething. "Then you refused to come to the Deathscape."

"And you treat me like I'm your little pet," I shot back. "Little Bird, Little Bird. I'm not your damn *anything*. Except that I'm the reason you get to be here, right?" I threw out my arms to show the room, the city, the whole freaking Living Lands.

The silence that followed was steeped in too much meaning.

In hurt.

In fury.

In something else neither of us wanted to name.

Death didn't move. But I could *feel* the coil of his magic, held barely in check. Like he was restraining himself from becoming more than he should be here—more than this plane could handle.

He might be pissed at me but... "You came anyway," I whispered.

He didn't deny it.

Didn't explain.

Just stood there, furious and ghostly and real in a way that made my chest ache.

I hated that he still showed up.

I hated that I still wanted him to.

I blew out a breath, dragging a hand through my hair. "Can we just...forget what happened in the locker room?"

His expression didn't shift.

"I mean it," I added, folding my arms tight across my chest. "I don't want to fight with you."

"You don't want to fight," Death murmured, voice soft—too soft. "But you also don't want to let it go. Not really."

I narrowed my eyes. "You don't know me as well as you think you do."

A ghost of a smile curved his lips—sharp, bitter. "No?" He drifted closer, the air tightening between us. "Strange. I've been paying *very* close attention, Sonia Byrd. Studying my *pet*, since I'm such a good *master*"—he spat the word, like it had soured on his tongue—"isn't that what you said?"

The smirk didn't reach his eyes. Not even close.

"You made it perfectly clear what I am to you. Just the cold hand on your leash. Nothing more."

I scoffed. "I don't care about what we said. That whole thing was—"

"You *cursed* at me."

His voice was a blade drawn in the dark.

I blinked.

The flickering shadows around him coiled tighter, crackling like they wanted to peel the room apart. His face was half lit by the magic sparking at his edges—one side eerily calm, the other writhing with the sharp undercurrent of pain.

"I have heard thousands of languages. Lived through eras of cruelty. Do you know how many souls have spit in my face?" His voice dropped, barely more than breath. "But not you. Not until then."

I swallowed, hard.

"You don't get to pretend it didn't happen just because you're tired of feeling guilty," he said. "We don't move forward until we have it out."

Like hell I feel guilty!

I gritted my teeth. "Fine. Say whatever it is you need to say." I just wanted this freaking conversation to move on so I could ask for my favor with the least amount of groveling.

His breath skimmed the shell of my ear, cold enough to raise goosebumps along my spine. How could I feel his breath? "Then tell me what's really clawing at you," he murmured. "Is it that I dared to lose control? That I showed up at all? Or is it the bond—that unbearable thread tying us together—"

The words ripped out of me, too fast to catch, too raw to filter.

"I don't care if the *only* reason you give a damn about my safety is because I'm the one idiot in the Living Lands bound to you."

Silence cracked open around us.

My chest heaved. The ache in my throat turned sharp, and behind my eyes—heat, pressure, something close to breaking.

He didn't move.

Didn't speak.

Just stared.

Like I'd tilted the world on its axis. Like he hadn't considered—*not once*—that that was what I believed.

And gods, somehow that look on his face made it worse.

Worse than the bond. Worse than the magic.

Because for the first time since I met him...he looked *human*.

And I hated how much that hurt.

Death dipped his head—slow, deliberate—until we were eye to eye.

He was so much taller than me. Always had been. But like this, lowered to meet me, it felt like the entire room contracted around us. Like the air between us belonged to him.

His gaze burned into mine. Not with fire, but something older. Hungrier.

His mark on my neck throbbed.

"Is that truly what you believe?" he asked, voice barely more than a whisper. "That I only care because of the bond? Because you connect me to the Living Lands?"

I scoffed. Sharper than I meant to, more brittle than I wanted to admit.

"You've made it pretty damn clear, haven't you?" I said, folding my arms to hide the tremor in my hands. "Always reminding me that I'm yours. That I'm *bound* to you."

His smile came slow.

Refined and smooth and just this side of pleasure.

And so, so dangerous.

Still bent close, he tilted his head just enough to make the air between us buzz—like magic was coiling beneath his skin, tethered only by the thinnest thread of restraint.

"You *are* mine," he said, the words silk and steel. "You would be—bond or not."

My breath caught.

I didn't know what to say to that. Didn't know how to respond when something warm bloomed in my chest and crept outward, loosening my lungs, softening the ache I'd been carrying all day.

His gaze dropped. Just slightly.

To the single tear sliding down my cheek.

His expression changed.

Fury still lived behind his eyes—but this time, it wasn't at me. It was *for* me.

"I do not like seeing you in pain," he said, voice low. Almost surprised. "Whether it bruises your flesh...or carves through your soul. I never want it to touch you."

And the Woods damn me, I believed him. Stupid—so stupid to believe the sweet murmurs of Death.

I didn't look away from him. Not even when his words sank beneath my skin like a brand, still glowing.

But I needed to breathe. Needed to think past the pulse in my throat and the ache that had nothing to do with my arm.

So, I did what I always did when the feelings got too sharp.

I reached for the next question.

The next mystery.

The next thread of chaotic thought that might pull me out of the wreckage.

"When I was at the med lab," I said quietly, voice steadying as I shifted the weight in my chest. "The House Doctor said something...interesting. When he was bandaging me up."

Death didn't move at first. Just kept watching me like I was the only thing holding him to this world.

But when I said *bandaging*, something flickered in his eyes.

A flare of silver. Bright. Cold. Possessive.

He didn't speak, but his body tensed—like his magic was bristling just beneath the surface. So much magic controlled so tightly I felt like I was just waiting for it to break loose. What would happen to the world if it did?

I pressed on, carefully. "What he said got me thinking. Matron Black told me I had to join the House if I wanted protection. If I wanted to continue my training. She gave me until the end of the week to decide."

Death's brow creased. "Slow down," he said, voice still low but tighter now. "You're skipping pieces. Start again."

I inhaled, deeper this time.

"The doctor mentioned these old texts," I said. "Folktales, really. Ones that talk about people who could see into the Veil. People who spoke to the dead. Sometimes, they were even called Ghost Whisperers."

His expression shifted—not subtly.

Gone was the glint of anger at my injury. Something heavier took its place. Older. Still. But I couldn't stop.

"And these stories? They're old, Death. Like, pre-1870s old. Before the Three Great Woods appeared. Before anyone knew what a Mage even was."

His eyes—storm-silver and unreadable—locked onto mine with that same, terrible intensity I was beginning to recognize. That weight of knowing more than he would ever say.

I couldn't tell if the flicker in his gaze was recognition or warning.

But I wasn't about to lose my nerve now.

"So, if Ghost Whisperers were already here," I went on, "then someone must've taught them. Right? They had to learn their magic *somewhere*."

I didn't realize I'd stepped closer until the toe of my foot bumped his and sank through the hazy edges of him.

Death hadn't moved.

He was just watching me.

And I could *feel* it—that intensity coiling between us like a drawn bow, aimed straight at the truth I was about to say out loud.

"I think..." My voice caught, then steadied. "I think I need to learn from the source. Or as close as I can get."

His power stirred.

Not violently. Not even visibly.

But it was there, wrapping around the room like breath fogging a mirror.

He had offered to train me before, but now...I honestly wasn't sure if he'd refuse me just to make a point, but I needed this training. I hadn't told him about the bloodline curse. What if it made me worthless to him? His ticket to the Living Lands would die in a few months. What if it caused him to seek another Mage to bond to himself? What if he refused to waste time helping me when he, of all creatures, knew how inevitable death was? What if he gave up on me too?

I swallowed hard.

"I want you to train me," I said. "To use my magic."

Death said nothing at first.

Just stood there, watching me.

The silver in his eyes churned slowly—like storm clouds thinking.

I hated how it made my skin feel too tight. Hated more that part of me wanted to fill the silence with more words. Just to keep him here. Just to stop that calculating quiet.

"You surprise me," he said at last, voice low and unreadable.

There was a note in his voice—not quite awe, not quite suspicion. Like he hadn't decided yet if this version of me was a gift or a threat.

His form shimmered slightly at the edges, like mist unraveling from shadow.

"You want to be trained?" he said, tilting his head.

My throat tightened.

He didn't wait for a response.

"Come to the Deathscape."

And then—

He vanished with a sudden emptiness where he'd been, like a candle snuffed in a tomb.

I was left staring at the place he'd stood. At the air still thrumming with the echo of his magic. At the tug inside me that led straight to that other realm.

That red desert.

That burning sky.

That place where his power could touch me. Where his skin had no barrier between mine. If he was still angry about what I said to him in that locker room, then going to a place where not just his magic could touch me, but his hands could too...it was reckless. So freaking reckless, but that was quickly becoming the theme of my life.

And if I didn't go, I wouldn't have too much life left to be reckless with.

I sat down slowly on the edge of my bed. The bracelet on my wrist—the twin's gift—gleamed faintly in the low light, like a warning or a tether. My arm still ached beneath the wrappings. My magic still hummed just out of reach, raw and unshaped.

If I stayed here, I'd be untrained. Vulnerable.

But if I went to him...

I didn't know what I'd become.

9

The world bent when I reached for the tether.

No chanting. No sigils. Just intent—like opening a door that was already cracked, like calling home a shadow that had never truly left. The bond hummed low and deep in my chest, and for one suspended heartbeat, I felt it all.

My magic didn't rise—it *remembered*.

It *knew* the way.

A surge of cold light licked through my veins, and then—

—I stepped sideways out of the Living Lands.

The red desert welcomed me with unnatural silence. Always silent. Always still. The air didn't breathe. The sky hung low and silver, thick with poisoned starlight, and the earth beneath my boots was a cracked wasteland the color of dried blood.

In the not too distant distance, the river of black fire writhed like a living wound, cutting through the desert and reaching toward the onyx mountains beyond. Obsidian flames curled from its banks, flickering like tongues tasting the air. And beyond it, the jagged teeth of the black mountains tore into the silver sky like a threat.

Death stood waiting.

Tall. Unmoving. Watching.

I swallowed hard, stepping forward even as every instinct told me *not* to. Even as my bones whispered *run*.

"Well?" I said, trying not to let my voice shake. "Will you teach me how to use my magic?"

He didn't speak.

Didn't move.

His silver eyes were burning—wild and resolute, bright enough to make the Deathscape feel darker in contrast.

And in that moment, my bravado slipped.

Because this wasn't some sarcastic, frustrating immortal with a soft spot for banter and human food.

This was *Death*.

The end of all things.

I had told the literal embodiment of death to *fuck off*. And I knew from being connected to him for the last so many weeks that he *liked* grudges and was not above acting petty.

And now I was in *his* domain.

Where his magic wasn't shackled. Where his will was law.

I took a step back.

He raised a hand.

Panic flared—sharp and sudden. *Was he going to—?*

Snap.

It wasn't pain.

It was *pressure*. A twisting, impossible drag behind my navel, a ringing flood in my ears like I'd been pulled too deep underwater. The air rippled. The sky cracked. The whole world turned inside out—and then righted itself with a lurch that stole my breath.

The sand was gone.

I staggered, catching myself against cold stone. Beneath my palms, the ground was obsidian—smooth, polished, faintly reflective. Like it had once been part of a mountain. Or a throne.

I pushed to my feet slowly; every muscle tensed like the floor might shift again.

But it didn't.

No sand. No windless sky. No black river clawing at the horizon.

Just stone.

Polished obsidian beneath my boots, smooth enough to catch faint reflections from the firelight veining the walls. Except...they weren't just walls. They were shelves. Towering, endless shelves built into the bones of the mountains—carved from some deep, smoky stone that glittered blue when the light hit it just right. Like starlight trapped in ash. Or magic petrified mid-breath.

Smoke—or something like it—drifted inside the shelves themselves, curling faintly through the cracks between books. Hundreds of them. Maybe thousands. Their spines whispered secrets in languages I didn't recognize.

The room was cathedral tall. Windows—thin and vertical like ancient watchtowers—rose into the black stone, framed with silver sigils that pulsed faintly with magic. But there was no sky out there. Only darkness. Layers upon layers of silver mist pressed against the glass, like the world beyond the mountain had been swallowed whole.

To my left, nestled between two massive shelves, sat a desk made of that same smoky-blue stone. It gleamed like moonlight frozen over water. The chair behind it didn't match—tall-backed, wide, and covered in the softest white fur I'd ever seen. I didn't know what kind of creature could grow fur like that in a place like this.

I didn't want to know.

But it made me shudder.

At the head of the room stood a dial—etched into the floor, wide as a summoning circle. Like a sundial without a sun. Its black metal was marked with curved lines and constellations I didn't recognize. No light reached it from above, but something shimmered faintly in its center. Moving. Turning slowly.

It looked like it was keeping time.

But *what* kind of time, I couldn't say.

I turned, pulse skipping, and found Death watching me.

His expression was unreadable. But there was something...*quiet* about it. Like he was waiting. Almost—*almost*—nervous.

And somehow, that rattled me more than any of the magic he'd just used.

"Where are we?" I asked. "Why did you bring me here—away from the desert?"

The words came out in a single breath. Fast. Too fast.

Death moved toward me. Slowly. Like every step required thought.

He stopped only when we were a breath apart, his gaze scanning my face like he was looking *for* something—not at me, but through me. Deep into the places I didn't show anyone.

And then he said, in a voice low and grave as earth:

"This is my home."

I blinked at him. "You...have a home?"

It sounded ridiculous, even to me. Death shouldn't have a *home*. A dominion, maybe. A throne forged from bone and misery, sure. But this?

This was a study.

His expression didn't flicker. "What did you think I did when I wasn't looming behind gravestones?"

"I figured looming was like...Not just a profession but a *lifestyle* for you."

His mouth curved—slow, razor-edged. "I've had centuries to accumulate bad habits. Nesting, apparently, is one of them."

I snorted. "So, what is this then? Did you bring me here to punish me for telling you off, or are you about to lock me in some Gothic tower until I behave?"

Death stepped forward, not quite closing the distance, but enough that the space between us felt suddenly scarce. "Would it make a difference?"

His voice was a velvet-wrapped threat, glinting like the edge of a blade just before it sank in.

"That's not a no," I muttered.

His smile deepened—feral, wicked. "I've never been fond of turning down possibilities, Little Bird."

And just like that, I remembered I was standing in the domain of the literal embodiment of Death...and I'd willingly walked into his lair.

But curiosity?

It always came first.

Even when it should be fear.

I drifted toward the shelves, curiosity a tether I didn't bother trying to break.

The air changed here—thicker somehow, like it had been holding its breath for centuries. The scent of parchment and something darker—time, maybe—pressed against my skin like dust soaked in shadow. Most of the volumes were journals. Leather-bound. Untitled. Just dates. Some written in notations I didn't recognize. Others burned along the edges or warped like they'd drowned in a century of rain.

I glanced back at him. "You journal? What, do you start each entry with 'Dear Afterlife'?"

Death didn't smile, but his voice curved with dry amusement. "I'm not that sentimental. These aren't mine. Most of them belong to the ones who came before me."

I froze. "Wait...what?"

His gaze didn't shift. No flicker. No reaction. Just silence that hit like a trapdoor opening beneath me.

"There were others?" I asked, turning to face him fully. "There were other *Deaths* before you?"

Still nothing.

Instead, he nodded toward the obsidian desk, toward the soft-furred chair behind it, still empty—its white fluff glinting faintly like moonlight caught in something unnatural.

"We're not here to talk about them," he said, and this time, the finality in his voice didn't just close a door. It slammed it.

"We're here to talk about *you*."

My throat tightened.

I tried to play it off, turning my attention to the shelves behind the desk. These weren't journals. No parchment, no ink. Just objects—strange and unsettling. Relics. Artifacts. A collection of forgotten things that hummed with quiet magic I didn't recognize and wasn't sure I wanted to.

Each piece looked like it had a story.

And some of those stories felt hungry.

"Right," I said quietly. "My magic."

But standing in Death's home—surrounded by the remnants of those who came before him—I wasn't sure I wanted to know what *mine* would become.

I tried to keep my focus on the shelves, on the reason I'd came, but it was hard to think when the air in this place hummed like a living thing—like it had its own pulse.

"My magic is connected to the Deathscape," I said, clearing my throat. "You're—well, you're *Death*. It's your magic this entire realm is built from, right? So, it makes sense. If I'm going to survive this—Matron Black... I need someone who understands where my power comes from. Someone who—"

He stepped closer.

I trailed off, blinking up at him just as his hand rose slowly, reverently.

His fingers brushed against my hair—those front strands that always slipped into my face no matter what I did with them. He gently tucked one behind my ear, and for a beat too long, his hand lingered there. Not touching. Just hovering. Watching.

Like the act of brushing my hair back had somehow unraveled him.

"Death," I sighed. "Are you even listening to me?"

"I am," he said softly, though his gaze didn't meet mine. It was still fixed on where his fingers had just been. Watching the strand like it might fall again and give him an excuse to touch it once more.

Then, slowly, he reached for my hand.

I didn't move.

Didn't stop him.

He pressed his palm to mine, lining up our fingers. His hand completely eclipsed mine—long and graceful, almost skeletal in shape, but warm. Not human-warm, not living-warm, but *something*. The kind of warmth that whispered, *I remember life. I remember touch.*

His skin was pale enough to glow faintly in the shadows—like the light of a soul just before it faded.

I didn't say anything.

Neither did he.

Until—

"Deals," Death said, voice low and precise, "must be made simply and clearly."

The contact of our hands was electric. Not magic, not exactly, but it felt like standing on the edge of something massive and ancient, knowing it could swallow me whole.

My breath caught.

"You...you want to make a deal with me?" I stammered, then cleared my throat and tried again. "Like—an actual deal?"

Death didn't answer with words.

He simply leaned in.

Not like a man drawn to a woman. Nothing as simple as that, but like *gravity* noticing something too bright, too rare, and aching to pull it into orbit.

He moved without hesitation but with a slowness that felt deliberate. Consuming.

And though the rest of him didn't touch me, our hands stayed pressed together—his palm against mine, steady and unshaking, while the rest of the world seemed to narrow to just this.

Just *him*.

Just *me*.

"I will teach you," he murmured, his voice a dark hush between us. "Not as the Mages would. Not with half-truths and leashes. I will train you as you were meant to be trained. As a true Ghost Whisperer."

I exhaled. Relief loosened something tight in my spine, and I nearly sagged with it. "You'll really do it?"

His lips curved.

Slight.

Dangerous.

And then he spoke again—soft and unhurried, like the strike of a blade that didn't need speed to draw blood.

"My terms are simple, Sonia Byrd. For every lesson..." His head tilted, silver eyes bright with something vast and unspoken. "You'll give me a kiss."

My pulse slammed against my ribs.

"Excuse me?" I croaked, but it came out too thin, too breathless.

He leaned just a fraction closer—close enough that I could feel the cool slipstream of his magic ghost across my skin.

"A kiss," he repeated, voice velvet dark. "One for each truth you demand. One for every fragment of power I teach you to wield."

He was watching my mouth again.

Like it held answers.

Like it might undo him.

Like he'd *let* it.

"That's not—" I tried, but the words crumbled in my throat.

Death's mouth curled—barely. Not a smile. A shadow of one. Arrogance dressed in velvet malice, dark and knowing.

"Don't worry, Little Bird," he said, voice low and smoky, the kind of sound that slips beneath armor before you realize you're bleeding. "I don't expect affection."

He leaned in—barely. Just enough for his breath to graze my cheek, a whisper of frost and fire brushing the heat blooming beneath my skin.

"Not yet."

My pulse stumbled. Staggered. Fell headlong into silence.

"We'll work on that."

As if my defiance were merely a delay. As if my surrender had already begun.

I hated that part of me agreed.

"You're unbelievable," I managed, heat crawling up my throat in a traitorous flush.

That flicker of a smile sharpened into something dangerous. Dark. *Sure.*

"I am Death, Sonia," he said, silver eyes glowing like distant stars about to fall. "Belief was never required."

My breath trembled. My spine straightened.

"Fine," I whispered. "I accept your deal—and its price."

Stillness followed. Not silence. Not absence.

Stillness.

Like the world had taken one long inhale and was waiting to see if I'd flinch.

But I didn't. Couldn't.

Because I'd seen the other roads. And every one of them was lined with the broken bodies of my ancestors. My birth mother. Of magic that called down ghosts and, eventually, who knew what else.

Only he stood there, unafraid of what I was becoming. What I already was.

His eyes searched mine. Not with triumph.

But something closer to disbelief.

As though a part of him had *counted on my refusal*. Braced for it.

Because if I turned away, he wouldn't have to want anything at all.

But I didn't.

And that truth bloomed between us, unspoken but blistering.

A smile cut across his face—crooked, brutal, *hungry*. But beneath it...the slightest hesitation. How long had he been alone in this red desert?

"Good," he said, voice sheathed in silk and shadow. "Then let us seal it."

He leaned forward.

Each movement deliberate. Slow. Like a man tracing the edge of a prayer he'd never meant to say out loud.

His hand rose.

Fingers brushed along my jaw—careful. Like he wasn't sure if I'd vanish. His thumb dragged up to my cheek, then slid into my hair. Not hesitant. *Claiming.*

But his eyes, those silver eyes like pools of mercury, watched me. The slightest crease formed between his brows and, for the first time since stumbling accidentally into his realm, I hadn't seen him so...unsure.

"What is it?" I asked, breath barely more than a whisper. *Was he changing his mind about our deal?*

"I cannot remember when I've felt someone else's skin beneath my fingers." His voice was just as soft, as if the scarce thread of space between us allowed for soft things. "Before you, that is. Have humans always been so soft"—a stroke of his thumb down the column of my neck—"or fit so perfectly in my hand?" His fingers dug harder into my hair, cupping the back of my neck and tilting my face up to his.

His pupils were blown wide, silver spinning around the black heart of them.

"I do not remember." He leaned in, warm breath tickling my lips, and I could not stop from looking down. He had a full mouth, tight and curved down. That crease still between his brows. "I find I do not care."

"Care?" I stammered on a breath. "About what?"

"If I remember anything more than this moment."

And then—

Death kissed me.

Slow. Searching. Like he didn't remember how to feel, but he knew I was the way back.

I meant to stay still. Eyes open. Detached.

But the second his lips moved against mine—

I broke.

My eyes fluttered shut. My breath hitched. My lips parted.

Any patience he had fled the moment my lips moved under his.

The kiss turned hard. Needing. *Hungry.*

It was *punishment* for every moment he'd been forced to wait.

His mouth crashed against mine—cold and heat colliding, hunger pouring from him like an avalanche of centuries starved. His grip in my hair tightened, and his body angled into mine like he needed to feel *everything*. Like the kiss was the only thing keeping him tethered to existence.

It wasn't gentle.

It was *brutal.*

Devouring.

A kiss that dared me to pull away.

A kiss that knew I wouldn't.

And gods help me—I *didn't want to.*

I kissed him back, gasping against the sheer force of it. My hands fisted in his coat, dragging him closer. My body *lit up,* every nerve sparked and screaming for more. There was no caution. No thought. Just *need.*

I moaned into him—soft, desperate, completely undone.

He drank that sound like he'd been dying for it. Like he'd *waited* through lifetimes just to taste that moment.

The hand not tangled in my hair slid up my back, tracing fire through every inch of me, shadows curling at his fingertips like they wanted to join in the claiming. The world tilted; I didn't know if I was breathing him in or if he was stealing the air from me—maybe both. His mouth was everywhere, wild and reverent all at once, until there was nothing left in me that wasn't his name in the shape of a breath.

When he finally pulled back, I swayed. Staggered.

His hand was still buried in my hair, holding me there, thumb dragging slow over the skin beneath my ear.

But his gaze—

His gaze was silver fire.

Shining.

Ravenous.

And far, far too *human* for the monster he was supposed to be.

I couldn't breathe.

Couldn't *survive* this.

What the hell was that?

"Our deal is sealed, Little Bird," he said, voice raw now. Frayed at the edges.

I tried to stand straight. To remember who I was.

Failed.

Because all I could think—drenched in magic and madness and the ruin of his kiss—was one unholy, undeniable truth:

I want him to do it again.

10

I was still frozen.

My mouth tingled. My breath wouldn't come right. And my heart—gods, my heart—was kicking at my ribs like it wanted out of my chest entirely.

Death just watched me.

Calm. Steady. The sharp curve of his mouth still laced with the echo of what we'd just done. None of that unsure reverence or hunger in his eyes. It was like he had thrown a shield over anything he had felt or could still be feeling.

It was not a skill I knew how to do, but damn if I didn't wish I could. My cheeks warmed just thinking about how all that *I* was feeling was written plainly on my face for him to see.

"Now with that out of the way," he murmured, thumb dragging once across the apple of my cheek before he stepped back. "Time to begin."

"Begin?" My voice cracked like dry kindling.

His eyes glinted silver in the shadows. "Lesson one."

Of course, he wanted to dive right into training. Of course, he wasn't the one internally combusting. I was the idiot still tasting his mouth and wondering if I'd gone insane for liking it.

I cleared my throat, trying to scrape together some dignity. "Now?"

Death smiled like a promise. "You came here for magic, not indulgence. Or was that kiss so good it changed your mind?"

I flushed. Violently. "It was fine. Maybe one day it will even be decent."

He stilled, something dark that edged his monstrous shadows peeked out of his eyes at me. Maybe teasing him on not kissing well wasn't the best idea. Could the embodiment of death feel self-conscious?

He prowled back to me, the steps he had taken away earlier gone in an instant.

"Decent?" His voice was deadly, the shade of afterlife I suspected only ghosts he personally reaped got to hear. I swallowed. "Was it just decent when you pressed against me Little Bird? Held on tight enough to do this?" He tapped the collar of his shirt that had felt like cool shadow beneath my fingers.

I glanced down. Two small holes sat at the seam of his collar like something small had dug in and ripped the fabric…Had I been pulling *Death* closer to me so hard I had ripped his freaking shirt?

My cheeks flamed, and I seriously considered making my magic take me back to the Living Lands. Lesson or no lesson.

"But if you're offering to let me practice," He slid a finger under my chin and tilted my burning face up. "I would enjoy the chance to learn how to get you to react like that again."

I couldn't speak. My tongue had died of embarrassment, and even if it hadn't, there was no way I would allow myself to speak. If I did, I might very well ask him to start practicing right now.

What was wrong with me?

He watched my face for another scattered beat of my racing heart, and then he turned, shadows peeling away from his frame like falling smoke. "Come."

The black, stone floor rippled beneath us, and before I could blink, we were moving—not walking, not teleporting exactly, but descending. The air thickened around me, rippling with blue ghostfire. The floor melted away, revealing polished onyx stairs that spiraled down, down, into silence.

We stepped into a vast chamber carved into the belly of the Deathscape itself.

The walls were the same haunting marriage of onyx and that blue, smoky stone—threaded with vein-like lines that pulsed faintly, as if the room itself were alive. Ghostfire sconces floated in the air like will-o'-the-wisps, casting eerie, flickering light across the space.

Death crossed the floor in a slow prowl, silent as sin.

"This is not Black House training," he said quietly. "You are not here to recite spoken sigils or to learn how to command sigils without words. That is for Mages. You are a Ghost Whisperer. Your magic is different and the way you call on it is born within your soul. It is instinct that cannot be trained into submission."

I stood still, trying to keep my breathing even.

He circled me, voice lowering to a murmur. "Your kind were never meant to beg the dead for answers. You command them. You bind them. You release them."

I swallowed hard. "How?"

Death lifted a hand—and the chamber darkened.

"You must remember that ghosts are at your mercy, not the other way around." He murmured. "Your magic will be drawn to them and want to guide them on instinct. It is about giving that instinct a clear path to moving the ghost through to the afterlife that has claimed them."

A low rumble stirred underfoot, and mist began to gather. It poured in from the corners of the room, a veil-gray fog that thickened into something more than air. I could *feel* it. Cold. Hungry.

Then...a presence.

A shape flickered in the mist. Human. No—*was* human.

A ghost, fractured and frantic, shimmered into being. A young soldier. His eyes wide. His mouth moved around names that weren't mine. His chest heaved with sobs that had no breath behind them.

"He's reliving it," I whispered. "His last moment."

"Don't speak," Death said. His voice came from somewhere near, though I didn't see him move. "Feel his memory. Don't fix. Don't comfort. *Anchor.*"

The ghost spasmed, reaching for something—someone—who wasn't there.

My heart twisted. Every instinct screamed at me to say something soothing. To offer comfort.

But I didn't.

Instead, I did as Death said.

I reached inward—deeper than before—toward that thread inside me. The one that had always hummed just beyond reach. This time, I didn't pull.

I *called*.

I whispered into it like a name. Like a promise.

And something whispered back.

Magic surged through me—raw, staggering, *real*. I opened myself to it. Let it move like breath, like blood. Let it touch the ghost.

He *stilled*.

For one moment, his eyes cleared—sharpened—and they *saw* me.

"S...Sam?" he rasped, voice flickering like the light around him.

My chest tightened. "No, but—I can help—"

The thread slipped.

I gasped as the magic jolted inside me, a current pulled too tight then suddenly slack. The ghost's gaze *changed*—soft confusion shifting to cold fear.

His mouth twisted. His body hunched, shuddering. He backed away with jerky, animal movements.

"No—wait—" I reached again, grasping for the thread, but it danced out of reach.

His hands curled into fists. The light around him flickered wildly.

Then he *screamed*.

A piercing, hollow wail that rattled the sconces in the walls.

I flinched as ghostfire roared up around us, my instincts screaming *danger*. But I couldn't move. I couldn't *leave him like this*.

"You have to *anchor*," Death said, his voice suddenly near, a blade of calm in the chaos. "You lost the connection."

"I'm trying!" I snapped, breath ragged. "He keeps slipping—"

Footsteps behind me. Silent, deliberate.

Then—*warmth*.

Not magic.

Just presence.

Death's hands settled onto my shoulders—cool, steady, *grounding*. Solid. Like a weight I could lean against.

My heart still thundered, but something inside me quieted. Just enough.

"If he sees you as a threat," Death murmured near my ear, "it's because your hold on him is wavering. Your thread is frayed."

"I don't know how to fix it," I whispered.

"You do," he said. "You think of the anchor as a bond. A need to comfort and help. That will do for today."

He stepped in closer, his chest pressing into my back and giving me the sense of a grounding presence—I wasn't at the whim of this ghost having a meltdown. I could do what Death said. My urge to comfort was really my need to anchor the ghosts. To direct him to the afterlife that he should go to.

"Feel," he said. "Not with your hands. Not with your voice. With *your magic*. Find the place where his pain rages wild. It will be easiest to see and latch onto. Let it thread between you."

I closed my eyes.

Let go of the panic.

The ghost was flickering again—shifting between a man and a scream—but I reached deeper this time. Not pushing. Not pulling.

Just...*offering*.

And there—it shimmered. That thread. Laced with sorrow. Tense with memory.

I exhaled slowly, let my magic slide along it, let it *settle*.

"Now," Death said, voice low and sure. "Lock it. Imagine a clasp. A knot. *Claim* it."

I did.

And this time, the thread didn't slip.

The ghost blinked. And for the first time since he appeared...*he didn't look afraid.*

The ghost stood still now—breathless, flickering in and out of shape like a lantern struggling to stay lit. His eyes, once clouded with fear, locked on mine. Steady. Waiting.

"I...I've got him," I whispered. "What now? How do I help him move on?"

Death moved to stand beside me, his hands no longer on my shoulders, but his presence still anchoring me like gravity.

"All ghosts carry the echo of their end," he said softly. "But beneath that—woven through the grief and fear and memory—is the *imprint* of their afterlife. It's etched into them the moment they arrive in the Deathscape."

I frowned. "How do I find it?"

"Look closer," he said, stepping past me, eyes locked on the ghost like a predator circling prey—but there was no hunger in him. Only purpose. "Don't focus on what he was. Focus on what waits for him. It will be a thread with no end."

I swallowed and turned my focus inward again, letting my magic trace the thread that tethered us together. All of them ended, a thread for adolescence, for different dreams, for anger. On and on, a million threads that made up this life in my hands. It hummed like a live wire in my chest—faint and fragile, but sure.

And then—I saw it.

A flicker. Not of memory, but of something *beyond*. A thread that was stronger, bolder than the rest. That had no end.

A field bathed in soft gold light. A child's laugh. The echo of a name whispered in peace. A woman waiting in the distance, arms open.

The ghost's shoulders sagged.

His breath hitched.

I felt his longing.

"I see it," I said, barely breathing. "I see where he's meant to go."

"Good," Death murmured. "Now *will* him to it. Not a push. Not a shove. A command given in mercy. You are a Ghost Whisperer, a command from you is something a ghost should not be able to refuse."

I closed my eyes and imagined the light of that place reaching for him.

And I whispered, *"Go."*

The ghost's expression shifted—relief, wonder...and then he was gone.

No scream.

No sound.

Just silence—and then a ripple of warmth in the air, like a soul finally *settling*.

I sagged, suddenly heavy. My legs nearly gave out beneath me, and I braced my hands on my knees. My joints burned, the bracelet on my wrist almost too hot for my skin, and my lungs shook.

"Gods," I muttered. "That was..."

"Draining?" Death offered, voice like a velvet knife.

I glanced at him. "Is it always like that?"

"For the untrained?" He lifted a brow. "Sometimes. But you did well."

I straightened, flexing my fingers, still catching my breath. My gaze drifted to the floor, to where the ghost had once stood. A small part of me still clung to the thread, even though it was gone.

And then another question came—unbidden. But I couldn't help it.

"Have you ever...seen ghosts who don't have an imprint?"

Death didn't answer immediately.

His expression shifted—just slightly. The faintest curl at the corner of his mouth. A glint in his silver eyes like a storm brewing beneath still water.

"Worse," he said softly. "I've seen the ones who run from it."

I went still.

Death turned, gaze sharp, dangerous, but almost...*amused*.

"That's why I have Reapers."

My skin prickled.

Because the way he said it—it was like the memory of anticipation. I supposed entertainment was scarce in the Deathscape.

I shivered at the word *Reapers*, but I couldn't stop the questions forming on my tongue.

"What do they do?" I asked, voice low. "The ones who run. What happens to them?"

Death turned back toward me, his expression unreadable at first...then slowly shifting. His mouth curled—not into a full smile, but something far more dangerous. Dark amusement laced with temptation.

"Careful, Little Bird," he said, stepping close enough that I could see the silver veins in his eyes pulse with magic. "Every answer comes with a price."

My breath caught.

He leaned in—not touching, but close enough that the air between us felt *charged*, like standing beneath a storm just before lightning strikes. The two little rips in his shirt mocking me and my racing heart.

"Our deal," he said, voice a low murmur. "One kiss for every lesson. Every truth."

His gaze dropped to my mouth.

Then lifted again, slow and deliberate.

"So unless you're eager to offer more," he added, *almost* gently, "you might want to save your curiosity...for another night."

I flushed.

Not just from embarrassment—but from the way he said *eager*. Like he *hoped* I was. Like he wouldn't mind in the slightest if I kept asking questions until I owed him a hundred kisses.

And the worst part?

I wasn't sure I would mind either.

I forced a scoff, lifting my chin. "You really overestimate how much I care."

Death didn't reply. Just kept watching me.

But something shifted in his gaze. That simmering heat cooled into something quieter. More observant. His head tilted, barely.

"You should rest," he said at last. "This taxed you more than I anticipated."

"I'm fine," I muttered, shifting on my feet and swaying immediately.

He took a single step forward, just enough to catch me if I collapsed, but not enough to touch me. That restraint somehow made it worse.

"There's a room here—quiet, warm. You'll have privacy. I'll—"

"No," I said quickly, sharper than I meant to. "I should get back."

His jaw twitched.

A beat passed. Two.

Then he inclined his head in a motion that felt...old. Formal. Like a predator amusing his prey. Would I find that, after one of our lessons, he would not let me go back to the Living Lands?

"As you wish."

I closed my eyes and reached inward—into that place where my magic lived. Where the thread connecting me to the Living Lands pulsed faint and distant. Normally, it took nothing to call it. A breath, a whisper, a flicker of intent.

But now...

I had to *force* it.

Gritting my teeth, I dragged power from a well that felt far too shallow. Heat bloomed behind my ribs, pressure mounting behind my eyes, and just when I thought I might fail—

The world shifted.

When I opened my eyes, I was back in my room at the twins' apartment. The air was cool, the light dimmed by the drawn curtains.

I took two steps toward the bed, and that was all I had.

My knees gave out, and I barely managed to flop onto the mattress before the world went dark around the edges. My body felt hollowed out. Like whatever I'd done in the Deathscape had scraped the inside of my magic clean.

That—I thought hazily, curling into the blankets—*can't be normal.*

And then I slept.

A heavy, dreamless, bone-deep sleep.

11

I woke to the taste of dust and magic still clinging to my tongue.

The room was dim, washed in the burnt-orange hues of evening slipping through the curtains. My body ached like I'd run ten miles through water, every limb heavy, mind foggy. When I sat up, the world tilted slightly.

My phone buzzed angrily on the nightstand.

Sixteen messages. Three missed calls. One voicemail.

All from the twins—except for the voicemail. That was from Keyleth.

I scrubbed a hand over my face and opened the most recent text.

> **The Nice One:** *You okay? We're stuck at the House for a meeting. If we're not back by 9, Keyleth's swinging by.*

> **The Other One:** *You missed training.*

Before I could process how much time I'd lost, a flurry of violet wings zipped into view.

"*You're alive!*" Phontine hovered at eye level, arms crossed and eyes glittering with too many emotions to count. "I leave for a few days to recharge on the *Other Side* and you go *full danger zone,* huh? What the hell happened? Why haven't you answered your phone? Did the Black House lock you in a crypt or something? Did a ghost drag you into a mirror—because I *told* you to stop talking to mirrors—"

"I'm fine," I croaked. "Sort of."

She flitted backward with a skeptical look, wings flickering like hummingbird glass. "Define *sort of.*"

I swung my legs over the bed, slow and dizzy, and reached for the glass of water someone—probably Calypso—had left on my nightstand. "Matron Black cornered me. Told me if I don't pledge to the House by the end of the week, I'm out."

Phontine blinked. "So just join the weird Mage club already. Get your training, get cured, stay alive. Easy."

I stood, swaying slightly. "It's not that simple."

"Why not?"

"Because," I muttered, stumbling toward my dresser, "joining the House means giving her magical control over me. Matron Black gets a tether to every member's magic. It's not just House rules and robes. It's leash and collar."

Phontine went still. "That's...horrifying."

"Exactly." I yanked my old jeans off and braced myself against the dresser, waiting for the spinning to slow. "That's why I went to the Deathscape."

Dead silence.

Then, "*You what?*"

"I needed training. I needed it now. There's no one else who understands my magic—*really* understands it. If I don't start fighting this curse with everything I've got, I'm dead by February."

Phontine's wings buzzed erratically. "Okay, but—Death? You went to Death? He was *furious* at you the last time you saw him, and you just...*walked into his domain?* Sonia, he could've crushed you like a firefly!"

"I know."

"*Clearly, you don't!*"

"I know," I said again, softer this time. "But I also know he's the only one who can help me."

Phontine hovered near my shoulder, uncharacteristically quiet. Then, in a small voice, she asked, "Is that why you're so drained? Did he do something to you?"

I sank back onto the bed and let my eyes fall closed. "We trained. Just...one lesson. It took everything I had."

She floated down to perch on my knee. "Was it bad?"

"No." I hesitated. "Not bad. Just...intense. Like peeling yourself open and hoping the power doesn't eat you alive."

Phontine didn't respond right away. She just sat there, tiny and solemn, her wings barely moving.

Then she whispered, "I hope he knows what he's doing."

"Yeah," I breathed. "Me too."

Clean clothes didn't fix everything, but they made me feel a little less like roadkill.

I tugged the second bow on my shoulder tie tight and glanced at the mirror. Dark-plum velvet clung to my ribs, the deep color washing out the tired circles under my eyes a little. My black jeans were ripped at the knees, frayed from too many nights on too many haunted streets, but they still fit. Still made me feel like I had armor, even if it was cotton and denim.

Phontine buzzed near my head, doing barrel rolls to try and break the heavy silence. "You sure you're okay to go out?"

"Nope," I said, grabbing my phone. "But I'm not staying here and marinating in my own exhaustion."

I tapped Keyleth's name and held the phone to my ear. It rang. And rang.

No answer.

"She's probably busy," Phontine offered. "Or dancing in a moon circle. You never know with Key."

I snorted and opened the group chat with the twins.

> **Me:** *Going to the Quill for a potion. Will check in later.*

No reply, but the "read" icon popped up. Good enough.

Phontine zipped toward the door. "Let's go get you something illegal in three provinces."

The Obsidian Quill didn't just specialize in tea and coffee. It was what you could get in those caffeinated beverages, or on its own, that the Quill was known for. And its ambiance, of course. Even if Keyleth had warned me that the Quill's sort of concoctions could toe the line between potion and problem—but at this point, I didn't care. I needed something fast-acting. Something that could hold my bones together long enough to fake it through the next twelve hours.

As I stepped into my boots, the thought came unbidden:

Call McDara.

He'd answer. Probably. With that clipped tone and barely leashed intensity that made it sound like he could bulldoze the problem if given a target.

I closed my eyes.

For one breath—one stupid, fleeting breath—I wanted that. Him. That quiet, take-charge way he had. The way his presence alone made chaos feel a little more ordered.

But I couldn't call him.

Not after everything.

Maybe he'd meant it when he said he still wanted to help with the curse. Maybe he even still cared in some distant, clinical way. But being the one I could lean on? Be messy with? Break down in front of?

He'd made it clear that wasn't his role anymore.

And that was fine.

I'm fine, I told myself as I opened the door and stepped into the cool, mist-edged night. The lie only echoed a little.

The Obsidian Quill pulsed with music and steam and the soft hum of spelled caffeine. It was busy, but not *too* busy—just the way I liked it. Enough people to disappear into.

I passed a table with a Gobin male and human woman, hands entwined as they smiled at each other. It was still disconcerting to me to see a Goblin smile. All razor teeth and black tongue, but you know what? Good for them. At least someone in this city was happy.

I slid into a corner booth, my haul of potions clinking in a paper bag that smelled like mint, ash, and desperation. Phontine flitted beside me, tiny hands on her hips.

"You're not seriously going to drink all five—"

I uncorked the first vial and downed it like a shot. "Yup."

She zipped back a few inches, wings twitching. "You're going to overheat your liver or, I don't know, explode."

"Don't care. I'm already half dead."

Potion two. Gulp. Burn. Gasp.

The relief was immediate and addicting—the weight pressing behind my eyes loosened, just a little. My limbs still felt like sandbags, but now at least I could pretend they weren't dragging me down.

I reached for vial three.

"That better not be my favorite flavor," said a voice behind me.

Keyleth slid into the booth without waiting for an invite, bracelets clinking as she crossed her arms.

"I heard my barista muttering about someone ordering *five* pep-me-ups," she said. "And I thought: Who's that strung out and reckless?"

She took one look at my face, and her expression softened. "You okay?"

I started to nod—then stopped. My fingers twitched. The third potion slipped from my hand and clattered to the table, rolling toward Phontine.

"I'm fine," I mumbled.

Keyleth leaned in. "Are they pushing you too hard at the House?"

"Something like that." I watched Phontine sit on the toppled vial, lazily rolling back and forth on its smooth glass shape. "Key, did McDara ever tell you...about what's going on with my, um, my—"

"Yeah," Keyleth's face, when I peeked up at her, was just this side of distraught. "The curse, on your bloodline, Sonia..."

In an instant she was out of her side of the booth and sitting next to me in mine. Warmth and the light, sweet scent of honeysuckle and cotton enveloped me. Keyleth kept hugging me, her words muffled.

"He was so upset, Sonia, I've never seen him more desperate, not even with—well, he told me and Dom." She pulled back enough to look at me, and I nearly collapsed without her hug supporting me. "We've been looking through the city archives on anything related to a curse like yours, but without knowing really what to research—"

"Yeah," I sighed, the sound hard in my own ears. My lungs fluttered until I sucked air down again. Maybe I needed one more potion. "I plan on combing through the Black House archives to see if they have anything on my birth mother Grace or another Ghost Whisperer. I mean they have to have some information on what keeps happening to them, right?"

"They should." Keyleth muttered.

"Meaning?" Phontine shot into the air to hover right before us.

"Look," Keyleth began, "Ever since I came to Blakewell, the only Ghost Whisperer I'd ever heard of was a part of their House. Actually, I'd never heard of a Ghost Whisperer before coming here."

"What, the Black House had a monopoly on Ghost Whisperers or something?" Phontine flitted to my shoulder and tucked her hands into my collar, like that would anchor me to the Living Lands. To The Obsidian Quill.

Before I could respond, a strange shimmer slid across the room—like heat rippling off asphalt, but colder somehow. The hum of conversation, the low hiss of the espresso machine, even the soft clinking of spoons and mugs—went silent. Not quiet. *Silent.*

The world seemed to hold its breath.

A table beside ours scraped as a chair was pushed back. A human woman staggered upright, her expression dazed, pale fingers pressed to her temple. Across from her, a Goblin male—humanoid in shape but unmistakably Magical with his dark, red-brown skin and pointed ears—reached out to steady her.

She recoiled like he'd struck her.

"Don't touch me," she gasped. Her voice carried in the sudden hush. "W-what the hell—what *are* you?"

He blinked, clearly startled. "Babe, it's me. Tom."

"G-Goblin. You're a—you're a Goblin."

His hand dropped. "Yeah. I've *always* been a Goblin. What's wrong with you?"

She shook her head rapidly, as if trying to dislodge a thought. "No. No, my Tom isn't—he's not—" She trailed off, her mouth working but no words forming.

"Amy?" The Goblin—Tom—reached for her again, but she flinched. The look on his face crumpled to something worse than devastation.

I felt the hairs rise along my arms. I glanced at Keyleth, who was already sliding out of our booth.

Keyleth approached slowly, arms loose at her sides, voice calm and even. "Hey. It's okay. You're okay. Take a breath."

The woman's gaze darted between Keyleth and the male—Tom. She looked ready to bolt.

But then it happened.

The shimmer returned—this time falling like a velvet curtain over the room. Sound rushed back in: spoons scraping ceramic, the grind of coffee beans, murmured conversation that hadn't stopped...except it had.

And just like that, the woman blinked and swayed. Her shoulders sagged like someone had just pressed a sleep spell on her.

"Tom?" she whispered, as if surfacing from a dream.

He caught her, gentle, unsure. "Yeah. It's me. I think maybe...I should get you home."

She nodded against his shoulder. "I feel so weird."

When Keyleth returned, her bracelets and necklace glowed. She didn't sit at first—just stood there, watching the door swing shut behind the couple.

"That's the third one this week," she muttered finally. "Humans flipping out mid-date. Magicals asking for tonics. Headaches. Bad dreams."

I rubbed the back of my neck. "What was that? It was like...a mist—something—I remember something about a mist."

Keyleth sank into the booth beside me and nodded slowly. "Mist?"

"Yeah," I rubbed at my temples, feeling like the thoughts were a second away from flying out of my head. "The mist and the Viel Towers. I remember something about them, Elias...He told me that the long thin poles that are all over Blakewell? You see them but once you look away you don't think anything of them."

"Yes," Keyleth's voice was quiet, her eyes unfocused and brow pinched. "Yeah, yesterday I saw one and the thought about what they were kept popping up in my mind all day, but I figured they were new because—"

"You never remembered seeing them?"

She nodded.

"Elais told me they release the mist throughout the city."

"But what does it do?" Keyleth asked, and Phontine fluttered down from my shoulder to sit on the rim of my discarded coffee and dunked her feet in.

"The mist, I think, it even affects us since we can't remember the Viel Towers or mist itself very well. It makes humans not freak out about magic or Magicals."

"Freak out?" Keyleth nearly hissed, it was the harshest sound I had ever heard from her. "That woman didn't even remember that her boyfriend was a Goblin."

Phontine, from her perch on my coffee cup, tilted her head. "That's not the weirdest part," she said softly. "We remembered. If the mist is supposed to keep humans and Magicals from remembering the Viel Towers, the mist and anything else they don't want, then why did we remember?"

Silence, different than the fall of the mist, shrouded our booth. Even now I couldn't quite recall what it felt like when the mist failed. Would I forget this whole conversation? Would they?

Needing the pep-me-ups more than ever, I uncorked the vial that had toppled over on the table and downed it to the stares of Keyleth and Phontine.

If the mist was failing, then would that mean all memories it had been suppressing came back? What would happen to the humans, and hell, the Magicals too, if the substance that they had been breathing in everyday for years was taken away?

Veil magic pulsed at my fingertips before I even knew it was rising.

It shimmered like heat, but colder—silver and smoke and the shimmer of water on stone. It spilled from my hands in delicate threads that danced like cobwebs catching moonlight.

The café lights flickered.

Someone screamed near the back counter, saying that a cold hand had touched them.

Oh no.

Ghosts.

They *sensed* it—Veil magic, the bridge between this world and the one they weren't ready to leave. My magic didn't just call them. It *ripped the veil thin* and made it impossible for them not to come through.

The first one appeared near the espresso machine, a woman with half her face melted and her eyes too wide, too wrong. She shrieked and knocked over a rack of enchanted mugs, which shattered in a spray of sparks and turned into butterflies that flew with fire tails.

More came.

A boy dragging spectral chains. A man missing half his torso. A translucent dog barking like thunder.

People couldn't *see* them. Just cold drafts, flickers, chaos with no source. But Keyleth knew what was happening. One look at me and the ghostlight glow of my magic spreading from my fingertips and she knew whatever was happening was coming from me—so did the handful of Mages in the Quill. Their arms lighting up with sigils or whispering protective spells, but the only target they could see was…well, me.

"Sonia," Keyleth said, voice taut. "Reel it in. *Now.*"

"I'm trying," I breathed, clutching my hands together—but the magic pulsed harder, brighter, sparking like starlight as it spilled down my wrists.

Phontine was shouting something, wings flaring, but the world was tilting.

Too much. I'd pushed *too* hard.

The floor felt like it wasn't there anymore.

I caught flashes—Keyleth's face above mine, her phone pressed to her ear. Then a car. A blur of city lights through the window. Someone's hand gripping mine tight.

Then stairs.

A hallway full of light.

I was being carried—strong arms, a steady heartbeat.

And then a white room. Gleaming counters. A sterile, lemon-and-salt smell I didn't recognize.

I tried to ask *where are we*, but the words slipped out of reach.

And then there was nothing but white and silence and the strange shimmer of Veil magic fraying at the edges of my mind.

The first thing I felt was the sting in my veins—like they'd been scrubbed raw with salt and then stitched together with ice.

The second was a hand around mine. Small. Warm. Fierce.

Keyleth.

I blinked my eyes open slowly, the sterile brightness of the med lab burning through the fog in my head. The walls here were always too clean, too pale—white marble veined with onyx, glowing faintly with sigils of containment and healing. It made my skin crawl.

"She's awake," Keyleth said, voice steady but tight. She leaned closer, brushing her thumb over my hand, her gold eyes sharp with fury and fear. "You scared the shit out of us."

My lips parted to respond, but my throat was dry—my body *empty*.

Like something vital had been scooped out of me and replaced with cold.

A gentle hand touched my shoulder. "Easy now."

I turned my head toward the voice and saw him.

The doctor.

Not just *a* doctor—the *one*. Dr. Corwin Fenwick. The kind one. The one with tired eyes and a quiet, steady way of existing. His presence was like balm on burned skin.

Relief unfurled inside me like a breath I hadn't realized I'd been holding. No one in the Black House was safe. Even though Calypso seemed to want the best for me, there were still too many secrets. But the doctor? He was kind down to his bones. It wasn't something that could be easily explained, it was just felt.

"You're safe," he said. "We've stabilized your vitals. You'll need to rest—deep, magical fatigue like this doesn't pass easily."

I nodded weakly, but my gaze had already slid past him.

To the tall, looming figure in the corner.

Matron Black.

Cold elegance. Sharp eyes. Her silhouette was a dagger of disapproval dressed in gray silk.

The twins stood beside her. Calypso's arms were crossed tight across her chest, her expression unreadable. Pandora's brows were furrowed, jaw tight like she was holding something back.

"You summoned ghosts in a public space," Matron Black said flatly. "Do you understand the risk you posed?"

"I didn't mean to," I croaked. "It just...happened."

"A lack of control is not an excuse. It's a liability." Matron Black took her time looking me over. "This is why you need advanced training. Why you need House membership."

Keyleth shot to her feet. "She needs *rest*. Not a lecture."

Matron Black's head tilted slightly, but Keyleth didn't flinch. If anything, her fingers tightened around mine.

"She stays," I whispered, dragging my gaze back to the Matron. "She stays until I can leave."

There was a beat of silence.

Then the Matron inclined her head. "Fine. You have until morning to recover. Then I expect you to be well enough to return home or attend class."

She turned on her heel, heels clicking like a countdown.

When the doors hissed closed behind her, the tension cracked.

"Holy hell, Sonia," Calypso breathed, stepping closer to the bed. "You had *everyone* panicking."

"I didn't mean for it to happen," I whispered. "I thought I had more control than that."

"You've been pushing yourself too hard," the doctor said gently. "This kind of collapse isn't just magical—it's *soul-deep*. Something is draining you, and the Matron is worried."

It was then that I saw Keyleth's blonde hair move like something was lifting it, but I saw nothing there until Phontine winked into existence.

She had been invisible. She had never gone invisible where I could not see her.

In a blink she fluttered down from Keyleth's shoulder and settled on my pillow, expression guarded and grim.

I looked away. Avoiding a room full of curious, anxious faces. Just let my gaze drift to the ceiling—where a sigil flickered faintly like a heartbeat.

I thought I knew what was draining me.

Training with Death wasn't just dangerous. It was *exhausting*. Because it wasn't just about magic. It was about *being seen*. Being unmade. And being rebuilt into something else.

Something that could survive.

But I couldn't say that out loud. Not yet.

So, I let my eyes flutter closed again, holding onto Keyleth's hand like an anchor, and whispered, "I just need to sleep a little."

12

The scent hit first. Clean, sterile. Too bright.

Then the ache settled in. A bone-deep exhaustion, the kind that curled beneath my skin like frost.

I stirred, blinking slowly as the sterile ceiling of the Black House's med lab came into focus. My body felt like lead, limbs sunk into the soft cot, breath dragging slow and uneven.

"Sonia?"

The voice was familiar—soft and worried. Keyleth.

I turned my head, sluggish and aching. Keyleth sat beside the bed, still in yesterday's clothes, her golden eyes red-rimmed but fiery with defiance. She was holding my hand like she'd been ready to throw down if anyone tried to make her leave.

Phontine was perched on the headboard, legs crossed and wings twitching. "Finally. You're awake. I was about to start poking you with your own hairbrush."

I gave a weak huff. "That'd be a new low."

Dr. Fenwick stepped into view then, dressed in khaki slacks and a navy-blue sweater, his presence a steady balm. His dark eyes swept over me with clinical precision—but there was relief in the subtle way his shoulders eased.

"Your vitals have recovered some strength now," he said gently. "No signs of magical collapse, though your output was...unusually high. It took a while to get you to stop leaking a low level of Veil magic. Since it is so rare and grossly under studied...well, we got you stable in the end." He glanced at the monitor sigils hovering beside me.

"Did I—?" I tried to sit up, but my body groaned in protest.

Keyleth helped steady me. "You passed out after Matron Black's little visit yesterday and haven't moved since."

Dr. Fenwick checked my pulse. "You're not to do anything strenuous until tomorrow evening. Your system needs to recalibrate."

I sighed and leaned back, wiping a hand down my face. "What time is it?"

"Well, you slept for fourteen hours," he said. "It's just past ten in the morning."

Phontine twirled in the air. "You missed breakfast, training, and three separate freak-outs."

I groaned. "The twins."

Keyleth nodded. "They're still in a Black House meeting. They asked me to check on you when you missed training." She hesitated, then added, "I stayed the night."

Warmth flooded my chest. I squeezed Keyleth's hand. "Thanks."

Keyleth stood. "I should drive you back to the apartment. You're still pale. And don't even think about going to training this afternoon."

I shook my head. "No. I need to go. I have to...talk to the Matron." My voice wavered on the last part, and I didn't miss the way Keyleth's jaw tightened.

As I slowly swung my legs off the cot and stood, Keyleth grabbed my elbow. "Sonia, seriously. You almost blew a hole in the Quill. You don't owe Matron Black anything."

"I'm not joining her House." My voice was quiet but certain. "That's what I need to say."

Phontine whistled. "Ballsy."

I didn't answer as I led Keyleth toward the glass med lab doors, needing to stretch my legs. Every step buzzed with weakness.

We were halfway down the corridor when I spotted a familiar silhouette on the other side of the glass.

Tall. Dark. Striking.

My breath caught.

McDara.

"What the hell is he doing here?" I whispered, heart stuttering. "He *hates* the Black House."

Keyleth followed my gaze, but I was already pulling away.

"Wait, Sonia—"

"I'll text you later," I said, voice too high, too rushed.

Ducking out of sight, I retreated deeper into the inner House corridor, my heart pounding.

My phone buzzed.

Hey. How are you? — McDara

I stared at the screen. My fingers hovered above the keyboard. *Say something. Say anything.*

But before I could decide...

A shift in the air.

Then his voice—cold and dry as shadow.

"Out of sight out of mind," a dark voice murmured, too close to my ear. "Until he happens to see you, that is."

I turned to find Death, materialized just behind me, his silver eyes burning with something sharp and unamused.

He was just...there.

Leaning against the corridor wall like he'd grown out of the shadows themselves.

"But when you're in his sights he doesn't waste time, does he?"

Death's voice slithered around me, low and precise, all bite behind a velvet edge.

My breath caught, and I turned to face him. "Seriously?" I said. "You weren't even here. Can you, like, see me even when you don't appear here?" I waved at the slightly translucent body that was still too close and leaning too casually against a wall that I knew he couldn't feel. "I know you follow me around, but you usually make yourself known. Are you actually stalking me though?"

"I don't stalk," he replied, pushing off the wall with infuriating calm. "I *watch.* When I have time, and what I see is you—still tethered to the Mage who left you easily."

I flinched. Just a flicker. But his eyes—those eyes that didn't miss *anything*—locked onto it.

"McDara didn't leave—" I started, then snapped my mouth shut.

"No," Death's smile was a shadow. "But he didn't stop you when you did, did he?"

Heat flushed my neck. I hated that he could see through me like this. Hated that part of me *still* wanted to believe McDara would show up for me when it counted.

Death stepped forward, slow and deliberate, and my spine straightened on instinct. He couldn't touch me in the Living Lands, but his presence wrapped around me like tension made flesh.

Then he paused. Tilted his head.

And something changed.

The bite drained from his expression. The venom in his voice faded. He went still. *Too* still.

He looked at me—not in that smug, serpentine way he always did—but like he was *assessing*.

"What have they done to you?"

The words struck low.

"It's fine. Just overworked my magic." I lifted my chin. "Dr. Fenwick worked spells and ran potions all night. I'm fine now."

Lie. It tasted bitter on my tongue.

Death's eyes dropped to my neck. His gaze sharpened, like he was looking *through* me. Then he moved—his hand lifting.

Fingers pale as moonlight, elegant and precise, reached for me like he meant to *touch*. And forgot.

The moment his hand passed through me, something in his expression closed.

No impact. No contact. Just air. Like I was smoke, and he was reaching for something already gone.

His fingers stilled inside the space where my skin should've been. Then, slowly, they curled into a fist.

A muscle in his jaw ticked. He exhaled, long and low.

"Your magic is unraveling."

I turned my face away. "I said I'm fine."

"Don't lie to me." That whisper sent a chill down my spine. "You lie to your friends and that Mage, but not to me, Sonia."

He was still close enough that the knuckles of his hand had sunk into my stringy, unwashed hair like he was my personal ghost. Still, those silver eyes caught me. Held me and threatened to unravel whatever supposed calm I was trying desperately to project.

Death didn't care how messy my life was. How *I* was. He had met every moment of my very chaotic life since coming to Blakewell without flinching. Lies were of no use with him and…Maybe I was starting to feel like I didn't need their thin veil of protection when it came to him.

I moved to step past him—because I couldn't keep standing here, not with him looking at me like that. Not with all this *feeling* clawing up my throat.

But I didn't make it far.

The air snapped.

Threads of shadow burst around my arms, my waist—cold and alive, coiling like smoke that had teeth.

I gasped. "Death—*don't*."

"I asked nicely."

"No—" I fought it. Pulled at the magic inside me, what was left of it. "I *said* I'm fine—"

But the world around me cracked like glass.

And I fell straight through it.

The moment the world split beneath my feet, I knew.

The Deathscape didn't *take* you gently. It *dragged*.

One blink, and my boots were skidding across black stone—cold air slicing my lungs, the red desert a blur in the distance.

I barely caught my balance before I was *seized*.

Death's hands closed around my arms, unyielding. Heat flared under his grip, his power burning bright through the threads that bound us.

"What the hell is wrong with you?" I snapped, shoving at his chest. "You can't just—"

"Be silent," he growled.

Not cold. Not cruel. *Panicked*.

His eyes roamed over me, frantic, furious, fixated. As if he expected to find me shattered.

And gods, maybe I was.

He touched my wrist, my cheekbone, the hollow beneath my throat—each pass of his hands more frantic than the last.

"Your soul," he bit out. "I felt it slipping."

"It was just training the other day. It drained me." I muttered, trying to pull away. "I'm fine, you overdramatic—"

"*Fine?*" His voice cracked open like thunder. "If your soul cracks, Little Bird, it will not heal. No amount of magic—*mine or yours*—can stitch it back together."

My breath stuttered.

He wasn't looking at me like I was annoying. Or inconvenient. Or fragile.

He was looking at me like I was *important*.

Like he'd burn the whole damn Deathscape down if I didn't get better.

My fury twisted in my gut. Tangled with heat. Hunger. A slow, aching pull toward him I didn't want to name.

"I told you I could handle it," I whispered, the fight slipping from my voice.

"No," he said, and stepped even closer. His forehead nearly brushing mine. "What you did the other night was basic. It should have felt natural to you as a Ghost Whisperer, but it taxed you far more than it should. Why?"

I didn't know, and from Death's searching, panicked voice, it felt like he was asking the very creators of my kind more than me. For one dizzy, dangerous second, I didn't want to fight him at all.

My breath shook as I stared up at him. "You said it could break," I whispered. "My soul."

The word tasted like frost.

Death didn't move. Not right away. Just stared at me with those eyes like molten silver—liquid and lit from within. Like the moment had caught him off guard.

Like *my fear* had.

And then—*the Wood help me*—he softened.

Only a fraction. But the whole of the Deathscape seemed to dim and turn liquid in its blood-red sands as Death's face gentled its harsh striking lines.

"I wouldn't let that happen," he said, low and rough. "Not to you."

It wasn't a vow. It was a *need*.

I should've questioned him. Argued. Asked what he got out of being bonded to me. Something. But the terror still lived beneath my ribs, sharp and skittering, and I hated that I needed reassurance from *him*. Hated even more that I *wanted* it.

"Is it really that bad?" I asked. "Am I—"

"Frayed," he murmured, and his hand hovered just above my sternum like he could see the place where the threads of me were unraveling. "But not lost."

My mouth trembled.

Death's hands found my arms, just above the elbow and he held on tight, and it took all of my splintered control not to fall against his chest and let him hold me up.

"I can help," he said. "If you'll let me."

That caught me.

My heart skidded against my ribs. "You're actually asking for permission?"

His eyes narrowed, mouth turning sharp and the soft bite of his fingertips dug into my arms. "It is something that you must willingly receive."

"Help how?"

A shadow of something darker curled behind his eyes, but his voice remained steady. Careful.

"A shot of my magic. Just enough to replenish what you've spent. It won't repair what's broken—but it will keep the pieces from falling apart. It will give you time to mend."

He stepped even closer.

The air between us pulsed.

"You'd give me that?" I asked. "Your magic?"

"I'd give you anything if it meant you wouldn't look at me like that again."

"Like what?"

He pulled me up to my toes, the expanse of his hands covering my upper arms, and made sure he had captured all of my attention before speaking. "Like, I would want your soul to break."

Like I was afraid of him.

Like I didn't trust him.

My lips parted. I didn't even mean to speak—but the words slipped out, bare and aching. "I don't know how to let you help me."

Death inhaled like the sound of my honesty stole the breath from him.

And then—*so gently I could've shattered*—he reached up and cradled my face in his palms. Cool. Steady. Reverent.

"Then let me show you," he said, his thumb brushing beneath my eye like I was something sacred. "Just this once."

And maybe it was a trick. Maybe it was a mistake.

But I needed someone to help me, and if he chose to because our bond was necessary for him, then...The consequences weren't something my tired brain wanted to think about right now.

I whispered, "Okay."

Death's thumbs ghosted along my cheekbones as he studied me—no, *devoured* me—with that gaze. Like he needed to memorize every part of me before he dared do more.

"This will feel...close," he said softly. "There's no other way to give you part of me."

I swallowed, peeking up at him. "Define close."

His lips curved in the faintest echo of a smirk. "You'll know it when you feel it."

Before I could question that, he drew me closer. Not yanked. Not demanded. Just *guided*—like he couldn't help himself. Like the space between us offended him.

His forehead dipped to mine, his breath brushing my lips. Cold and electric.

I barely managed a whisper. "What do I do?"

"Nothing," he said, voice low and reverent? Content? Something that seemed as foreign for him to feel as it was for me in this moment because being held like this...it was close to peace. "Just...*accept* what I offer you."

Then his hand slipped from my face and found mine—pressing our palms together. Again. Like before when we made our deal.

Magic flickered at the edges of my skin.

It started in his fingers—a slow, deliberate seep of energy that curled over my palm like smoke and settled into me with a shiver. Scorching and deep.

My breath caught.

Because it didn't stop at my hand.

His magic slid up my arm like a lover's caress, winding through my veins and tugging gently at the places where I felt frayed. Not repairing. But holding. Cradling. Like he *refused* to let me fall apart.

"Oh gods," I breathed, because it felt like he was *everywhere*. Not just in my magic—but under my skin, in my ribs, behind my teeth.

Death shuddered. Actually *shuddered*. His eyes fluttered shut, jaw clenched.

"Sonia..."

The sound of my name on his tongue—it was almost a growl.

And I realized—*this* was intimate for him too.

His magic trembled through me like it recognized something. Like it *wanted* me.

"Is this normal?" I asked, voice shaking.

"I don't know," he rasped. "I've never shared my magic before."

He opened his eyes, and they were glowing—pure molten silver, burning with something I didn't have a name for.

His free hand hovered, then slowly—almost reverently—slid through my hair, tangling gently in the strands near my neck.

"This," he said, voice a breath against my mouth, "is what happens when you give part of your soul to someone who could break you."

My lips parted.

"And yet I'd still do it again," he whispered. "For you."

My heart was hammering. My skin burned where his magic lived inside me. I couldn't think. Could barely breathe.

"You're...insane," I managed.

He smiled, slow and dark. "About you? Maybe."

And then—like he couldn't help himself—he leaned in again.

Close.

So close I swore he could taste my next breath.

But he didn't kiss me. Something kept him from covering that small space between us, and I didn't know if it was because of our deal. I hadn't asked for any information or lessons...Would that be the only time he'd kiss me?

He slowly withdrew his hand from mine, his magic trailing behind it like smoke slipping from a flame.

I almost reached for him.

Almost begged him not to stop.

But then his voice—quieter now—cut through the silence.

"You'll feel better soon."

Liar. I already felt *too* much.

13

The Deathscape shimmered around us, still as starlight on black glass.

I sagged against him, body boneless. Not because I was so desperate to touch him, or that I didn't try to stand on my own, but because I *couldn't* hold myself upright anymore. I let my head fall to his chest, pressing against the cool, quiet steadiness of him.

And he just...stood there.

Frozen.

I could feel it—his disbelief. The weight of it wrapped around me as surely as his arms did. As if my trust was something sacred. As if he didn't know what to do with it.

His chest didn't rise and fall like a human's. There was no heartbeat beneath my ear. Only a silence so profound it echoed.

But his grip tightened—just a little. Like maybe, just maybe, he didn't *want* to let go.

Then the world shifted.

A ripple, like fog bending around light, and—

We were in my room.

The Living Lands.

His arms vanished.

No fanfare. No warning. One second, I was wrapped in Death's stillness.

The next, I was falling.

Luckily, he'd placed me right beside my bed. I crumpled onto the mattress with the grace of a dropped marionette, half-draped over the covers.

"Sonia? I saw you disappearing into thin air and assumed Death took you and I kept Keyleth from worrying but—" Phontine zipped into view, her tiny wings beating a nervous hum. "Are you—did he hurt you?"

I managed a groan.

She hovered a little closer, watching my half-lidded eyes flutter closed. "Okay. That's...not encouraging."

I didn't answer. Sleep pulled me down like quicksand.

Phontine

Phontine gasped.

Her glow dimmed to a flickering violet as she turned. Her stare locked on the corner of the room.

Right where *he* stood.

A faint outline shimmered in the shadows—barely more than a ripple in the air. But it *was* him. Broad shoulders. Tilted head. Unmistakable presence.

"I can *see* you," she whispered.

Death didn't reply.

"How are you here?" Her wings buzzed with unease. "How are you *visible*?"

Still silence.

Then her awe twisted to suspicion. "You've been hovering around her ever since she touched the Deathscape. Pulling her in. Keeping her close. Why?"

She flew a little higher, puffing herself up. "She's weaker every time she comes back. Don't pretend you don't notice it."

She flew closer, voice rising. "What do you *want* from her?"

Death's head turned, ever so slightly.

"I asked you a question, corpse god."

His form sharpened. A little clearer. A little colder.

"You forget," he said, voice like soot sliding over steel, "who you speak to."

Phontine jolted backward, but her wings didn't falter. "Then remind me. Because from where I'm standing, you're just a shadow with boundary issues. And you can't use your magic in the Living Lands. So how is it that I can see you?"

He stepped forward—and though his form remained incorporeal, the pressure in the room shifted. Like the air itself remembered what it meant to fear.

"I allow your sharp tongue," Death said, "for one reason."

Phontine blinked.

"It would hurt her," he said simply, "if I tore your soul from your body and cast it somewhere even she could never find."

Phontine's glow dimmed to a pinprick. "You wouldn't."

His outline flickered, a slow, rippling smile in the dark. "I would. I *want* to."

He looked at Sonia then. At the way she curled into the bed, lashes brushing her cheek, the brand on her neck faintly glowing.

"I'm beginning to find," he murmured, more to himself than anyone, "that the idea of her hurting makes me...uncomfortable."

Phontine said nothing. Just watched him. Sure that *uncomfortable* was not the word he was looking for.

"You speak as if she cannot trust me." Death's form flickered, but those silver eyes sparked brighter. "But she doesn't even know what *you* are. Does she...Pixie?"

Evening light slanted across the room, thin and silvery through the gauzy curtains. My body felt heavy but warm, the kind of warmth that came from magic still humming beneath the surface. It pulsed low in my belly, a slow, echoing rhythm—like something had been kindled and was still burning there.

I blinked blearily at the ceiling. Death. His arms. His magic.

The memory came back in pieces—how I'd gone limp against him, how he'd held me like something precious. How he'd filled me with his power, dark and ancient and *intimate*, like he'd slipped it beneath my skin and left it curling in my veins.

Gods. I flushed. My entire body *throbbed* at the memory, as if it remembered too.

It had been the most sensual thing I'd felt in...longer than I cared to admit—and far more dangerous than it had any right to be.

I turned my head slowly.

Phontine was curled up in the armchair, snoring softly, wings twitching like she was chasing something in a dream. I smiled faintly and reached for my phone on the nightstand.

Two unread messages blinked at me.

> **~~McHotty~~ McDara:** *Are you feeling any symptoms of the curse yet?*

> **~~McHotty~~ McDara:** *I still want to help. Any way I can.*

The texts were from earlier. Before Death had dragged me into his realm. Before his hands had brushed my skin like a vow.

I stared at the screen.

The messages were...clinical. Detached. Like checking on an assignment. Like I was a *task*—not the girl he'd once kissed like he was coming apart.

I swallowed hard, the hollow behind my ribs aching.

No. I couldn't deal with that right now. Not when my pulse was still carrying the echo of someone else's magic. Someone who'd held me like he wasn't sure he'd let go.

I powered off the screen and let it drop to the bed beside me.

I rubbed at my head and the messy mop of black hair that was making a sad attempt at a styled bob.

The heavy fatigue that had dragged me under earlier was gone. In its place was a low, persistent thrum—energy curling through my limbs like wildfire licking up dry timber. I felt *buzzed*, electric. Like my body couldn't sit still another second.

I swung my legs over the side of the bed, planting bare feet against the cool floor.

No dizziness. No weight dragging me down.

Just *movement* begging to happen.

"Phon," I whispered.

She stirred, groaned, and rolled toward the back of the chair, her wings fluttering once.

I decided to shower and dress since she was dead to the world.

Leaving the adjoining bathroom, I padded over to the closet, dressed, then turned back to my Pixie. I nudged her gently. "Phontine. Hey. Wake up."

Her eyes cracked open, blurry and violet. "Whassit...Are you okay?"

"Yeah." I glanced toward the door. "Actually...I think I'm better than okay. Come on. Quietly."

That got her attention. She blinked once, then pushed herself upright with a muttered curse, wings stretching as she shook off sleep. "You're glowing weird. Not, like, literally—but close. Where are we going?"

"Just follow me."

We eased the bedroom door open. The apartment beyond was quiet. The T.V. in the living room glowed softly, flickering over the sleeping form of Pandora sprawled on the couch, a throw blanket half-tangled around her legs. No sign of Calypso.

I crept across the hardwood floor, motioning for Phontine to follow.

We slipped out the front door and into the shadowed quiet of New Town.

The street was nearly empty. Just the whisper of wind through the alley and the faint, blue haze of Magelight from the streetlamps above. Magic lingered in the air here—too quiet. Too still. As if the whole district knew to breath softly. Sometimes I felt like New Town acted as if a slumbering beast lived under its perfectly paved streets and if they were too loud, lived too brightly, it would wake.

Phontine caught up to me on the sidewalk, brushing her tangled lavender strands from her face. "Okay, you're worrying me. Where are we going?"

I didn't slow. "The Black House."

"What?" she hissed. "Are you joking? That place nearly *ate* you last time."

I didn't stop walking. "I need answers. I've got three days until I'm supposed to tell Matron Black whether I'm in or out. And if I say no, I lose access to everything—training, resources...if I don't learn more about this bloodline curse while I have access to their archives, I won't survive my birthday."

Phontine hovered off my shoulder and buzzed in front of my face, hands on her hips. "Okay, but—why *tonight*? Why not after another nap? Or food? Or, I don't know, *therapy*?"

"Because my birth mother was a Ghost Whisperer too. Because she trained there. Because she died at twenty-five just like every other one of us. And if there's anything the Black House is hiding about *why* that keeps happening, I need to find it now."

"Yeah," Phontine's wings fluttered fast as she angled her tiny body to look at me while flying. "Search the archives before telling The Dark Matron we're not joining her weird Mage cult."

I nodded absently as we crossed the street. "I actually have the energy to think about all this let alone *do* something."

Phontine's wings slowed. She looked at me—really looked at me—and I saw the worry flicker sharp behind her eyes.

"You were practically dead this morning," she whispered. "And then *he* dragged you away. You were drained down to your *soul*, Sonia."

"I'm better now."

"You're *glowing*. You look like you've been kissed by an arcane moonbeam."

I hesitated. Then—"Death gave me a little of his magic."

The words fell soft. Uneasy.

Phontine froze midair. And dropped three feet. I scrambled to grab her before she became a Pixie size smear on the perfectly even cement.

"He *what*?"

"It wasn't—he offered. Said it would help me recover faster. And it did."

She stared at me. Not blinking. Not breathing.

I shifted. "What?"

"I don't know if I'm more horrified that *he gave it to you*...or that he *could*."

Her voice was thin. Small.

I swallowed. "I feel fine."

"Yeah. Until you wake up one day and realize you're tethered to the Lord of Corpses with no way out."

I didn't answer. Because part of me *was* afraid.

But the louder part? The part that was humming with energy and resolve?

That part said *I want more*.

"Let's just focus on the plan," I murmured. "We get into the Black House. I want to find whatever records they have on the year Grace died. Any about the curse. Whatever records they're hiding. If there's a way to break this thing—I'm going to find it."

I turned to look at her. "You don't have to come with me."

Phontine snorted, folding her arms. "Are you *kidding*? If you think I'm letting you break into creepy Mage headquarters while glowing like a half-possessed banshee, you clearly don't know me."

A breath escaped me—half laugh, half relief. "Good."

We turned, and together, vanished into the shadows. Toward the truth.

Toward whatever the Black House was still hiding.

14

It was nearly nine p.m. by the time the bus hissed to a stop, and the sharp scent of cold glass and restrained magic hit the back of my throat.

The neighborhoods surrounding the end of New Town were unsettling—slick, modern things with reflective windows and not a whisper of human warmth. The kind of houses that looked like they could watch you breathe and report it.

The Black House sat at the center of Blue Lane like a jagged blade hidden in silk.

Phontine perched on my shoulder, quiet as I stepped through the iron-framed entry.

No one stopped us.

There wasn't another soul in sight which...was odd. It wasn't that late, and I knew a lot of the House Mage's lived in apartments on the top floors. Still, the halls were as quiet and empty as a tomb.

I couldn't see anyone but that didn't mean I couldn't *feel* anything.

"She knows," I murmured, more to myself than to Phontine. "Matron Black probably feels every time I cross the threshold."

"Then let's make it quick." Phontine's whisper buzzed in my ear as we slipped deeper into the House, the wards and candlelight shifting around us like breathless ghosts.

The hallways were too quiet. Too sterile. Like even sound didn't dare linger here.

We passed the training hall, then the ceremonial wing. I took the stairs that curved into the lower levels, my fingers grazing the cold banister.

"What is your plan for after we hit the archives?" Phontine asked softly.

I didn't look at her. Just kept walking. "I'll get Death to keep training me. If we can find anything useful here—anything that tells us how the curse works—maybe we can figure out how to break it before my birthday."

Phontine hovered off my shoulder, wings flickering with violet light. "I don't think you should trust him. Anything he says could be lies."

I paused at the bottom of the stairs.

"He's Death," she whispered. "There's no way he's doing all this out of the goodness of his shriveled, little heart. He wants *something*."

I stared ahead at the corridor that led to the archives, heart pounding. Of course, she was right.

I'd been thinking the same thing since the first time he smiled at me like I was a puzzle he'd already solved.

The bond between us—this invisible tether that let him pull me into the Death-scape—let him *feel* things through me. It had to benefit him somehow. Maybe even more than it benefited me.

And still.

Still.

There were moments—quiet, terrifying, beautiful moments—when he looked at me like I mattered. When his touch steadied me instead of stealing something. When he held me like the world was something he could keep at bay if I just let him.

I didn't tell Phontine any of that. Not the way I sometimes craved his hands on me. Not the way I still felt the thrum of his magic moving through my bones.

Instead, I slipped through the threshold of the archives and whispered, "I'm not stupid. I'll use him to learn what I need. And when I survive my birthday, I'll figure out how to end the bond between us. Whatever it takes."

Phontine hovered beside me for a long second.

Her face was tight with something unreadable. "Right," she said eventually. "Let's start digging."

She didn't sound convinced.

Neither was I.

But I stepped into the archives anyway.

Because time was bleeding out.

And if I didn't find answers soon, I wouldn't need to worry about Death's bond or Matron Black's control.

Because I'd already be *dead*.

Dust coiled in the stale air, the deeper we moved into the archives.

The stone walls whispered with the weight of centuries—records and relics from every Mage generation buried in towering metal drawers and sigil-locked cabinets. The kind of room designed to suffocate secrets rather than share them.

I ran my fingers across the spines of cracked-leather tomes, eyes scanning for dates. Anything cataloged around the year Grace died.

Phontine flitted overhead, her glow casting long, flickering shadows as she darted through the air like a violet spark.

"No sign of bloodline stuff yet," she muttered. "Unless it's filed under *Inevitable Doom*."

I didn't laugh.

Because I'd just felt the temperature drop.

Not gently or slowly.

But with the swift cruelty of an open grave.

Phontine let out a yelp and darted toward me, her wings icing at the edges.

"Not again," she hissed, voice trembling. "Sonia—"

"I know," I said, breath ghosting into a fog.

It was *freezing*. That sharp, brittle cold that burned more than it chilled. My skin prickled. My breath hitched.

And then I saw her.

She wavered at the end of the corridor, a pale blur peeling itself out of the shadows. The Faceless Woman. Her movements were wrong—unsteady, like she couldn't quite remember how to make her body obey. Each step dragged, feet whispering against the floor as if sound itself resisted her.

Her face—or where it should've been—was a smooth, colorless void. A smear of skin wiped clean of every human feature, every trace of who she once was. The absence of eyes, of a mouth, of *anything* made her look less like a ghost and more like the memory of one—unfinished, unraveling.

She tilted her head toward me, as though she could *see*, but the motion was jerky, disjointed. Her hands lifted, trembling, fingers grazing the air like she was reaching for a face she no longer had. A soft, hollow sound escaped her—a sigh, a sob, maybe both.

Where she passed, frost followed.

Crystalline veins of ice unfurled across the floor, spiraling toward me in delicate, living threads. The air grew sharper, heavy with the scent of old stone and winter. Near the base of a shelving unit, the frost thickened, spreading wide until letters began to take shape—etched in a fine, shimmering sheen.

FOLLOW. ME.

Phontine gripped my shoulder. "Sonia don't. All the ghosts that come from the Black House are *wrong*."

"No," I whispered. "She's not wrong. She's...trying to communicate with me."

The ghost turned.

And the air grew even colder.

I followed.

Down through the winding rows of forgotten histories and misfiled spells. Past artifacts that pulsed faintly with old magic. The ghost's burned back guided me, every step painting frost across the floor like a trail only I could read.

She paused at a heavy wall in the far corner. There were no shelves. No drawers.

Just blank stone.

Phontine hovered beside me, muttering something about how this felt like a terrible idea.

I pressed my hand to the wall.

It *shivered* under my touch.

A pulse. A beat. A rhythm not my own.

The Faceless Woman raised a delicate, nearly transparent hand and pointed to a patch of wall just above eye level. The frost bloomed there again, a single word this time.

PUSH.

I hesitated.

Then pushed.

The stone groaned inward, revealing a narrow, pitch-black crevice behind it. Not a hallway. A crawlspace.

"You've got to be kidding," I muttered.

The ghost waited.

No flicker of impatience. Just...stillness.

Resolute.

Phontine's tiny voice cracked. "Please don't go into the creepy death tunnel."

"I have to," I whispered.

Because whatever was hidden in that space wasn't meant to be found by anyone else.

And that could only mean one thing.

It had to be about the curse. I hoped.

I dropped to my knees.

And crawled into the dark.

The crawlspace was tighter than I expected.

Rough stone scraped at my shoulders. Dust choked the air, thick and ancient. I couldn't lift my head—had to keep my body hunched, hands dragging me forward as the cold closed in behind us like a second skin.

Phontine landed on my shoulder, wings folding tightly. Even she seemed hesitant to fly in this space.

"This is—" she whispered, voice barely audible in the stale dark, "—officially the worst idea you've ever had."

She wasn't wrong.

My breath echoed too loud in the tunnel. The silence pressed down like a weight. The crawlspace sloped downward—barely—but enough that I could feel gravity pulling me deeper with each drag of my limbs.

And then, suddenly, the air changed.

Not warmer. Just...older. Horribly stale.

My hand slipped past the last edge of stone—and met open air.

I blinked into the black, heart thudding, then slowly pulled myself forward.

And emerged into a chamber that *should not exist*.

The space opened around me like a breath held for centuries. A low, vaulted ceiling stretched overhead, crumbling in places where the roots of the Black House had pushed through. The air tasted of limestone and long-dead things. Moss and decay clung to the walls, but beneath it—etched into the stone—were remnants of something sacred.

Archways. Columns. A cracked basin that might've once been used for ceremonial water.

Tomb.

This was a tomb.

Not just for the dead. For memory. For magic that had been *buried*—on purpose.

I stood slowly, taking it in. Stone sconces jutted from the walls, though their fire had long since gone cold. The floor was uneven, pitted, with faint traces of a sigil carved into its center. Something that might have once been used for protection—or imprisonment.

Phontine hovered beside me again, silent for once. Her glow reflected off something near the far corner. My eyes followed it—

And there, carved into the stone just above shoulder height, were two names. *Celeste & Theo.*

The lettering was worn, but still graceful. Below the names bloomed an intricate rose, its stem winding down like a curl of memory etched into time.

Phontine floated closer. "This looks...pre-House. Like...*way* older than anything upstairs."

I nodded, heart heavy with something I didn't yet understand. A name carved in a place like this was no accident.

"Maybe this was the *original* Black House," I murmured, fingers brushing over the rose. "Or what came before."

But we hadn't come for ghosts of love stories past.

We'd come for *Grace.*

I turned from the carving and scanned the chamber. There were niches along the walls, once used to house bones or relics. Broken shelves. A collapsed bench in one corner with a strip of torn velvet still clinging to the stone like it had been placed there just yesterday.

But it was the altar that drew me.

Half buried beneath crumbled brick and vines, it stood at the far end of the room. Squat. Quiet. Waiting.

I approached slowly. The ghost hadn't followed us in. I was alone in this decision.

One breath. Then two.

And then I knelt beside the altar, hands sweeping across the vines until I found it.

A seam.

A hollow tucked into the base—barely noticeable unless you were looking. Added by Phontine's natural Pixie glow I was looking at everything my eyes could see.

Heart hammering, I slid my fingers inside and pulled out a thick, leather-bound book. Its edges were warped from age and moisture, but the binding glowed faintly—sigils pressed into the spine still pulsing with quiet, Veil-slick magic.

I turned it over.

Grace Guen

My birth mother's name, burned into the cover like a brand.

The breath left my lungs.

Phontine gasped, then clamped her hands over her mouth.

This was it.

The answers she had died for. The reason I was cursed to follow in her footsteps.

And maybe—just maybe—how to *stop it*.

I stood there in the tomb, holding Grace's ledger to my chest, and for the first time since stepping foot into the Black House...

I felt hope.

15

My hands were coated in dirt and crumbling dust, my knees ached from crawling, and Grace's ledger was clutched to my chest like a lifeline. Phontine hovered close to my cheek, wings fluttering in near-silent bursts. Neither of us spoke.

Not since we came up through the crawlspace and back into the archives.

Because something had changed.

The moment we'd emerged, the air had felt...wrong.

Heavier. Like the walls were listening. Like the floors were waiting.

We were halfway to the atrium when I felt it again—an unmistakable prickle at the back of my neck.

Someone was watching.

"Don't look behind you," I whispered, barely mouthing the words.

Phontine didn't need the warning. She pressed close to the side of my neck, nearly disappearing into my hair, her glow dimmed to a faint lilac hum.

We crept toward the back corridor, but before we could round the corner, someone stepped into our path.

I stopped short, heart lurching.

"Miss Bryd?" Dr. Fenwick stood before us, holding a steaming mug of tea in one hand. His blue and white striped pajamas were rumpled, his hair slightly mussed—he must've just come from the kitchen.

He blinked, gaze sweeping from my dirt-covered knees to the wild, slightly crazed look I knew I wore. "What are you doing here this late?"

"I—" I hesitated, clutching the ledger tighter. "I'm looking for answers, Dr. Fenwick. My curse..."

How was I supposed to explain what I was doing? That I was looking for a way not to die in a couple of months, and if I needed to rob the Black House archives blind before turning down Matron Black's offer, I would?

His brow creased. "You shouldn't be in the House."

"Why not?" I asked, voice low, tight.

He opened his mouth. A flicker of something passed across his face—hesitation, conflict, maybe even guilt. Like he was about to say something important. Like he *wanted* to say more.

And suddenly, I remembered—

Calypso and Pandora had been caught in mandatory House meetings all week. Every day. Long hours, no explanations. I hadn't thought anything of it at the time—just chalked it up to more Black House politics. But now?

Now my stomach twisted.

Had something happened?

Had the House changed around me, and I'd been too distracted, too drained, to notice?

Was that what Dr. Fenwick had been about to say?

But he didn't speak.

Because that was the moment, we both heard it.

A sound that silenced every thought.

Footsteps.

Measured. Precise. Unhurried and deliberate.

My pulse spiked.

Dr. Fenwick's head snapped toward the sound, and without a word, he yanked me into a small alcove just behind a curved wall beside a tall corner window. The space was barely large enough to hide me. Phontine zipped into the shadow beneath the window ledge.

Dr. Fenwick flattened a hand against the wall to keep me tucked against it, body angled as a shield.

We waited.

The click of heels on marble drew closer—sharp and distinct, like teeth on bone.

Then I saw her.

Matron Black.

Reflected in the dark glass of the window in front of me.

She glided like a phantom through the corridor beyond, wrapped in a silk robe that shimmered with sigils. Her slippers—glass, I was almost sure of it—clacked with every step. Her hair was coiled high atop her head, a white crown.

But it was her *eyes* that sent a ripple of cold through my blood.

She was prowling.

Not walking. Not passing through.

Hunting.

She moved past the junction, pausing only once to glance down a side corridor. My body locked still. I didn't breathe.

Was she looking for me?

My fear surged so violently it snapped like a signal through the Veil.

And then—I saw him.

For the briefest flicker, Death's face formed in the window's reflection. His eyes wide, furious. But before I could speak, before I could even think, he vanished again.

Just a breath of him, then gone.

Dr. Fenwick moved fast. Too fast for a normal man of his age. He took my wrist and guided me through the winding inner hallways with such precision it felt...unnatural. Like he knew every creak of every floorboard. Like he could *sense* the Matron's movements before they happened.

He didn't speak until we reached a side door half-hidden behind a tapestry of the twelve original Mage House crests.

The cool night air hit me like a splash of water.

I turned to thank him—but his gaze had dropped to the ledger in my arms.

Recognition flared.

And something else. *Dread.*

He met my eyes. "You need to leave. And Sonia..." His voice was softer now. "Don't come back."

I froze.

"What?"

"Not here. Not again." His jaw worked like he wanted to say more. Needed to. But instead, he looked back toward the House and stepped into the shadows.

The door clicked shut behind him.

I stood there, dirt-streaked and full of questions, clutching Grace's ledger while the Matron hunted ghosts in silk.

And for the first time, I wasn't sure if the House was more afraid of me—

Or if it knew what I was about to learn.

We didn't stop at the nearest bus station.

Didn't even glance at it.

Phontine flitted silently beside me, her wings barely stirring the air, her tiny form hidden beneath the blunt ends of my slightly grown-out bob. We walked for miles—away from the manicured streets that cradled the Black House, away from the knowing eyes that might've watched us crawl out of shadows we were never meant to find.

By the time we made it deeper into New Town, the streets were deserted. Midnight hung heavily above us, the flicker of Magelights catching on the slick pavement. Somewhere far off, a horn wailed like a dying thing.

I dropped down on the edge of a perfectly white painted bench at the next bus stop, hands still tight around Grace's ledger, heart louder than the silence.

"Do buses even run this late in New Town?" I murmured. New Town was always strangely quiet, even at midday when there were Fairies and Mages walking the streets, but there was no one out right now. It was such a startling contrast to any time I had been in Old Town at night. It sat just a handful of miles away, never sleeping and thumping with music and life, and here...silence. Just unending silence. I supposed some might call it peace.

Phontine landed on the crook of my elbow, arms crossed over her chest. "You're just now wondering that?"

I opened my mouth to answer—

And the temperature *plummeted*.

Frost exploded across the glass of the bus sign in a fast, searing sweep. The metal groaned under the cold. My breath hitched as the ice spiraled in curling letters.

She was here.

The Faceless Woman.

Phontine let out a choked curse, wings buzzing frantically as she darted higher, her glow flickering. "Oh, no—you've got to be kidding me. Sonia, get rid of her!"

But I didn't move.

Didn't even blink.

Because the frost was shaping words across the sign.

I will help you find the truth about Grace.

My pulse stumbled. More frost bloomed, spreading outward in intricate veins before scratching out a second line:

But you must do something for me.

I swallowed hard, still clutching the ledger to my chest. "What do you want?"

"Sonia!" Phontine hissed, flying a tight, panicked circle around me. "You've still got magic left from Death—use it! Send her away!"

I shook my head. "Not yet."

The air behind the sign thickened—then she appeared. The Faceless Woman wavered in and out of focus, gliding closer, her head tilted as if listening for a sound she could no longer hear. Her facelessness was worse in the streetlight—a smooth, featureless oval that seemed to droop at the edges of her jaw like her face was literally melting off her right then and there. She lifted a trembling hand toward me, palm out.

Another surge of cold hit, sharp enough to sting. New words bled through the frost, letter by letter:

Keep away from the Blacks. Matron. The boy.

The chill of it crept through my veins, burrowed deep.

Phontine's voice came small and frightened. "Sonia..."

But I couldn't answer. I just stared at the frost still clinging to the glass—those words breathing cold against the night.

The boy? What boy?

"What do you mean? Stay away from what boy?" I whispered, more to myself than to Phontine.

The Pixie was clutching a strand of my hair like a lifeline, her tiny wings buzzing in slow, anxious beats. "She said stay away from the Blacks. Like Matron Black?"

The only Black I knew of was Matron Black...

"No," I swallowed hard. "McDara is related to the Black's remember?"

Phontine cursed.

"He's Matron Black's nephew." I looked to the slowly fading form of The Faceless Woman. "Why do you want me to stay away from the Blacks? From McDara?"

Keep away from the Black's flared with a renewed layer of frost, and then, appearing beneath it, like it was carved by an unsteady hand, was: *Cillian McDara.*

Before I could say anything else, the air shifted. The kind of shift that tasted like thunder and felt like the moment before lightning struck skin.

A shadow peeled into the space in front of us—and just like that, the Faceless Woman dissolved. Like ash on wind.

"*No!*" I snapped, a spark of fury cutting through my exhaustion. "Why would you do that? She was trying to help me—"

"I didn't force her to move on," Death said, voice smooth as smoke. "She'll find you again. If she wants to."

He stepped forward from the dark, fully formed, dressed in that storm-slick coat of his, silver eyes gleaming like mercury.

"Sonia..." Phontine sunk onto my shoulder, I could feel her tiny hands gripping strands of my hair.

"I was in the middle of something important," he said, tone cool but...off. "And then I felt it. A wave of fear so sharp it nearly choked off my magic—" He pressed a hand to his chest like he still hadn't recovered. "And then I was *there*. Standing in front of you. You looked terrified, and then—just as quickly—I was back in the Deathscape."

I swallowed hard. "I don't know what happened."

Death tilted his head, like he was watching a puzzle shift into place. "I think I do."

"Well, then tell me," I said, too tired for games. "Stop killing me slowly with anticipation."

That made him laugh. *Gods help me*, that *laugh*—low and rich and warm enough to curl around every nerve I had left. The sound startled Phontine and I felt a slight wind as she darted off my shoulder and backed away from us.

"I think," he said, stepping closer, "you were scared...and you called me."

I scoffed. "You think my first instinct, when I think Matron Black is going to filet me alive with her Wood-forsaken magic, is to call *you*?"

Death smiled. Not his usual smirk, but something more...lethal. Intimate. "Who else do you have to call?"

The words landed like a knife to the chest. Clean. Sharp. Too damn true.

I looked away, jaw tight. "Leave me alone. I just want to go home and take a shower."

He didn't move. His gaze dipped lower, trailing down my dirt-streaked jeans, the grime on my hands, the ancient leather-bound ledger pressed tight to my chest.

His voice turned curious, almost amused. "What *have* you been doing?"

I sighed. "Broke into the archives. Found my dead birth mother's journal. Barely escaped getting caught by the House's evil mistress in glass slippers. You know—normal, middle-of-the-week things."

He raised a brow. "You found her ledger."

"Cliff notes version. I'll explain tomorrow in the Deathscape." I looked up at him, one brow arched, voice a little too soft to be innocent. "Unless you're too busy brooding over dead empires or doing whatever *important work* the embodiment of death gets up to."

That earned another quiet laugh. "I'll make time."

Then, softer—something like velvet over a blade—he murmured, "Sweet dreams, Little Bird."

He looked past me—his dark gaze locking onto something just over my shoulder. The change in him was subtle but sharp, like a predator scenting something unexpected.

I felt a jolt against my scalp as Phontine gripped a strand of my hair a little too tightly.

"Hey," I murmured, glancing sideways. "What—"

But when I turned to look, all I saw was the iced-over bus sign still dripping frost. Shadows pooling in the corners of the street.

Most of the ice words were melted, but I could still make out McDara's name.

I'd bet the newly transferred money in my bank account from Mom that Death had seen it too.

Behind me, Phontine was dead silent.

And when I turned back, Death was already gone.

Gone like he'd never been there at all.

We waited.

Waited long enough to realize the bus wasn't coming.

Of course it wasn't. New Town didn't care that we were exhausted and haunted and carrying a book that could save my life.

So, we walked.

Down the too clean sidewalks, past shuttered cafés and magic-lit lamp posts that buzzed with the kind of charm that felt *forced*. Like everything here had been scrubbed spotless, polished to perfection—and cursed to stay that way. One foot in front of the other. Ledger pressed tight to my chest.

And the echo of Death's laugh still in my ears.

16

The smell of black coffee hit me before I turned the corner into the kitchen, but it wasn't what made my pulse ease for the first time since last night's descent into tombs and terror.

It was the sound.

Laughter. Soft and real and edged with the usual chaos of Calypso and Pandora arguing over whose turn it was to clean the stovetop. Something normal. Something blessedly mundane.

For a second, I just stood there, leaning against the doorway like a ghost haunting my own life.

Pandora was cross-legged on the counter, her curls piled into a gravity-defying bun, face flushed from sleep and irritation. Calypso was wearing one of her obscenely short robes, pouring syrup like she was mixing a potion, her tongue sticking out in concentration.

Phontine was already fluttering above the fruit bowl, a grape between her legs like she was riding into battle.

The twins didn't know what I'd found. They didn't know how close I'd come to being caught. Or how it still felt like something had followed me home from that crypt beneath the Black House.

"Look who decided to grace us with her presence," Calypso said without turning.

Pandora grinned and held out a mug. "Fresh coffee, sainted by my very hands."

"Then I better boil it again," I murmured, stepping into the kitchen and taking the cup anyway. The warmth grounded me. "What'd I miss?"

They launched into a flurry of updates, like we hadn't been living separate lives in the same apartment. Apparently, there was a new club downtown where the floors lit up like Fairy wings and you had to kiss a Siren at the door to get in. I tried to smile at that, and managed something that might've passed.

"There's a Fairy party next week," Pandora added, grabbing half a bagel. "Not the court. Just the ones who think glitter is a lifestyle and live like eternal spring break."

"Sounds fun," I said. "Actually, I was wondering if you could tell me about something."

Across the table, Pandora raised a perfectly shaped brow. Calypso looked up from her plate, fork paused midair.

I shifted in my seat. "It's probably nothing, but when I was at The Obsidian Quill the other day with Keyleth, something...weird happened. There was this shimmer, like heat in the air, and then everything went completely silent. And then this human woman—she was sitting next to us with her Goblin boyfriend—she suddenly freaked out. Like, full-on panic. It was like she hadn't even realized he was a Goblin until that moment."

Pandora stilled, eyes sharpening. Calypso slowly lowered her fork.

I went on. "It only lasted a second, and then it was like...it rewound. The mist came back, and the woman didn't remember anything. But *I* did. So did Keyleth. And now I'm starting to remember more of these moments—little flickers. People acting confused or afraid, and then suddenly...forgetting."

A soft rustle came from the corner of the kitchen.

Phontine, curled up on the windowsill beside the potted herbs, had gone unusually quiet. Her wings were still. Her eyes wide.

Calypso and Pandora shared a look.

"No one's supposed to remember the mist," Calypso said carefully. "Or the Veil Towers that distribute it."

I knew all about the Veil Towers, well I remembered what I'd read on McDara's laptop. What Elias had told me. Still, I frowned and asked, "Veil Towers?"

Calypso sighed and leaned back in her chair. "The mist is old magic, but its distribution system is...newer. Veil Towers were built in Blakewell to test how the mist would work on humans. If it could keep them from fearing magic and in turn Magicals. But the sigils that are used to create the mist...Rumor has it the Mage Council found them in our world, but they predate the Woods. Most people can't even perceive the sigils. Even *we* wouldn't remember they exist without a charm."

My stomach tightened. "So, you're saying people like me aren't supposed to remember any of this?"

"Exactly," Pandora said, tone clipped. "And we shouldn't be talking about it too openly. Matron Black made it clear—Veil Tower interference is classified. But...Elias is leading a task force. Quietly. They're trying to find out who's tampering with the Towers and why the mist is glitching."

"Glitching?" I echoed. "Like it's a program?"

"It was designed to be seamless," Calypso said. "Invisible. But something—or someone—is corrupting the sigils. And that makes people notice what they're not meant to."

I wanted to ask if anyone had thought about the longer-term effects on humans, or even Magicals, who breathed this crap in everyday, but...as much as I liked the twins, as much as they'd helped me without asking for anything in return, they were still Black House Mages. I knew they didn't like how Matron Black ran things, but I also knew that to become one of her Mages you had to allow her a bit of control over your magic.

So, I swallowed my disgust at these Veil Towers and the mist and instead asked, "Who would even be able to remember they exist? Who would want humans to see the truth?"

Calypso hesitated. "Only people who can remember the mist when it *is* working. And that's rare. You'd need a charm from Matron Black herself or the Mage Council to retain memory while inside the influence."

"Elias thinks it's a rogue group of Mages," Pandora added after a moment. "The kind who don't think Magical secrecy is worth preserving."

I let that settle over me like fog. Across the room, Phontine remained silent, eyes flicking between them, her mouth drawn in a tight line. She hadn't said a word the entire conversation.

"Anyway, you feeling better?" Calypso's voice gentled as she looked at me over the rim of her mug. "You were wrecked yesterday."

I nodded. Lied. "Yeah. Just needed rest."

Calypso didn't push. "I talked to Matron Black this morning. Told her you needed a break. She agreed to excuse your training for the rest of the week."

That stopped my breath cold.

"She just...agreed?" I asked, forcing casual.

"She even wants to meet tonight. Says she just wants to check on you." Calypso pinned me with her emerald eyes. "Seems...interested in your well-being."

Yeah. Right. Because Matron Black had the same level of maternal instinct as a basilisk.

"She's not checking on me," I muttered into my cup. "She's checking *me*. Like she's still trying to figure out where I fit into her plans."

I still had no clue what Matron Black even needed a Ghost Whisperer in her House *for*. Why care if I join or not?

Pandora's brow arched. "She said it wasn't mandatory."

But we all knew what *not mandatory* meant in the Black House. Decline an invitation, and you might wake up to find your lungs spellbound to someone else's will. Enchantment magic being illegal hardly seemed like it mattered anymore.

I stared into the dark swirl of my coffee, the echo of Dr. Fenwick's words pounding through me. *Don't come back.*

I didn't plan to.

"So," Pandora said, stretching like a cat, "Elias and I were supposed to go out this weekend. But he's caught up again—still looking into that rogue group."

I blinked. "What exactly do rogue Mage's do? Besides mess with magical towers. Do they graffiti Blakewell's city center with sigils that act out rude holograms?"

My real question was, how could a Mage go rogue if their Matron or Master had a hand on their magic? Did every Mage House operate like the Black House? Or was it not a group of rogue Mages at all but an entire House going against Matron Black's precious Towers?

Her smile faltered. "They poke into things they shouldn't. Elias thinks they're messing with raw magic. Ancient stuff. Nothing sanctioned."

My spine prickled.

"Like...the kind that eats people alive?"

"Basically." She shrugged like it wasn't terrifying. "He hasn't told me much. Says it's tied up with Council oversight and politics. But something about it makes his shoulders stay tense even when he sleeps."

I filed that away, deep in the part of me that knew threads always pulled tighter eventually.

"Anyway," Pandora said with a grin that didn't quite reach her eyes, "I told him he owes me three dates and a bottle of muscadine wine when this is over."

I guess that answered my question on whether Pandora and Elais were more than best friends. Honestly, she'd always sidestepped any leading questions I asked in that I'll-gut-you-if-you-keep-prying-into-my-personal-life sort of way Pandora had about her.

I made myself laugh. Made myself finish the coffee. But inside, I felt it building again. The weight of what I'd seen. The ledger I hadn't told them about. The meeting with Matron Black looming like a blade.

And beneath all of it...the memory of Death's magic still humming through my veins.

Something was coming.

And I didn't know if I was going to survive it.

Phontine landed lightly on my shoulder, but even her wings seemed slower today. Her lavender glow was dimmer, too, like someone had pulled a shade over her.

"I'm gonna need to recharge," she whispered, rubbing one tiny hand across her eyes. "Didn't sleep while you were practically dead in the Black House Med Lab, in case you were wondering."

Guilt twinged low in my chest.

"I'll be back soon, promise." She gave my ear a tired pat before she shimmered, then blinked out of sight—like breath vanishing from a mirror. Just gone.

I barely had time to feel her absence before my phone buzzed on the counter beside my coffee.

My heart stuttered. For a second, I thought—*McDara?* Or maybe my mom, finally checking in—

But it wasn't a number I recognized.

> **Unknown:** *Can you meet me today. The university library. 1st floor. Back west alcove. Please come alone. —Dr. Fenwick*

I stared at it. The word *alone* pulsed like a heartbeat.

Just as I began typing my reply, Calypso looked up from her mug, lashes fluttering as if some inner thread had just plucked her into alertness.

"What's your plan for today?" she asked, casual on the surface—but her tone carried that breezy sharpness she used when she was fishing for something beneath it.

I blinked down at the message, thumb hovering.

"Thinking I'll walk the university campus a bit," I said, crafting the lie as smoothly as I could. "Take it slow. Clear my head."

Calypso's smile curved, unreadable. "Perfect. I've been dying for a reason to stop by the market district on that side of town. I'll drive."

Damn it.

There wasn't a good way to tell her no without raising suspicions, and if I'd learned anything about Calypso, it was that suspicion was her native tongue.

So, I just smiled, finished typing *I'll be there,* and sent it. I'd figure the rest out later.

We drove in her tidy, silver Toyota—windows down, some haunting, Fae indie band pulsing from the speakers like a spell you couldn't quite shake. The farther we moved into Blakewell city center, the more New Town's glittering polish gave way to old academic stone and thorn-choked ivy.

The university was a Gothic fever dream—spires and shadows and steps that creaked like they remembered too much.

And I did remember.

The last time I was here, McDara had been beside me—his shoulder brushing mine, his voice warm in my ear as he tried to distract me from the chill crawling down my spine. I remembered the way his eyes had narrowed when Orlla's ghost practically froze me in a lecture room, how fast his hands had steadied me, like he couldn't help himself.

Orlla had haunted these halls like grief with a purpose. A murdered Black House Mage, her death tangled in secrets.

Now, McDara was silent. Distant. And Orlla was gone. Forced to move on to her afterlife by Death.

The memory pressed against my ribs, soft and cruel.

And still, I walked forward.

Calypso walked beside me in a flowing, crimson cardigan that looked like it belonged on a cathedral window. She pointed out details as we moved across campus—most of them laced in whispers.

"That lecture hall?" she murmured, nodding toward a sandstone building with a broken gargoyle. "There's a rumor the old Archmage who taught there went mad and sealed his office from the inside with blood sigils. It's still locked. No one's figured out how to unbind it."

"Comforting," I muttered.

She grinned. "And that garden? The one behind the Language Wing? Supposedly blooms year-round. But only for students who've cheated death."

I paused. "Cheated it how?"

"Doesn't say. Just...death." She looked at me, one brow lifted. "You'd probably light the whole garden on fire."

I didn't answer. I couldn't. Not with Dr. Fenwick waiting. Not with Grace's ledger burning a hole in my bag. Not with Matron Black's silk-robed image still haunting the back of my mind like smoke that refused to clear.

And definitely not with Death's voice still echoing beneath my skin.

Desperate to shake Calypso, I pulled out my phone and texted Keyleth.

Me: *Need an emergency favor. Call Cal in two minutes. Tell her something dramatic.*

She replied instantly.

Literal Sunshine: *You got it.*

One minute later, Calypso's phone rang. Her eyes widened.

"I need to run over to The Obsidian Quill real quick," she said, already moving. "I'll be back in an hour. Stay out of trouble."

I waved her off, turned on my heel, and headed for the library.

Dr. Fenwick wasn't in the alcove yet. My nerves buzzed as I chose a central table—dead middle of the library floor, impossible to miss. I reached into my bag, fingers curling around the soft leather of Grace's ledger.

I cracked it open.

The first page was simple:

```
GRACE GUEN
Private Observations, Theory Notes, and Experiments
```

Below it, a single sentence written in slanted, elegant ink:

```
What kills us is not fate. It's design.
```

The next ten pages unfolded like a desperate diary. Grace's voice felt young but razor-sharp—half furious, half terrified. She'd tracked the ages of every Ghost Whisperer in the Black House for the last seventy years. None had lived past twenty-five. All orphans. No known parents. No exceptions.

David—my birth father—refused to accept the curse as a magical inevitability. His notes were blunt. Almost angry.

No active magic. No casting. No surge patterns comparable to Mages.
   Conclusion: cause of death cannot be inherent magic failure.

He believed the deaths were a cover for something else—though at the time, he didn't know for what. Grace hadn't written any theories yet. Only questions, repeated in different hands, different inks.

If Ghost Whisperers are cursed, who placed the curse? And why now?

Later entries shifted in tone.

Grace hadn't rejected David's theory outright—but at first, she'd tried to reconcile it with what she'd been taught. Her handwriting softened. Doubt crept in.

Raised to believe this was fate.
A balancing mechanism.
A curse placed on Ghost Whisperers because their magic carried too much weight.

This is what we were told.
This is what the Houses believe.

The words trailed off there, the rest of the page left blank—like even she hadn't been able to convince herself.

Then the notes became different. Grace had started by wanting to find a way to get rid of her magic. Thinking the curse, fate, would not need to seek out her death for balance if she no longer had a Ghost Whisperer's magic, but then...her beliefs started to shift. She wrote about dreams that didn't feel like hers. Shadows that clung to her even in daylight. A sense that the House was watching her.

And then came the experiments. Spells that tested the resilience of soul-bound magic. Rituals to sever inherited ties. Pages of sigils, notes on bleeding rites, mirror chants, and something called *Veil-threading,* a forbidden ritual that hinted at using the Deathscape to burn clean a tethered fate.

The most disturbing part? I wasn't sure who was doing the experiments. If it was Grace and David or the Black House. Grace had just listed out the experiments, almost like she was racing to get down as much information before she forgot it...or died.

The symptoms she'd listed...

```
· Nosebleeds during strong emotional surges
· Feeling phantom hands around the throat during
nightmares
· Weakness and extreme fatigue after using magic
· Physical weakness that escalated closer to the
25th birthday
```

My heart kicked hard.

I hadn't experienced all of them but...weakness after using magic? Check.

Grace had circled one line three times:

If soul-bound magic can be created, it can be undone. The price will be steep. But what is steeper than death?

The next page was sealed with a spell tag I didn't dare break in public.

I looked up.

Still no sign of Dr. Fenwick.

I flipped back a few pages, heart in my throat, rereading the part about David. About his certainty that the curse wasn't natural. Wasn't fate.

That it was engineered.

That someone wanted us dead.

I closed the ledger, fingers pressed tight to the leather, pulse hammering.

This wasn't a curse.

It was a blueprint.

17

T hirty minutes passed.

Still no sign of Dr. Fenwick.

The library had thinned to a few scattered students, but it felt…off. Like the walls were listening. Like the glass skylight above was an eye pressed wide open.

The feeling wrapped around my spine and pulled.

I glanced toward the back west alcove which currently housed the Veil Theory section. Still empty. My pulse quickened. That weight in the air—like breath held too long—was growing heavier. Wrong.

I whispered it.

"Death."

The word barely passed my lips, but it tore through the quiet like a spell breaking.

He appeared three shelves away.

And he didn't look like *my* Death.

He looked like something conjured from the deep. Something the world shouldn't see.

Shadows poured from his skin like reversed blood—liquid night sliding off muscle and bone. He was bare beneath them. The darkness clung to him like smoke with intent, curling around his hips, coiling low on his abdomen, trailing down powerful legs like it *wanted* to be touched.

His chest rose and fell with ragged breaths. His silver eyes burned too bright to look at for long.

He looked like hunger made flesh. Made ruin. The monster beneath clawing to get out. There was no skin where his joints met. Just shadow, an endless night that sewed his body together.

What did he *do* when he wasn't in the Living Lands with me? And...what did Death really look like if he wasn't wearing the familiar guise he had always shown me?

"Shit—" I started, stepping back, heart sprinting. "I—I'm sorry. I didn't mean to—"

His head turned, slow and predatory.

And then...he changed.

One breath. Two.

The storm inside him folded in on itself. Shadows settled, slicking back over muscle, smoothing into something more elegant. His form still shimmered with power, but it became quieter. Sharper. *Focused.*

He became...familiar again. Not safe. Never that. But known.

"I shouldn't have called you," I blurted, voice too high. "Not without warning. I just—Not that I know how to reach you, not really, and I thought something was wrong, I panicked and—"

He raised a hand.

I went silent like he'd pressed a key.

Then he motioned, wordless, and I followed—heart thudding—through the stacks, deeper and deeper, until the shadows grew long and the scent of paper and dust drowned out the rest of the world. We stopped at a corner cloaked in quiet.

I opened my mouth again—

His fingers pressed to my lips.

Only...they passed through me.

The chill of it swept down my nerves. Not cold like frost. Cold like starlight. Like breath held in the dark.

I froze. Eyes wide. His touch vanished a heartbeat later, but the echo stayed. Right there. On the bow of my lips.

"You don't need to apologize," he said softly, voice edged like velvet wrapped around a blade. "I am not...bothered. When you call."

"But what if you're working?" I whispered. "Doing something important?"

I couldn't even think to ask what that something important would be. One crisis at a time.

He stepped closer. Too close.

The stacks behind me felt like walls. His shadow cut across mine.

"It is your right," he murmured, "to summon me. For anything."

"My...right?" My throat went dry.

He smiled then. Just a flicker of teeth. The kind of smile that made promises in dark places.

"You think this bond goes only one way? I am yours," he said, voice low and certain. "As much as you are mine. So yes, Little Bird—you may demand my attention. Whenever you crave it."

My breath caught.

What power that would be. To call the god of death whenever I wanted him. If I believed him, that is, about our bond. Tapping on the thread inside of me that led to him seemed to be the only thing I could gain from it. Everything else had been gifted by him.

Training.

Lessons.

His magic.

No, I did not believe I inherently gained anything from the bond, but that didn't mean I found his words any less pretty.

Because part of me—some broken, burning, aching part—*wanted* to believe him.

I didn't mean to lean toward him.

Didn't mean to linger in the comfort of that voice. That promise.

But the ache in my chest felt less like weakness and more like...relief. Like something fragile inside me had finally been caught, and I hoped he wouldn't crush it.

"I don't get it," I murmured, still staring at him. "You're Death. You're probably planning to use me. And yet—"

He tilted his head slightly. "And yet?"

"I almost feel safe with you."

That earned a breath of a smile. Not mocking. Not cruel. Just...there. Like maybe I'd surprised him.

"That," he said quietly, "is far more dangerous than feeling afraid."

I huffed out a laugh, shaky and tired. "Thanks. That's comforting."

"I will not promise you that I am safe." Death seemed to float a hair closer, and I found myself wishing that he could be corporal in the Living Lands. "But I will never lift a finger to hurt you."

"Hmm," I watched him, the word *okay* a breath from slipping past my lips, but I held it back. Barely. Just because I was desperate to trust someone didn't mean I should give all my trust to the first person asking for it.

Easier said than done.

His gaze didn't waver. "Tell me why you called me. What frightened you?"

The weight of the night folded in around us again. The silence. The ledger in my bag. The strange text from Dr. Fenwick. The way everything felt like it was unraveling thread by thread, and I was the only one holding the needle.

I shifted my weight, glancing toward the far shelves.

"There's a doctor at the Black House. Fenwick. He's been...kind, I guess. One of the only ones who treats me like a person. After the attack during training and then finding me in the Black House trying to get out with Grace's ledger without Matron Black finding me..." My fingers brushed the satchel at my side. "He helped me get out of the House last night without her finding me. Then this morning he messaged me and asked to meet here. Alone."

Death's entire presence changed.

Subtle. Lethal. His hands curled at his sides like he was resisting the urge to drag me away from this place entirely.

"Alone," he echoed, voice turning dark as soot.

"I know." I swallowed hard. "I shouldn't have come, but Phontine would have been with me. She needed to recharge though and...I needed to know if he had answers. About the ledger. About—about my birth mother."

The fact that I hadn't told Death about my curse sat like poison in my chest until each breath practically ached with the need to tell him. But I still didn't know if that would make me worthless to him, and right now, I needed to be priceless. Needed his training and any protection he could give me. And in the desperate, guilty part of my soul I needed someone who knew everything about my abilities, the ghosts, the Mage Houses yet chooses to stay. Right now, that was Phontine, and I loved her, but she couldn't help me survive what was coming any more than Keyleth or the twins or...McDara.

Death didn't speak for a long moment. Only watched me—too intently. Like he was looking at something he didn't yet understand.

Then he held his hand out, directing me from the stacks.

"Come. We'll wait where we can see who arrives."

We crossed the library in silence, the soft squeak of my boots on marble the only sound as I slung the satchel over my shoulder. His shadow moved beside mine, tall and deliberate.

The wide, glass doors whispered open at our approach, revealing the small courtyard beyond.

Rain drifted like mist across the open space. It beaded on the ivy-choked walls, slicked the stone benches, turned the courtyard into a quiet basin of gray light and shallow puddles. The carved stone buildings of Varitas loomed around us—old and reverent—but the modern skylight overhead glinted faintly, streaked with droplets that blurred the star-shaped design into something fractured.

There were no students out. No voices. Only the steady patter of rain and the distant echo of water rushing down gutters.

We stepped out.

Beyond the courtyard, the stone steps spilled toward the heart of the university grounds—quiet paths winding between old dormitories and halls lit by Magelight. The place looked abandoned in the downpour. Ghostly.

Death stood beside me, his gaze fixed forward, like he was already watching for the danger I hadn't seen yet.

And somehow, despite everything, I wasn't afraid anymore.

The rain caught me in a burst of wind, spattering cold against my cheeks and soaking the tops of my shoulders. I darted beneath the narrow awning to my right—a stone overhang carved into the side of the library entrance—and pressed back against the wall, tugging my hood forward.

But when I looked to my side...he wasn't there.

Death was gone.

Panic prickled until I spotted him a few paces away, standing beneath the wide, lilac umbrella of a small coffee cart.

Lavender's Honey Brews was painted in soft gold, elegant, curling script across the wooden front. Rain slid off the umbrella in gentle arcs, charmed to spill away from the delicate operation beneath. The space was just wide enough for the Fairy who worked the cart—and, apparently, for the embodiment of death.

I blinked.

He wasn't brooding or looming or shadow-stalking.

He was...inspecting.

Head tilted slightly, he leaned in to examine the espresso machine like it was a relic from an ancient temple. His fingers ghosted near a row of tiny, labeled jars filled with flower petals, dried fruit, and bright syrups in iridescent vials. His expression—sharp cheekbones and midnight-silver eyes lit with open curiosity—was boyish in a way that made no sense.

I didn't know what I'd expected from a coffee cart encounter with Death.

But it wasn't...this.

The Fairy working the cart didn't seem to notice him at all. Of course she didn't. She chatted with a student who stood under the umbrella, her soft, lavender hair curling to her hips and gossamer wings folded carefully behind her, glowing like woven starlight. Her body pulsed with restrained power, brightening around her fingertips, the corners of her lips, and eyes—like the magic barely tolerated being crammed into a humanoid shape.

Maybe it was ridiculous of me, but I didn't think Fairies...worked. Not in Blakewell. I'd passed them on the streets of New Town looking important and otherworldly. To see one working a coffee cart on a university campus was...strange and kind of cool.

This was only the second Fairy I'd seen up close since coming to Blakewell. The first had been back in New Town when the twins took me to that velvet-drenched not-really-ly-a-pub. Those Fairies had been aloof, all grace and clipped words and glittering jewelry that hummed with spelled protections.

But this one?

She didn't glow with cold superiority. She glowed because she *was* power. Wrapped in mortal skin. Pouring coffee like she was pretending not to be divine.

And Death—he was pretending to be interested in coffee. Or he actually was...

He leaned closer to the row of jars. Peered into one filled with candied violet petals like it might hold the secrets of the cosmos. When the Fairy bent to reach something beneath the counter, he startled slightly, then blinked at her like he'd just remembered she couldn't see him.

I clutched my satchel tighter and stared, caught between amusement and bafflement.

This was the one I was supposed to fear. The monster who haunted the Deathscape, silver-eyed and cruel, bound to me only because he wanted something. He'd whispered promises like knives. Touched me without touching. Made me forget how to breathe. He was literally unspooling into a shadows and dark void magic back in the library before he contained himself, but here he was...fascinated by human food.

And now, he was inspecting a rosewater syrup bottle like a mortal man on a first date with caffeine.

A wet laugh slipped out before I could stop it—just a breath. I covered my mouth with the back of my hand and tried not to smile.

Tried.

He glanced over, eyes catching mine across the drizzle-soaked courtyard.

His smile curved, slow and secret.

Like he knew *exactly* what I'd been thinking.

And worse...like he liked that I was watching him.

The student under the umbrella gave a quiet thanks and darted off into the rain, clutching her drink like it might dissolve before she reached the doors.

I exhaled, stepped out from beneath the awning, and made my way toward the cart.

Death's stare trailed me as I came closer, but I kept myself from looking at him, or at a blank space which is what the Fairy at the cart would see.

The Fairy turned toward me with a smile so radiant I forgot how to breathe.

By the Woods.

Up close, she was stunning. Ethereal in a way that didn't feel natural. Her lavender curls shimmered like dusk-lit water. Her skin gave off a low, golden glow that brightened with each movement—hands, mouth, even the quick flare of her nostrils as she took me in.

I forgot what I was supposed to say.

And apparently, forgot how to stand like a normal person. My limbs felt too long and too light, like I might float off the cobblestones. Was this a spell? A side effect of standing too close to raw magic barely pretending to be a person?

"Hello, lovely," the Fairy said, her voice like sparkling citrus and cello notes. "Raining and gloomy—perfect for something warm. What can I get you?"

I fumbled, glanced at the hand-painted menu. "Uh—Caramel Divine?"

"Excellent choice." She beamed and moved like silk, her fingers dancing over jars and levers. Her wings glowed brighter as she worked.

I kept my eyes on the espresso machine and *not* on Death, who stood right at my back and bent over my shoulder, studying the entire process like he was observing some sacred ritual.

Moments later, the Fairy handed me a cup that smelled like sugar and sin and everything I didn't deserve. I paid her, muttered a thank you that sounded far too human, and walked stiffly back toward the awning.

Death followed.

His silver eyes locked onto the drink in my hands like it held answers he'd been chasing for centuries.

"You know," I said softly, careful to keep my face angled toward the street and not toward him, "for someone who's supposed to be the literal embodiment of death, you're weirdly obsessed with lattes."

His grin flashed sharp. "You mortals cling so tightly to it. I find it amusing that you worship it in such tiny cups."

"Just admit it," I said, lifting the lid and inhaling the scent. "You're jealous."

"I have no need of envy."

"Uh-huh."

"Try it."

I arched a brow at him but lifted the cup to my lips.

Buttery caramel, rich espresso, and a hint of sea salt and something floral—maybe lavender—coated my tongue like a spell. I let out a quiet hum and closed my eyes, tipping my head back just slightly as warmth slid down my throat and pooled in my chest.

When I looked up, Death wasn't watching the coffee anymore.

He was watching me.

And the hunger in his eyes had nothing to do with food.

The look pinned me where I stood. My heart tripped over itself, my pulse jumping as heat skittered down my spine. He didn't move. Didn't blink. Just... *looked.*

I panicked.

"So," I blurted, gripping the cup like it might anchor me, "what do you eat in the Deathscape?"

He moved closer.

Slowly. Deliberately. Like a predator who already knew exactly where the cage door was hidden.

His gaze dipped to my mouth.

A drop of caramel clung to the corner of my lips. I went to wipe it, but he raised a hand—fingers brushing the air like he wanted to do it himself. He didn't touch me.

He couldn't.

"There is nothing," he murmured, voice like smoke curling down my skin, "to satisfy hunger for me in my realm."

I swallowed. "Sounds...bleak."

"It is."

A beat of silence passed. And another.

The rain fell steadily around us, dimming the world. My breath clouded faintly in the cool air. Death's gaze didn't waver.

He stepped closer still—close enough that I could feel the air shift between us, could almost taste the cool slipstream of his magic. That overwhelming, beautiful pressure.

But then—his head turned sharply.

He went still.

Statue still.

I blinked. "What?"

He didn't answer right away.

His silver eyes narrowed, focused on something past the courtyard.

"What is it?" I asked again, quieter now.

He didn't look at me.

Only stared at the stone steps beyond the library's courtyard.

18

The rain had softened into a silver curtain.

It whispered against the courtyard stones. Slid in gentle sheets over the library's glass skylight. Clung to the ivy trailing down the old stone walls like weeping vines.

Lavender's Honey Brews still glowed beneath its floating umbrella, a little pocket of warmth tucked into the gloom.

But Death was still unmoving.

He stood beside me, motionless, eyes locked on the far steps like a gargoyle sensing a storm.

The shadows around him had stilled.

No teasing smirk. No clever reply. No trace of the wicked, seductive magic that had shimmered between us moments ago.

Just stillness. Sharp. Focused.

Wrong.

A pit opened in my stomach.

"Death," I said again, my voice quieter now. "What is it?"

He didn't answer.

Didn't even flinch.

I turned to look at him—really look—and felt cold bloom beneath my skin.

His expression had hollowed. The mirth was gone. What remained was something ancient. Watching. Waiting. Like a blade held steady before the strike.

The sound came a heartbeat later.

A wet *drag*.

Then a choking gurgle.

The hairs on my arms lifted.

I turned toward the steps.

"Don't," Death said, but not in warning. Not a command. Just a quiet, inevitable truth.

He knew I would.

I took a step forward. Then another.

Rain slicked the stone path, turning the air metallic and strange. My boots made soft, traitorous sounds against the wet.

And then I saw him.

A man. Crawling. Soaked to the bone, one arm trembling beneath his weight, the other pressed tight against his ribs like he was trying to hold something *in*.

But it wasn't just any man.

The breath caught in my throat.

He was at the bottom of the steps—barely more than a silhouette in the misty light—but I knew it was him. Knit sweater soaked by rainwater and pressed khaki pants. The dull glint of his watch flashed through the dropping rain as he grasped at the step right above him.

The thought came careening into me: *He looks like my dad.*

He was crawling.

No—*dragging* himself.

One arm trembling beneath the weight of his body. The other curled tight against his ribs, like he was holding something in. Or holding something *together*.

"Dr. Fenwick?"

The name cracked out of me.

He lifted his head just slightly.

I rushed forward, slipping on the last step as I dropped to my knees.

"Hey—hey, I've got you—"

His head lolled toward me.

Blood ran down his jaw. His lips moved, but only a whisper of sound escaped—wet and broken and *wrong.*

Behind me, I felt Death arrive.

Felt the air ripple with the weight of him.

And still, he said nothing.

Dr. Fenwick's eyes fluttered. His hand clawed weakly toward me, fingers shaking.

I caught it.

Held on.

"Stay with me," I whispered, heart in my throat. "Please—just stay with me."

The rain fell harder.

But all I could hear was the sound of him choking on blood and the silence where Death should've spoken.

As gently as I could, I shifted his head from the stone steps. It was heavy in my lap, rain slicking through his hair as I tried to shield his face from the downpour.

"It's going to be okay," I whispered, but my voice was shaking. My gaze dragged to where his arm clamped tight across his stomach—blood blooming through his shirt, spilling between his fingers. Stab wounds. More than one.

My stomach turned to stone. Who would do this to him? The kind doctor who patched me up, who spoke in gentle riddles about Ghost Whisperers and fate?

He choked, body convulsing. I hunched lower, cupping the back of his head, turning his face so he could cough up the blood pooling in his mouth.

"The...ledger..." he rasped, words wet and broken. His breath hitched. "She was right...tell no one..." His chest seized, another coughing fit tearing through him. "It's...in Larkend..."

Tears blurred the world. "Don't talk. Please, just—don't. We'll get help."

But his breathing was already unraveling, shallow and jagged.

I looked up wildly, desperate.

Death stood only a few steps above us, silver eyes burning, face carved into stillness. Watching. Waiting. His silence pressed down on me like a judgment I didn't understand.

And at the top of the stairs—the Fairy from the coffee cart. Her hands flew to her mouth, wings trembling with shock.

"Call for an ambulance!" I screamed. "Now!"

She darted off, light flickering as her glow trailed into the rain.

I looked back down.

Too late.

Dr. Fenwick was still.

Gone.

The sound that ripped out of me was raw, unmoored. My chest caved as if I was back in my family's house, decorations for a birthday that would never be celebrated hanging around me, and a police officer, hat in hands, telling me and mom the worse thing we'd ever heard.

The same hollow ache. The same echo of loss I would never recover from.

I bent over him, clutching his shirt, sobbing until the rain and my tears blurred into one.

And above me, Death didn't move.

The rain had stopped, but everything still smelled like it—wet stone, soaked ivy, blood.

I sat at the top of the steps, wrapped in a scratchy gray blanket someone from the ambulance had shoved around my shoulders. The police officer's voice was steady, low, his notebook open, pen scratching as he asked me to recount what happened. Again.

I answered on autopilot. My throat felt scraped raw. My body hollow.

Beside me, Death sat in utter silence. Only I could see him. Only I could feel the weight of his presence. I tried not to look his way, tried not to make the officer's pen pause with the suspicion that I was talking to shadows.

But my mind was already unraveling.

Why would anyone stab Dr. Fenwick?

The EMT had whispered that there was no trace of magic in his wounds. Just knives. Blades. Human brutality. Which made it worse. More deliberate.

Was it because he wanted to meet me? Because of what he knew about Grace? About the ledger?

About *Larkend*.

That word spun in my head like a hurricane, ripping through every other thought.

The town sealed off by raw magic. The place everyone avoided. The place marked by a Death Echo that had never faded.

And now...the place where my answers waited?

My chest constricted.

That's when I noticed it.

A hand on my knee. Not solid, not warm—his fingers sank partway through, spectral, but the intent was there. Enough to drag my gaze sideways.

Death's expression was...strange. Withdrawn, shadowed, but threaded with something I couldn't name. Grief. Maybe worry. Maybe both.

"Come to the Deathscape," he said at last. It didn't sound like a command. More like...a plea.

I just stared at him, heart a mess of splintered glass. Lost.

He drew in a sharp breath. His jaw flexed. "I can't..." His voice halted, then darkened. "You are needing comfort, and I can't—"

"Sonia."

The sound of my name cut through everything.

I jerked my head up, breath catching in my throat.

McDara.

He stood on the steps in front of me, rain-dark hair a mess, shadows carved deep beneath his eyes. Like he hadn't slept.

And the look on his face...

Relief. Worry. Longing. Like he wanted nothing more than to gather me into his arms, shield me from the world, carry me far from this bloodstained place.

Like he had before. When he was my protector.

At the bottom of the steps, Dom lingered—watching, waiting. But McDara didn't take his eyes off me.

McDara opened his mouth, closed it again, swallowed hard, then tried once more.

"Are you alright? What happened?"

My gaze slipped down the steps. Rainwater still ran in thin rivulets down each one, carrying streaks of blood into the cracks between the stone. Fenwick's blood.

"He wanted to meet me," I whispered. My voice broke, trailing off before I could shape the rest. I couldn't. Not again. Not when the words would taste too much like memory.

McDara's jaw worked, something hard in his eyes. "He was a good man."

Of course he'd known him. McDara had been part of the Black House once, before he walked away. That connection twisted inside me, sharp and unwanted.

I only nodded. My throat was too tight for anything else.

The officer had already told me I could leave after my statement. I needed to be gone. Away from the steps. Away from the echo of Fenwick choking on blood.

I shoved to my feet, blanket sliding from my shoulders. My legs shook as I started down. Death was right there, close enough that his form pressed into mine, shadow at my side.

And then McDara's hand caught my arm.

I froze.

Death's spectral body tightened, merging so close with me it felt like we shared the same breath. His silver gaze burned into the place McDara touched, sharp enough to shred.

"Let me drive you home," McDara said. His voice carried that mix of command and care I'd once leaned on too easily. "After what you've been through—you shouldn't be on a bus. Keyleth said you're staying with Calypso"—A tight breath—"New Town is far away."

Of course, Keyleth would have told him where I was staying. It's not like I had said not to but…His worry was so familiar. His determination too. One part of me ached to just give in, to let him steady me the way he used to.

But I glanced sideways. At Death.

He was staring at McDara's hand like if he had form, he would rip McDara's hand apart with his very teeth.

I pulled my gaze back to McDara, pulse thrumming. "I'll be fine."

His eyes narrowed. Too sharp. Too knowing. "Is there a ghost here?" He'd caught me looking. Thought he understood.

I shook my head. Tried to move past him, but his grip tightened. My name on his lips this time was edged with detective steel. "Sonia."

I looked him dead in the eye.

"It's not a ghost," I said. "It's Death."

The words landed like a blade between us.

McDara's grip stiffened, his breath catching—caught between disbelief and dread.

And behind me, Death smiled. Feral. Shadows rippled across his shoulders, crawling like claws eager to tear free. He looked almost pleased, almost hungry, as though my confession was a victory he'd been waiting for.

19

The look on McDara's face gutted me. Shock gave way to fear, fear to that rigid, bone-deep protectiveness that lived in his every breath.

Once, not so long ago, I'd told him about falling into the Deathscape. About the shadowed figure waiting for me there, whispering that he might never let me leave. McDara had sworn then—sworn with fire in his eyes—that he'd never let Death have me.

But Death *did* have me.

And the truth that chilled me most wasn't fear. It was how little that thought frightened me anymore.

"When did you go back to the Deathscape?" McDara's voice was sharp, insistent. His detective's edge.

Dom had reached the top of the steps now, brows shooting up as if I'd just confessed I'd been cozying up to the apocalypse itself. Which, maybe, I was. But McDara didn't spare him a glance. All of his attention was on me, his eyes storm-dark, burning.

"Tell me," he pressed, stepping closer. "How is he here? How can he be in the Living Lands?" His jaw clenched, his hand tightening on my arm. "Are you hurt? What has he done to you?"

Behind me, Death hissed.

Not human. Not even close. The sound scraped the marrow of my bones. Shadows writhed at his feet, stretching forward like claws. He took one lethal step toward McDara, silver eyes flashing with pure fury—as if the very idea that he'd harm me was the gravest insult imaginable.

"Stop."

My hand flew out, catching the air between them before Death could advance farther. My pulse thundered. McDara stiffened at the gesture, his gaze darting to where my palm hovered in empty space.

Dom's voice broke the silence, low and uneasy. "Sonia...what's he doing right now?"

The air between us thrummed, thick with storm and shadow, and I couldn't bring myself to answer.

Not yet.

"Little Bird." Death's voice slithered through me, low and feral, like the scrape of claws over stone. "Get rid of the mortal Mage before I do."

The words burned.

I bristled, spinning toward him even though only I could see, could hear. "Just stop." My voice shook, but not from fear. From anger. From grief. "You can't hurt him."

McDara's hand was still warm on my arm. Too warm. Too steady.

And all I could see was Dr. Fenwick's blood slicking my palms. His broken breaths rattling out against the rain. The way his eyes had gone glassy in my lap.

It slammed into me like a fist. My dad's mangled car. The silence after the officer talked to Mom. Six months clawing at my own useless magic—six months of failure—begging to see him one last time. That desperation leading me here to more struggle than I've ever known. And now Fenwick, kind, steady Fenwick, gone in the exact same, shattering way.

Gone, and I was helpless. Again.

The grief hollowed me out and poured me full of fire all at once. It burned behind my eyes, seared in my throat.

I couldn't let Death take another. Not McDara. Not anyone.

"Don't you dare," I choked, my voice shaking as I stepped toward Death, rage and anguish tangled into one. "You can't."

Death stilled. Those molten-silver eyes locked on mine, his fury caged but trembling, the edges of it razor-sharp. And beneath it—just barely visible—something else. Discomfort. Scrutiny. As if the end of all things had never found himself needing to consider pushing someone too far.

My heart tugged painfully. For Dr. Fenwick. For McDara. For Death. All of it.

I dragged in a shaky breath and let it out in a sigh. "I just want to go home." The words spilled raw, not aimed at either of them, not really. Just...out.

"I'll drive you," McDara said immediately, his voice steady, resolute. The protector to the end.

I nodded. Too tired to argue.

Death snarled. The sound curled through me, black and hungry, and shadows surged around my feet. His magic pressed against me hard, pulling, dragging—my stomach flipped with the telltale lurch that said he was a heartbeat away from yanking me into the Deathscape.

I gasped, panic cracking my chest. "No—" The word ripped free, desperate. "I just want a ride to Calypso's. You can follow."

The pull eased. Barely. Enough that I stayed planted on stone instead of sand.

McDara and Dom were both watching me, alarm sharp in their eyes, their bodies tense like they were ready for a fight they couldn't even see.

Death lingered at my side, shadows licking the edges of his form, silver gaze hot with barely leashed violence. He let me walk down the steps, McDara and Dom flanking close.

But he followed. Always.

And for the first time in days, real fear stirred in me.

Not for myself.

For what Death might do to McDara.

The SUV smelled faintly of leather and old coffee, the hum of the engine too steady against the chaos clawing inside me. I sat in the back, pressed against the door, blanket still clutched around me like flimsy armor.

And Death.

He was right beside me. Silent. His silver eyes locked on McDara with a predator's patience, as if he were cataloguing all the ways he could drag him from the driver's seat and peel him apart bone by bone.

I kept waiting for the snap. The drag into shadows. The end.

We cleared the university grounds, the wet streets gleaming under passing headlights. Dom finally broke the silence. "He still here?"

"Yes." My voice rasped, raw.

McDara let out a breath, long and controlled, like he was trying to exorcise a demon from his chest. His knuckles tightened on the wheel, tendons stark. In the rearview, his eyes flicked to mine, brief but heavy.

"You told me," he said quietly, regret bleeding through every syllable, "about him threatening you. And I—" He cut himself off with a curse. "Instead of helping you, I pushed you away."

The words should've warmed me. Validation that he thought, even for a moment, he shouldn't have pushed me away, but the words only scraped me raw.

Because Death had shifted his gaze. Off McDara. Onto me.

All that sharp, monstrous focus hadn't lessened, but underneath it...something churned. His stare held me captive, dissecting, calculating.

And my stomach dropped.

He'd just heard that I'd essentially told McDara that he freaked me the fuck out. That I hadn't wanted anything to do with him and wanted McDara to help keep me safe.

Would it tip him over the edge? Would he drag me into the Deathscape now, chain me there, keep me tethered as long as he could?

McDara's voice kept unraveling in the front seat, guilt spilling like he could patch up the damage with words.

I couldn't let him keep going. Not with Death watching me like that. Not when every apology scraped against the raw edges inside me.

"Stop," I cut in, sharper than I meant. "Just—it's fine."

Dom's head tilted, sharp eyes flicking up to the mirror. He must've heard the hysterical crack in my voice because he slipped in smoothly, like only Dom could. "How'd you know Fenwick well enough to meet him at the university?"

I clung to the lifeline of the question. "He saw that I'd found my birth mother's ledger. Grace's. He wanted to talk to me about it. I think."

McDara's knuckles flexed on the wheel. "Did it say anything about the curse?"

The word dropped into the car like a blade.

"Yes," I whispered. "It...my birth father didn't think it was inevitable. He thought something caused it. Something unnatural. The ledger has theories, rituals, notes. He believed it wasn't fate—that it was designed."

I risked a glance to my left.

Death's magic had gone still.

Not the sharp fury he'd aimed at McDara. Not even the hunger I'd come to recognize. This was worse. A coldness so absolute it felt like it might hollow me out from the inside.

Because I had never told him.

Not about the bloodline curse. Not about the countdown that ended on my twenty-fifth birthday.

That meant I wouldn't be useful to him for much longer. That he'd have to find another tether to keep clawing into the Living Lands.

And the look in his eyes told me everything.

He knew there was a curse now. There was no way I could keep from answering his inevitable questions.

I was so, so fucked.

The drive back blurred. By the time we pulled into the pristine, asphalted lot of Calypso and Pandora's building, I felt scraped hollow, running on nothing but nerves and dread.

Despite telling them I didn't need an escort, both McDara and Dom walked me up the stairs and down the hall. The weight of their steps at my back was suffocating.

I unlocked the door and pushed it open. "Cal? Pandora?" My voice echoed into silence. No answer.

The apartment was empty, the air stale and too still.

"They must be at the House. Or on assignment," I said quickly, remembering the rogue Mages Elais and Pandora were investigating. About them messing with the mist. About everything spiraling tighter and tighter.

"Thanks," I muttered, trying to shut the door.

Before the latch caught, McDara's hand pressed flat against it, steady, immovable. His eyes locked on mine. "I'll check on you tomorrow."

It wasn't a request.

Some small, foreign part of me was relieved. The rest of me was just bone-deep exhausted.

I nodded once, forced the door closed, and leaned my forehead against the wood until their footsteps faded down the hall.

When I turned, Death was still there. Silent. A shadow threaded through the room, all silver eyes and unreadable quiet.

My chest tightened. He knew now. About the curse. About the ticking clock that made me useless to him. Whatever he was getting out of our bond wouldn't last much longer. The training I needed...I had nothing to bargain for that now. Not when his ability to come to the Living Lands would end soon. He was better off finding another Magical to bond to. I braced for the blow—for him to tell me I wasn't worth it anymore.

I drifted into my room, shut the door behind me, and stood there. Just stood, staring at nothing, lost in the storm tearing through me.

Then he moved.

Death stepped into my line of sight, blocking the blur, forcing me to look at him. He didn't speak right away, just waited until my eyes found his.

"Come to the Deathscape," he said at last.

My heart thudded.

He could drag me there whether I agreed or not. That had always been true.

But tonight, it broke something in me.

"Will I..." My voice cracked, quiet and small. "Will I be safe from you if I do?"

Death didn't answer right away. He only looked at me, and it was like he was taking me apart, measuring pieces of me I didn't even know I had. His expression shifted—strange, elusive, something I couldn't pin down. Beyond human.

He bent lower, folding himself down until his face was nearly level with mine. The air thickened. I sucked in a quick breath, pulse a frantic drum in my throat.

His voice was velvet and blade in one. "What do you think I will do to you, Little Bird?"

The trembling started in my hands, spreading until my whole body betrayed me. I forced words out anyway, my voice wobbling despite my teeth clenched tight.

"You'll keep me there. In the Deathscape. Not let me leave." The words tumbled out faster, harder. "Or you'll—smite me for not telling you about the curse. That after my next birthday I'll be dead, and I won't be useful to you anymore, and that'll make you angry, and you'll—" My throat burned as the words broke. "You'll kill me."

Rambling. Spiraling. Tears slid down my cheeks before I could stop them.

His eyes flared bright silver—so sharp it nearly gutted me to look at him. But when I finally forced myself to meet his gaze again, he wasn't mocking. He wasn't wrathful. He just...watched. Every tear. Every shudder.

And then, softly, with an authority that made my bones ache, he said, "Come to me."

I swallowed hard and shook my head, fear tangling itself up inside my chest.

He didn't lash out. Didn't snarl.

"Why," he murmured, voice low and dangerous, "would I damage what is mine?"

That single word—*mine*—slid over my skin like a brand.

"Come."

I closed my eyes because I knew. I never really had a choice.

The tether between us thrummed when I reached for it, and it cost me more than it should have. Using my magic to step down into the Deathscape left me lightheaded, weak, like every attempt was scraping something raw inside me. It hadn't always been like this.

But still—I went.

The world lurched, the air snapped cold, and when I opened my eyes, I was in his realm. With him.

Where his magic could finally touch me.

The spinning slowed. The red desert steadied beneath my boots—until it didn't.

Arms closed around me, iron and inevitability, and the Deathscape dissolved. The sand, the horizon, even the sky itself collapsed into a storm of black shadows, swallowing everything whole.

I stiffened, breath locked in my throat, waiting for pain. For wrath. For the punishment I knew he had every reason to deliver.

But when the world reassembled, I wasn't crushed beneath it.

I was standing—no, held—in a new chamber of his home.

The same onyx stone stretched across the floor, threaded with dusky veins, blue veins that pulsed faintly as if alive. The walls rose high and severe, but here, they opened into tall, slender windows. Through them, I could see the Deathscape sprawling in the distance—the red desert flat and endless, the black mountains looming all around. It struck me, for the first time, that his home wasn't apart from those mountains. It was inside them.

A massive fireplace dominated the far wall, carved in the shape of a beast crouched mid-snarl. Its head—somewhere between wolf and lion, but too jagged, too monstrous to be either—gaped wide to form the hearth. Flames roared inside its maw, the fire burning with unnatural brilliance, gold licked through with veins of shadow. It looked like it wanted to devour the room whole.

And yet, there was a couch.

Formed from the same stone as everything else, yes, but softened—if that word could even apply here—by streaks of that strange blue, smoky mineral. Piled high with furs that looked impossibly soft. Mortal comfort in a place where comfort had no business existing.

My heart thudded as the thought struck me: he'd made this. For me.

Before he knew I was dying.

Still, his arms tightened, adjusting me as if I weighed nothing. My head found his chest, his chin settling with disarming ease atop my hair. I realized, with a jolt, that my hands had fisted in the back of his shirt. I hadn't even felt myself grab hold.

My voice came out small, cracking at the edges. "Why are you holding me?"

His answer was immediate, smooth—too smooth. "Mortals need this, do they not?"

Confidence, on the surface. But I'd spent too much time studying him. His tells. His shadows. I could feel it—the strange hesitation beneath the words, the fragile newness of the contact.

A war raged inside me.

Every instinct screamed that he should be furious. That I had deceived him, used him, stolen his training while knowing it would all end at twenty-five. That he should break me for the audacity.

But this was also the same being who had poured his magic into me when I was drained to my soul. Who had told me he liked being called when I was afraid. Who had kissed me like eternity had finally bent in his favor.

I didn't know whether to tremble harder or melt. Whether to brace for destruction or...lean in.

And that was the part that scared me most.

After a while, I shifted—feet sore, body aching in ways that had nothing to do with muscles.

Death loosened his hold, silver eyes cutting down to me before flicking to the couch. He guided me there with a careful hand at my back, every movement deliberate, almost stiff. Like he was trying on something he hadn't worn in centuries and wasn't sure it fit.

I sat. He didn't. Not at first. He studied the fire, the shadows licking from that monstrous hearth, as though making sure the flames were enough for me. Then, finally, he lowered himself beside me—only to rise again, stride across the room, and pull another fur from a carved stand.

He draped it over me without a word.

When he sat again, his gaze swept over me with grim intent. His hand tugged the fur snug around my shoulders, and then—hesitant—his arm slid around my waist.

The Wood damn me, but that uncertainty of his...it was almost endearing. Which was probably why the question slipped out before I could stop it.

"So," I murmured, turning a little toward him. "You're not going to smite me for keeping the curse from you?"

He exhaled sharply, like the sound alone might burn away his irritation. "I've already told you, Little Bird. I do not damage what is mine."

I frowned up at him. "But you're not mad?"

His expression shifted—sharp edges breaking through, that beast under his skin pressing close to the surface. His voice came low, dark. "I am furious that you didn't tell me. But..."

He stopped, redirected—like he had to drag himself back from some darker conclusion. His eyes gleamed with something ancient. "I am not mortal. I cannot be. I will not promise you safety as if I were. To touch the living...to integrate with them...has been centuries. You fear me. I know that. I understand why you were afraid to tell me."

The firelight cut across his jaw as he tilted his head, voice dipping lower. "What I do not understand is why you would waste breath bargaining with a mortal. Why not with me? I am Death, Sonia. If you are cursed to die, why beg a Mage for help instead of the one being who ferries souls?"

I swallowed hard, twisting in his arm to face him fully. "Because we're already bonded, and I didn't know what you'd do if you knew. I didn't know if you'd kill me sooner. Replace me. Find someone better to tether you to the Living Lands." My voice cracked. "I told McDara because I knew he'd help. Because he felt safe."

His head tipped, eyes like molten, silver fire locking on mine. "And you thought I wouldn't?"

The words scraped raw in my throat. "No, I didn't think you would."

For a beat, silence stretched—thick and cutting, heavy with the weight of truths neither of us had wanted spoken.

Then his voice slid into the space, low and feral. "Are you mine, Sonia?"

My breath stuttered. His arm still anchored me at the waist, his body caging mine without even trying. I blinked up at him, startled, throat tight. Technically, I was his. The bond made it so.

He leaned closer, the fire throwing silver across his face. "Answer me. Are you mine? Because if you are not, then your desire for the mortal's help makes sense." His mouth curved, sharp and dangerous. "And if that is true, then you can have his help."

There was no explicit threat. Not in the words.

But his eyes, his tone, the way his magic pressed like storm clouds into the edges of my skin—it said enough .

"I'm not McDara's."

The words slipped out before I could stop them—bare, shaking, true.

Death's gaze didn't waver. For a long, suffocating moment, he only watched me, silver fire burning behind his eyes, unreadable and endless. Then he nodded once, slow.

"No," he said, voice low and rough, "you are not his and never will be."

He shifted closer, shadows coiling languidly around us. "You can tell me about the curse tomorrow."

That was...unexpected.

I blinked, caught between relief and confusion. He wasn't pressing. He wasn't demanding every secret or trying to peel me apart with questions. He just—let it go.

I supposed he knew I would answer his questions whenever he decided he wanted the answers. It's not like I could refuse, not really. But whatever reason he had for not pressing tonight, my muddled brain and aching heart were grateful.

Slowly, I sank back, which meant I leaned into him. His arm was still around my waist, solid and unyielding, and the movement brought me flush against his side. The fire popped softly in the hearth, sending flickers of gold and scarlet across his sharp features.

After a handful of breaths, the tension drained from me. My head found its way to his chest, the cool thrum of his magic meeting the faint echo of his breathing.

He didn't speak. Didn't move.

Just held me.

The thought almost made me laugh—quiet, disbelieving. Literal Death, content to just sit and hold someone in front of a fire. His shadows twined lazily through the air, dancing with the flame's light like they couldn't help but reach for its warmth.

I watched the fire, its rhythm hypnotic, and the weight of the day started to creep back in. The memory of Dr. Fenwick's body. The cold, rain-slick steps. The blood.

My chest tightened.

I sniffled before I could stop myself.

Death's head tilted slightly above mine, his voice a rumble against my ear. "Tell me what you're thinking."

It wasn't gentle. It was a command.

For all the talk about mortals needing comfort, I didn't think that even when Death was human he could step away from his demanding nature.

Still, something in me wanted to answer him. "It's just..." I swallowed hard. "Dr. Fenwick reminded me of my dad. They even looked a little alike." My voice cracked. "Seeing him—seeing him die like that—it brought everything back. Losing my dad. How it happened. How fast it all was."

He was quiet for a long time. I could feel the weight of his stare, the question unspoken until it wasn't. "Tell me about your parents."

So, I did.

Curled against him on the couch, the fire painting the walls in shifting gold and shadow, I told Death about my dad's perfect coffee, something he would surely be mesmerized with, and my mom's laugh, the tiny brownstone in Chicago that always smelled like lavender and ink. I told him about the library visits, the foster homes before them, the way they'd made me feel wanted in a world that hadn't before.

He didn't interrupt. Didn't even breathe.

He just listened. Completely.

And for one, fragile, impossible moment, Death felt almost human.

It was the biggest lie I would let myself believe.

20

I woke curled in the nest of furs, softer than anything I'd ever touched. The fire still roared as if it hadn't burned a single log down, flames snarling in the maw of the beast-shaped hearth. Beyond the tall, narrow windows stretched the same bloodred desert and jagged, black mountains, frozen in time like a painted backdrop.

But my bones...they felt as if I'd been asleep for ages.

I pushed upright, blankets slipping from my shoulders, and the silence struck me first.

No Death.

Cautiously, I stood. My boots whispered against onyx veined with that dusky blue, every step too loud. The room felt different without him anchoring it. Bigger. Colder.

I hesitated, then wandered toward the single hallway that stretched beyond. Its stone walls pulsed faintly with threads of shadow, like veins just under skin. The corridor branched off—some paths short, ending in doors, others long with countless thresholds yawning into darkness.

A maze.

My stomach knotted.

I could use my magic. Drag myself back to the Living Lands. But the thought of leaving without a word, of disappearing from his home as if I'd never been here—

I shoved that thought down before it could take shape.

Instead, I chose one of the shorter halls. Two doors waited at the end. The one on the left stood ajar, revealing only a slip of darkness, thick and strange, as though the room itself breathed shadow.

But before I could edge closer, a voice curled out from the other door.

Low. Smooth. Unmistakable.

Death.

The crack of light between the doorjamb and door glowed pale, spilling across the floor like a blade. Through it, I caught a glimpse of him—silver fire tracing the hard edges of his form—as he strode across the room toward a figure made entirely of shadow.

My breath caught.

I wasn't sure if I should watch...or run.

I froze, breath lodged high in my throat. The language spilling from Death's lips wasn't meant for mortal ears. Ancient. Bone-deep. Each syllable scraped along my spine as if the words themselves remembered burial shrouds and last breaths.

The thing opposite him replied in the same tongue, the sound low and guttural, like a grave growl wrapped in ritual.

I leaned closer—just enough to catch the curl of the sounds—when Death's head snapped toward the door.

Silver eyes flared, blinding bright, lit from within by something unholy.

"You are awake, Little Bird," he murmured, voice sliding over me like silk cut with steel.

The door groaned open on its own, willed by him. His hand extended toward the hall, fingers long and impossibly steady.

My pulse stuttered. Still, I stepped forward and pressed my palm to his, guessing that was what he wanted of me. His skin was cool as he closed his hand around mine, like he meant to keep it. The barest tilt of his mouth curved upward before he turned back to his...companion.

I dragged my gaze from him. Looked—really looked—at what I thought was only shadow.

My heart kicked hard.

Not shadow. A shape. A figure.

I startled, a small sound slipping out before I could stop it.

Immediately, Death looped my hand through his arm, anchoring me to his side. His other hand caught mine, idly stroking across my knuckles, slow and deliberate. I couldn't tell if he meant to soothe me—or remind me I belonged to him.

The thing wasn't shadow at all.

It stood, humanoid in shape but wrong in every way. Its body was thick with muscle, corded and heavy, smoke curling off it in ribbons that clung like rot. Its claws flexed as though the air itself resisted them. Its eyes—if they were eyes—burned like pits of coal fire, hollow and endless. And its jaw...stretched too far, filled with jagged teeth meant for tearing.

It spoke in that same bone-deep tongue as Death, each syllable vibrating low in the walls. A sound like earth splitting open, like something buried clawing its way free.

Glowing red orbs that sat within the shadow maw that was this creature's face shifted toward me, and I swore this thing was looking at me, but at a low snarl from Death the thing's orbs shifted back to him and they...Blessed the freaking Wood they looked like they had sunk deeper into the shadows. This creature, that looked like every kid's nightmare that had come crawling out from under their bed, was afraid of Death.

I peeked a look at him, standing tall and solid next to me. Silver eyes pinning the creature as words ancient and foreign flew like daggers from his sinfully shaped mouth.

Damn right this creature was afraid of Death. Beautiful things were always more dangerous than the ones that seemed easily marked as bad. And the most dangerous thing in this entire realm was holding and stroking my hand like I was his favorite pet.

My stomach twisted, but I didn't step back. Not with Death's hand folded around mine, his fingers tracing idly over my knuckles as if reminding me that I was tethered here, anchored. That I was safe. With him, I *was* safe. From this creature at least.

The creature bowed its head once, shadows rippling around it, then dissolved into smoke at a flick of Death's fingers.

The silence it left behind made the hair on my arms stand on end.

I swallowed hard, dragging my gaze to him. "What...what was that?"

His silver eyes cut back to mine, lips curving slow. Dangerous. Disturbing.

"What do you think it was, Little Bird?"

My throat worked. "A Reaper?"

That grin sharpened. "Only a Grim. My Reapers are far worse."

I opened my mouth to ask about the Reapers, because of course I did—curiosity and terror had always danced too close in me. But Death's hand tightened just enough on mine, guiding me across the room, and before I knew it, we were at his desk.

Two chairs waited there. I didn't remember them before. High-backed, carved of the same black onyx that seemed to pulse faintly with his power. One of them was draped with furs white as bone.

"Sit," he said.

I glanced at the fur-covered chair. Obviously for me. He took the other, the bare stone, as if the cold meant nothing to him. Maybe it didn't.

With a sigh, I lowered myself into the seat, shifting against the surprising softness. My gaze flicked to him. He looked...pleased. But determined too, as if some decision had already been made. The combination unsettled me.

Another sigh slipped out before I could stop it. "That look on your face? It can't mean anything good."

His mouth curved, sharp as a blade. Wolfish.

He leaned back in his chair, elbows resting on the arms, fingers steepled over his stomach. His eyes dragged over me, slow, lazy—like I was already his answer to whatever question he hadn't asked. Heat crawled up my throat, fireflies lighting under my skin, because the last time he'd looked at me like that, it had ended in a kiss that had changed everything.

But instead of claiming another...

"Tell me," he said, voice low, commanding, "all about this curse you think you have."

The way he'd said it—*the curse you think you have*—grated, like he'd brushed aside everything I'd been choking on for weeks.

I dug my fingers into the white furs draped over my chair, trying not to notice how deliberate it felt, how he'd chosen this one for me. Trying not to think about how much easier it would be to sink into them and pretend I wasn't about to hand Death the sharpest blade he could ever use against me.

If he knew I was already living on borrowed time, why would he keep me alive? Why would he waste himself training me, guarding me, pretending he cared?

What was his plan? Because beyond desire, or the odd comfort of his arms around me, there wasn't an inch of me that didn't think he had one.

He must've felt my hesitation because his voice cut through the silence, low and unrelenting.

"What age are you, Little Bird? When is your birthday?"

The air lodged in my throat. "I'm twenty-four." I forced the words out. "February."

It was mid-November now. Less than four months left.

His silver eyes flared, bright enough to sting, but he didn't move. Didn't speak. He only...calculated. And that silence—gods, that silence—was worse than if he'd bared his teeth.

I swallowed hard and looked at my hands. "Every Ghost Whisperer in my family dies at twenty-five. All of them. My birth mother, Grace. Her father before her. Records in the Black House go back decades, and it's always the same."

The words thickened as I pushed them out. "And it's not just them—their partner's too. Like Grace's mother who wasn't a Ghost Whisperer according to her ledger. Grace says her mom left her to be raised by the Black House. That she couldn't stay after her dad died. I need to find the records at the Black House about the partners for the Ghost Whisperers in my family line. The parent with the Ghost Whisperer ability dies, and then the other parent just...leaves? It doesn't make sense to me."

The words thickened as I pushed them out. "The closer it gets, the worse it gets. That's what Grace wrote. Fatigue that deepens every time magic is used. Nosebleeds during emotional surges. Nightmares that feel like choking. Ringing in the ears near Black House artifacts. Weakness that escalates until the end."

I forced myself to look at him then, searching for a flicker of understanding, but his face was carved from shadow and stone.

"I haven't had them yet. Except the draining from using my magic. You've seen that," I whispered, the words scraping. "But she experienced all of them. She says they all did."

Saying it aloud was like naming the monster already stalking me, watching the hourglass run dry.

"Your birth mother kept a ledger." It wasn't a question, and the way Death's gaze tracked every breath that passed my lips with razor-edge precision, he was not in the mood to be the calm and patient man that had held me on the couch last night. Who was almost...soft. This Death before me was more akin to the one that I had met over a month ago in a red desert. Who had clasped my throat and bound me to him. At the thought, the skin of my neck burned. His eyes flicked down, and it seemed he could see the impression of the mark his fingers had made on me just as surely as I could feel them. "Tell me all that Grace has learned."

I dragged in a shaky breath. "I haven't finished reading it, but what Grace said was that at first, she thought the bloodline curse was fate. Something inevitable. But David—my birth father—he wouldn't accept that. He said it was engineered. Murder disguised as curse."

The words scraped raw as I pushed forward. "She started experimenting, trying to find ways to sever the tie. Sigil bleeding rites. Mirror chants. She even wrote about something called Veil-threading."

The second I said it, Death went still. His silver eyes flared—violent, sudden. Shadows flexed like a storm breaking against stone.

"When did your mother die?" His voice was a blade.

I startled at the sharpness. "I—I was about one. So...twenty-three years ago."

His jaw tightened, a flicker of something grim crossing his face. He said nothing. And I couldn't stop myself, not when my chest was burning with fear that had nowhere to go.

"Do all Ghost Whisperers die at twenty-five?" My voice cracked. I leaned forward, desperate, as if I could shake the truth out of him. "Or is it just my family?"

Silence. It stretched until my heart ached.

"I have never heard of such a curse." His silver gaze pinned me. "The Ghost Whisperers I once knew lived long lives. Full lives."

The floor fell out from under me.

Not fate. Not destiny. Not something written in blood and bone.

Targeted. Engineered. My family alone.

My thoughts spiraled. *Who would want my bloodline dead?*

The first name clawed up like bile—Matron Black. But I shoved it down just as fast. No. She wanted me in her House. Desperately. She threatened to withhold real Ghost Whisper training to get me to join. Why go through all that just to kill me? And I knew she wanted me trained. She pushed me to take it seriously, again and again. If she wanted me dead, it would be simple. I didn't have defensive magic, not really. She wouldn't need to orchestrate decades of curses to make it happen.

But someone else in the Black House?

The thought coiled cold in my stomach.

"Back when I was allowed to walk the Living Lands without tether," Death said, voice smooth but edged with something colder than steel, "Ghost Whisperers were revered. No one could do what they did. Every village wanted one to anchor them, to ferry their dead safely onward."

The word lodged in my chest. *Allowed.*

My breath caught. "Allowed...meaning you weren't always bound to the Deathscape? Like locked away here?"

His gaze slid to me, silver burning. "The Veil Keepers." He spoke their name with such venom the air seemed to thin, the fire at his back shuddering lower. "They are not lenient when their rules are broken."

A chill raced down my spine. "Who are they?"

"The guardians of the balance. Jailors of the gates. Cowards who fear time moving toward its inevitable end." His mouth curled in disdain. "It was they who locked me in the Deathscape."

My throat worked as I swallowed. This—this was the first real truth he'd given me about his punishment, and it was worse for the restraint in his voice.

"Gates?"

"Gates to the two other Bone Veils. I assume you know that the Deathscape is only the first layer of...this realm," he said. "Gates to other worlds as well."

"Why?" The word scraped out of me before I could swallow it back. "Why did they punish you?"

His stare cut through me. For a long, heavy moment, I thought he wouldn't answer. Then, quiet and lethal, "For doing something unforgivable. Something that would make you as terrified of me now as you were the first moment we met. More so."

The silence that followed was cavernous. I couldn't look away from him. I couldn't push further either, because whatever truth lived in those words—it wasn't ready to be unearthed.

So instead, I asked, "When did they lock you away?"

"1347." His answer was immediate, unflinching.

My mouth went dry, the fire's heat suddenly doing nothing to chase the chill crawling my spine.

"You've been stuck in the Deathscape since...1347?" The number caught in my throat, splintered and sharp.

Death didn't move, didn't blink. His silver gaze remained fixed on me, unflinching.

"That's—" My voice broke, horror catching in my chest. It was 2024 now which meant... "That's 677 years. Alone. With only...things like that"—I jerked my chin toward the door where the Grim had been, my hands trembling—"for company."

The weight of it pressed down on me. Six centuries of silence. Of punishment. Of nothing but monsters and ghosts and the endless, red desert.

I shook my head, unable to stop the words spilling out, too horrified to swallow them down. "No one survives that. No one should."

And still, he sat before me. Eternal. Unyielding. Watching me like *I* was the storm that threatened to undo him.

677 years.

The number rattled in my head like a curse I couldn't shake. My pulse wouldn't calm, my breath coming in shallow bursts. I couldn't stop seeing him standing in that endless desert—alone, trapped, only monsters for company—centuries grinding by with no one to speak to. No one to touch.

And yet, here he was. Watching me with that unbearable patience, as if my reaction was more fragile than his prison had ever been.

The questions broke out of me before I could stop them.

"Why only my bloodline? Was it punishment?" My voice cracked, bitter. "The Mage Council? Someone in the Black House? Could these Veil Keepers have done it?"

"Why would they punish your bloodline?" The question was steady. Everything that I didn't feel in this moment.

"*I don't fucking know.*" It was nearly a scream. "Why would anyone want to curse an entire family, generation after generation?"

My hands clenched in the fur draped over the chair, knuckles white. "If it was the Council, then *why*? Why suppress Ghost Whisperers at all? What did we do?"

The fire popped, harsh and loud in the silence.

My throat burned. "Are Ghost Whisperers even Mages?"

That got him. Death tilted his head, eyes gleaming like moonlight sharpened to a blade. "Not in the way you think."

Nothing more. Just that.

And somehow, that was worse.

The words slipped out before I could think better of them.

"Dr. Fenwick told me...he read texts that mentioned Ghost Whisperers long before the Woods ever appeared. You remember me talking about that, right? What he read made it clear that Ghost Whisperers could have been here before the first Mage was even created." My voice felt too loud in the firelit study, like I was confessing something dangerous.

I turned toward Death.

He was already watching me. That look again—silver eyes sharp as blades, measuring me with a cool calculation that made my stomach flip.

If he had known Ghost Whisperers back in the 1300s...then that was centuries before the Woods tore into our world in the 1870s.

My pulse stuttered. "So that means..." My mouth had gone dry, but I forced the words out. "Ghost Whisperers can't be Mages. We aren't from the Wood at all...are we?"

Death leaned back in his chair, shadows curling over the sharp lines of his face as if even the firelight refused him. His eyes glinted like silver cut from the night sky.

"No, Little Bird," he said, voice low and absolute. "You never were."

The air seemed to drop, heavy and final.

His gaze didn't waver. "As far as I know, Ghost Whisperers have always walked this world. Long before the Woods scarred it. Long before Mages learned to twist their power into sigils and call it law."

My throat was dry, the words scraping out raw. "Will you help me?"

For the first time since I'd started talking, his silver eyes cut sharp with offense. He rose in his chair, shadows draping off him like smoke. "You still ask me that?" His voice was a low rasp, dangerous. "Are you not mine, Sonia?"

The air left my lungs. He hadn't moved closer yet, but it felt like he had—like the space between us was gone. My pulse hammered, my fingers twisting the fur in my lap.

If I told him yes, maybe he would help me. Maybe he'd fight for me. But I didn't want the only reason to be my magic.

So, I forced my chin up. "If you help me break the curse, I'll use my magic for you."

His eyes flared bright, molten silver, and he stilled as if I'd struck him. Then, with sudden violence, he was on his feet, pacing—his shadows scraping the floor like claws.

"Stupid girl," he hissed, fury curling in every word. "Do you not hear yourself? You offer me your magic with no safeguard. No limits. Do you have any idea what you've just placed at my feet?"

Heat flared in my chest, anger mixing with fear. "It doesn't matter if it's dangerous for me! I'm already going to die in a couple months." My voice broke, but I powered through. "If you want my magic, then once the curse is broken, I'll train with you. We'll...we'll make an agreement about how it's used."

He stopped pacing and turned on me. In two strides he crowded me, his presence swallowing the chair, the air, me. I went rigid, every nerve sparking with terror and something darker I didn't want to name.

"Stop." His voice was jagged with restraint, his face inches from mine. "Stop offering me temptation of your magic." His breath shuddered, his gaze devouring me. "Do you not think I would want you alive for any other reason?"

The words landed like a blow. My heart stumbled, my body trembling with the weight of it.

Was that real? Did he actually want me safe because I...mattered? The only way I was useful to him was through my magic and, well, 677 years alone...

But he could have taken my reckless offer just now. Demanded anything in return. Did that mean Death was starting to care for me, or was this a long-planned ruse for an end much darker than I could guess? For all that he looked like a man, he wasn't. I needed to remember that. He was Death. Not human. It wasn't until I had left McDara's apartment that I started to really get a glimpse of anything close to humanity in him. Maybe caring for someone wasn't possible for a creature like him.

A flash of our last bargain narrowed my vision to his hesitation when we kissed. To the gentle and unsure way he had tucked the furs around me last night.

I suddenly realized that I wanted Death to be capable of caring.

We stood there, breathing like we'd just fought a war, shadows curling hungrily between us. Then, with a sharp inhale, he tore himself back. "You will keep searching for answers in the Living Lands," he said, voice cold, command laced into every syllable. "I will search here. Tomorrow, we resume your training."

My breath stuttered. "So...you're going to help me? No bargaining?"

His eyes flicked over me, molten and unreadable, before narrowing darkly. "When I find something that can help you, Little Bird, then we will bargain."

The promise—the threat—hung between us like a noose.

21

Death rose slowly, deliberate as the turning of the tide, and drew me up with him. His hands settled firm at my waist, then slid around me, caging me in his arms as if he could read the tremor beneath my skin. His eyes—silver, fathomless—searched mine with an intensity that rooted me to the spot.

My heart stuttered. Was he about to kiss me? Or...rip my soul straight out of my body? Honestly, with him, either seemed equally likely.

The air between us stretched taut, ready to snap. My breath caught in my throat, my nerves screaming with anticipation. And before he could do anything—before I could unravel any further—I whispered, "Thank you."

His head tilted, a flicker of something sharp in his gaze.

"For listening to me last night," I pressed on, my voice small but clear. "For asking about my dad. For...holding me. I didn't realize how much I needed comfort until you gave it."

For the first time, his expression softened. Not much—not nearly enough for anyone else to notice—but I saw it. The shadow of satisfaction. The smallest release of tension, as though he'd been waiting to hear if he'd done it right.

He didn't speak. He didn't have to. The silence felt like his answer.

Shadows licked around us, curling tighter, colder. The Deathscape dissolved, the red desert and its endless horizon unraveling into smoke. My stomach swooped, head light as the world shifted.

And then we were in my room. The twin's apartment.

His arms were the last to go—once solid, now nothing but smoke, fading from around me until I was clutching empty air. A final glance at me, the room, and then he was gone, snapped back into the Deathscape.

I exhaled a shaky sigh, pressing a hand to my chest.

And froze.

Pandora sat on the edge of my bed. Watching me. Like I had just walked straight out of hell.

All the blood drained from my head, leaving me lightheaded, dread slick and heavy in my veins.

What had she seen?

Before I could shape a word, she shot to her feet, cutting a sharp line through the air with her arm as though to stop me. Her eyes narrowed, dark and piercing.

"Where were you?" she demanded. Then, before I could even open my mouth, she slashed the question away with a flick of her hand.

"Better yet," she said, her voice a blade now, "who were you with?"

My mouth opened, some excuse half-formed, but what could I say? No Mage could just...*portal* without a chorus of sigils and half a House boosting them. Any lie I tried would crumble in my hands.

So, I forced the words back down, steadied my voice, and asked instead, "What did you see?"

Pandora's glare cut through me like sharpened glass. She knew I was dodging her question, but after a long, taut beat, she answered anyway.

"An onyx stone room," she said flatly. "Then smoke. Black as night. And then it was gone. But *you* remained."

A shiver ripped down my spine. So, she hadn't seen him. Death hadn't been visible to her, even with the veil between realms open. For one heartbeat, I'd thought maybe...maybe he could be seen by someone else. But no. Of all the living, it was still just me.

Which meant I had no excuse left.

I didn't trust Pandora. Not like I did Calypso. I probably needed to stop holding her ties to the Black House against her. But Pandora? Ruthless to the bone. What would she do if she knew I'd been letting Death touch me? Train me?

Still...what else could I give her but a shard of the truth?

I dragged in a breath, bracing myself to admit I could slip into the Deathscape—

My phone rang.

The sound sliced through the tension like a reprieve from the gods.

My heart jolted at the name on the screen. *McDara.*

I answered without hesitation, clinging to him as an escape rope. "Hello?"

Relief crackled through the line, though his voice was clipped, detective-sharp. "Will you meet me at the corner of your block? Now."

"I—yes." Too quickly. Too eager.

I turned to Pandora, already backing for the door. "I'll explain later."

She opened her mouth, but I lifted the phone higher, pressing it hard to my ear, pretending I was still on the call. McDara had already hung up, but I didn't care. It gave me the shield I needed.

And then I bolted. Out of the apartment, down the hall. Running like the walls might cave in if I stayed a second longer.

The block was nearly deserted, the night heavy with low clouds pressing down against the streetlights. A kind of hush lingered over everything, broken only by the occasional drip of rain from gutters.

And there he was.

McDara stood at the far end of the block, coat dark as shadow, shoulders squared but taut with tension. His head was lowered, as if bracing against more than just the cold. Haunted eyes. Broad frame I knew too well. He looked the same. Gods, he *looked* the same.

But it didn't *feel* the same.

My chest constricted painfully. I remembered what it felt like to step into his orbit and feel safe—like the world couldn't touch me if he was there. That feeling was gone, fractured the moment he pushed me away. And yet the ache of it gnawed at me, as if my body still hadn't accepted the loss.

He lifted his head. His eyes locked on mine.

His whole face shifted, softening in a way that gutted me. "Thank the gods. You came."

I stopped a few feet short, breath uneven, every muscle wired with conflict.

His gaze flicked around me, sharp and searching. "Is he here?"

The question hit like a stone. My pulse skipped. I didn't know if I should feel offended or oddly...seen. "No," I managed, voice rough. "Death isn't here."

His shoulders lowered, only slightly, but enough that the tension in his frame eased. A careful exhale. "Good."

Then his eyes came back to me, steady and determined. "Will you come with me? To the university. There's something I want to look into. You might be able to help."

My stomach dipped. The university. Which meant his car. Which meant *alone*—in the same space, with his scent, his voice, his presence pressing against all the cracks in my chest. I hesitated. The ache of what I still wanted warred with the sting of the rejection I couldn't forget.

And more than those familiar aches was the ghosts warning. The words the Faceless Woman had written in frost telling me to stay away from the Black family. From McDara.

For one wild heartbeat, I thought about calling Death. Bringing him here to cut through the silence, to shield me from this ache. This uncertainty about the ghosts' warning. But I shoved the thought away. Death and McDara in the same space...one of them wouldn't walk away.

McDara must have read the hesitation in my face because he stepped closer.

His scent wrapped around me—cedar, smoke, and storm air—and it wrecked me. My breath caught.

His eyes softened, sincerity written there like a confession. "I'm sorry," he said quietly. "For not reaching out sooner. Other than being a coward...I have no excuse."

The words burrowed deep, prying at the ache I'd been trying to bury. My throat burned. I swallowed, staring at him like maybe if I looked long enough, I could read the truth in his bones.

Finally, I forced out the words. "I'll go with you."

Even if it shattered me all over again.

22

The drive to the university was brutal. Every second trapped in McDara's red sports car was a reminder of how wrong things were between us. His hands gripped the wheel too tightly, the leather groaning under his knuckles. The silence pressed in, thicker than the rain-streaked windows. Every time I caught his scent—woodsmoke and storm air—it was like being dragged backward into memory, into safety I no longer had. I sat there with my arms folded tight across my chest, pretending the ache didn't still live in me.

When he finally pulled into the parking lot, my lungs felt raw, like I'd been holding my breath the whole way.

We got out, doors slamming in unison, and the night swallowed us. The university loomed, Gothic and eerie, spires and ivy-streaked stone heavy against a sky choked with clouds. The rain had slowed to a mist, but the air still smelled like wet stone and old leaves.

We didn't speak as we crossed the dark campus, footsteps echoing too loud in the hush. When the library rose before us, its stone steps gleaming slick and black, I stopped. Yellow police tape webbed the entrance, cordoning off the place where Dr. Fenwick had dragged himself up to die. My stomach twisted at the sight.

McDara cleared his throat, breaking the silence. His voice came low, rough. "I want you to try and contact him. Dr. Fenwick."

I blinked at him, studying his profile in the dim light. His jaw was iron, but there was something in his eyes—something raw. "Why tonight?" I asked carefully. "Why right now? Why do you care so much?"

He blew out a breath so heavy it seemed to drag the air with it. "Because he was my doctor, Sonia. Mine and Deidre's. He delivered her. He's been in my life since I was a kid." His throat bobbed, his voice going softer, frayed at the edges. "I just need to know that the doc is okay. And if he can give us answers...all the better."

That punched something hollow in my chest. I nodded, words catching in my throat. "He treated me too, you know. He was kind."

McDara's brow furrowed, sharp confusion flashing across his face. "Why would he be treating you? For what?"

Panic snapped through me. I mentally slapped myself. *Idiot.* I hadn't wanted to bring this up—not here, not with him. I forced a shrug, aiming for casual. "One of the trainings in the back courtyard...there was a misfire. Grazed me. He patched me up."

McDara stilled. Every muscle in his body went rigid. His jaw clenched so hard it looked painful, and I could almost see the implosion simmering in his chest. We both knew the truth: Misfires like that didn't happen at the Black House. Not unless someone *wanted* them to.

I turned away before he could say anything, throat tight, pulse racing. "Doesn't matter," I muttered, refusing to let him continue this conversation.

Closing my eyes, I reached inward, grasping for that tenuous thread of magic—the one I'd been learning to pull on in the Living Lands, sharp and draining. My stomach twisted as I began to pull.

The night held its breath.

I tried to do it the way Death had shown me. To quiet the noise of my mind and body, to slip past it, to grip the thread of power that tethered me between worlds. But every time I reached it slipped like water through my fingers.

Heat prickled along my skin, a slow burn rising under the surface. I looked down and my stomach lurched. The veins around my wrists and hands were glowing faintly silver, bright and eerie against my skin—like moonlight trapped beneath flesh. The gold bracelet at my wrist gleamed like molten fire against my moonlit veins. My pulse jumped.

"Come on," I whispered to myself, shaking out my hands, trying to rid them of the glow, of the frustration building in my chest.

I walked a little ways from McDara, closer to the steps, but the slight distance did not ease the weight of his expectation.

I could feel McDara watching me—his gaze heavy, assessing—but he didn't move closer. He didn't say a word. Not like before. Not like when he'd once guided me with steady patience, his calloused hand warm over mine.

My throat tightened.

I shut my eyes again, forcing myself not to think about him, not to think about the fact that my own body was betraying me. My heartbeat thundered, erratic, my breath catching as sweat broke out along my spine. The curse. It had to be the curse already dragging me under.

No. I couldn't fail. Not this time. Not when McDara was asking. Not when I wanted—needed—to do this for Fenwick. For a moment, just the breath of a single second, I saw my dad's face in my mind before it flickered to the doctor's, and my chest began to ache even more. I couldn't contact my dad, but this...Fenwick had been gone only a day, and I had some training now...maybe I could do it this time.

I did the only thing that my body would allow. I called him.

Not with words. Not out loud. Just with the desperate pull of my mind, like throwing open a door inside me. *Need you.*

The answer was immediate. His presence swept through me like cold flame, like shadow cutting through fever. My heart, frantic moments ago, slowed into something steady. A calm I shouldn't feel. A calm I didn't *want* to feel.

But the Wood help me, I leaned into it.

I opened my eyes.

Death stood at my side. His grin curved sharp, silver eyes catching like storm light. "Already begging for me, Little Bird? Careful. You'll spoil me."

I rolled my eyes, even as relief thrummed traitorously in my veins. "I need help. With my magic."

His attention shifted, gaze gliding over the campus around us, over the police tape and the looming dark of the university library. His grin slipped. "Why here? Why tonight?"

I swallowed hard. "To try and contact Fenwick. McDara thought—"

But I never finished.

Death turned. Saw him.

The second his eyes locked on McDara, everything about him changed. The sharp amusement vanished, his whole presence curdling into something darker, sharper. The air thickened, the shadows at his back coiling as if eager to strike.

And the storm between them sparked to life.

"Are you talking to Fenwick?" McDara's voice cut through the night, low, measured. Too measured.

He came to my side, close enough that I could feel the heat of him through my coat, but still left a handsbreadth of space—as if that distance could save him.

Death tracked him like prey, silver eyes narrowing, shadows restless at his back.

I glanced at McDara, my chest tight, then forced my focus back to Death. Tried to catch his attention, to anchor him to me. But he wasn't looking at me. He was already calculating McDara's end.

"I—it's the same," I murmured, voice rough. "The same problems when I try to use my magic."

I didn't add the part about how the drain left me trembling, about how every attempt hollowed me out a little more. That weakness felt too raw, too shameful to bear in front of McDara.

That made Death look at me. And gods help me, I stepped closer, as if proximity alone could steady him, steady me.

"Will you help me?" I asked softly.

Something eased in him. The storm pulled back, his edges less lethal, like my nearness was tether enough to keep him from breaking into violence.

But before he could answer, McDara's hand slid over my arm. The contact shot through me, familiar and yet too sharp now.

"Who are you talking to?" he asked, jaw tight, eyes searching mine.

Death's shadows exploded, magic snarling outward like black fire. The entire air around us went razor-edged, hungry.

"McDara—stop." I turned, trying to put myself between them. "It's Death. I called him. Just—calm down. Both of you."

McDara froze. Then his expression hardened, horror cutting deep into the lines of his face. His magic flared to life across his hands, sparking violent light into the dark.

I darted between them, pulse pounding. "Enough! Death is the only one who can help me. He's the only one who's ever made my magic work."

That seemed to shake McDara. His eyes snapped to me, wide, stricken with something between disbelief and fury.

Behind me, Death moved. Closer. His presence pressed hot and cold all at once against my spine, shadows coiling until they tangled with my own breath.

"The mortal should see," he said, voice like velvet dragged across blades, "who holds his end."

And then the shadows peeled away.

Death *became visible.*

Right there, in front of McDara.

I couldn't breathe. Couldn't *think.*

Death stood beside me, not as smoke or shadow or something half-felt—but *real.* His edges were clean and sharp, the blur I'd always seen when he pulled himself into the Living Lands utterly gone. He was solid. Visible.

"Gods," I whispered, my voice cracking. "How the hell can you do that?"

His silver gaze never once left McDara. A smile curved his mouth—slow, terrifying, like a blade unsheathed.

"My magic is strengthening here," he said.

The words dropped into me like stones hurled into a well, sinking and sinking with no end. Strengthening. Here.

Our bond. My pulse stuttered, panic clawing at my chest. Was *I* the reason? Was my tether letting him gain more purchase in the Living Lands? Was this why he wanted me? Why he had bound himself to me? Not because I was me, but because I was useful?

When did he realize he could become corporal here?

Suddenly, I felt foolish and small. So unbelievably small. I would only know what Death wanted me to. Only see him how he decided to design himself. The realization that there was so much about him that I did not know slammed into me and left my knees hollow, but Death's shadows tied themselves tighter around me, supporting, caging.

McDara's sharp inhale dragged me back. He was pale but steady, shaking on the inside maybe, but still braced like a soldier ready to go to war. His magic slipped outward in a controlled rush, cool and crystalline—icy threads weaving around me like a shield. The air tasted sharp, metallic, like biting down on winter itself.

"Back away from her," he said, voice low, commanding. "Now."

I felt Death's shadows snap in fury, restless against my skin. His magic was the opposite—dark and hot, heavy like molten smoke, pressing closer with every breath. It wanted to *consume*. To pull me into him.

And gods, I couldn't do this. Not between them. Not tonight.

"Enough!" The word tore from me, louder than I meant, but I didn't care. My whole body shook with it. "Both of you—*enough!*"

They froze, caught in the sound of my voice.

I shoved out from between them, stepping to the side, forcing space into their battleground. "I am here to contact Fenwick. *Not* referee your egos." My throat burned, my voice rising. "So, calm the fuck down. Both of you."

For a long, heavy moment, Death's shadows writhed against McDara's frost, black fire straining against winter's bite.

Then slowly, reluctantly, two pairs of eyes turned toward me.

One silver, unholy, and burning with possessive fury.

One coffee-dark, sharp with protectiveness and pain.

And I was caught between them.

I turned to Death, pulse thudding in my ears. "Can you calm down enough to help me control my magic?"

McDara stiffened at my tone, like he expected Death to tear me apart for daring to talk to him like that.

But I didn't look away. I held his silver stare, even as shadows rippled off him like smoke rolling across the ground.

Death moved closer, as if the space between us was an illusion he refused to tolerate. His voice was low, dark silk. "Using your magic in the Living Lands is a risk, you know this. If you wanted to speak to your doctor..." His head tipped, unholy light flaring in his eyes. "You could have come to *me*. To the Deathscape. I would have helped you find him."

The breath caught in my chest. *My father.* The thought slammed into me like a fist. If he could help me find Fenwick...could he help me find—

"No." McDara's voice cut hard, furious. He stepped forward, his still like ice, tightened like a noose around me. "What the hell does that mean, Sonia? What exactly are you doing with him?"

Before I could get a word out, Death laughed. It was low, merciless, like smoke sliding beneath the skin. "She comes to me when she wants control over her power. She comes to me when she needs a place to breathe. Tell me, little mortal—what does it feel like to know her refuge is with *me*?"

McDara's jaw locked, fury sparking in his eyes.

I was so. Fucking. Done.

I reached for Death's arm—needing to *ground* him, ground myself—but my hand went straight through. Solid edges, but nothing beneath. Just smoke. Just shadow.

He looked at me then, softer, but no less dangerous. "My magic still needs to strengthen more in the Living Lands."

The words hit me like a slap. My stomach dropped. Strengthen. That was all I was to him. A means to claw his way further into this world.

Used.

"We need to talk," I said, anger sharpening my voice to steel.

He tilted his head, measuring me. Shadows rippled like wings at his back. "So talk, Little Bird."

"Sonia." McDara's voice—pleading this time, desperate—cut in. His hand almost brushed my arm. "Come away from him. Please."

I turned from them both, chest heaving, tears burning at the edges of my fury. No more.

I shoved my magic outward, forcing it through me even as it clawed and drained and burned. The world spun, silver light cracking in my vision—

And then the Deathscape took me.

23

The Deathscape swallowed me whole.

I hit the red desert hard, knees buckling, sand searing hot against my palms. The air was poison-silver, cutting into my lungs until I couldn't breathe. My chest heaved, gasping, choking.

And then he was there.

Death materialized out of shadow and firelight, hands already reaching, silver eyes sharp with concern. All that ego, that sharp-edged hunger, gone the instant McDara wasn't here.

I batted his hand away. Hard. "Don't."

It was probably stupid—striking Death himself—but wasn't I supposed to matter to him? Wasn't I the tether that let him dig claws into the Living Lands again? What would he really do to me if I lashed out?

Tears pricked at my eyes. Fury rose hot in my throat. I hated both.

He only watched me. Silent. Like he knew I was seconds from breaking.

"What do you get out of this?" My voice cracked, ragged. "Our bond. What's in it for you?"

He didn't answer. Just stood there, watching me fall apart like it was a damn spectacle.

My chest burned hotter. I stormed toward him, tilting my chin up though he towered over me. "It's the bond, isn't it? That's why you're gaining more ground in the Living Lands. That's why you're so"—my throat closed on the word—"*possessive.*"

His silver eyes flared. Shadows rippled off him like storm waves.

"You still have feelings for the Mage," he bit out, voice dark as ash.

I threw my arms wide, tears sliding hot down my cheeks. "So what? What does it matter? You get whatever you want out of this bond whether I like you, or him, or no one at all! You don't need me to *choose* you."

Shadows surged. And then he was on me—crowding close, towering like a storm about to break. His hands curled into shadow claws, black fire licking down his knuckles as he hooked them near my face.

"What if I *want* you to choose me?"

The breath ripped out of me. My head shook, frantic. "It's all about winning with you. That's all this is. You want to win over McDara. But you know what? I'm done. I don't have anything left to give you."

I shoved at his chest, palms colliding with stone-hard muscle that didn't move an inch. His sheer, immovable strength made my stomach twist with fear.

Slowly—so slowly—like the air itself had cracked, he pulled back.

I ripped my jacket tighter around me, stepping back like I could shake him off. My voice shook, raw. "You know what is so pathetic? I was relieved when you showed up at the university." My laugh was a jagged, half-sob. "My gods, what's wrong with me? Comforted. Because *you* had shown up. And isn't that so fucking stupid of me?"

The tears wouldn't stop now, no matter how hard I scrubbed them away.

"All I am to you is a means to an end," I spat, even as my voice broke. "So, let's just stick to our bargain. You train me, I try not to die on my birthday, and you get whatever the hell you're bleeding out of this bond. Because I can't—" My voice cracked to a whisper. "I can't take you and McDara shredding me apart anymore."

I turned, back rigid, shoulders shaking, the tears falling fast now. It was the last defense I had—denying him my face.

And I knew. The way my soul knew his pull in my marrow. The way the air stilled.

When he left me.

Alone in the red desert of the Deathscape.

The desert swallowed me whole.

I walked without knowing where I was going, boots sinking into the shifting red sands, each step heavier than the last. My chest burned from everything I hadn't said—everything I *had* said. My heart felt cracked open, bleeding into the endless silence of the Deathscape.

Wind picked up, tugging strands of my hair across my face, and the sand began to whirl in restless circles. The horizon blurred until I couldn't tell earth from sky.

The storm was building, winds clawing at my hair, red sand biting into my skin. I squinted through the haze—

A figure.

Tall. Broad-shouldered. Moving slowly, dragging one leg like it was wounded. For a heartbeat I thought—Dr. Fenwick.

"Doctor!" I shouted, my voice torn away by the wind.

The figure turned.

And it wasn't Fenwick.

It was my dad.

I staggered, heart dropping into my stomach. His face—blurred by distance, but familiar enough to shatter me. My throat burned. "Dad!"

He lifted a hand, like he was reaching for me. I swore I heard him call back—my name, carried on the storm.

I ran. Sand stung my cheeks, my eyes, but I didn't care. "Dad!"

No matter how hard I pushed, he stayed the same distance away. Always just beyond reach. A mirage made of hope and memory.

The storm swallowed him whole.

The world dissolved into a maelstrom of red and black. No horizon. No ground. Just shrieking wind and suffocating sand.

And then—

A voice.

Low. Drawn out. Notes bent strange, like a song that had rotted in the throat of whoever sang it. The sound wrapped around me, echoing from everywhere and nowhere, too close and too far at once.

The melody coiled like smoke, lilting, almost sweet—if sweetness could crawl over your skin like a thousand spiders.

I spun, chest heaving. Nothing but sand. Nothing but storm.

The song came again, higher now, sliding into words I didn't recognize. My heart slammed against my ribs.

It wasn't a song.

It was a lure.

And I was the prey.

The song wound tighter, circling me like a noose. My skin prickled. Every instinct screamed *run,* but there was nowhere to go. Nowhere to hide in the endless expanse of red desert.

"Who's there?" My voice cracked, torn raw by sand and fear.

The storm answered with laughter—high, shrill, sharp enough to slice. It was woven into the wind, impossible to tell if it was beside me or a mile away.

My breath hitched. The song returned, soft again, as if mocking me. A cradle song turned wrong. My chest constricted. I didn't know what lived in the Deathscape. I hadn't wanted to know. And here I was, running headlong into it like a fool.

I stumbled over a jagged rock half-buried in the sand and caught myself on my hands, grit grinding into my palms. Tears stung my eyes, though I didn't know if it was grief or sand or pure terror.

The laughter came again, closer this time.

And then the storm *parted.*

She was there.

At first glance, she looked human—too human. Skin like marble veined in pitch, glinting with unnatural light every time lightning cracked in the sky. Her long, black hair was woven into braids that clattered with bone beads, her mouth opening in a grin full of black, serrated fangs.

Her wings unfurled.

Not feathers. Not angelic. Leather stretched taut, monstrous, each tip ending in a hook that gleamed like wet obsidian.

She swung her scythe once, easy as breath, its curved blade hissing through the storm.

"Well, well," she purred, voice thick with delight. "So, this is the mortal making our Death so foul-tempered."

Her grin widened.

I bolted.

She shrieked after me, the sound half laughter, half hunting-cry, chasing me through the storm.

And gods, she was *enjoying it.*

I ran blind, the storm clawing at me from every direction. The song twisted through the gale, sometimes sweet, sometimes jagged, always close.

I zigzagged between the jagged stones jutting from the sand, my lungs burning, my boots slipping. For a heartbeat I thought I'd lost her—until a shadow dropped out of the haze, those monstrous wings blotting the storm itself. She swung the scythe low, sparks hissing where the blade kissed stone, and laughed as I shrieked and stumbled the other way.

Every path I took, she was there. Always ahead, always waiting.

"Faster, mortal," she crooned. "Run harder. I want to hear you *scream.*"

My pulse thundered in my throat. Terror made me clumsy. I tripped again, scraped my palms bloody, forced myself up. The laughter followed.

A sudden gust tore the haze apart—and I realized too late I had cornered myself.

A wall of obsidian loomed at my back, slick black spires rising like teeth. To the other side, the river of black fire burned molten and merciless, throwing waves of blistering heat into my face.

The creature landed between me and the storm with a graceful snap of her wings. She looked at me the way a cat looks at a pinned mouse—gleeful, cruel, savoring.

I bolted sideways, desperate.

She swung her scythe, not to cut me down but to *catch.* The flat of the blade slammed into my ribs like a steel bar, the force throwing me off my feet.

I smashed into the obsidian spires. Pain burst white-hot in my arm where it struck the rock, and I crumpled at the base, clutching it to my chest.

The storm shrieked around us.

And the creature smiled, stepping closer.

The pain in my arm was a steady throb, hot and nauseating, but I forced myself upright against the obsidian wall. My lungs still burned from running, and every hair on my body screamed *don't speak,* but silence felt worse. Silence felt like surrender.

"What are you?" My voice came out ragged, but steady enough to be defiant.

The creature tilted her head, braids sliding over her shoulder like black rope. The scythe twitched in her grip, and then—slow, deliberate—she lowered the curved blade until the flat, gleaming edge brushed against my bangs, pushing them from my damp forehead. The cold steel grazed my skin. My stomach twisted.

Her grin was full of night. "I am a Reaper, little morsel."

The word dripped like venom.

"Death's pride and joy," she went on, voice purring and poisonous. "His blades. His wings. His teeth." Her eyes—those obsidian pits veined with silver—flared with cruel delight. "And when he is done wringing you dry for what he needs, none of us will be shackled here anymore. We will walk your Living Lands again. We will feast."

The scythe's tip tapped my chin, forcing my head up. I didn't dare breathe too hard, afraid the edge would split my throat open.

But even through the pulse of terror, something inside me snagged. Something curious. Hungry.

"What he needs from me?" My throat bobbed, my voice barely more than a rasp. "That's what this is about? That's why he's so—" I faltered, searching for the word that could hold Death's obsession. "So...possessive?"

The Reaper's grin widened, feral.

I hated the way my heart pounded, hated the fear slicking my palms, but the words tumbled anyway. "Is that what he wants? To be free in the Living Lands again?"

For a beat, the storm howled around us, and the heat from the black fire river scorched my cheek. It *didn't* sound so terrible, not on the surface. For Death to walk free again. To not be trapped in this nightmare wasteland.

But the Reaper's laugh was soft and cruel, as if she could taste every tremor in me.

The Reaper leaned in, close enough that the heat of her breath ghosted over my lips. Her obsidian teeth gleamed in the firelight, sharp and endless.

"All Death wants," she whispered, voice curling like smoke into my ear, "is to be free."

My blood iced.

Her gaze dragged down the length of me, slow, deliberate, like she was deciding which part would taste sweetest. "Unfortunately..." Her tongue flicked across those black fangs. "...I am hungry. So, he'll just have to find another mortal to use."

The scythe tipped, angling toward my throat. I tried to shove myself back into the obsidian, but there was nowhere to go. My heart thundered as her arm arched back—ready to strike.

Then her head snapped sideways, a vicious crack ringing out, and she was wrenched off me.

Death.

He loomed behind her, his hand fisted in her braids, his silver eyes burning like molten moons. His shadows writhed, alive with fury, and the air itself bent beneath the weight of it.

The Reaper shrieked and tried to pivot toward him, one of her monstrous wings lashing out. It struck his side with a wet smack.

The sound Death made—low, guttural, inhuman—curdled my stomach. His grip shifted, and with one, brutal motion he seized the joint of her wing and *snapped it backward.*

The crack of bone and membrane echoed through the storm.

The Reaper's scream was animal, ragged, and piercing. She thrashed, but Death caught her second wing and tore it in the opposite direction. Another sickening break. Another scream that split the sky.

And still he didn't let go.

He was rage incarnate. Beautiful. Terrifying. Endless.

And barely keeping that beast of shadow within him contained.

Death wrenched the Reaper upright, her broken wings dragging against the stone with wet snaps. He hauled her close until her snarling mouth was inches from his. Shadows poured off him in sheets, swallowing the storm.

"I said," he roared, voice so deep it rattled the obsidian at my back, "that the mortal is not to be harmed. Not to see any of you."

The Reaper flailed, black firelight searing across her marble skin. "She stumbled into Reaper territory," she spat, trying to sound defiant through her screams. "No mortal walks into Acheron and lives."

Death's lips peeled back in something between a snarl and a smile. He spun her and shoved her down, hard, into the river of black fire.

The sound—her body plunging into molten dark—was horrific. Steam hissed. Her shrieks cracked the sky. Only her torso, arms, and the upper, ragged tips of her wings remained above the surface, the rest blistering and burning as the current tried to drag her under.

But Death held her there. One massive hand clamped around her skull, forcing her half-submerged as she writhed.

"Sonia goes anywhere in my domain she pleases," he said, low and lethal, each word vibrating through the storm. "And none will harm her. None."

The Reaper's voice turned frantic, desperate. "Our numbers are already thinned! We starve without the Living Lands. If you kill me, you cannot replace me—you *need* us. You can't afford—"

Death leaned in, shadows wrapping tighter around her struggling form. His teeth flashed, feral. "You are right." His gaze flicked sideways—toward me—and my heart froze. "I cannot afford to lose *her*."

Then, with a violent thrust, he shoved her fully beneath the lava. His arm plunged into the river too, his skin smoking where mortal flesh would have been consumed, his grip unrelenting.

The river swallowed her screams. Only the roar of molten current and Death's shadows twisting above it remained.

Horror crashed over me as I watched him hold her under, as easily as someone drowning an insect. The Reaper's shrieks cut off, but the image seared into me—the wings, the marble skin, devoured by black fire. And yet, beneath the terror, another pulse thrummed: the words he'd said. That he couldn't afford to lose *me*. A claim so possessive it felt like shackles and salvation all at once. Revulsion warred with something shameful, something hot and trembling in my chest, until I couldn't tell if I wanted to run from him—or reach for him.

The Reaper went still. Death let go.

When he pulled his hand free of the black fire river, it was nothing but bone—charred sinew clinging to scorched ivory. The sight should've made me sick. Instead, I couldn't look away. He barely spared it a glance, shadows already stitching over the ruin, before turning and coming toward me.

I pressed harder into the obsidian, heart clawing at my ribs. Half of me wanted to recoil—run from the monster who could kill one of his own without blinking. The other half...gods help me, the other half wanted to fling myself into his arms, to feel safe in the very place that should terrify me.

He crouched in front of me, so close I could see the faint silver glow threaded through his dark lashes. He didn't speak. Just *watched*, as if measuring whether I'd shatter or strike.

"You killed one of your Reapers," I whispered, my voice raw.

"I did." His tone was simple, unrepentant.

"But—I thought you were mad at me." The words slipped out before I could stop them, small and shaking.

"I am," he said, silver eyes burning into me. Then his mouth curved, not quite a smile, not quite a snarl. "But that does not change the fact that you are mine."

My pulse stuttered. The Reaper's taunt echoed in my mind—that all he wanted was freedom, to walk the Living Lands again. That didn't sound so terrible, not compared to the nightmare I'd just seen. My fury at him frayed, replaced by a hollow ache, by the dangerous temptation of believing him when he'd said I belonged to him.

My gaze snagged on his arm. The ruin of it—charred, skeletal, ash clinging to the bone where flesh should've been. The breath caught in my throat, and I lifted my hand before I could think better of it. I didn't touch him—just hovered inches away, trembling.

A sound rumbled out of him—half scuff, half laugh, like I'd surprised him. He lifted that ruined hand, the sharp white of bone stark against the shadows coiling over it, and with one skeletal finger he tipped my chin up.

"Do not look at me like that, Little Bird," he murmured. "It will be whole again before we return home."

And then he swept me into his arms.

The desert, the river, the storm—gone. Shadows curled tight around us, and when they fell away, we stood in a chamber so grand it stole the breath right out of me. A bathroom—if something so magnificent could be called that. Black stone gleamed with veins of red firelight, carved into elegant arches that soared into shadow. A tub, massive and perfect, sat sunken into the floor, steam curling off its surface as if it had been waiting for us all along.

His home kept expanding in ways that made me dizzy. Just how big was this place?

My body trembled as he set me down, the shock of the Reaper still in my bones. When I glanced at his hand, I blinked—whole again. Only the ash remained, clinging like a memory.

Without asking, he helped me out of my jacket. Then my boots. His touch lingered at the hem of my shirt, knuckles grazing the bare strip of skin above my jeans. Every brush of him was a brand—cold and hot at once, like the grave dressed in fire.

I should have pulled back. Instead, I let him ease the fabric upward. His body shifted closer as he helped me out of it, and the breath stuttered in my throat when his chest nearly brushed mine. The shirt caught for a moment, and his hands smoothed it free, fingertips trailing along the slope of my spine as if he had to memorize every inch.

My skin prickled. The ache in my arm almost forgotten beneath the awareness of *him*.

When the shirt was gone, his hand rose—slow, deliberate—to the black velvet ribbon at my throat. He leaned in, the scent of smoke and storms wrapping me as his fingers slid beneath the clasp. For the smallest beat, he rested there, not unclipping it yet—just letting me feel the cool weight of his touch against my skin. My pulse fluttered against his knuckles, betraying me.

Click. The choker fell away, and the absence of it made my skin feel naked.

Then his gaze dipped lower. To my wrist. To the golden band biting into it. His fingers brushed mine as he slipped it free—tingles ripped through me—like pins and needles woven with lightning as his fingers tugged the last of my jewelry off. My whole body seized, nerves alight, and I gasped. His expression darkened at the sound.

By the time I caught my breath, I was standing in just my bra and jeans, my chest rising too quickly, heat flooding places I didn't dare name.

Death looked anything but unaffected. His brow furrowed, his jaw tight, and his entire frame drawn taut as a bow. The way he held himself—it was like every ounce of control he had was being tested.

When his hand went to the buckle of my belt, slow and careful, my body jolted. I caught his wrist, my voice unsteady but firm.

"I can do that."

He moved away only long enough to retrieve something from a carved stone shelf. A dish of soap—dusky blue, threaded with petals, the scent of it heady and clean even from here. He set it beside the bath with reverence that felt almost absurd, given who he was.

"You're...preparing a bath for me?" My voice came out hushed, incredulous. My scattered and overwhelmed thoughts catching up to me. "I thought you'd just throw me back into my room. Pretend none of this happened."

His head snapped toward me.

And then he was there. In front of me in less than a breath, skeletal fingers reformed and gripping my chin, holding me still. His face carved in fury, shadows ripping free of his body like a beast unfurling.

"Do not," he snarled, his voice a rasp of storm and grave, "ever mistake me for so little. You may be convinced I care only for the bond, but hear me, Sonia"—his silver eyes burned into mine, molten and merciless—"I would *never* leave you broken by *my* realm."

The words were a vow and a threat, all at once. His shadows shivered against my skin like claws poised to rend.

Then he released me, stalking away, his fury leaving a hollow in the air where his body had been.

I stayed frozen, my chin aching where he'd held me, heart pounding, a whirlwind tearing through me. Relief. Terror. A strange, devastating tug in my chest that wanted to believe him.

And the Wood help me—an ache that wished he'd stayed.

24

The bath was...gods, it was heaven. Steam curled around me, scented with whatever that soap was, and for the first time in days the ache in my muscles began to fade. The heat pulled the sting from my arm, loosened the tight knot of fear in my chest. I didn't want to get out, but eventually, I forced myself to rise, skin flushed and trembling.

A robe waited for me. Black silk, cool as water when I slid it over damp skin. It felt indecently soft, clinging, as if he'd chosen it for the way it would feel on me. My clothes were grimy, torn, but I folded them carefully and set them on the bathroom counter. I stacked my velvet choker and the gold bracelet neatly on top.

There was only one door leading out.

It opened it into a bedroom so vast and magnificent I froze in the threshold. Floors and walls carved of the same dark stone, veined with threads of dusky blue, glowing faintly in the firelight. Tall windows bared the Deathscape beyond—red sands, black mountains like a jagged crown. A bed dominated the center, massive and draped in layered furs the color of smoke and bone.

My stomach turned over. Was this *his* room?

The thought rattled me. But exhaustion made the decision for me. I crossed the space, slipped beneath the furs, and let their impossible softness swallow me.

I lay there too long. Listening. Waiting.

Some part of me—pathetic, foolish—expected him to come back. To hear the tread of his boots or feel the sudden hush of air when his magic filled the room. But nothing came. No sound. No shadows curling in the corners.

He left me alone.

Sleep dragged me under before I could decide if that disappointed or relieved me.

Morning—or whatever passed for morning here—was no different. A fire had been started at some point while I was sleeping. The sky beyond those windows still hung silver and poisonous. Death wasn't there.

I wrapped the robe tighter and left the bedroom, bare feet silent on the cold stone. I tried doors as I passed them, but one after another refused to open. The house—or whatever this place was—didn't want me inside its secrets. Only the rooms I'd already been in opened for me, as though I wasn't allowed deeper access into his world than what I had already been given.

Eventually, I found myself in his study.

The shelves behind his desk caught my eye, lined with odd relics from decades—or centuries—past. Trinkets from wars, tools worn smooth by use, coins that no longer held value. All of it placed without order, without care.

Except one thing.

Prayer beads. Simple wood, strung and worn by hands long gone. Resting not on the shelves but on a stand of velvet and stone, as if this was the most precious artifact of them all. There was a wooden tassel at the ends of the prayer beads. It had an odd symbol that adorned its face but if it belonged to a religion, it wasn't one that I had ever seen. But...it did remind me of a House crest, but that couldn't be right. Each Mage House claimed one of the first twelve House symbols to show what kind of magic they specialized in. This symbol wasn't one of them. Then what was it? My gaze lingered there, questions pressing like weights against my ribs. Why these? Why not the gold, the jewels?

Why did the beads matter to him?

The silence offered no answer.

Disappointment pressed in heavy when I realized he wasn't coming. No matter how far I wandered, he didn't appear. Not last night. Not this morning.

And I hated myself for the ache of wanting him to.

Maybe I was wrong. Maybe my assumptions about him had been too harsh, too narrow. If all he wanted—*all*—was freedom to walk the Living Lands again, to not rot in this red desert forever...was that so terrible?

I didn't know anymore.

With a breath, I tapped into my magic, bracing for the familiar drain. But it came easy. Like stepping sideways, like opening a door. The Deathscape bled away, and I gasped, startled at how effortless it was.

It felt like the Deathscape had charged me somehow, filled my veins with its pulse.

I landed in my bedroom with a thud, the silk robe whispering around me like a guilty secret. The first thing I realized was how much I missed him.

And how much I wanted to make things right.

Voices drifted from the living room—low, tense.

Shit.

I dressed fast, fumbling with cotton and lace like the fabric itself was conspiring against me. My hands shook. Gods, I wished Phontine was here. She'd know what to say, how to make me laugh so I didn't feel like my lungs were collapsing in on themselves. But Phontine was still gone, recharging wherever it was she went. It wouldn't be long before she came back—I clung to that thought as I slipped on my boots.

By the time I opened my door, I was armored in my version of normal. Fishnets under black shorts, a velvet tank layered beneath a chunky wine-red sweater ripped in just the right places. Black boots stomping a rhythm on the floor.

I stepped into the living room—and froze.

Calypso and Pandora stood like drawn blades, sharp and waiting. And Elias, eyes so sharp it felt like they could shred me from where he stood across the room.

Before I could get a word out, Pandora snapped forward, already on her feet like she'd been waiting for a fight. Her eyes glittered like poisoned emeralds, sharp and merciless. "I saw you," she spat. "Coming from a place of black rock and burning sands."

My blood iced.

Which meant—of course—Pandora had told Calypso and Elias she suspected I was...well the Deathscape would be the only place for her to suspect wouldn't it? The question, that soured my stomach and made my pulse scream, was if they had told Matron

Black that I've been to the Deathscape. I didn't think the twins would rush off to the Matron before talking to me. Pandora would probably want more information to lay at her House Matron's feet, but Elias…Had he already told Matron Black?

I swallowed hard, steel lodging in my throat. No. No. I would not let them make me feel like I'd done something wrong.

I was an adult. My choices were mine. If I deemed bargaining with Death the only way to survive my curse, then so be it. None of them had the right to stand in judgment. And I didn't belong to the Black House anyway.

I lifted my chin, forcing my hands not to shake, forcing my breath not to quake. And I stared them down—Elias's narrow gaze, Pandora's lethal glare, Calypso's unreadable calm.

Let them look. Let them assume.

I had nothing to apologize for.

Pandora pounced. Impatient with my silence. "How do you go there? What do you do there? What is it like? Nothing living can go there, survive there. Do the dead claw at you? Wouldn't it be overwhelming to be surrounded by the dead?"

Her questions were like blades—one after another, no space to dodge, no time to breathe. My pulse hammered in my throat.

"Pandora," Calypso's voice was a ribbon of calm, silken but firm. She reached for me, her hands cool and grounding as they closed around mine. Her eyes darted down—caught on my wrist.

Her breath pinched. "Where's your bracelet?"

Guilt lanced through me like a hot needle. Our bracelet of friendship. My throat dried out. "I…accidentally left it. In Death's home."

The silence that followed was absolute. A void.

I couldn't look at Elias—his eyes already pressed down on me. Instead, my gaze slid to Pandora, whose stare could have flayed flesh from bone.

"You wanted to know how I can go there?" I forced the words out, my voice thinner than I wanted. "Because my magic originates from the Deathscape. It's like second nature to step into it. For a Ghost Whisperer, it's just…there."

"What's it like?" she pressed, sharp.

I shook my head, a bitter laugh catching in my throat. "That's hard to explain." Too hard. Too much. Too personal.

But the last question—I couldn't dodge it.

"What do you do there?"

I met the twins' eyes one by one, my stomach churning, and gave the smallest sliver of truth I could survive. "I practice my magic. It comes easier there."

I didn't add with Death.

Calypso's hands slipped from mine, her retreat slow, deliberate. Her eyes narrowed, weighing every word like it was her heart on the scales. "Are you making more progress there than in the Black House?"

The truth burned bitter on my tongue, but I gave it anyway. "...Yes."

The knock splintered the apartment's quiet.

All three of us froze.

Pandora narrowed her eyes, already moving toward the door. "If that's the team"—A pointed glance at Elias over her shoulder—"I don't know why they're here so early. We're not meant to meet them until this evening to track those Rogue Mages fucking with the mist."

She swung the door open.

Not Black House Mages. Thank the Wood but maybe worse...

McDara.

The charge that hit the room was instant, brutal. Like the very air caught fire, burning across my skin. His gaze landed on the twins, sharp as a blade—hatred, history, everything unspoken flashing in his eyes—before sliding to me. And once I was in his sights, he didn't look away.

His voice was low, rough, and threaded with something that made my chest ache. "We need to talk."

Calypso stepped forward, her tone careful, strained. "Now isn't a good time."

Pandora scuffed, folding her arms, venom in her stare. "We don't owe him explanations. Least of all now." She shoved at the door, already trying to slam it shut.

But McDara's hand shot out, bracing against the frame. Unmovable. His magic thrummed beneath his skin, a warning in the air.

"Stop." My voice cracked sharper than I intended. I slid between them before the whole apartment combusted, before past grudges boiled into something bloodier. "I'm helping McDara on a case. I need to go. I'll be back tonight and we can...talk more then."

Talk more. Gods, I wanted nothing more than for them to forget Pandora's words, forget the image of me stepping out of black stone and burning sands.

I didn't give them time to argue. I slipped past McDara, coat forgotten, cold November air already biting through my sweater. My pulse drummed like I'd run miles, not three steps.

He fell in stride beside me, silent, tense.

And I didn't look back.

25

The silence stretched between us as we walked down the corridor. Every tile gleamed too perfectly, every wall whispered with warding charms. Even the air carried that faint shimmer of spelled cleanliness, lavender and lemon laced into the breath of the building. It made my skin itch.

New Town always felt like this—polished to a shine that had nothing human left in it. The kind of perfect that rang hollow.

Beside me, McDara looked like he was barely holding himself upright, all tension and willpower, his long stride measured as if each step kept him from shattering.

We stepped into the elevator. The mirrored doors closed us in, sealing the hush tighter.

I glanced at him, at the exhaustion carved deep in his features. Not detective McDara. Not even the Mage. Just Cillian—fraying, fractured, and still pretending he wasn't.

Before I could stop myself, I reached out and gave his arm a small squeeze.

His gaze flicked to mine, wary, uncertain.

"How are you holding up?" I asked quietly. "With...recovering from the dark magic. With Deidre." Now Dr. Fenwick, but I didn't add that. I honestly didn't know how much more even he could shoulder before breaking.

His eyes fractured then, raw grief spilling through the cracks. "Some days it feels like breathing glass. Others...like I'm already buried next to her." His jaw tightened. "But I'm managing."

The honesty hung between us, sharp as broken stone.

The elevator hummed, carrying us down. Neither of us spoke again until the doors slid open at the ground floor. He hesitated, shoulders rigid, before his voice dropped low, rough, almost guilty.

"You scared the shit out of me when you disappeared."

The words hit like a blade to the ribs.

The thought gutted me. He was already dealing with so much, and then to find out Death followed me around. That I was going to the Deathscape with him, and then I just disappeared—with Death right on my tail. I think if our places were reversed, I would have already had a heart attack just from that, but he had more that plagued him.

What must it have been like for him, holding Deidre as she slipped away? I'd lost my dad in a blink, one phone call, one crash, one grave. If I'd had to *watch* it happen, if I'd had to hold him in his last breaths...my chest squeezed so tight I could hardly stand it.

I felt guilty that I...well, I wasn't making his life any easier, was I?

I squeezed McDara's arm again, softer this time. "I'm sorry," I whispered. "For stepping into the Deathscape like that. I just—Death was getting to me, and I couldn't take the two of you tearing into each other anymore. I needed space to breathe."

Something in his expression flickered. A crack in all that armor.

We pushed through the lobby doors together. Early evening had settled over New Town, dusk blurring the skyline. Fairies with glowing wings and Mages in crisp coats walked the streets in subdued clusters, humans weaving among them like they'd learned long ago not to look too closely.

McDara's red sports car was practically climbing the curb, hazard lights still winking. He must've thrown it into park and bolted without a thought. That was so far from the controlled, precise man I knew.

The blast of heat when I slid into the passenger seat made me realize how badly I was shivering. He cranked it higher, jaw tight, hands braced on the steering wheel. But he didn't pull away from the curb. He just sat there, the engine ticking quiet, his profile sharp in the dim streetlights.

Finally, he turned to me, voice low. "What did you need to talk to him about?" His throat worked, like he was forcing the words out. "I get that I...*we* didn't handle it well. But what was so damn pressing you had to vanish into the *Deathscape* to talk to him?"

My mouth went dry.

How was I supposed to tell him the truth? That I'd spiraled into an existential crisis over whether Death cared about *me* at all, or if I was just a tether, a means to his end? That part of me was relieved when Death appeared at the university, like some twisted comfort, and wasn't that the most messed up thing of all?

Not exactly the kind of confession you drop on the man you were once head over heels for.

I stared at the dashboard instead, my pulse drumming in my ears, scrambling for words that wouldn't unravel me.

"I know he gets something out of it," I said finally, voice as steady as I could make it. It still felt like lying, like I was peeling only half the truth out of myself and hiding the rest. "The bond. It's not just me tied to him. He's...pulling something from me too."

McDara turned his head, watching me. His eyes were dark pools, unreadable but heavy. I pushed forward before I lost my nerve.

"At first," I went on, "he could only come into the Living Lands as—" I faltered. "As something only I could see. Like one of the ghosts that follow me. But now—he can make himself *visible*. Not just to me." I swallowed hard. "That means his magic is strengthening. Here. Like he said." My chest tightened. "And that terrifies me, McDara."

The silence that followed was a strange kind of relief. Like bleeding out a wound I'd been pressing my hands over for too long. And telling him—it was like handing the fear to someone made of stone. Because that's what he was. Solid. Steady. It was in his marrow, in the way he carried weight that should have broken him.

His jaw flexed. "Spending time with him could be strengthening the bond," he said at last. His voice was rough, controlled. "That's not a good idea, Sonia."

I sighed, my breath fogging faintly against the window. "I know. It's dangerous. I don't know what all he gains from it. But I need his training." My throat ached around the words. "For my magic. For the curse."

McDara's gaze flicked away, then back, thoughtful, like he was turning every word into something heavier. Finally, he asked, "Has he told you more about the bond? About what it gives him?"

I shook my head. "No."

His mouth flattened, grim. "Then how can you be certain he can help with your curse?"

A small, bitter smile curved my lips before I could stop it. "Because, McDara...he is *Death*."

The words lingered between us like a tolling bell, reverberating through the small car until it felt like even the air held its breath.

"And you're sure you're safe with him in the Deathscape?" McDara gripped the steering wheel with a strangling hold and watched out his review mirror. "He could keep you there, Sonia." A darted, heated look at me before he pulled out into traffic.

"I don't think he will." He totally could though, and that was terrifying. Or it had been before he ran me baths and held me on a fur-covered couch after I had a breakdown. "He hasn't hurt me."

"I don't like you being at his mercy."

That made two of us.

Silence stretched between us as McDara pulled the car through New Town, the glittering shopfronts and pristine stone façades blurring past in the dark. My thoughts had gone brittle and looping—Death's skeletal hand in the lava, the twins' narrowed stares, the weight of February creeping closer every day.

It wasn't until the sharp turn onto the bridge into Old Town that I startled, realizing how far we'd gone. The glow of the city center behind us, the shadowed spires of Old Town ahead. "Where are we going?" My voice came out thinner than I meant.

McDara's grip on the wheel tightened just a fraction. "I might have...freaked out," he said, jaw working. "When you vanished into thin air with him last night."

Heat crept up my neck. "McDara—"

"I told Dom and Keyleth what happened," he pressed on, as if he couldn't stop now that he'd started. "Keyleth's losing her mind. She needs to see you. We're meeting her at the Quill."

For a moment, all I could do was blink at him. Then, to my own surprise, a laugh tumbled out. A real one, shaky but warm in my chest. I rolled my eyes. "Of course she is."

Because it was kind of nice—more than nice—that I had someone in my life who wasn't dissecting my magic, weighing what I could do or what I might become. Keyleth didn't care about any of that. She just cared that I was *okay*.

It made something in me ache.

The Obsidian Quill was winding down for the night when we walked in. The warm, spiced air of coffee and cinnamon wrapped around me, and I nearly sagged into it. A pair of baristas were wiping down counters, the hiss of the last milk steamer letting out a weary sigh before it clicked off for the night. The shelves glowed low with their sigils, like stars dimming out one by one.

And then Keyleth was there.

She flew around the counter, practically barreling into me. "Gods, Sonia!" Her arms crushed around me, her white-blonde hair catching against my cheek, gold eyes shining too bright. "You can't just vanish like that. You can't—" Her voice cracked, and she shook her head, squeezing me tighter.

Something hot and wet pricked at my eyes. I hadn't realized how much I needed this. Just...someone who cared I was *here*. Not for my magic. Not for what I could do. Just me.

Behind us, McDara cleared his throat, awkward as hell. Keyleth shot him a look that could have been molten if it weren't wrapped in worry. "Kira will lock up," she said briskly, nodding toward one of her workers sweeping near the door. "Dom's waiting upstairs."

Upstairs.

I knew Keyleth lived above the Quill, but I'd never been invited up before. My chest gave a small, curious twist as she tugged me toward the back.

We passed through a narrow hallway lined with quirky art—half of it shifting with quiet glamours—and she pressed her hand against a massive portrait of a wolf drinking coffee from a porcelain cup. The canvas shimmered, rippling like water, and then swung open to reveal a tight staircase.

The moment we stepped into her apartment, I stopped breathing.

It was the Quill, but *hers*.

Velvet drapes the shade of sage fell heavy over tall windows. A dozen mismatched lamps with stained-glass shades spilled honey light across bookshelves bursting with titles. Plants dangled from the ceiling—some glowing faintly, some whispering when brushed. The air smelled like roasted beans and lavender incense. A grand, battered sofa sprawled across the middle of the room, blanketed in knitted throws and tasseled pillows.

On the far wall, a record player spun something soft and jazzy, and near it, shelves lined with teacups—each one a different pattern, a different mood.

It felt alive, whimsical, entirely Keyleth.

And the Wood help me, I loved it immediately.

Movement caught my eye near the big sofa.

Dom was sprawled there like he owned the place—legs stretched out, broad chest rising under a soft henley, his sandy-blonde hair a little mussed like he'd run his hands through it one too many times. Hazel eyes flicked up as we entered, warm and sharp all at once, and that damn grin tugged at his mouth. Mischief. Always mischief.

"Well, well," he drawled, pushing himself up with lazy grace that didn't match the sharp attention in his gaze. "The ghost girl returns."

Something in my chest unclenched at his voice—bright and teasing in a way that scraped against all the dark edges still clinging to me from last night. But it was also jarring, stepping from the haunted silence of Death's realm into this apartment brimming with color and life.

Dom's eyes flicked over me, taking in the sweater, the boots, maybe the exhaustion stamped all over my face. His grin faltered, just for a second, before it returned, softer. He didn't ask what had happened—didn't push. Just gave me that look, the one that said he noticed *everything*.

I swallowed hard, suddenly hyper-aware of McDara standing stiff at my side. The tension in the room was thick enough to choke on, like three storms had just collided in one space: Keyleth's worry, Dom's sunshine barely leashed, McDara's shadows looming close.

And me, caught in the center of it all.

The apartment smelled like cinnamon and roasted coffee beans, like warmth trying to chase the chill still lodged in my bones. Keyleth hummed as she set a pot of tea on the low table, the steam curling up like ghostly fingers. Dom grabbed a mug without hesitation, sipping like it was the cure to everything.

I wasn't hungry, but that didn't stop Keyleth from shoving a croissant into my hand. I held it, the flaky pastry warm against my palm, but the thought of eating turned my stomach. My insides were already a knot of fear and exhaustion.

I slid down onto the rug, grateful for the anchor of something soft beneath me. Keyleth immediately dropped down too, tossing me a pillow edged with crooked beads and lopsided stitches. Her work. I knew it without asking. Somehow that made the unevenness perfect.

"So," Keyleth said, her gold eyes sharp despite the gentleness of her voice, "tell us why you look like you've been dragged through all three layers of the Bone Veils. Start with the curse. McDara told us the basics but just start from the beginning."

The word landed heavy. I tugged my bag into my lap, fingers brushing the worn leather, and pulled out Grace's ledger. It still smelled faintly of old paper and ink, even after all this time. I passed it to Keyleth. She touched it reverently, like she knew she was holding something sacred, and set it beside the tea.

I told them.

About the curse. About how every Ghost Whisperer in my bloodline had died at twenty-five. About Grace's notes, her desperate experiments. And—finally—about Death. That he was training me, pushing me to wield the thing inside me I barely understood.

"He's teaching you?" Dom's voice was sharp, cutting through the air like an arrow.

I nodded. "If I'm going to survive this, I need to learn. And he's the only one who can show me how. The only one that knows my magic enough to truly help."

Keyleth leaned in, her beaded earrings swaying with the motion. "But is it helping? Really?"

I hesitated. The truth tasted bitter, but I forced it out. "Yes. But...it costs me. Every time I use my magic it's like something inside me is scraped raw. I get so tired. Drained down to my soul. I think the curse is starting to affect me."

The reaction was instant.

McDara's face went white, like he might actually be sick. Keyleth clapped a hand over her mouth, her golden-brown eyes wide and horrified.

"That's—" McDara swallowed hard. "Sonia, that's beyond dangerous. You're burning yourself alive."

Dom had been lounging, but his lion tail flicked sharply now, betraying the tension coiling in him. His hazel eyes locked on me, suddenly serious. "And you think that's safe?"

I straightened my spine, even as the weight of their fear pressed against me. "I don't know if it's safe," I admitted. "But I know it's necessary. Training with Death is the only time I've felt like I might actually have a chance at breaking this curse. I can't afford to turn away from that."

The silence that followed was suffocating. The tea steamed. Pastries sat untouched. And three pairs of eyes—gold, hazel, storm-dark—burned into me like I'd just told them I was walking willingly into the jaws of a monster.

But I held their stares, because maybe I was. And maybe it didn't matter anymore.

The tea on the table had long gone cold, the steam faded to nothing. The pastries Keyleth had piled onto little plates sat untouched, their buttery sweetness turning heavy in the air. The only light came from lamps and the scattered candles she'd lit in her fireplace, wax dripping down the brass holders, their flames throwing restless shadows across the walls.

I rubbed my thumb along the edge of my mug, though I hadn't taken a single sip. My throat felt too tight for tea. "Grace's notes…" I forced the words out, low, steady. "She wrote that the more her magic drained her, the closer the curse came. That's where I am now. Every time I reach for it, I feel less like myself. More like something's pulling me apart, thread by thread."

McDara's jaw tightened, storm-dark eyes flashing. He leaned forward on the couch, forearms braced against his knees. "And you think letting *him* push you harder will stop it?" His voice was sharp, but the tremor underneath it wasn't anger. It was fear. For me.

I met his gaze, refusing to flinch. "I don't know. But doing nothing isn't an option. If I don't try, if I don't use every single path open to me—then I won't make it to twenty-five."

The silence that followed was thick, suffocating. I let it sit a moment before adding, "I need to know what Dr. Fenwick was trying to tell me. About my birth parents. About Larkend." My voice cracked on the town's name. That cursed, half-buried place felt like a stone in my chest, waiting to crush me.

McDara cursed under his breath, shaking his head. "Sonia, using your magic—even with him—could kill you faster. You're gambling with your life."

I swallowed hard. "Maybe. But my life's already a gamble. If risk is all I have left, then risk doesn't matter anymore."

The words hung there. Heavy. True.

Keyleth's gold eyes cut through the weight of them. She reached across the rug, squeezing my hand hard, her expression fierce. Determined. She didn't look scared—not for herself, not for me. She looked like fire.

"Then call him," she said, her voice ringing with iron. "If this is the path we need to take, let's walk it. Call on Death, Sonia, and let's get this show on the road."

I stared at her, the candles flickering in the shine of her hair. She was the embodiment of determination, sitting cross-legged on a too bright pillow like she could take on the world with sheer will alone. Beside her, Dom shifted uneasily on the couch, his lion's tail flicking tight arcs. McDara's stare burned into me from the shadows, unreadable and unyielding.

The tea was cold. The pastries forgotten. My heart, however, was anything but still.

I grimaced, tugging at a loose thread on the edge of Keyleth's pillow. "Calling on him...might be an issue."

Her brows rose, gold eyes narrowing with sharp curiosity. "Why?"

Across from me, McDara's whole body shifted—like the weight of the air itself doubled. His intensity was already a lot, but somehow he managed to make it worse. Like he was bracing for an answer that would break him.

I rubbed my palms down my thighs and muttered, "He's...mad at me right now."

Keyleth opened her mouth, but McDara's voice cut in first. "And what reason," he said, low and biting, "would Death have to be mad at you?"

Something about the way he asked it prickled at me. Like maybe he thought it had to do with *him*. Like maybe he suspected there was more between Death and me than there should be. My throat tightened, and I gave myself a sharp mental shake. Gods, I was reading too much into it. It didn't matter. None of this mattered.

"Never mind." The sigh left me like smoke. I pushed to my feet, turning from all three of them so I wouldn't have to feel their eyes on me. The fireplace flickered with its modest collection of candles, throwing shadows that felt safer than their stares.

Closing my eyes, I reached inside myself, tugging at the thread that was always there. That impossible tether.

For a long moment—too long—I thought he wouldn't come. That he'd ignore me.

Then the air beside me thinned, folded. Death materialized in the wavering light, edges hazy, as though only I could pull his form into being. His gaze found me instantly, and my chest went cold.

Because he wasn't the Death who had teased me, or held me, or brushed his fingers over my lips as if the touch meant something.

No.

This was the Death I'd first met—the one who had stared at me with eyes like a void, his magic stretching bottomless and inhuman. Detached. Dangerous. A predator that could strip the soul from my body and not even blink.

The sight of him like this hollowed me out. My stomach dropped, and tears pressed hot and stinging at the backs of my eyes. I didn't expect the ache that cut through me. Didn't expect to feel so...melancholy.

But there it was.

I missed him. Even as terror clawed at my ribs, I missed the way he had *looked at me* before.

And now, standing here, I wasn't sure if I'd ever see that Death again.

I couldn't find my voice. My throat felt clamped shut, my heart a drumbeat of panic and yearning all at once.

He said nothing. Just watched me. Expectant. Patient. A predator in no hurry.

Finally, words scraped out of me. "McDara, Dom, and Keyleth have been looking into the curse. They're trying to help." I kept my voice even, careful, even though the words tasted like surrender. "With my birthday so close...February isn't far. I need all the help I can get."

It was my olive branch. My way of acknowledging McDara's involvement—hoping it would temper the storm I'd felt brewing in him last night.

"And I..." My hands twisted at my sides, useless. "I need to call on Dr. Fenwick. To know what he wanted to tell me about Grace's ledger."

The air tightened.

And then—he became *visible*.

Keyleth gasped behind me, a sharp intake of breath, but I couldn't turn. Not when Death's entire presence filled the space, pressing against my lungs like I'd forgotten how to breathe. He stepped closer. So close the edges of my awareness went blurry, my body tilting toward him as if he'd rewired my gravity.

Every nerve lit at once. His nearness was unbearable. And intoxicating.

His voice was low, dark silk. "You remember the price, Little Bird. For my help with your magic."

Heat crawled up my neck, treacherous and raw. Gods. He was reminding me. Making sure. And it didn't feel like it was about the bargain itself—it felt like it was about me. About my choice.

He could have demanded. He could have said nothing, helped me and then collected every kiss that I owed him. But instead, he was *asking*.

Even now, when I had accused him of using me.

I nodded, throat thick. "I know." My voice trembled, but I forced it steady.

Something cracked in my chest, sharp as glass. I hadn't expected this—this flicker of gentleness buried in the shadows. It left me touched, shaken, and aching all at once.

Maybe I had made a mistake accusing him. Maybe I had been wrong, thinking I was nothing but a tool.

But how could I not ask those questions? How could I not fear being used when my life itself was ticking down like sand in an hourglass?

The turmoil burned under my skin, impossible to silence.

And yet...his nearness made it so damn hard to care about anything but him.

Death's gaze dragged over me one last time—slow, deliberate, unreadable—before he straightened.

"Then let us begin," he said, voice all command, no softness. "Call him."

That tone snapped my spine rigid. He didn't wait for acknowledgment; just started giving crisp, exact instructions, like the air itself was his to order.

But something snagged in my brain. "Wait—don't we need to go to where he died?"

The temperature in the room plummeted.

McDara and Dom moved instinctively—shoulders squaring, magic humming low and ready. I saw the sharp flash of claws snap out of Dom's nail beds, both on guard. Death didn't so much as glance at them, but shadows licked up his boots, curling into the air like smoke, and the look he leveled at me was ice and fury wrapped in beauty.

"When I tell you to call a *common ghost*," he said, voice low and terrible, "you do not need the place of death. You need focus."

His power rolled off him like a tide, and even Keyleth's usual brightness dimmed beside it.

Then—like he couldn't be bothered to waste another word—he flicked his hand in a *hurry up* motion.

It was so perfectly, infuriatingly *him* that my temper flared right through my fear.

I rolled my eyes. "Fine."

McDara made a strangled sound, somewhere between a groan and a prayer, but I ignored him and sank to my knees in front of the low coffee table. The wood was cool beneath my palms. The flickering candlelight brushed over Death's sharp profile as he came to stand behind me—his shadow spilling over my hands like liquid night.

"Quiet your mind," he instructed, voice softer now, deliberate. "You are the bridge, Sonia. The threshold. Call not with sound—but with knowing. There is a thread inside of you that will form and take you to the one you seek. Call that thread into being and follow it."

I exhaled slowly. Let the world blur around the edges. I thought of the way Dr. Fenwick's blood had felt hot against my hands. The way his eyes had rolled to mine. *It's in Larkend.*

A pulse fluttered deep inside my ribs. My magic rose to meet it—hungry, instinctive.

It came easier than it ever had before. Like breathing. Like Death himself steadied the current under my skin, even without touching me. The room dimmed; candle flames stretched long, as though bowing. Cold seeped into the floor, up my legs.

I felt the veil *shift.*

A whisper rippled through the air—hollow, fragile. And then a shadow began to form beside the window.

McDara's hand twitched, magic sparking, Keyleth's eyes went huge, and even Dom's tail lashed once, restless.

But all I could think was: *It's working.*

Death's voice ghosted near my ear, low enough only I could hear it.

"Good. Now, Little Bird—bring him through."

And the Wood help me, I did.

26

The air turned glacial.

Candles shuddered in their glass jars, their flames guttering low and long, casting stretched shadows against the walls of Keyleth's apartment. My breath misted, a cloud in the dim light, and my magic—what little I could grasp—trembled in my veins, threatening to slip.

"Hold," Death's voice murmured, low and commanding behind me.

The temperature plummeted another degree, and my vision hazed with ghostlight. A sound like brittle glass cracking rippled through the room. Then—he began to form.

Dr. Fenwick.

His outline came first—a faint shimmer that pulsed, then solidified into the shape of a man. The details bled through like watercolor spreading across paper. His white coat was torn and stiff with dried blood. The wound on his stomach—where the blade had torn through him—still gleamed wet, spectral light dripping from it like ink.

"Miss Byrd," he rasped. His voice carried that same careful gentleness he always had—but warped, like it was being pulled through water.

My chest clenched. Gods, hearing that nearly broke me.

I wanted to tell him I was sorry. That I was sure it was because of me that he died. If he hadn't tried to meet me, to tell me whatever information that was important enough for him to be murdered, he would still be alive.

Death's hand lifted as if he meant to touch me but stopped short just above my shoulder. Those long, elegant fingers flicking up once. It was a deliberate motion, and I found it odd.

Keyleth moved to my side, steadying me by the elbow as the room seemed to sway. Dom's lion tail flicked once behind him, tension rippling through his massive frame, and McDara stood a step closer than he probably meant to—his dark eyes scanning every corner, protective and haunted all at once.

Realization hit me. They could see him...I or, no, it was Death. He had pulled Dr. Fenwick far enough through the veil that....holy shit they could see the ghost!

His power was indeed strengthening, but then...He had forced Orlla's ghost to move on to her afterlife all those weeks ago when our bond was a new, weak thing.

I peeked over at Death...

He stood a breath behind me. A stillness that devoured the air itself. Shadows gathered at his feet like smoke curling toward their master. Watching. Waiting. Judging.

Dr. Fenwick's pale gaze found mine. "I've been wondering...wondering...wondering. But why did you call me, Miss Byrd?"

"I need to know," I whispered. My voice cracked. "About my birth parents. About Larkend. That night...when you—I mean..." I forced a deep breath. "You wanted to meet to tell me about Grace's ledger right? The last words you said were about Larkend."

He hesitated. The ghostlight in his gut dimmed and flared again, unstable. "Then you must understand...Larkend was sealed for a reason. The Mage Council put the dome in place—raw magic was tearing reality there. The Black House, being the strongest House in Blakewell, was chosen to guard the entrance."

My breath caught. "Guard?"

His head tilted. "Only two keys exist. One belongs to the Council. The other to Matron Black." His translucent expression twisted, regret clouding the fading features. "You'll never get her to hand it over, Miss Byrd. Not willingly."

Behind me, Death's presence sharpened. I didn't look at him, but I felt it—the cold edge of his focus, the silent calculation that always followed any mention of the Black House.

I swallowed hard. "What if..." I hesitated, thinking of the burned ghost—the one who'd haunted the bus stop, who'd written in frost and warned me to keep McDara out of this. "What if someone else could help? Someone already bound to the House?"

Fenwick's spectral eyes flicked toward McDara, though I doubted he truly *saw* him. "Be careful, Miss Byrd. Lineage can mean death in a House like this one, as you well know. Trusting anyone in the Black House did not help Grace—." His voice faltered midsentence, words thinning to smoke. The air around him rippled, distorting the edges of his form until his face looked like it was being dragged through water. For a heartbeat, his features blurred—eyes stretching too wide, mouth trembling like he was trying not to scream.

A pulse of unease slithered down my spine. The Faceless Woman had said something similar, hadn't she?

"Dr. Fenwick?" I swallowed and forced my voice to steady. "Are you alright?"

The ghost flickered, his outline stuttering. "The Matron will not give you the key. The Council would rather Larkend rot behind their dome than risk what lies within spreading again."

"Spreading?" Keyleth breathed, her usual brightness stripped down to awe and fear.

The ghost's head tilted slightly, as though listening to something none of us could hear. Then, in a low, trembling voice, he said, "The dome suppresses the raw magic that once bled into the world. Without it, the Death Echo would spread—consume more than a single town. The Council feared it might infect every living Mage line. It would surely reach Blakewell should the dome be destroyed."

A cold shiver ran down my spine. "In the university texts," I said, forcing my voice steady, "it says Larkend's raw magic came *after* the Echo—that the two were connected."

He turned those pale eyes on me. "The scholars are wrong. The raw magic came first. Long before the Death Echo. It ran beneath the earth, pure and wild. You could tap it with a breath, a heartbeat. That power doesn't vanish—it festers when caged."

His transparency deepened, bones beginning to show through the shimmer of his form—white and luminous beneath the ghostlight. His head snapped to the side like he'd heard something that wasn't there. "I can't—" he rasped, and his voice fractured, breaking into two tones that echoed off the walls.

Dread began tapping insistently down my spine. A warning my instincts knew to head but there was still too much for me to learn to send Dr. Fenwick back now. I shifted an inch back toward Death's shadows, worried about what the doctor kept looking at.

McDara's voice cut through the electric quiet, deep and clipped. "Then why the Death Echo? Every record says it appeared about twenty years ago."

At the question, Fenwick's ghost seemed to shudder—his image glitching, the air rippling around him. "No," he said hoarsely. "It wasn't twenty. It was twenty-three." His expression twisted with grief. "Grace and David ran there. It was the closest magical town they could reach before the House caught up to them. When we got word that the raw magic had started to destabilize in Larkend the Matron was so scared that something would happen to Grace and you, Sonia. Grace had you by that time, though you were a little thing. The Matron ordered half the House to Larkend to retrieve them before the raw magic consumed the town."

My stomach dropped. "The House?" My voice broke on the word. "The Black House?"

The doctor's spectral gaze softened with pity that made my skin crawl. "Yes, Miss Byrd. Grace wished to leave her magic behind. The Matron then—Matron Black's mother—used her Ghost Whisperer abilities constantly. Grace feared that every time she channeled her gift, it brought her one step closer to the curse's fulfillment."

His face, more glowing white bone than anything alive, still echoed eerily with human emotion—was drawn tight with sorrow. "Grace believed if she stopped using her magic, she could break it. I always suspected that there was more to why your parents ran to Larkend other than it just being another Magical city, but when the raw magic there started to destabilize, it didn't matter. The Matron at the time sent Mages to go bring Grace and David and you back. I remember the Matron was so worried that something would happen to them."

The air crackled, the lights dimming until only the candle-flames flickered. I could feel the strain through my magic—my hold on him thinning, slipping.

"Dr. Fenwick," I pushed, desperate now, "what happened when they got to Larkend? What caused the raw magic to destabilize? Did the raw magic kill Grace or did the curse?"

The air was brittle with cold, my breath fogging in front of me. I couldn't stop shaking—whether from exhaustion, the drain of holding Dr. Fenwick's ghost, or the ache clawing its way up my throat, I didn't know.

For a split second, Dr. Fenwick's face was not his own. The features melted into something elongated, predatory. His eyes hollowed into pits of white fire. The kind man who'd helped me was still there—but buried beneath the thing that clawed its way up through his magic.

I startled when his head snapped around too far than should be possible to the side. Looking, searching.

Then a hand touched my shoulder. I nearly screamed, but this hand was followed by shadow.

Not the phantom chill of a ghost. *Solid.* Warm, for half a heartbeat.

Death.

I sucked in a sharp breath and turned my head just enough to glimpse him—his silver eyes stark against the dim apartment light. His hand stayed there, steadying me. Real. Until it wasn't.

The warmth bled away, his fingers turning to smoke that coiled through my sweater like mist.

But it had happened. He'd touched me—in the Living Lands.

I barely had time to process it before Dr. Fenwick's ghost drew my attention back, his voice a hollow rasp as he stared at something far away. His transparency wavered with each word, his outline flickering in and out of the candlelight.

Fenwick's expression folded into something like grief. "It was chaos," he murmured, and his hand—half light, half memory—lifted to his chest. "By the time we arrived..."

He trailed off. His glow pulsed once, then dimmed. "The magic had already begun to twist. It was like standing inside a storm of the Veil itself—every breath a thread away from unraveling. The Matron tried to control it, but the raw power lashed back. She was the first to fall."

I pressed a shaking hand to my mouth. "Killed by the magic?"

"Unmade by it," he said quietly. "The air burned her name out of existence. We couldn't even retrieve her body."

Keyleth gasped softly beside me. McDara's jaw flexed, his hand clenched against his side.

Dr. Fenwick went on, his gaze unfocused now, voice thick with memory. "Many from the House died that night. Grace and David...they had already fled deeper into Larkend by the time we reached the outer circle. Grace protected you—you were barely a year old. She'd hidden you beneath a warding cloth, something woven with Whisperer sigils. I don't know how you survived it."

The air around us quivered. Candles flickered.

"The last I saw," Fenwick continued, "David was running from the heart of the town. He was wounded, dragging his leg through the dust but holding you. Orlla was there too—standing on the ridge. She told me Grace was just ahead of him, that we should let them go. That they wanted nothing more to do with the House."

My pulse stuttered at the mention of Orlla. "And you did?"

He nodded faintly. "We did. Grace had gone through such lengths to find a way to survive her curse. She deserved to have the rest of her life without House involvement if that is what she wanted. But the Matron's inner circle was still inside. We turned back to help them."

"And that's when the Death Echo formed," I whispered.

Fenwick's features twisted with pain. "I believe so. The raw magic destabilized completely. The town folded in on itself, and every soul trapped inside—Mage, Magical or human—was consumed. I believe the Death Echo was born from that devastation."

I shook my head. He spoke with such conviction from what he remembered he saw but...Matron Black had told me my birth parents died *in* Larkend. My eyes flicked over Dr. Fenwick's spectral shoulder to those dark, searing eyes that had never once seemed to leave me since Death appeared. McDara had told me that my birth mother died because of the bloodline curse and that David had left because the memory of Grace was too much for him to bear.

Three different accounts, and I had no clue which one was true.

I was beginning to think that none of them were.

Behind me, I could feel Death's presence shift—heavy, aware. Watching.

But my mind was spinning too fast to care. The timelines didn't add up. The cause didn't make sense. Grace and David weren't victims of an accident. They had been *hunted*. I could feel it, like a splinter under my skin.

"Something's missing," I murmured.

Dr. Fenwick's form flickered violently then, like something unseen had pulled at the edge of his soul. He grimaced, his light stuttering. "The truth about Larkend was buried for a reason."

I leaned forward instinctively, desperate. "Tell me what you mean. What reason? Who buried it?"

But his outline faltered—edges crumbling, eyes hollowing into white light.

His hands convulsed, fingers stretching into talons of mist. The air around him howled—actually *howled*—as if the room itself was trying to push him back from the edge. Shadows coiled around his torso, twisting like they were feeding on his unraveling soul.

He lunged forward suddenly, not at me, but like his body no longer knew the difference between pleading and attack. The glow in his chest flared, bright and violent, the ghostlight burning through the remnants of his face until only the hollows of eyes and teeth remained. "Sonia," he gasped—or maybe screamed. "Sonia—" The word shredded into static. And then his form began to shudder, threads of his spirit whipping through the room like torn silk caught in a storm.

I recoiled into Death. The spectral edges of his form sinking into my back and shoulders, and even without his physical form I felt safer. After watching Dr. Fenwick shake his head and growl with an inhuman whine, I was ready to crawl inside Death and let his shadows conceal me forever.

"Enough," Death's voice cut through the air, low and sharp. It vibrated through the floorboards.

Dr. Fenwick went silent, but his body continued to shake, flickering between glowing skeletal bones and the translucent flesh of his face and hands withering away. Over and over as the structure of his face fought to retain some kind of human form.

"What's happening?" I whispered.

"When you called on him he was moving through the veil to his final resting place. We must not keep him any longer." Death answered with a calm voice that made me risk taking my eyes off Fenwick to look at him. He was completely unbothered.

"Why?" My hands shook.

"Because if we keep him from finishing his journey once started he will become a Wraith." Death pressed closer to my back, and even with his body incorporeal, I knew his presence like my skin was attuned to any scrap of him it could get. "I cannot let that happen."

"Wait," McDara came forward with his burning presence and piercing eyes, but they were not looking at Death or me. They were wholly fastened to Dr. Fenwick. "Who killed you?"

For a moment, Dr. Fenwick's face sharpened—like he was forcing himself to stay present. "I...I didn't see much." His outline rippled, bones showing through the ghostlight before knitting back into shape. "A tall figure...cloaked..."

He broke off with a ragged, inhuman gasp as his spine arched, a ripple of wraithlight tearing through him. Bleeding a ghostly pale green over the room. I instinctively reached out, magic prickling beneath my skin. "Their voice," I said quickly. "Did they speak? What did they sound like?"

His head jerked toward me—too fast, too sharp. The air around him crackled with the beginning of a scream that hadn't yet formed. "A woman," he rasped. "It was—a woman's voice."

Then the fight inside him surged.

His form split and reformed in violent shudders, eyes hollowing into pits of white fire, fingers stretching into hooked shadows. He let out a sound that wasn't a word—wasn't human—before the ghostlight exploded outward, tearing him away from the conversation and into the full, terrible thrashing fight against turning wraith.

"Dr. Fenwick—!"

The temperature dropped so fast frost crawled over the teacups on the table. Death's shadow rose taller behind me, his presence pressing the room into silence.

Dr. Fenwick's ghost looked at him—and for the first time, fear crossed his spectral face.

Then to me, quiet but absolute, *"Let him go, Little Bird."*

I hesitated—torn between desperation and obedience—but my grip on my magic was already faltering. The cold in the room grew unbearable, my breath coming in short gasps.

Dr. Fenwick's ghost thrashed, half-formed talons ripping through the air as wraithlight burned under his skin. He lunged—blind, anguished, dangerous.

Death lifted a hand.

Just a hand.

The entire room obeyed.

Fenwick's spirit froze mid-lunge, suspended in a snarl of unraveling ghostlight. His form ruptured and reknit in violent spasms, like something was clawing at him from the inside.

Death's voice rolled through the apartment, low and resonant, the kind of sound that wasn't meant for living ears.

"Be still."

The command wasn't spoken so much as *embedded into the world.*

The transformation halted.

Fenwick hovered, shaking violently, trapped between soul and Wraith. His jaw distended. His form warped. His scream fractured into a thousand echoing tones—too many voices for one throat.

Death stepped around me but many of his shadows remain twined around my legs, and with the sight before me they were comforting.

The rest of the shadows followed him like loyal beasts.

They wound around his arms, his torso, his hands—forming tendrils of ink-black magic that pulsed like veins. Sigils flared under his skin, silver and ancient, lines and runes I didn't recognize but instinctively feared.

He reached toward Fenwick, and the shadows braided themselves into a spear of pure night. Not sharp, but precise—like the tip of a needle poised above the most delicate thread.

"Please—" Fenwick choked, voice two tones at once.

Death's expression didn't change. Not cruel.

Not kind.

Just the stillness of inevitability.

"I know," he said quietly.

"Death—wait—" I choked, reaching for them both. My magic sparked painfully against the weight of his shadows. "Please—don't hurt him."

A soft look flickered through his eyes—brief, real.

"Sonia," Death murmured. "This *is* mercy."

He pressed his hand—not to Fenwick's chest, but *into* the place where the ghost's soul was fraying. The spear of shadow sank in, threads of Wraith-light screaming as they recoiled.

The room shook. Actually *shook*.

Fenwick's head snapped back. A beam of pure white fire burst from his mouth, then another from his chest as Death's magic threaded through him like a surgeon stitching shut a wound in reality.

And then it happened—

Fenwick's form ripped apart in a flare of brilliant, silent light.

Not destruction.

Release.

His essence rose like steam catching moonlight, soft and bright and impossibly gentle.

Death guided it upward with both hands, shadows parting around the soul like reverent sentries. For a moment, he looked carved from starlight and nightmare all at once. A being capable of mercy so fierce it bordered on violence.

Fenwick's spirit shimmered—whole, unbroken—and ascended.

Then it was just gone.

The shadows sank back to the floor.

The cold receded.

Death's glow dimmed to its usual silver.

But the silence he left behind…felt like a cathedral emptied after a prayer.

I exhaled shakily. "You—is he—?"

"Moved on," Death said, his form still haloed in cold shadow. "Whole. Safe. Beyond the reach of corruption."

But behind his calm, I saw it—a flicker of strain.

As if freeing Fenwick had cost him something.

And when his eyes met mine, they were silver and ancient and unreadable.

What did it cost him to use such magic here in the Living Lands? Was he powerful enough now to do things like that whenever he wanted, or was this the first time he used such magic here?

Oh my gods, could Death come to the Living Lands without appearing to me?

I shook my head, forcing my racing and twisting thoughts to slow down. There was no proof that Death could come to the Living Lands and do whatever he wanted without having to be where I was.

I looked at him, at where I stood half covered in his shadows. He could have forced Fenwick into the Deathscape and dealt with him there. It probably would have been easier for him than trying to manage his magic in the Living Lands when he couldn't even become fully corporal!

I swallowed as Death stepped back over to me, those mercury eyes liquid and searching. He'd done it for me. The realization slammed into me with a force that stuttered my breaths. I'd told him how Dr. Fenwick reminded me of my dad. Sitting on his couch, wrapped in furs and his arms, I'd cried about losing my father, and here Death had just kept me from watching a man that reminded me so much of him turn into a monster.

What the hell was I supposed to do with that? Did Death truly care for me or not?

In moments like this, I wanted to believe he did.

"Well," Keyleth said, but there really wasn't anything that could be said as we all processed what had happened.

Only silence engulfed us once more.

And I stood in the middle of it, feeling like the entire world had just shifted—like a piece of truth had been ripped away before I could grasp it.

I believed that Fenwick had told me the version of events that he thought to be true. Like McDara had, but Matron Black…I wasn't sure, but I knew more than any one person's account of what happened was that the real answers lay in the town over. A town that was ravaged by a Death Echo and locked away by the Mage Council.

A lock that Matron Black had a key to.

27

The candles burned low in Keyleth's apartment, wax puddling across the bright enamel of the holders, soft light flickering against the kaleidoscope of color that filled the room. It should've felt warm here, safe. Instead, every hue felt dulled—like the air itself was grieving what had just happened.

Dr. Fenwick's ghost was gone.

But the image of him lingered behind my eyes—his hollow, unraveling face, the way his voice had broken apart when Death's shadow filled the room. I couldn't stop seeing the way the ghost's edges had frayed, *nearly wraithlike.*

Because Death had held him back. *Held him here.*

If I asked Death to find my father...would he do the same? Would he drag my dad from the edges of peace—keep him hovering in this half-existence—just so I could say goodbye?

The thought made me sick.

And yet, the craving for it—the desperate, selfish ache—burned in my chest like a fever.

I barely noticed when movement drew my attention.

McDara.

He'd crossed the small distance between us, closing the space like it cost him something. Death was still there, visible and silent at my back, silver eyes a blade against the candlelight, but McDara didn't seem to care. He stood in front of me, tension etched into every line of his frame.

"Sonia."

His voice cut through the fog in my head. I blinked up at him, startled by how raw his expression was.

I hadn't realized I'd been picking at my nails until he reached for my hands, prying them gently apart. I froze. His hands were warm, steady.

"Hey," he said softly, voice breaking into something that was half plea.

For a moment, I just stared at him—his dark hair falling over his forehead, the shadows under his eyes. He looked...tired. Haunted.

The first thing that left my mouth wasn't what I meant to say. It wasn't even what I *should've* said.

"You told me Grace died because of the curse."

The words came out quieter than I intended, laced with accusation and disbelief.

Every movement in the room stopped.

Dom stilled, muscles tense beneath his easy façade. Keyleth's eyes, brightening to gold, darted between us, worry etching into her expression.

And Death—Death cocked his head, a slow tilt, predatory and fascinated. He watched McDara like he was studying a new species of creature—one he might decide to dissect if it said the wrong thing.

McDara's fingers tightened around mine. His throat worked as he swallowed.

"That's what I was told," he said finally, voice rough. "What everyone in the Black House was told. That every Ghost Whisperer in your line dies at twenty-five because of the curse. Grace included."

He paused, eyes flickering with something that looked like regret. "And that David couldn't handle it. He left soon after."

My breath hitched, and I forced myself to pull air into my lungs. It came sharp and trembling.

The candlelight danced over McDara's face—the softness there breaking something fragile inside me.

I took in a shaking breath, the question clawing at my throat but refusing to leave.

Because if that was the truth...

The words left my mouth before I could second-guess them.

"Matron Black told me Grace and David both died in Larkend."

The air snapped tight again.

McDara's head jerked up, the muscle in his jaw ticking. Keyleth's brows knitted, and even Death's attention sharpened—his silver eyes glinting like frost catching the candlelight.

Dom let out a low whistle and sank back into the couch, throwing his arms out in mock defeat. "Brilliant. So we've got the House version, the Council version, and the ghost version. All different. Love that for us."

I shook my head, pulling my hands from McDara's before he could stop me. The warmth of his touch clung to my skin like guilt as I began to pace, too full of energy to stand still. Even Death's presence felt like a weight at my back.

"None of these stories matter," I said, voice sharper than I meant it to be. "None of them actually *tell* me what happened. Every version contradicts the last. Fenwick thinks they escaped. Matron Black says they died in Larkend. The archives say the raw magic killed them."

McDara frowned, but I didn't stop. The frustration had built too long, coiled too deep.

A bitter laugh clawed up my throat. I threw my hands up. "But it doesn't even matter, does it? Either way Grace is dead. Either the raw magic consumed her or the curse did. The end result's the same."

No one said a word.

The silence pressed down until I couldn't bear it. I dragged a shaking hand through my hair and forced myself to keep going. "Grace went to Larkend because she thought there was something there—something that could help her break the curse. And Orlla..." I exhaled sharply. "Orlla was tasked by Matron Black to find a way to *control* that same magic. It all circles back to the same damn place."

That got Keyleth's attention. Her eyes widened, golden irises bright in the low light. "You want to go to *Larkend*?"

Her voice pitched high enough that Dom's head snapped up.

Keyleth leaned forward, incredulous. "The town sealed by the Mage Council? The one they literally put under a death order because if anything happens to the dome the Death Echo will spread and *consume anything in its path*?"

I nodded once. "Yes."

McDara swore under his breath.

"I have to," I said quietly but firmly. "Everything points to Larkend. Whatever my birth parents were trying to find—it started there. And if there's even a chance I can finish what they couldn't, I have to try. I'm dead anyway if I don't."

Keyleth stared at me like I'd just announced I wanted to jump into an active volcano. "Sonia, you can't. That town eats magic—and people. It's not just the raw magic. The Death Echo inside twists everything that enters."

"I know." I met her gaze evenly. "That's why I need the key from Matron Black first. She's the only one who has one outside of the Council. If we use the key it won't damage the dome."

"We hope," muttered Dom.

The room fell silent again, each of them looking at me as if waiting for me to realize how insane this sounded.

But I already knew.

And still, beneath the fear, the grief, the exhaustion—there was something else simmering.

Determination.

Grace had walked into Larkend searching for answers...then I would too. What choice did I have?

I dragged a hand down my face, exhaustion pulling at every bone like lead weights. My head was buzzing with everything Fenwick had said, every version of my birth parents' deaths colliding into noise.

"I need to figure out how to sneak into the Black House," I said finally, voice rough. "Matron Black's expecting my answer about joining, and the next time I see her she's going to press the issue. I'd rather deal with a wraith than her right now."

Dom let out a low whistle, but Keyleth cut him off with a quiet, steady tone. "You need to rest first."

I started to argue—because rest wasn't going to solve anything—but the look she gave me was the kind that brooked no argument. Soft, but unyielding.

McDara, still standing near the window where city lights bled through the glass, finally spoke. "I'll drive her back to the twins' apartment."

The thought of being in a car, warm and quiet, sounded like mercy. I nodded.

Behind me, Death hadn't said a word. His silence stretched so long that I finally turned toward him. His posture had gone unnervingly still—like a predator scenting something only it could perceive. Then his head jerked slightly to the side, and the light in his silver eyes went distant, unfocused.

"Death?" I asked, heart tightening. "What is it?"

For a moment he didn't answer. Then he blinked, refocusing on me, his expression carved from something unreadable. "I must return to the Deathscape."

The air around him pulsed with a faint ripple of cold. His gaze cut briefly to Mc-Dara—sharp, lethal, promising violence. The kind of look that could gut a man with nothing but intent.

If Death's magic were at full strength in the Living Lands, McDara wouldn't have survived that look.

A shiver rolled through me. "Will you be gone long?"

His eyes flicked to mine, and for the briefest moment something almost gentle lived there—softened silver, edged with shadow. "No, Little Bird," he said, voice low, rich with that ancient weight that always made my stomach tighten. "Not long."

But he wasn't *looking* at me when he said that last part.

His gaze slid past me—locking onto McDara. The words lingered in the air, dark and heavy with a second meaning.

Don't touch what's mine.

The temperature in the room dropped, cold seeping into my skin like mist off a grave. McDara didn't flinch, but the line of his jaw went rigid, his magic stirring beneath his skin like a growling thing.

Death's expression didn't change. Just that quiet, terrible promise in his eyes—before the shadows rippled outward and swallowed him whole.

And then he was gone.

The air rushed back into my lungs all at once, and McDara let out a slow breath, dragging a hand through his hair before murmuring, "Let's get you home."

I nodded, trying not to think about the unspoken message Death had left behind—or how much it terrified me that part of me *didn't* want him to stay gone.

The drive back was quiet—one of those silences that felt too full, too fragile to break. The city blurred past in ribbons of silver and red light, rain beginning to speckle the windshield. I could feel the weight of McDara's thoughts beside me, heavy as my own, but neither of us spoke.

When he finally pulled up in front of the twins' apartment, the car idled for a beat longer than it should have. The hum of the engine filled the small space between us.

He turned toward me, his expression softer now, but shadowed by worry. "Are you really okay?"

I stared down at my hands, the faint shimmer of residual magic still clinging to my skin. A sigh slipped out before I could stop it. "I don't know." My voice cracked on the words. "I'm just so damn tired of finding nothing but more questions. Every time I think I'm close to understanding something, it just splinters apart. I need answers, McDara. I *have* to start finding them, or I'm going to lose it."

He didn't say anything for a long moment. Just looked at me, like he wanted to fix it—*fix me*—but didn't know how.

Finally, I unbuckled my seatbelt and reached for the door handle. "Thanks for the ride," I said quietly, forcing a small, tired smile. "And for...everything else."

Slowly he reached out. His fingers brushed a strand of hair from my cheek, tucking it behind my ear. The touch was so careful, so gentle, it nearly undid me.

"Hey," he said softly, voice low and rough with everything he wasn't saying. "You're not alone in this, alright? Dom, Keyleth, me—we're working around the clock to find something. Anything. And now with..." He hesitated, jaw tightening before he forced the words out. "With Death helping you, even if I hate it, your chances are better. We'll find a way to break this curse."

His eyes held mine, fierce and unflinching. "Grace's fate won't be yours, Sonia. I won't let it be."

Something in my chest cracked open. The conviction in his voice, the heat of his hand still lingering against my skin—it all tangled into a painful, beautiful ache. I wanted to lean into it, to him, to the safety he used to mean.

But there was something that stopped me. A quiet, inexplicable pull under my skin, a whisper that wasn't his. It left me feeling split down the center, torn between the comfort right in front of me and the shadow that had wrapped itself around my soul.

So instead, I gave him a small, tired smile. "Don't make promises you can't keep," I whispered, my voice too soft to be a challenge.

He smiled, sad and stubborn all at once. "Then I'll just have to keep them."

And gods, part of me wanted to believe him—wanted it so badly it hurt. But another part of me, the one that still carried the echo of Death's voice in the back of my mind, stayed silent.

I opened the door and stepped into the cool night air.

The rain had started to fall in earnest now, soft and steady. I tilted my face up for a second, letting it hit my skin, letting the chill sink in before I headed toward the building.

Behind me, McDara's car engine revved, then faded into the distance.

And for just a heartbeat, standing there in the rain, I swore I felt Death's presence again—like a cold breath against the back of my neck, reminding me that he *hadn't* gone far.

Calypso was sitting on the couch when I walked in, her hair piled on top of her head in a messy bun and a stack of old spell journals open around her. The moment she looked up and saw my face—whatever was written there—she raised both hands in surrender.

"Okay," she said gently. "No questions. Not a single one."

She slid a mug across the coffee table and poured steaming tea into it, the scent of chamomile and something floral curling through the air. "Drink before you pass out."

I sank into the chair across from her and wrapped my hands around the mug, grateful for the warmth even if my fingers were still trembling faintly.

"Where's Pandora?" I asked, taking a sip to keep my voice from shaking.

Calypso leaned back, one leg tucked under her. "She and Elias are working on the mist issue tonight. Apparently, the Council's throwing a fit about the numbers rising again." She paused, then tipped her head toward the door. "That was McDara who dropped you off, wasn't it?"

I nodded, staring into the tea. "Yeah."

Her lips curved in something that wasn't quite a smile. "How'd that go? Things getting any better between you two?"

I blinked, wary of where this was headed, but Calypso just tipped her head, a playful glint breaking through the concern in her eyes. "Are these questions okay? No magic talk, I swear—just *boy talk.*"

The smallest smile tugged at her mouth, soft and conspiratorial, like we were just two friends chatting and being close for once instead of dancing around curses and death. The gesture disarmed me, melting a little of the tension that had been strangling my chest since I'd stepped through the door.

A humorless laugh escaped me. "Things with McDara are...not great." I took another sip, trying to ignore the heaviness in my chest. "It's...tense. Awkward. I don't know how to feel around him anymore. My instinct is to—" I cut myself off, shaking my head. "Never mind."

Calypso's gaze softened. "To what?"

"Nothing important," I murmured. *To want him close. To feel safe again. To believe he still could be that for me.*

But I didn't say that aloud. I couldn't. Not when the truth was that he didn't want me—not when he already felt too far in and was terrified of losing another person. I couldn't blame him but...

Calypso reached forward, covering my hand with hers. "You don't have to figure it all out tonight."

I nodded, the lie automatic. "Yeah. I know."

After a few more sips of tea and quiet conversation about nothing important, I excused myself and headed to my room.

The moment I opened the door, I froze.

Death was waiting there solid and still, his silver eyes cutting through the dim light. The air around him crackled like static before a storm. Agitation radiated off him in waves.

He didn't move closer, didn't even blink. His voice was a low command, curling through the air like smoke.

"Come to the Deathscape."

And then he vanished.

Confused, my pulse stumbling, I closed my eyes and pulled on the tether between us. The world folded in on itself, shadows clawing at the edges of my vision until the red sands of the Deathscape bled into view.

28

The Deathscape met me like a held breath—too still, too heavy, the red sand shifting underfoot as if it had been waiting. The air shimmered with shadow and heat, a pressure that crawled along my skin and whispered of something ancient stirring.

And then he was there.

Death emerged from the darkness like he'd been carved out of it, eyes burning silver-white. His movements were too smooth, too fast—predatory. Before I could even form his name, he crossed the distance between us.

His hand caught my chin, firm enough that my breath caught in my throat. The faint tremor of his magic brushed over my skin, sharp and cold as steel.

"You have an unpaid price," he said, his voice a low, dangerous melody—smooth as polished obsidian and twice as sharp.

My pulse faltered. *The kiss.* The one I'd promised him for his help.

But the look in his eyes wasn't the cool detachment of a collector claiming what was owed.

It was hunger—molten, furious, and wounded.

I opened my mouth to speak—to tell him to take his bargain and choke on it—or maybe to beg him for exactly what he wanted. I didn't know. My lips parted on a breath, and he took that as surrender.

He kissed me.

The world shattered. The red sands, the endless horizon—gone. All that remained was him. Cold and fire in one impossible body, his power pressed against mine until my knees threatened to give. Every time I tried to draw breath, he took it, like he was unmaking me one stolen inhale at a time.

This wasn't a transaction.

This was an undoing.

He tasted like storm light and old fury, like every forbidden thing I'd ever wanted.

And gods, I kissed him back.

It hurt. It healed. It ruined.

When he finally pulled away, the Deathscape itself seemed to tremble. He didn't retreat far—his breath slid over my mouth, his hand still cradling my jaw, possessive, reverent. Silver eyes burned with something terrible and tender all at once.

For one dizzying heartbeat, I swore the embodiment of death looked almost *human*.

His thumb lingered at my jaw, the sharp edge of his control fraying. Shadows coiled around us like breath.

"Tell me something, Little Bird," Death murmured. "What you said to your friend—Do you still want the Mage?"

The question landed like a blow. I faltered, the words clawing up my throat only to die there. I didn't know how to answer him. *Did* I still want McDara? Or did I just miss the way I'd felt when I believed someone like him could choose me? When I felt protected.

Death's eyes darkened, silver rimmed in black. His hand slid from my chin to my mouth, tracing the curve of my lower lip with unnerving gentleness.

"Has he ever tasted you?"

The air fractured. His voice shouldn't have made my pulse leap, but it did. I nodded once, barely.

Something in him *snapped*.

Shadows flared outward like wings unfurling, swallowing the horizon. His form distorted—less man, more the creature beneath. The red wind tore at his hair and cloak, his magic shaking the air between us.

I should have stepped back. I didn't.

He looked like fury given shape, like the end of all things—and my pulse only quickened. Fear threaded through me, sharp and fleeting, but beneath it...fascination bloomed. Because even as the monster rose in him, some part of me *knew* he wouldn't harm me.

His voice, when it came, was a growl that brushed my skin like heat.

"Did he satisfy you or leave you aching?"

I could barely breathe. "We only kissed," I whispered.

Something in Death stilled. The rage receded by degrees, though it left a storm behind. His gaze softened—not gentled, not quite—but it burned less like wildfire and more like worship.

When he spoke again, the words were silk over steel.

"Then he's a fool."

The words were a growl, a vow, a promise I didn't know how to brace for. The shadows around us pulsed with his breath, steady and lethal, like the Deathscape itself had bent to listen.

He tilted my chin higher, forcing me to meet that impossible, star-split gaze. "I will not make that mistake."

My pulse stuttered.

He leaned closer, until the air between us burned—cold and heat tangled together, impossible to separate, like we were the contradiction holding this realm together.

"When I touch you," he murmured, his breath sliding against my skin, "you will not be left wanting."

Every word sank into me like a spell. The Deathscape faded; even the red wind went still, listening.

My lips parted, but no sound came. His power pressed against me—not crushing. Just *there*, relentless as gravity.

Death's gaze roamed over my face, tracing each flicker of breath, each tremor of disbelief. "Do you know what it means to wake something like me?" he asked softly. "To make the end itself...desire?"

"I didn't mean to," I whispered.

A faint, pained smile touched his mouth, as though I'd told him the cruelest kind of truth. "Neither did I."

For one breath, we were motionless—two forces caught between ruin and surrender.

And then the world exhaled, and I realized I was trembling, not from fear...but from the unbearable pull of everything I wanted.

"It would be reckless for me to get attached to you, Sonia."

The space around us felt strung too tight, like one wrong breath would shatter it. Like he was deciding something.

Then Death's restraint cracked.

He caught my face again, his fingers cool and sure, the storm in his eyes breaking free. The first brush of his mouth was nothing like the last—it wasn't fury or punishment now. It was a claiming, an unspoken apology, a promise whispered against my skin.

The world tilted. The Deathscape blurred to nothing but shadow and heartbeat. My heartbeat. His breath. They merged until I couldn't tell which was which.

He deepened the kiss, every movement deliberate, reverent, devastating. The taste of him was winter air and lightning, and somewhere in it was the ache of everything we'd never said.

My hands found the front of his coat, clutching like I could anchor myself to the impossible. For a breathless moment, the monster, the man, and the myth all became one being—and I yielded to it.

The darkness around us pulsed once, hard enough to steal the air from my lungs.

The world broke apart in a rush of cold and shadow.

One heartbeat we were standing in the open Deathscape; the next, the air folded inward, dragging the cold of his magic around us. Reality snapped back into place inside his home—stone walls, the deep hum of ancient wards, the scent of smoke and iron.

The great hearth loomed before us, carved in the likeness of a beast whose molten eyes still burned with the memory of its life. Pale furs blanketed the couch before it, soft as starlight. The air shimmered with leftover power, pulsing in time with my pulse.

I realized we were still close—too close—his breath mixing with mine, his hands braced against my spine. Firm and unmoving and I knew he was not letting me go.

The silence was unbearable. My heart thundered against him, a traitor's rhythm, and when I finally lifted my eyes, the light from the hearth gilded his features in gold and shadow.

He looked nothing like the thing I'd accused of being incapable of feeling.

He looked... *undone.*

My breath fled as his mouth took mine again, and then impossibly soft furs replaced the hard press of his hands. Sensation caught me captive and I barely managed to flutter my eyes open as those hands moved with possessive intent around my waist, one flattening on my stomach. The other braced him above me.

And without conscious thought, my legs were tangling with his on this stone couch in the Deathscape. His knee wedged between my thighs, and I opened readily for him.

Then too soon his lips pulled from mine and a soft, needy sound left my throat, but my disappointment was short lived as I looked up into eyes that roared with a desire that sent the silver there into churning, devouring depths.

He watched me, eyes never leaving mine, as his hand trailed from my stomach upwards. The tips of his fingers brushed the underside of my breast, and my breath caught, fluttering in my throat as he ghosted a touch so soft over my breast, tracing torturous lines down the edge of my top until he finally met skin.

A whimper seeped from my lips, a sound I didn't even recognize from myself, but it made something snap in Death.

His other hand found my hair, threading his fingers there and keeping my eyes pinned on him.

"Do you need satisfaction, Little Bird?"

Bless the freaking Wood, yes.

But all I could manage was a nod and another soft whimper.

His hand slipped into the neckline of my top, not needing to go far from the deep-V design to find the fabric of my bra. I watched as Death felt the delicate lace, the thin line of dark-blue velvet I knew bordered its edges. His eyes never left mine, but his glazed as if he was consumed with what his hands felt and soon those hands found a raised nipple, quickly pebbling in the wave of my need.

His thumb swept over the tender bud, and my breath caught. Awareness flared back to life in Death's eyes. His hand cupped my breast perfectly, thumb playing a torturous game as his fingers rolled my nipple. I couldn't help but let out a moan, arching into his touch.

"Sensitive," he murmured, a wicked gleam sparking into his eyes as he repeated the motion. "We will have fun with that."

He moved his attention to my other breast, the sensation heightening as he touched more of my skin.

"Death," I whimpered, not knowing why I called to him, but knowing I needed more than this exploration of touches.

He leaned down to kiss my neck, sucking on the sensitive skin until I moaned again. "Such sweet sounds." The words vibrated against my skin, and I couldn't help but shift my hips restlessly against his thigh. He nuzzled his face into the curve of my shoulder and neck, and as my hips pressed more insistently, he bit down.

I gasped at the sensation. It was hard enough to bruise, and the primal action had my legs clenching around him.

He pressed his thigh harder between my legs, right against my heat, and I couldn't stop myself from clutching at him, wanting to tear the silken fabric of his shirt right off him.

Death's mouth found my jaw, his hand wandering in a lazy trail down my stomach. It wasn't fast enough for me, but he kept me pinned in place. His hand in my hair, and his thigh sending delicious pressure against my core.

"Death," I panted, feeling like I'd go mad with anymore teasing. I wanted the blissful relief he could give me. A reprieve from the stress that had become my life. "*Please.*"

"Oh, Little Bird," Death murmured into my ear, his fingers stilling on the button of my jeans. Tapping once. Twice. "If you start begging me for things, I might become addicted."

It just made me whimper again, hand going to his, slipping under and trying to undo the button he had been playing with.

"No." His hand gently captured mine. He found my eyes, and his were dark, pupils blown wide enough that only a thin sliver of silver ringed them. "I'll give you what you want. Did I not say I would?"

He watched me, and I realized he wanted a response. I blew out a breath and nodded.

He gathered both of my wrists in his hand and pinned them above my head. A shocking thrill raced through me. My wrists were easily held in one of his hands and I was reminded of just how big he was in comparison to me.

At some point I had stopped being intimidated by Death, but with him looking like he wanted to taste every inch of me, butterflies with razor wings erupted in my stomach.

I swallowed, and nerves skittered across my skin. Death, his focus never leaving me, paused.

"Do you want me to stop?" He asked, and I shook my head. If he left me aching now, I would implode. He crowded me then, what little space there was between us vanished. He blocked out any light from the fireplace, and his eyes glowed a dark, haunting light all their own. "If you want me to stop, Sonia, at any point, you will tell me."

His eyes pored holes into my own, and I nodded again.

"Words, Little Bird." His hand holding my wrists squeezed once.

"Yes," I whispered, sounding embarrassingly breathless, but it was hard to continue to feel that way when he looked at me like I was the answer to a lifetime of prayers he had lived.

"Good," He dipped down to press a kiss to my lips that started soft, tender, but quicky fell into a blaze that had us both panting when he pulled back. "Let me learn you, my Sonia, and make more of those sweet sounds pour out for me."

His finger began tapping the button of my jeans, and I could not stop my hips from rocking into his thigh, needing him to do more than tease.

With a wicked smile that I'm sure sent souls to eternal damnation, he popped the button of my jeans open and slowly pulled the zipper down.

I lifted my hips the best I could, willing him to take them off. Tendrils of shadow crawled over my body, hooking into the waistband, and tugging them clean off my legs. The little scrap of black lace and cotton panties was all that separated me from Death's fingers, and it was already horribly wet.

For the first time, his eyes slid from mine, tracking down my body until he saw my barely covered core. His nostrils flared, and the muscle in his jaw worked as he looked his fill of me. Slowly, he slid a finger down the soft panties to the steadily growing dampness there.

A part of me wanted to cover myself, to feel embarrassed by how wet I had gotten, but I stilled my trembling body as much as I could.

I had no reason for being embarrassed. For enjoying what we were doing. For feeling pleasure.

"So beautiful, Little Bird," he whispered, reverent. His finger pressed down into the wet depths of my panties, sliding between my folds, taking the fabric with him. I hissed as he slid over my clit.

His eyes flicked back to me, finger returning to the spot that had my hips jerking involuntarily.

I closed my eyes as he circled my clit through the fabric, breathing turning to needy panting. Suddenly, his hand pulled away.

My eyes snapped open, a complaint on my lips, but just as quickly as his touch had left, his hand slid under my panties, and then his skin was on mine.

His eyes found mine again, taking in every minute expression and reaction that I could possibly give as his fingers slid back to my clit, sending bliss through me, but he did not stay there long. Those searching fingers slid through my folds, catching at my entrance and gently circled there.

"You're overflowing with pleasure, my Sonia," He growled approvingly. "Just for me."

His stare was more effective at pinning me in place than his hands or body. Shadows curled off his shoulders in a spiking pattern. His back seemed to thicken and grow into a glimmer of that shadow beast I'd seen hints of before.

"Mine, Sonia." It was not a question but an oath that gave no margin for argument. His breath was warm against my lips, and I tried to lean forward to kiss him, but he had me too tightly pinned. A slow, feral smile stretched his lips. "You are mine. Your body, your protection, your pleasure. I will give you those things, and no one else will touch you."

His finger sank into me.

My eyes went wide, my hips squeezing against where his leg kept mine open. His finger was thick, thicker than I had realized with the elegant lines of his body and tall frame, but as the last knuckle of his finger sank into me, I felt myself clench around him, feeling invaded by something I had not felt in too long.

He watched me rock my hips against him, watched me pant and whimper as he started to pump into me, finding a rhythm.

"More," I whimpered and tugged on the hand pinning my wrist. "Please."

I could not believe I was begging Death, but my breathless words seemed to break down any resistance he had in giving me what I wanted.

Without slowing his motions, he gently slipped a second finger into me. The fullness was delicious and nearly too much.

I was swimming in bliss, climbing higher to that edge of unbearable pleasure, when he curled his fingers slightly. I gasped, bucking up on his hand. He did it again but more purposeful this time, and my vision blurred.

Death braced over me, hand in my panties, sending me to heave from the Deathscape. If I was capable of anything other than moaning pleasure, I would have laughed.

I looked to Death, expecting him to be watching his hand, but he was once again watching me as I shuddered beneath him. His face a raw mask of concentration and soul-deep hunger.

It hit me then that Death hadn't touched anyone in millennia. He was watching my reactions so closely to know what I liked.

Warmth exploded in my chest alongside the pleasure, and I held his intense predator's gaze.

"It feels so good," I managed to whisper, and the tightness in his shoulders seemed to loosen.

His thumb came to my clit again and I threw my head back, hips canting in a wild rhythm. "*Yes.*"

The combination of firm circles on my clit and the deep, driving force of his fingers with that perfect, curling motion sent me over the edge, falling into a heady pool of pleasure and sensation where everything felt intense and perfect. Bliss so acute there wasn't a good enough name for it.

I came down in degrees. The world slowly painting my reality back around me, and the first thing I saw was silver eyes, messy silver-white hair, and a grin so satisfied it was as if he had concurred the world.

I lay there under Death, tingling and mesmerized by the shadow-swathed look of him. He slowly pulled his fingers from my tight channel, still clenching tight to the aftershocks of pleasure. I shuddered, goosebumps pebbling my skin.

Death's shining eyes narrowed, and suddenly fluffy, white fur was covering us. He released my wrists, and I gingerly pulled my arms down. They were a little sore from being held in that position, but nothing some rest couldn't fix.

Death, however, was still watching my every expression and had me wrapped in his arms, my cheek pressed to his chest, and hands gently squeezing my shoulders in an instant.

I sighed and burrowed into his chest, surrounded by the night-dark scent of him and the warmth from his skin and the furs. Relaxed for the first time since coming to Blakewell, I closed my eyes.

"Thank you," I murmured into the sliver of skin that was bared from the buttons of his shirt being undone. I wondered if, after a little rest, I could get that shirt off him. The pants too.

"For what, Little Bird?" The words were whispered into my hair, the heat of his lips pressed against the crown of my head. "It was I who wanted to touch you. I should thank you."

"I feel," I shook my head, wanting him to understand that it wasn't just physical release, it was that even after I pushed him away, even after learning about the curse, he was still here, wanting me to be his.

"What do you feel?" I felt more than heard his words.

"I feel"—I pressed my lips to his chest—"safe."

29

I woke to cold air and silence.

Not the kind that belonged to morning, but the kind that thrummed through the bones of a realm that had never known sunlight. The kind that reminded me I was still in his world.

Death's bed.

The thought hit like a spell to the chest. My body was tangled in the sheets, and my pulse started racing even though the room was still. The memory of his mouth burned on my lips—the hunger, the reverence, the release.

And the space beside me was empty.

The air still carried the echo of him, that low hum of power that lived in every shadow of this place, but the man—*the being*—was gone.

I sat up slowly, pressing a trembling hand to the sheets where his body should have been. Cool. As if he'd been gone for hours.

The ache that followed felt stupid. Mortal. I shouldn't have expected him to stay.

I touched my lips, the swollen sting proof that last night had been *real.* That for one impossible moment, he hadn't been a god or a monster or my executioner in waiting—he'd just been *him.* And I'd wanted him. Gods, I'd *wanted* him.

The rush of memory made my breath catch. And it hadn't been a bargain or a transaction. There had been no tally, no demand. Just want.

My want.

Heat climbed my throat before guilt crushed it flat. I'd fallen asleep—just drifted off in his arms, like some mortal fool who hadn't realized she'd been kissing Death. I hadn't even...returned what he'd given—

I shut that thought down, hard.

It didn't matter. None of it did. Because the next one that crawled in was worse: What if it hadn't meant anything to him? What if it had just been another step in whatever this thing between us was—our bond, our bargain, his endless need for power?

What if I was just a doorway he kept prying open?

Or worse, what we'd done was nothing but curiosity for him. The first touch in his lifetime as Death.

My throat burned. I swung my legs off the bed, needing to *move.* The air itself seemed too thick, humming with a power that still remembered him.

The bathroom's black-veined marble glowed faintly under my feet. My destroyed clothes sat folded where I'd left them the other day—the fabric dark with blood, the gold bracelet resting neatly on top. He hadn't moved them.

For some reason, that hurt the most.

I told myself maybe he hadn't been in here. Maybe he didn't need things like baths or sleep. But the thought didn't help. Because if he didn't need any of this...why make a place that could hold someone like me?

My reflection caught my eye—messy hair, lips bruised, eyes too bright—and I hated how *alive* I looked in a place that wasn't meant for the living.

I wanted him to want *me.* Not my bond, not my magic, not the pieces of me that made his prison crack open. Just...*me.*

But wanting that from Death was like begging the sea not to drown you.

I closed my eyes, clutching my ruined clothes and the bracelet tight enough to hurt. I needed to leave before he came back, before I saw that careful distance in his eyes again.

Before I remembered how it felt when he *didn't* keep his distance. Not when every nerve in my body still remembered the way he'd said my name.

The air shifted around me, silver-edged and trembling. I reached for the thread of my magic—the part that was always anchored to the Living Lands—and it answered instantly.

One step. One breath.

And I was back in my room at the twins' apartment, standing barefoot on the rug, my heart racing like I'd run through the red desert itself.

The Deathscape's heat lingered under my skin, the memory of his touch a ghost I couldn't banish.

And even though I was home, I'd never felt farther away.

The moment I was back in my room, the silence pressed in—thick and suffocating. The only sound was the frantic pounding of my heart.

My ruined clothes were wrinkled in my hands, the faint, impossible scent of smoke and him still clinging to the fabric. I shoved them into the trash with a violence that made the metal rim rattle.

I didn't want the reminder.

Didn't want *him* on me.

Except I did.

That thought made my stomach twist. I snatched clean clothes from the dresser, movements jerky, angry. It wasn't until I turned toward the bathroom that I realized—mortifyingly—I wasn't wearing pants.

For one dizzy heartbeat, I just stood there, breath caught halfway up my throat. Then the memory hit: the way his shadows had slid them down my legs, the rough whisper of his power against my skin.

Heat rushed through me so fast I thought I might actually combust.

"Gods," I muttered, cheeks flaming, and stomped into the bathroom like I could scald the thought out of my head.

The shower roared to life, steam swallowing the small space. I stood under the hot water for what felt like forever—scrubbing until my skin was pink, until the scent of Death's power and shadow and smoke was gone. Or mostly gone. Because no matter how long I stayed there, I could still feel him. His touch. His breath. His voice.

Thirty minutes later, I shut the water off and leaned against the tile, water streaming down my face. Clean. But not free.

I pulled on fresh clothes—a fitted black sweater, jeans, boots. Practical. Grounding. Human. The kind of outfit that said *I'm fine* even when I wasn't.

If only my mind would stop betraying me. Every few seconds, another flash—his mouth at my throat, the sound he made when I said his name, the way the world felt like it had finally stilled between us.

Then I woke up alone.

I exhaled sharply, frustrated with myself, and shoved Grace's ledger into my bag. I needed a distraction. A purpose. Anything that wasn't *him*.

"I'm not going to think about Death," I muttered as I slung the strap over my shoulder. "Not today."

The apartment was quiet when I left my room. The twins were gone—probably out dealing with whatever new chaos the Black House had stirred up.

Good. I didn't have it in me for explanations.

But the silence wasn't comforting. It was empty. *Too* empty.

I found myself glancing toward the small space on my dresser where Phontine usually perched when she was home. She'd been gone longer than usual this time, recharging somewhere between realms, and though she'd always come back before, worry still pressed behind my ribs.

That worry mingled with the rest of it—the constant hum of dread over my bloodline curse, the guilt of not calling mom enough, the sharp, hollow ache of still wanting to see my dad again. All of it layered in my chest like bruises that never healed.

The only time those bruises ever stopped throbbing—the only time all the noise went quiet—had been in Death's arms.

That thought gutted me. I hated it. Needed it.

I shoved the keys in my pocket and left before I could think too much about it.

The door clicked shut behind me.

Outside, the crisp air bit my cheeks as I made my way toward Old Town. The walk helped steady me a little—the hum of traffic, the distant chatter, the faint shimmer of magic bleeding through the city's pulse.

And I told myself—lied to myself—that I was going there to plan, to talk to Keyleth, to figure out how to break into the Black House.

Not to forget how it had felt when Death held me and the whole world finally stopped hurting.

The walk to the Quill shouldn't have been this long. I had just passed Blakewell's city center and the change from sterile uniformity to the almost rough, magical cadence of Old Town was a relief. But even with my destination nearing each step, it felt like dragging myself through molasses, like the city itself had grown heavier.

The sun had nearly dipped below Blakewell's skyline, and the first of the enchanted streetlamps were sputtering to life, their gold light catching on the fog that had started to linger, low and soft, over the cobblestones. Key had said it was normal during the fall and winter months. Just another Blakewell oddity.

Through the dwindling evening haze, I could just make out the black and gold sign of The Obsidian Quill swinging gently above the door. Safe. Warm. The promise of Keyleth's voice and the smell of roasted coffee beans and honeyed milk. I focused on it like a lifeline.

But the closer I got, the stranger the air felt.

Heavier. Thicker. Like the city was holding its breath.

A faint vibration moved through the soles of my boots—subtle at first, then stronger, humming up through my bones. My magic reacted instinctively, flaring under my skin. I stilled, every sense sharpening.

The lamp post nearest me flickered once. Twice. Then steadied, burning too bright.

I rubbed at my arms as a chill ran down my spine. The fog wasn't its usual pearly drift—it looked *alive*. Pulsing faintly, like a lung inhaling light.

Something deep in my chest whispered, *danger*.

The hum became a low, thrumming note, a heartbeat that didn't belong to me.

Something was wrong.

Very, very wrong.

The hum reached a pitch that made my teeth ache.

Then the world *snapped*.

A single, splitting crack shuddered through the air —like glass fracturing in the bones of the world.

Everything went still.

And then, too *clear*.

The colors around me sharpened until they hurt to look at—every neon sign, every brick, every drop of rain on the cobblestones blindingly vivid. The air lost its softness, stripped bare of the quiet haze I hadn't even realized was always there. It was as if the whole city had been muffled and someone had just ripped the fabric from its mouth.

The mist—the magic that blanketed Blakewell, hiding the truth from human eyes—was *gone*.

I felt it before I could think it.

The pressure in the air vanished, and what replaced it scorched across my skin like invisible fire. My magic surged to meet it, panicked and raw. My breath came out in bursts, frosting in air that felt suddenly too thin.

Every Ghost Whisperer sense I had flared to life.

The dead whispered all at once—a thousand unseen voices brushing against my consciousness. Magic pulsed in every direction, no longer disguised.

I could *feel* the absence of it, like the silence after a scream.

And then the city began to unravel.

A woman gasped nearby, stumbling back from the Goblin vendor she'd been buying flowers from. The way he looked hadn't changed—he still looked exactly as he always had—but without the mist dulling her mind, she *saw* him. Saw the jagged line of his teeth, the faint shimmer of his magic, the light green skin.

"Oh gods," she whispered. "What are you—"

Her words turned into a shriek.

Others followed.

A Shifter's tail flicked once in alarm before he was shoved against a wall. Spells cracked in the air—wild, defensive flares as panic rippled through the crowd. The comforting murmur of city life shattered into chaos.

My breath stuttered. The air burned hot and cold at once, my Ghost Whisperer senses sparking like live wires. I could *feel* the ghosts pressing closer—drawn by fear, by violence, by the sudden thinning of the barrier between life and death.

Humans screamed. Magicals shouted warnings. The world had been holding its breath for years, and now it had exhaled—sharp and furious.

And in that exhale, the city began to fall apart.

A terrified wail split the air.

It cut through the noise of the street like a blade, shrill and human and terrified.

Then another. And another.

The crowd fractured.

People shoved and stumbled, their fear rolling off them in waves. The mist had always softened their instincts—blurred the line between fear and fascination. But now that veil was gone, and the truth of Blakewell was too sharp to bear.

The Goblin vendor hissed as the woman threw her shopping bag at him. A Fae man turned, confusion flashing across his face as humans recoiled from his gold-lit eyes. A Shifter's tail whipped out as he tried to push through the crowd—and someone screamed, "Monster!" before hurling a bottle that shattered against the street.

I froze mid-step. My heartbeat thundered in my ears.

It was chaos. Unfiltered.

A couple stood near the edge of the street, a Vampire female and a human man—she was beautiful, pale, her dark curls reflecting the lamplight. The human man with her had been smiling, fingers laced with hers as they walked. He blinked. His gaze snagged on her too sharp fangs, the bright shimmer of red threading her irises. Confusion rippled over his face, soft affection hardening into disbelief.

"Clara?" he whispered, his voice small and uncertain.

Three other men nearby—humans who'd been laughing together only moments ago—saw the exchange and moved toward them, faces twisted in disgust.

"She's one of *them!*" one snarled. "Let him go!"

The Vampire raised her hands, backing away. "Stop—he's my—"

They didn't listen. One man shoved her hard, slamming her into the wall.

That was when the human man snapped out of his shock.

"Stop!" he shouted, lunging forward, trying to push them back. "She's not—she's not hurting anyone!"

The three men ignored him, rage and fear feeding on each other like wildfire.

His words were lost in the noise.

My stomach twisted. I'd seen death, seen blood, seen ghosts—but this? This was hysteria turned human. The ugliest kind of fear.

The street boiled with movement. Magic flared in raw, uncontrolled bursts. Someone summoned fire, the spell streaking wild across the cobblestones. A window shattered overhead. People ran, shoved, tripped.

A cup hit the ground and spun, clattering. Another scream rose.

The world I knew—the fragile balance between human and Magical—was unraveling before my eyes.

And somewhere in the distance, through the chaos, I saw the faint glow of The Obsidian Quill's sign.

Safety. Maybe.

If I could reach it.

I started toward the Quill. Its sign glowing through the chaos like a promise—black and gold against the blood-orange light of the failing evening.

One block. Just one block and I'd be safe.

But the crowd surged, shifting like a living tide, and the group with the Vampire woman spilled directly into my path.

The three men were shouting now—faces red, movements jerky with fear. The Vampire had been knocked to the ground, her palms scraping the cobblestone as she tried to crawl backward. Her lover—her *human* lover—was screaming for them to stop, his voice cracking, torn between horror and disbelief.

"She's not hurting anyone!" he yelled. "Get away from her!"

One of the men kicked at him, another grabbed the Vampire's arm. She hissed, fangs bared on instinct, and that only fueled them.

"She's controlling him!" one of them spat. "She's got him under some spell!"

The air around us burned—wild, erratic. Someone's magic flared nearby, a blast of wind ripping through a street sign, tearing bolts free. The noise was unbearable—people shouting, spells detonating, glass breaking.

My heart hammered. This was going to get someone killed.

The Obsidian Quill's door burst open.

Keyleth stood in the frame, her white-blonde hair glowing in the light, gold eyes scanning the street like a weapon. Even in the chaos, she was radiant—fierce and otherworldly, every inch the Mage she was.

When she spotted me, her expression sharpened.

"Sonia!" she shouted, her voice cutting through the din. "Get over here!"

I shoved forward, elbowing through bodies, trying to reach her. The air tasted of ozone and fear.

But I didn't make it.

The Vampire's human lover lunged toward her, just as one of the other men swung. The motion sent both of them stumbling—straight into me. The man's arm caught my shoulder, hard, and I was thrown sideways.

My back slammed into the wall of a building.

The impact knocked the air from my lungs.

Sound warped around me—too loud, too close, too alive. Screams and shouts blended with the thrum of magic, the smell of blood, the raw, electric taste of panic.

The world tilted.

And the last thing I saw before I tried to push myself up was Keyleth's eyes blazing gold as her magic ignited.

An air-thin bubble encased my body, shimmering like iridescent stars. I thought it would pop the moment anything touched it, but one of the men stumbled back as the human lover desperately shoved at them, and the bubble held firm.

I looked up, just barely able to see Keyleth through the jumble of their fighting.

A shield. Eye contact and immense concentration was needed to create one, but how had Keyleth done it? She belonged to no Mage House. I'd assumed she was untrained.

The air split with a snarl.

The Vampire lashed out—feral, terrified—her claws catching one of the men across the cheek. Blood sprayed in a thin, bright arc.

The man screamed. The crowd screamed with him.

Someone shouted for help, another for the police, but there were none. Just chaos. Just panic.

Then—

A flash of silver.

A gun.

My breath froze in my chest. "No—!"

The shot detonated the air.

The sound ricocheted through my bones, through the magic humming beneath my skin.

People scattered. A woman fell. The Vampire's lover dropped to his knees beside her, his voice breaking into a sound I would never forget.

Blood glinted dark on the cobblestones.

And something in me—something old and buried deep—cracked.

The world lurched. My magic roared to life, drawn to the death, to the anguish bleeding through the street. I could *feel* the souls unraveling, the sharp rip as life left a body.

Too much.

Too fast.

Too many.

The air burned in my lungs. My vision went red at the edges. The veil between life and death buckled around me—thin as wet paper. I could almost see through it. Hear whispers clawing from the other side.

The crowd blurred. Keyleth's voice became static. McDara's name—someone's name—echoed, distant and hollow.

I couldn't breathe.

I couldn't move.

I could *feel* them.

Ghosts stirred. Souls untethered. They were everywhere, and the city, the shimmering shield, was all gone, and all I saw was ghostlight racing down threads to the dead.

The mist was gone.

And Blakewell was burning without it.

I dragged in one ragged breath as the world titled. The air scalded my throat.

I could *feel* the ghosts now, hundreds of them pressing at the edges of the Veil. Hungry. Frantic. Whispering my name.

A hand gripped my shoulder.

Then another.

"Sonia—hey—look at me."

McDara's voice. Low. Fierce.

It cut through the noise like an anchor line.

I blinked hard, trying to focus. His face came into view—blood splattered across his cheek, eyes wide and wild. His magic burned blue along his arms, trying to steady mine, but it only made my skin ache.

"She's burning out," Keyleth shouted somewhere near my ear. "Her magic's overloading."

The air was still screaming with ghosts and sirens and gunfire, but I could barely hear it over the rush of my own pulse.

Then McDara scooped me up.

Just—lifted me off the street like I weighed nothing.

I should have protested, but my limbs wouldn't move. My magic was clawing its way out of me, searching for the dead it couldn't touch.

"Got you," he murmured, half to me, half to himself. His jaw was tight, his voice rough. "Just hold on."

Keyleth was already ahead of us, her gold eyes bright with power. She threw her hands out as we reached The Obsidian Quill's door. The wards sparked to life, flaring gold and white before slamming down like a cage of light.

The air *thumped* as her lock spell sealed.

Inside, the café looked hollow without its usual glow. Tables overturned, the scent of coffee and ozone thick in the air. The candles flickered, their flames bending toward the windows as if trying to watch the chaos outside.

McDara set me down on the nearest table still standing, his hand still braced on my shoulder like he thought I'd shatter if he let go.

Keyleth moved quickly, sealing the last window, her lips moving in a rush of words that vibrated against my bones. The wards shimmered through the room—layers of spellwork clicking into place like a lock turning.

"Shields up," she breathed, turning to us. "Nothing's getting in or out."

Outside, the city screamed.

Inside, the silence was suffocating.

McDara knelt in front of me, his hand still on my arm. His thumb brushed the inside of my wrist, grounding, careful. "Sonia. Talk to me. You with me?"

My magic was still humming, a fever under my skin. I looked at him—at the worry in his eyes, at the faint glow of his magic wrapping around mine—and managed a rasp of a laugh.

"Barely," I whispered. "But I'm here."

He exhaled, shaking his head. "Good. Stay that way."

Keyleth turned toward the door, her expression grim. "Because whatever just happened out there?" She swallowed. "It's not over."

The words hung between us—thick and heavy and true.

30

Keyleth crossed the room in a rustle of color and candlelight. Her slippered feet were silent on the tile, her rich brown complexion wane but steady.

"Hey," she murmured, crouching beside me. "Breathe for me, Sonia. You've got to pull it back in."

I tried. Gods, I tried.

The ghosts still howled at the edge of my mind, brushing cold fingers along my skin. My magic wanted to answer, to rip the Veil open and let them all through.

Keyleth's hands came up, warm against mine. A faint shimmer of her magic—soft, honey-gold, and laced with wildflowers—threaded through the chaos in me.

"We need to get you calm before you can steady your magic. Ready?" she whispered. "Match my breathing."

I focused on the rhythm she gave me—inhale and hold for four counts, a long exhale for five counts, again—and slowly the storm began to still. The air cooled. The ache in my chest eased.

Her magic wrapped mine like silk around barbed wire, smoothing every edge until I could breathe without feeling like I'd swallowed fire.

McDara had moved to the front windows, his broad frame a dark silhouette against the fractured light outside. Every few seconds I saw the blue pulse of his warding magic skim over the glass, a protective heartbeat against the madness beyond.

Then—

Something shifted.

A pressure rolled through the city like a sigh. The air thickened, cooled, *settled*.

The mist was coming back.

We all felt it.

The pull of it, the smoothing of fear. The hum that seeped into the stone and water and blood of Blakewell.

The screams outside turned to quiet cries, confused voices calling names.

Keyleth's head snapped toward the window, her eyes wide and gold with disbelief.

"It's returning," she breathed. "The mist's reforming."

And just like that, the ghosts retreated.

The whispers faded to nothing. My magic—still humming—finally stilled enough that I could sit without shaking.

I pressed my hands to my face, drawing in a long, trembling breath. "It's...gone."

McDara turned from the window, his shoulders lowering a fraction. "People look dazed," he said. "Scared, but not violent anymore. Like they just woke up from a nightmare."

Keyleth stood and looked toward me, her expression a mix of relief and dread. "Maybe they did."

The silence that followed was fragile. Outside, the city was breathing again.

But under it all—the faintest echo of fear, of something broken in the air—lingered still.

I could feel it in my bones.

The mist had come back...

...But it would never feel the same again.

The silence stretched until it felt like it would snap.

Keyleth finally broke it. "If the mist's going to keep failing like that..." She trailed off, staring toward the window, gold eyes reflecting the faint shimmer of the wards. "We can't just sit here and wait for it to happen again."

McDara scrubbed a hand down his face, his voice gravel-rough. "If we don't find what's causing it to fail—and fast—this city's going to eat itself alive."

He turned to me. "You saw what happened out there. That wasn't just hatred, it was *shock*. Half those people didn't even know they were living next to Magicals."

I swallowed hard, the memory of the Vampire woman flashing behind my eyes—the way she'd looked at her lover, the way his expression had changed from tenderness to fear in the span of a heartbeat.

"The mist," I said quietly, "it's doing more than hiding us. It's *controlling* them."

Keyleth's gaze snapped to me. "What do you mean?"

"That man didn't even realize his girlfriend was a Vampire." My throat tightened around the words. "And the other day, the Goblin with the human woman? Same thing. She looked at him like he was a monster she'd never seen before. He looked *shattered*."

The room went still.

McDara leaned back against the counter, arms crossed, eyes shadowed. "You're saying the mist isn't just a veil—it's manipulation." His eyes narrowed. "That wasn't what the mist was supposed to do."

"According to your evil aunt," Keyleth said with as much bitterness as I'd ever heard. "She got you to help get the Veil Towers cleared by the city and to implement them. She probably told you and anyone else helping with it whatever she needed to get you to do what she needed."

McDara scrubbed a hand down his face. "But the mist is from the Mage Council. Besides having a city whose human occupants don't object to Magicals, what would Matron Black get out of such an arrangement?"

"Maybe that's enough. It's clear the mist manipulates humans more than she told you, and maybe that is perk enough for her," I said. "It dulls human instinct, makes them ignore what's right in front of them. If they ignore magic, it makes them easy targets and maybe it keeps the peace, but it's not *real*."

Keyleth sighed and sank into one of the chairs, elbows on her knees. "Bless the Wood. You're right. We thought it was just glamour woven into the air, but if it's that deep—if it's rewiring how humans think..."

"It's wrong," I said, sharper than I meant to. "Maybe it prevents riots, but it also steals their choice. Instead of Magicals and humans coming together and being aware of what they're doing and choosing each other anyway, the mist is dulling any part of a

Magical that would alarm a human. And Magicals don't even know it's happening, well the Magicals that aren't behind the mist at least."

McDara looked between us, jaw flexing. "The mist has to come down. I should have never…I didn't question it like I should have when she asked me to help set up the Viel Towers."

"Not all at once," Keyleth countered immediately. "We just saw what that looks like."

Her voice dropped, tired and resolute. "If it drops again without warning, all of Blakewell will burn."

I wrapped my arms around myself, staring at the faint glow of her wards trembling over the door. "So, we need to find a way to lower it safely. Gradually. Let humans *see* again—but not…break."

Keyleth nodded slowly. "Controlled dismantling of the glamour field."

McDara's tone was grim. "If doing slow is even possible."

For a long moment, we just sat there, listening to the muffled quiet outside—the uneasy calm after the storm.

The wards still hummed faintly, soft, golden veins pulsing across the door and windows like the heartbeat of a creature standing guard.

The silence had settled heavy again—too thick, too still—when I finally found my voice.

"Where are your employees?" I asked, glancing toward the back of the shop. The counters were abandoned, coffee cups half-filled, a broom lying where someone had dropped it mid-sweep.

Keyleth blew out a breath and raked a hand through her pale hair. "In the bunker. The one under the storage cellar. I sent them down as soon as the mist started failing. They're safe." Her tone was resolute, but the flicker in her golden eyes betrayed how rattled she still was. "I'll go get them once I'm sure everything's calmed down out there."

I nodded, but the unease gnawed deeper. "And Dom?"

Before she could answer, McDara's phone buzzed. The sharp sound fractured the quiet like a spell breaking.

He checked the screen, his brow furrowing before he answered. "Ashford?" His voice dropped, all business now. "Yeah. We're at the Quill."

A pause. Then his expression shifted—confusion, then irritation. "That's not our sector. The Vampire quarter's ours."

Another pause, longer this time. He sighed. "Fine. We'll hold position."

He hung up and slipped the phone into his pocket. "Change of plans," he said. "All units are being pulled to the city center and the closest surrounding areas like the Quill. Dom's on his way here."

Keyleth frowned. "Here? Why?"

"Apparently, the Chief decided we're securing this territory." His jaw tightened. "Says there were no riots anywhere else. It's safe to assume that the mist only failed in this area."

"So, the Veil Towers in the city center were messed with?" I asked, and McDara, holding my eyes, nodded once.

The front door thudded a second later, but the door didn't budge. There was a deep voice cursing with passion on the other side.

"Shit," Keyleth jumped to her feet and snapped her fingers. The shimmering gold ward winked out. "Sorry, Dom," she called as Dom stepped inside, his usual sunlit grin replaced by a frown. His sandy hair was damp with sweat, his badge half-hidden under a torn jacket.

"Wards still pack one hell of a shock, Key," he quipped, though his tone was tight. "Chief says to stay put and keep the coffee-witch safe."

"Witches aren't real." Keyleth's mouth curved despite everything. "He knows I'm perfectly capable of keeping myself safe."

Dom grinned, a flash of the old mischief returning. "Yeah, but your enchanted muffins apparently made you a forever admirer. Chief doesn't take chances with his favorites."

Keyleth rolled her eyes, muttering something about sweet-talking lions as she moved to double-check her warding sigils.

I managed a small laugh—weak, but real. Then I turned to McDara. "It'll be dangerous out there, won't it?"

He looked at me, his expression softening just slightly. "It usually is." Something flickered in his gaze—concern, maybe something more—and before I could look away, he added quietly, "You worried about me, Byrd?"

We'd been tiptoeing around each other for weeks that the normal, teasing words caught me off guard. My chest tightened, guilt pricking deep.

Because for one reckless heartbeat, I *had* been worried. Not as someone in love, but as someone who couldn't stand the thought of him being hurt.

But after last night—after Death—every emotion felt layered and wrong.

I forced a faint, crooked smile. "Maybe a little. Don't let it go to your head."

His answering smirk was small, but it reached his eyes. "Too late."

Keyleth snorted softly. "Children, please. I have enough chaos without the two of you flirting in my locked-down café."

Dom barked a laugh. McDara shot him a look. I sank back into my chair, my pulse still uneven.

Because beneath the humor and the tension, one truth pulsed steady in my chest—

If the mist could fall once, it could fall again.

And next time, there might not be a Quill to hide in.

McDara's phone buzzed again, and this time he didn't hesitate. Dom was already shrugging out of his torn coat, that restless energy rolling off him like heat.

"Orders," McDara said, tone clipped. "They're moving us out to help the containment units. Too many scared people still wandering around."

Keyleth crossed her arms, her expression softening despite the tension. "Go. We'll hold things down here."

McDara met my eyes, and for a heartbeat something unspoken passed between us—worry, maybe. "Keep the wards up."

"Of course," Keyleth said.

Then he nodded once and followed Dom out into the night. The door closed behind them with a quiet click that somehow felt too final. With a few words, Keyleth had the wards shimmering back in place.

For a moment, I just stood there, listening to the faint hum of the wards and the distant sirens winding through Old Town.

Then Keyleth exhaled and rolled up her sleeves. "Alright, Sonia," she said, forcing a smile that didn't quite reach her eyes. "Let's clean up before Blakewell decides to implode again."

We worked in silence at first, wiping down tables, righting chairs, gathering the shards of mugs shattered when the chaos hit. Every sound seemed sharper—the sweep of the broom, the faint crackle of the hearth still burning behind the counter.

When it was done, Keyleth went to the cellar door, whispering a quick unlocking charm. The hidden hatch groaned open, and one by one, her workers emerged—pale, shaky, but alive.

I helped her hand out water, murmuring quiet reassurances. A few of them hugged her, eyes wet with gratitude and fear. Keyleth's warmth never faltered; she moved among them like sunlight through smoke.

Together we arranged transport—safe routes, trusted drivers, enchantments to keep them calm until they were home. When the last of them stepped out into the night, Keyleth locked the door again and leaned against it, shoulders slumping.

Her voice was soft when she spoke. "I don't think I've ever hated the quiet this much."

I didn't trust my voice enough to answer, so I just nodded.

We turned out the lights, the Quill sinking into shadow, and climbed the narrow staircase hidden behind wolf drinking tea portrait.

Upstairs, the warmth from the fire reached us first. The familiar scent of cinnamon and old paper followed.

By the time I sank onto her couch, exhaustion had dulled everything—the fear, the guilt, even the echo of Death's touch.

Keyleth joined me on the couch, two steaming cups in hand. She passed one to me, her bangles clinking softly in the dim light.

The scent of chamomile and honey drifted between us, warm and grounding.

For a few minutes, neither of us spoke. The fire cracked softly, painting the room in gold and shadow. Then Keyleth turned her body toward me, studying me the way she did a complicated coffee order that was void of sugar, gluten, and anything that resembled real milk—slow, deliberate, eyes full of calculation and concern.

"I wanted to ask you about the other night," she said finally.

I blinked, already tired enough to feel the words land like a weight. "What do you mean?"

"When we spoke to Dr. Fenwick," she clarified, brows arching. "*Death*, literal Death, was standing in my living room." Her tone hovered somewhere between disbelief and fascination. "I'm still trying to process that."

I gave a weak laugh, blowing on my tea. "Yeah, that makes two of us."

She hummed low in her throat, eyes narrowing just slightly. Then, with the kind of wicked curiosity only Keyleth could pull off, she said, "He's handsome."

I almost choked on my drink. "What?"

"Handsome," she repeated, unbothered. "I didn't think that was even *possible*. I always imagined Death as more...cloak and scythe, less brooding god with perfect bone structure."

Despite myself, I laughed—soft, startled. "Keyleth—"

She tilted her head, her grin turning sly. "But it wasn't just that. He seemed...*consumed* by you."

My laugh cut short. "What?"

Her grin sharpened. "Oh, don't pretend you didn't notice. The way he looked at you? Like he'd murder time itself if it meant keeping you in one piece."

Heat climbed up my neck. "You're reading way too much into that," I muttered.

"Am I?" she pressed, eyes glinting.

I groaned, setting my cup down on the table. "There's nothing to tell."

"Uh-huh," she said, voice singsong. "You're blushing. Spill, Byrd."

I buried my face in my hands, the mortification immediate and absolute. "I don't know, okay? I really don't."

That, at least, made her pause. Her expression softened, the teasing melting into quiet concern. "Are you sure you're safe with him? Training with...*Death* sounds like the worst idea I've ever heard—and I've had some spectacularly bad ones."

I looked at the fire instead of her, letting the flickering light blur. "We made a bargain," I said carefully. "As long as I pay the price, nothing bad will happen."

I didn't add that I didn't *believe* he'd ever hurt me. Not physically. He needed our bond too much for that.

Keyleth frowned. "What price?"

My face went nuclear. "You don't want to know."

"Oh, I absolutely do." Her grin returned, bright and predatory. "Spill."

I groaned into my hands. "He wanted...a kiss."

Her brows rose. "*One* kiss?"

"For every magic lesson," I mumbled.

Keyleth froze. Then, like a firecracker, she *squealed.*

"*He* made up that bargain? The supposed, soulless embodiment of death?"

I nodded helplessly.

"Oh, my gods," she said, practically bouncing in place. "Death has a *crush* on you!"

"Keyleth," I hissed, half mortified, half hysterical, "you cannot say that like it's a good thing!"

But she just laughed, eyes bright with delight. "Sonia Byrd, you are literally flirting with Death. And he's flirting back."

I groaned into my teacup, heat burning in my chest for reasons that had nothing to do with the fire.

Because deep down, beneath the embarrassment, I knew she wasn't entirely wrong.

I stared at her, bewildered. "Why are you so excited about this?" I asked, brow furrowing. "Shouldn't you be rooting for McDara? You're his friend."

The teasing spark in Keyleth's eyes faded. She set her cup down and reached across the space between us, her fingers warm as they folded over mine.

"I am his friend," she said softly. "But I'm *your* friend too, Sonia. Whatever choice he made—it was because it was what he needed. Maybe this is what *you* need. You deserve to be happy, no matter who it's with."

Her voice was gentle but unwavering, every word landing like something sacred.

I blinked hard, throat tightening. Words refused to come.

For so long, I'd felt like I was orbiting everyone else's battles—McDara's grief, the Black House's politics, Death's hunger for freedom. I couldn't remember the last time someone had simply *chosen* to stand beside me without wanting anything in return.

Keyleth gave my hand a squeeze, eyes glimmering gold in the firelight.

Tears burned hot behind my eyes. I tried to laugh, half-hearted. "Gods, I'm ridiculous."

She smiled and, because she couldn't let the mood linger too long, said lightly, "Well, for what it's worth, you and Death make a cute couple."

I groaned. "Please don't say that out loud again."

"I'm serious!" she said, grinning. "You were a mess of nerves before he showed up, but the moment he was in the room—bam. Calm. Like his presence *grounded* you." Her tone turned thoughtful. "It was...oddly comforting. Like he had it handled. I never thought I'd say that about Death."

I stared into my tea, the surface rippling faintly from my unsteady hands. "Whatever's happening between us," I said quietly, "it won't last long if I can't break the curse."

Keyleth's expression softened. She leaned back, tucking her legs beneath her. "Then we make sure you do. Because losing you? Completely unacceptable."

A small, wobbly smile tugged at my lips.

She lifted her cup again, clinking it gently against mine. "Now," she said, all determination and sunshine, "let's brainstorm how to cheat fate and piss off a Matron. I think we're overdue for a good miracle."

I laughed through the lingering sting in my eyes. And for the first time in days, it didn't hurt quite as much to hope.

31

I could still feel Keyleth's words echoing inside me—soft, steady, impossible to ignore.

You deserve to be happy.

It rattled me more than I wanted to admit.

The idea of her supporting...*whatever* this thing with Death was made my pulse stumble. I didn't even know what I wanted, only that the thought of him—and what had happened between us—set my heart racing and my stomach in knots.

So, instead of thinking about it, I latched onto the one problem I could actually face. That I had to face.

"The curse," I said quickly, straightening in my seat. "We need to focus on breaking it and to do that I need to *understand* it."

Keyleth raised a brow but didn't argue. She just gestured for me to continue.

"I think I need to go to Larkend," I said, the words spilling out in a rush. "Grace must've found something there. She wouldn't have risked the raw magic if she hadn't believed it could save her."

Keyleth's expression sobered, all traces of teasing gone. "Dr. Fenwick said Matron Black holds the key. Without it, you'll never even reach the dome."

I nodded, already feeling that familiar buzz of restless determination in my chest. "Then I'll find it. I just need to figure out *where* she keeps it."

Keyleth drew in a deep breath, holding it for a moment before exhaling slowly. Her gaze flicked toward the window, the city beyond still cloaked in uneasy silence.

When she looked back at me, something in her eyes had shifted—wariness, maybe. Or resolve.

"I might be able to help with that," she said quietly.

I frowned. "How?"

For a heartbeat she didn't answer. Then she sighed, closing her eyes, as if bracing herself for what she was about to admit.

"My magic..." she began, voice softer now. "I'm not entirely a Mage. My magic is...different."

I blinked, confused. "What do you mean?"

A small, knowing smile touched her lips. "It means I can do things other Mages can't. *Find* things other Mages can't."

I stared at her, the firelight dancing over her gold-flecked eyes, and for the first time it occurred to me that maybe Keyleth was more than just bright colors and warmth and mischief.

Maybe she was dangerous too.

"My magic," she went on, eyes glinting gold in the firelight, "it doesn't always follow the structured order of Mage magic. There are facets of it that...are purer to the origin of a Mage's magic. Something that came straight from the Wood instead of created by it." Her throat worked, and I watched as Keyleth took a deep breath. "I can project myself—send a thin version of my essence to another place. It's not full travel, more like...a spectral thread. I see through it, feel through it."

For a heartbeat, I just stared. "You can *project your essence*? Like—your soul?"

Her mouth tilted into a rueful smile. "A fraction of it, yes. Think of it as a soul-echo. It's dangerous if I push too far, but if I stay tethered here, I can search without being seen."

A grin bloomed across my face before I could stop it. "That's incredible, Key. Finally—someone else whose magic isn't *normal*."

Her expression softened at that, but there was a flicker of caution beneath it.

"Can you try to locate the key?" I asked, the words tumbling out. "Matron Black probably keeps it in her office at the Black House."

She hesitated only a moment, then nodded with grim resolve. "Alright."

She crossed the room, bare feet silent on the polished wood, and settled in the center of her riot-bright rug. She tucked her legs beneath her, spine straight, hands resting palm-up on her knees. The fire's light played off the copper thread woven through her skirt, catching on the gold jewelry circling her wrists.

"Okay," she murmured, closing her eyes. "I've been in the entryway of the Black House and the med lab. If I'm able to push my soul-echo there, then I can try and walk around the House until I get to Matron Black's office."

And then the air changed.

Her magic unfurled like sunrise—slow, searing, beautiful. Light threaded through her veins, glowing along the lines of her throat, her wrists, her temples. The faint seams of her eyes and lips shimmered gold, as though molten light pulsed just beneath her skin.

My breath caught.

Her hair—normally pale as starlight—blazed golden, every strand a filament of living magic. It cast the room in a warm, otherworldly glow, and the walls seemed to hum with it.

She whispered something under her breath, words that didn't sound Mage-born at all. A language older. Wilder.

I couldn't look away. This—this was the first time I'd seen someone else whose magic didn't fit the neat, little boxes the Mage Council liked to shove people into. It was wild and luminous and *real.*

My pulse raced with something like joy.

And then the air went cold.

A subtle shift. A faint whisper of displaced magic.

The door to the apartment clicked open behind me.

I turned just as McDara and Dom stepped inside—silent, tense, the faint tang of ash and night air clinging to them from the chaos outside.

Dom's brows shot up at the sight of Keyleth glowing like a living sun. McDara's expression was harder to read, shadowed and watchful as his gaze flicked between Keyleth, me, and the shimmering light spilling across the floor.

The temperature in the room dipped another few degrees.

Keyleth didn't notice them. She was already far, far away—her essence slipping beyond the walls of The Obsidian Quill and into the heart of the Black House.

Keyleth gasped. The golden light flaring through her skin snapped out, plunging the room back into its normal, candlelit warmth. She blinked hard, looking disoriented, sweat beading along her hairline.

Dom was suddenly on the couch beside me, one muscled arm braced on his knee, and McDara...gods, McDara was perched on the couch's arm, close enough that the heat of him licked along my skin. His magic always felt like embers—contained, but waiting for fuel.

I forced myself not to lean away, even though every inch of me felt too aware—like Death's touch had branded me and McDara could see it, glowing under my clothes. Ridiculous. Absolutely ridiculous.

Keyleth blinked, steadying her breath, and her gold eyes met mine. "It didn't work," she said flatly.

"What do you mean?"

Her mouth tightened. "The Black House has new wards. Strong ones. I couldn't even reach the areas I've been in before. It's like the whole place is sealed tight."

I slumped back against the couch, the fragile bubble of hope I'd been clinging to collapsing. "Okay," I said softly, though it wasn't okay at all.

Dom and McDara didn't look remotely surprised—no confusion about what Keyleth had just done. So, they knew. They already knew her magic wasn't normal either.

Keyleth rubbed at her temples, frustration flashing in her eyes before she looked at me again. "I'll need to be inside the Black House instead," she said finally, her voice calm but edged with determination.

My head snapped up. "Inside?"

Before she could answer, McDara's low growl of a voice cut through the room. "What the hell are we doing?"

The question wasn't directed at any of us in particular—but his eyes were locked on Keyleth, then on me. His jaw flexed, the muscle ticking hard. The mention of the Black House always hit a raw nerve.

Keyleth lifted her chin, meeting his glare without flinching. "We're finding a way to save Sonia," she said simply.

Silence stretched—thick and hot and full of unspoken history.

And I sat there between them, my heart pounding, feeling like the air itself might catch fire from the tension.

I took a slow breath, my pulse drumming in my throat. "The key," I said quietly. "I need to find it—but I can't risk confronting Matron Black."

McDara's gaze sharpened on me, the faintest flicker of dread threading through his expression. I pressed on before I could lose my nerve. "She's expecting an answer from me about joining the House. If she thinks I'm even *considering* declining, she'll never let me out of her sight again. I need to sneak around her. Get the key. Then go to Larkend and figure out what Grace found there that could—"

My voice cracked, the word *save* catching in my throat. "—that could stop the curse."

The room went still.

Dom blinked, his eyebrows shooting up. "You're planning on stealing from the most feared Mage House in Blakewell?" A slow, wicked grin tugged at his mouth. "Gods, I *love* how much trouble we get into together. We'll have to leave our badges at home, or better yet, pretend we heard none of this." He shot McDara a crooked grin.

Despite everything, I huffed a shaky laugh. Leave it to Dom to find mischief in potential suicide.

McDara, though, looked carved from stone. His jaw flexed. The shadows around his eyes made him look older, harder. Finally, he scrubbed a hand down his face, exhaling through his teeth. "If Keyleth needs to be inside the House to locate the key," he said at last, "then I can act as a distraction for Matron Black."

For a heartbeat, I thought I'd misheard him.

"You—what?" I managed.

Keyleth and Dom both looked at him, equally startled, but McDara didn't look at any of us. He was staring at the floor, a storm gathering behind his dark eyes.

"What do you mean?" I said, the words catching somewhere between disbelief and dread.

Keyleth and Dom looked just as stunned, but McDara didn't meet any of our eyes. He was staring past us, jaw tight, like he was bracing for a blow.

"You hate her," I said softly. "After everything that happened to Deidre—"

I stopped. The name hung between us like smoke.

McDara's shoulders went rigid, tension snapping through him so sharp it made my breath hitch. For a moment, I thought he wouldn't answer. Then he exhaled—slow, heavy, like it cost him.

"I've already been to see Matron Black," he said finally, voice low and scraped raw. "She won't be surprised—or suspicious—if I show up again."

The room went silent except for the faint ticking of Keyleth's enchanted clock.

Then he looked at me. Really looked at me. And the grief in his eyes hollowed me out.

"I haven't gotten Deidre's body back yet," he said quietly. "No funeral."

Something in me cracked.

I reached for him before I could think, my hand finding his arm, my fingers curling around the tense muscle there. "McDara..." His name was barely a whisper. Anger rose in me, hot and helpless. "She won't even let you bury her?"

He didn't answer, but the muscle in his jaw jumped. His silence said enough.

I squeezed his arm harder, wishing I could give him something, anything, to make that kind of pain less cruel. But all I could do was sit there, the fury burning in my chest, and the knowledge sinking in that the woman who ruled the Black House didn't just control power.

She controlled grief.

It didn't take long before a plan began to take shape.

Why wait until morning when every hour felt borrowed?

Dom leaned over Keyleth's coffee table, tracing the air with his finger as if he could draw their route into existence. "So, we go tonight," he said, tone uncharacteristically serious. "McDara and I will go to the Black House, talk to the Matron. I'll keep her guards from snooping, he'll keep her occupied."

McDara nodded, his expression dark but resolute. "We'll tell her I want Deidre's body back. She won't be suspicious. She'll think I'm desperate enough to beg."

The quiet that followed made my chest ache.

Keyleth exhaled and met my eyes.

"While they're inside," I said, "we'll slip through the courtyard entrance. The back door is always left unlocked for evening training sessions. If we're quick, you can set up in an alcove to project into her office and search for the key."

It sounded almost simple said like that.

Almost.

"Right," Dom said, straightening. "We'll check in at the precinct first. Chief'll want an update after the mist collapse."

McDara's mouth twitched like the very thought of bureaucracy made his teeth hurt, but he didn't argue.

When the group finally began to move, the air felt charged—like static before a storm. Dom and McDara headed for the door first, murmuring low between themselves.

I followed them into the hallway, catching McDara's sleeve before he could leave. "McDara," I said softly.

He stopped, looking down at me. The dim light made the shadows under his eyes deeper, sharper.

"Thank you," I said. "For being willing to talk to her again. About Deidre. I know how much that costs you."

Something flickered across his face—pain, maybe, or something heavier that didn't have a name.

He took a step closer, his voice a low rasp. "I told you I'd do whatever I could to help save you." His gaze caught mine, steady and burning. "And I meant it."

The world seemed to go still. The stairwell light hummed above us, the air thick between our bodies.

It should have felt comforting, the promise in his voice, the devotion in his eyes. It should have made me feel relief. Proof that he still cared in some way.

Instead, it made my stomach twist.

Because all I could think about was another promise—one made in a red desert, sealed by Death's mouth on mine.

McDara's loyalty felt like a weight pressing down on my chest, while Death's pull still throbbed like a pulse beneath my skin.

I forced a shaky smile. "I know."

He nodded once, lingering a second longer before turning away, his footsteps echoing down the hall.

I stood there for a long moment after he was gone, my heart split down the center between the man who was trying to save my life—and the one who already owned my soul.

When the guys left, the apartment felt strangely hollow without their restless energy. Keyleth let out a long breath, brushed her hair off her shoulder, and said, "Since we're waiting for them to finish at the station, I'm making us dinner. Something with potatoes. You look like you need it."

I nodded, even though my stomach was a knot of nerves and adrenaline. "Yeah. Sure. Food sounds...great."

It didn't. I wasn't sure anything sounded great. My pulse wouldn't slow. For the first time in weeks, it felt like there was a real plan—a path toward actually saving myself. But the excitement tangled with unease, a fluttering current beneath my ribs.

And gods, I wanted to tell Death.

The thought came unbidden, sharp as a heartbeat. To tell him, to see that flicker of approval in his eyes, to lean against him for just a moment and feel that strange, impossible calm his presence brought. I wanted—no, *ached*—to hug him.

Then I froze.

Because what if this—what I felt—was one-sided? What if I was letting myself crave something that didn't exist beyond the bond and the bargains? If I gave in too much, it would destroy me.

As if summoned by the thought, the air went cold.

A shimmer rippled through the space beside the kitchen counter, and he appeared—hazy at the edges, all shadow and impossible grace.

Death.

He looked at me like I was a secret he already knew, his mouth curving in a slow, dangerous smile. "Sneaking out on me now, Little Bird?" he drawled, the teasing lilt in his voice almost human. "I'm wounded."

But his words barely registered, because the moment I saw him, I moved.

I crossed the room in a rush and reached for him—my chest tight, my body acting before my mind caught up. My arms went right through him, and the cold of it sent a shiver down my spine.

He stilled. Surprise flickered across his face—real surprise, the kind he had never let me see.

Then that slow, knowing smile returned. "Careful," he murmured, voice low and rich. "If you need to touch me that badly, Little Bird...you'll have to come to the Deathscape."

The words curled through the air between us, intimate as a promise.

And gods help me—my pulse answered.

I swallowed hard and forced myself to take a step back. The air between us was charged—too full of him, too full of what I wanted. My fingers found the gold bracelet on my wrist, worrying it against my skin like it could ground me.

"We—uh—we have a plan," I said.

Death tilted his head, studying me. The smirk faded, replaced by something quieter, heavier. "A plan," he echoed, his tone unreadable. "And yet you look like you're about to fly apart."

He moved closer, shadows whispering at the edges of his form until he stood just a breath away. The silver in his eyes dimmed to smoke. "Are you alright, Little Bird?"

That simple question almost undid me.

"I'm fine," I started—but the words came out brittle. My thoughts scattered. "It's just...the mist—it failed. Earlier today. People were—humans were panicking, attacking Magicals, and there was blood and screaming and someone had a gun—"

I didn't get to finish.

Because in the space of a heartbeat, his whole demeanor changed.

The teasing, the half-smile—all gone. The air darkened, the shadows around him deepening until he was more beast than man.

"Come to the Deathscape," he said, voice low and edged with something that was not a request.

My pulse jumped.

One look at him—at the tension in his shoulders, the restrained violence of his form—and I understood. My fear, my exhaustion, the chaos I'd seen had bled through the bond between us. He felt it too. And it was driving him mad.

He needed to touch me.

And I—the Wood help me—needed him to.

"Sonia." His voice softened, dangerous in a different way now. "You need comfort, my Sonia. Let me give it to you."

The words tangled in my chest. My resolve, thin as paper, tore clean through.

"I'll—be right back," I called toward the kitchen, where Keyleth was stirring something on the stove. "Just...need to talk to Death."

"What—?" she started, but I didn't let her finish.

I turned, reached inward for that familiar thread of cold power, and the world folded.

The smell of spice and magic from Keyleth's kitchen vanished, replaced by the dry, burning air of the red desert.

The world lurched sideways as I stepped through the Veil.

Heat crashed into me first—the dry, blistering air of the Deathscape filling my lungs like smoke. The red desert stretched, endless and shimmering, black mountains clawing at the horizon. I swayed, lightheaded from the pull of my magic.

And then he was there.

Death didn't hesitate. His arms came around me, firm and unyielding, shadows curling over my back like a cloak. I didn't even think—my body just *moved*, melting into him. I buried my face against his chest, breathing him in. Cold and spice and something ancient, like rain that had never reached the earth.

My fingers fisted in his shirt. "I hate how dizzy this makes me," I mumbled into the silence.

He huffed a sound that might've been a laugh, the vibration low against my cheek. "Does being close to me affect you so?"

"I meant using my magic to come here." I huffed, and after a moment, "But maybe a little that too."

That earned me silence—and then a gentle brush of lips against the top of my head. The faintest kiss, but it felt like a promise.

After a long moment, his hand slid down my spine, his tone softer. "Tell me about this plan you mentioned."

I stayed pressed against him, letting my words soak into his stillness. "We're going to sneak into the Black House," I said quietly. "We think Matron Black has the key in her office—the one that unlocks the dome around Larkend. Keyleth can project herself to find it, but she needs to be inside the House because of the wards."

He didn't move, didn't even breathe.

"And McDara and Dom will distract Matron Black," I added, voice smaller than I meant it to be.

His arms tightened—just a fraction, but enough that I felt the strength behind it.

"I see," he said at last, each word weighted.

I didn't look up. Didn't want to see what that quiet, dangerous tone meant.

I just stayed where I was—pressed against the chest of Death, in a realm that didn't belong to the living—and let myself believe, for one fragile heartbeat, that I was safe.

Death's embrace didn't loosen. If anything, it grew tighter, as though the desert wind might steal me away if he didn't anchor me to him. His voice came low, threading through the red hush around us.

"Having the Mage's help," he said, his tone curdled with disdain, "is necessary for your survival."

I almost smiled—almost. Even now, he couldn't say McDara's name.

Death's thumb brushed over the back of my neck in slow, absent circles. "But understand this, Little Bird," he went on, quieter now, the heat of his words sinking under my skin. "I do not *like* it. And while you walk through that cursed House, I will be there. You may not see me, but I will not leave you."

A breath slipped from me, part sigh, part relief. "Okay," I murmured against him.

Because the truth was, I *wanted* that—wanted him close, wanted that tether of dark, steady strength beside me. Even if some small voice deep in the back of my mind whispered that getting attached to Death was like stepping off a cliff and expecting not to fall.

Still, I leaned into him.

He tilted my chin up, forcing my gaze to meet his. His eyes caught the Deathscape's strange light—silver one moment, black flame the next.

"The Mage," he said softly, "will not touch you."

My breath hitched.

"Only I," he continued, voice dropping to a growl that curled through me like smoke, "have that privilege. Only I give you pleasure. Only I get to hold you. Do not let him get ideas in the Living Lands because I do not have a physical form there."

The words were molten—danger disguised as devotion. His thumb traced the edge of my jaw, slow and deliberate, as if memorizing the shape of defiance he could already taste there.

Then, quieter still, his tone turned lethal.

"If the Mage does touch you, Sonia"—His gaze burned into mine, silver swallowing every other color—"it will be the beginning of his end."

A shiver rippled through me, my pulse a staccato of fear and want. I knew I should've told him to stop—to stop saying things like that, to stop being this possessive, this dangerous—but what terrified me most was how much I *didn't* want him to.

Because some foolish, yearning part of me wanted to believe that I mattered enough to be worth the threat.

A chill chased down my spine before I could stop it. I hated that he saw it, hated more that the corner of his mouth lifted, satisfied.

It was...hot. Gods help me, the possession in his voice didn't irritate or scare me like it once had. I *liked* being the one person Death coveted.

And it scared me just as much as it thrilled me.

32

By the time I made it back to Keyleth's apartment, I was still lightheaded from the magic. Or maybe from him. Death followed me in silence, a shadow in my wake, the air cooling as he stepped through the magical doorway that led from one realm to another.

The scent of garlic butter hit me before the sight of Keyleth did. She was barefoot in her kitchen, humming under her breath, her white-blonde hair catching the lamplight like molten thread.

Then she looked up—and stopped cold.

"Oh," she said slowly. "You brought a guest."

Behind me, Death materialized fully, visible now, shadows peeling off him like smoke. The temperature dropped by several degrees.

"Guest," he repeated, amused. "I haven't been called that in a long time."

Keyleth arched a brow, completely unruffled. "Until you give me a reason to call you something else, yeah. Guest works fine."

I was already fighting a smile. *Gods, I love her.*

Keyleth motioned toward the table. "Sit. I made grilled cheese and tomato soup because I'm emotionally sophisticated like that, and I was, tragically, out of potatoes."

Death glanced at the chair. I sighed, pulled it out for him, and he lowered himself gracefully—as if humoring me.

It was domestic and absurd and utterly surreal. Death. Sitting at Keyleth's dinner table.

"So," Keyleth began, ladling soup into our bowls, "you're the infamous Death."

He inclined his head. "In the flesh, so to speak."

"Uh-huh." She studied him, eyes narrowing slightly. "And what exactly are your *intentions* with Sonia?"

I nearly choked on my water. "Keyleth—"

"No, it's a fair question," Death interrupted, his tone smooth as glass. "What I want is simple. Everything—but we've started with a boon. To exist again in the Living Lands without being tethered. To walk in sunlight and shadow, as I once did."

Her gaze sharpened. "And you think Sonia can give you that?"

"She already has."

I froze.

He looked at me then—really looked at me—and the world tilted a little. "Our bond lets me touch the edge of life. Even now, sitting here, I am closer to it than I've been in centuries."

Keyleth frowned. "And when you have what you want, what happens to *her*?"

Death's smile was faint and not entirely human. "Then she lives. That is my goal, as much as hers."

Keyleth held his gaze for a long, tense beat, then huffed out a breath. "Fine. But if you hurt her—"

"She won't be hurt," he said, softly enough to make me forget to breathe. "I take very good care of what is mine."

The way he said it—low and wicked and dripping with implication—turned my face into a furnace.

Keyleth blinked. "Oh," she said faintly. "*Ohhh.*"

"Keyleth," I warned, voice strangled.

Death glanced at me sidelong, and the faintest smirk touched his lips. "It's true. She hasn't complained as of late."

I groaned. "You *can't* just—say things like that!"

Keyleth looked utterly delighted. "Wait. Wait. Are you two actually—?"

"No!" I squeaked, which was apparently all the invitation she needed to grin even wider.

"Hmm," Death mused, silver eyes glinting with mischief. "No complaints, but no confirmation either. How disappointing."

"Death."

He tilted his head toward me, voice dipping softer. "You're blushing, Little Bird."

And damn him, he sounded pleased.

Keyleth laughed outright now. "Oh, this is *so* happening. You two are ridiculous."

I dropped my face into my hands, mumbling something about betrayal and friends, but when I peeked through my fingers, Death was watching me—fond, fierce, and impossibly alive.

Dinner had ended in a blur of warmth and nerves. Keyleth, Death, and I cleaned up the dishes—well, *we* cleaned up while Death observed like an amused wraith—and just as the laughter started to fade, McDara called. He and Dom were already en route to the Black House, ready to keep Matron Black busy. It was our cue.

Now, we were crouched in the damp shadow behind the House, the courtyard's obsidian tiles gleaming faintly under the moonlight. The back door loomed ahead—smooth glass framed in black steel, spelled to blend with the walls unless you knew exactly where to look.

Death materialized beside me, half smoke, half man. Only visible to me, it seemed, from the hazy edges of him. I had been surprised by him staying visible throughout dinner, but there were clearly still limits to the power he had access to in the Living Lands.

"It would be rather convenient to have your little Pixie here," he murmured. "She would be excellent at flitting ahead unseen."

I stiffened. "She's still recharging," I whispered.

"What?" Keyleth quickly looked at me, and I gritted my teeth. I looked crazy, just talking to thin air. Hopefully she knew that Death would be following me. Surely, she had assumed that? *Shit, I should have just told her instead of sounding like a mad woman.*

"Death," I muttered.

"Mm," he hummed, eyes narrowing toward the dark roofline. Not even sparing Keyleth a glance as he continued. "The Pixie has been gone longer and longer, hasn't she?"

The quiet weight of his observation chilled me more than the night air. I shoved the worry aside. "Don't distract me. We need to get inside."

Keyleth nodded once, lips pressed tight, and together we slipped through the courtyard—shadows among shadows. The glass walls shimmered faintly with their own inner light, each panel humming with wards. From the outside, the Black House looked hollow, a cathedral of reflections. Inside, the corridors twisted like veins of polished obsidian and mirrored gold.

Death moved silently behind us, invisible to everyone but me. I could *feel* him more than see him—a pressure, a pulse in the air that made my skin prickle.

We ducked into a side hall, steps muffled against the glass floor. Most of the rooms here were used for combat training; open spaces, enchanted mats, faint scorch marks still etched into the walls. We needed somewhere enclosed. Somewhere Keyleth wouldn't be seen.

"There," I whispered, pointing to a narrow door tucked behind a staircase—the kind of room the House used for storing training weapons and supplies.

Keyleth exhaled shakily. "Perfect."

Death's voice curled through the dark, low and sardonic. "Let's hope it stays that way."

And as the door closed softly behind us, the hum of magic in the Black House rose—like the building itself knew we didn't belong here.

The storage room was small—too small, really. Tucked beneath the sweeping staircase, it felt older than the rest of the glass-built House. The walls here weren't transparent; they were black stone, veined with silver and faint traces of something darker.

The air tasted like dust and copper. There were faint sigils scorched into the floor—so faded I might've missed them if not for the way my Ghost Whisper senses stirred when I looked too long. Not training marks. Not accidental. Something *older*. Something that shouldn't still hum beneath the surface.

Keyleth closed the door behind us, shutting out the echoing emptiness of the hall. The small light fixture overhead flickered once, then steadied. She exhaled, brushed her hair out of her face, and lowered herself to the ground, crossing her legs in the center of the faded sigil.

"I'll need silence," she murmured. Then, with a faint smile toward me, "and focus. So, if you and Death can pause the flirting that would be great."

Death leaned against the far wall, half shadow in the low light. "That will be a challenge," he said dryly.

"Not helping," I whispered, glaring at him.

Keyleth closed her eyes. The change began instantly. Her skin gleamed as threads of gold seeped from her pores, tracing the shape of her veins until she looked half made of light. The glow spilled from the seams of her eyes, nose, lips—beautiful and unsettling all at once. Her magic hummed like a soft chord through the air, resonant and alive.

When she spoke again, her voice wasn't her own. It was layered—hers and something echoing beneath it, hollow and powerful.

"What...does the key feel like?"

I blinked. "Feel like?"

"Yes." Her eyes flickered open, but they were glowing pure gold. "Every artifact hums with a pattern. A frequency. A...soulprint. What would this one *be*?"

I glanced helplessly toward Death.

He was already watching Keyleth, thoughtful, the weight of centuries in his eyes.

"The key to Larkend," he murmured, "would not hum—it would *seethe*. It would feel like raw magic pressed into obedience, thrashing beneath its chains. Power that was never meant to be contained."

A shiver crawled up my spine. "So...alive," I whispered. "But wrong. Like the air before lightning hits—charged, but tasting of ash. Like raw magic chained."

Death nodded once, gaze distant. "Yes. Tainted. It would bleed the scent of corruption and creation both. The echo of something ancient trying to claw its way back into the world."

I relayed Death's description and hoped to the gods it helped.

The golden light around Keyleth flared brighter, answering that description like a struck chord. Her magic rippled through the room, through the House, seeking that pulse of twisted power.

Keyleth nodded, her breathing deepening. "Good. Keep talking."

"Dark," Death added softly, with my voice repeating his words to Keyleth. "It will reek of old magic—raw, hungry. But it won't want to be found. It will hide in a place that has bled."

The golden light around Keyleth flared brighter. I could *feel* her magic moving through the House, reaching, searching. My stomach twisted as faint whispers crawled along the edge of my awareness—her power brushing the wards, tugging at doors not meant to open.

Then her eyes snapped wide. "I think..." Her voice trembled. "I think I've found it."

My pulse jumped. "Where?"

Her expression faltered. The glow flickered like a candle in wind. "It's behind something."

Death straightened, tension rippling through the air like static. "A concealment spell?"

"Is it warded or spelled?" I asked.

Keyleth shook her head, voice rough. "No. Not a spell but a *blood*-ward."

The room went still. Even the faint hum of the glass beyond the walls seemed to hush.

Blood-wards meant only one thing—someone's blood, willingly or not, bound to keep others out.

And if Matron Black sealed it that way...whatever was behind that door wasn't just powerful. It was personal.

Keyleth's glow dimmed to a faint shimmer as she dragged in a shaky breath. "If the ward is blood-tied, it has to belong to Matron Black."

My stomach dropped. "Her blood?"

"For blood-wards." She nodded, jaw tight. "Only her lineage—or something that carries her essence—can open it."

Frustration burned through me so hot it felt like static under my skin. "Perfect. How in the world are we supposed to get Matron Black's blood?"

The air behind me shifted. A cool, familiar calm slid over the edges of my panic. Death's hand hovered near my shoulder, his voice a low murmur. "Easy, Little Bird." His tone smoothed over the sharp edges in my chest, dangerous in how quickly it soothed me.

I turned to him, searching those silver eyes. "I could go to her," I said quietly. "Tell her I've decided to join the Black House. It would give me access—close enough to—"

"No." Death's answer was instant, glacial. The faint mist coiled off him like smoke, and his form solidified, becoming visible to more than just me. "You will not give that Mage your allegiance. Not even as pretense."

Keyleth's light flickered with agitation. "He's right. If you go through that ritual, she'll have a tether to your magic. Once she's in, you'll never shake her loose."

I sighed, dragging a hand through my hair. "I don't like it either, but what choice do we have?"

Neither of them answered. The silence pressed heavy—until a faint echo of footsteps drifted down the corridor.

I cracked open the storeroom door, peering through the sliver of light. My heart jumped. Calypso was walking briskly down the hall, arms full of papers, her long curls bouncing with each step.

An idea hit—reckless, half-formed, but *something*.

I looked back at Death and Keyleth. Their expressions were identical—wary, questioning. "I have another plan," I whispered. "And with the time we have left, you'll just have to trust me."

Before either could stop me, I slipped out the door and bolted after Calypso.

"Calypso!"

My voice came out too loud. She turned, startled, the folders in her arms wobbling.

"Sonia? Hey, what's—"

"I need to talk to you. Privately."

Something in my tone must've reached her because she didn't argue. She just blinked, nodded once, and followed me. As we walked, she glanced sidelong at me, concern flickering behind her emerald green eyes. "You're scaring me a little. What's going on? Are you okay?"

I didn't answer. Not until I'd ushered her through the half-open door of the storeroom and shut it behind us.

Her gaze immediately found Keyleth, still faintly glowing from her magic. "Okay, what's happening?"

She didn't look at Death. Most people did—even if they didn't *see* him, they still *felt* him. But she didn't even flinch. I turned slightly, confirming what I suspected. He was hazy around the edges again, blurred in the way that meant only I could see him. He had let Keyleth see him when he stated his thoughts on me joining the Black house, but no one could see him now. Only me. Interesting.

"We don't have much time," I said, facing Calypso again. "So, I'm going to need you to trust me."

Calypso's expression hardened, that older sister kind of calm that always came before a storm. "That's usually the line people say right before they ask me to do something stupid."

"Then you're going to hate this." My pulse thudded in my throat. "We found something. In Matron Black's office. Something that could help me break the curse."

That got her attention. Her head tilted, eyes sharpening. "What kind of something?"

"It's a key," Keyleth said softly from behind me. "To Larkend."

Calypso's lips parted, but no sound came out.

"It's blood-warded," I added quickly, before she could interrupt. "With Matron Black's blood. We can't touch it, can't move it, can't even get close unless…"

"Unless you have her blood or something from her lineage to act as a counter," Calypso finished quietly.

I nodded, breath catching. "Can you help us?"

The silence stretched. She just *looked* at me—long and level, as if weighing every decision she'd ever made that led her to this moment. Then she inhaled slowly, set the folders on a nearby crate, and pulled out her phone.

My heart stopped. "Calypso, wait—"

She didn't look at me. "I need you two to meet me in the archives."

You two? My stomach dropped. Gods, she was going to call the Matron. She was going to turn us in.

But then she ended the call, pocketed her phone, and met my eyes. Her expression softened, almost wry. "Pandora and Elias will meet us there. Between the three of us, we'll find a way to get you that key."

It took me a second to process the words. Then joy and relief slammed through me so fast my eyes burned. "Calypso—thank you."

She opened her mouth to say something, but I didn't let her. I threw my arms around her and hugged her tight.

For a heartbeat, she didn't move. Then she sighed, hugging me back. "You're lucky I like you, Byrd," she muttered into my hair. "Because this is exactly how people end up in detainment wards."

Behind me, Death's low laugh curled through the air like smoke.

33

The archives of the Black House had always felt like another world. The walls were carved from dark stone that swallowed sound, the air humming faintly with wards and age. Lamps flickered in glass sconces, throwing pale light across endless shelves of grimoires and preserved relics.

After a whispered sprint through the lower corridors, Keyleth and I reached the archives with Calypso at our heels—and Death, shadow-still and invisible, gliding beside me. Pandora and Elias were already waiting amid the stacks, their faces caught between curiosity and unease.

In a few quick, breathless sentences, I told them everything: the key in Matron Black's office, Larkend sealed beneath a dome of corrupted, raw magic, and the desperate hope that what Grace found there could still save me.

Pandora, ever the straightforward twin, crossed her arms. "Alright," she said briskly. "We need access to the key. That means breaching a blood-ward. There are only two ways to do that—either the original caster's blood or their lineage."

Elias frowned. "The first option's out of the question. Getting Matron Black's blood is suicide."

"Agreed," Pandora said without hesitation. "So, lineage it is."

Calypso nodded slowly, eyes gleaming in thought. Then she turned to me, lips quirking. "That means you'll need to call your detective."

The words hit like a spark in a powder room.

Behind me, the temperature seemed to drop. Shadows rippled outward from where Death stood, his shape fracturing into something monstrous—horned, half-formed, the raw echo of his power. His silver eyes burned, the air vibrating with an almost animal growl that only I could hear.

I glanced at him sharply, heart pounding. *It's just a phrase,* I wanted to say. But his gaze stayed locked on Calypso, a promise of something lethal shimmering in the space between them.

That shadow beast—his other self—had been showing through more and more lately. I didn't know how long he could keep it leashed.

"I'll text McDara," I said quickly, cutting through the tension.

Calypso's smile returned, small and relieved. "Good. His blood, mixed with the right reagents, should counter the ward for a short window. Long enough for you to grab the key."

Pandora nodded. "We'll prep the potion."

Death said nothing. But as I pulled out my phone and typed McDara's name, I could feel his eyes on me—heavy, possessive, and burning with a fury that tasted almost like fear.

Boots scuffed against the stone steps. A second later, Dom appeared in the archway, his lion tail flicking behind him, and his usual grin nowhere in sight. "Couldn't find a better welcome committee?" he muttered, barely casting a look at Elias and the twins, then he held up an evidence bag pinched between two fingers.

Inside was a single, sealed vial of dark, red liquid.

"McDara couldn't exactly go traipsing around the House without Matron Black hovering over his shoulder," Dom said, his grin edging back in. "But he managed to get me this with a well-timed bathroom break. Pretty sure the Matron was shocked he's decided to sully her porcelain seat." He tossed the bag to Calypso, who caught it with quick fingers. "Fresh from the detective's toolkit."

Calypso held the vial up to the lamplight, the crimson glinting against the gold on her nails. "That'll work perfectly." Her tone was brisk, focused. "Is he still with the Matron?"

Dom shrugged, leaning against the nearest shelf. "He'll keep her attention for as long as she'll tolerate him. Or until he tries to kill her. Whichever comes first."

Pandora clapped her hands once. "Then we'd better move fast."

She and Elias fell into rhythm at the long oak table. I'd seen them work together before, but not like this. Pandora's magic sparked first—gold threads flaring at her fingertips, fine as spider silk, webbing through the air until the entire room seemed to hum with the pulse of invisible strings.

She moved like someone plucking at harp strings only she could hear. "I can see the wards in layers," she murmured. "Every tether has a pulse—like mineral tracks in stone."

"That's the tether magic," Calypso whispered beside me. "She can read the bonds between living and nonliving things...and snap them, if she needs to."

Elias said nothing, his attention fixed on the bowl before him. His magic was quieter, denser. Where Pandora's shimmered, his *rooted*. Silver fluid thickened and began to coil in the bowl, every strand locking into place. "And he binds things," Calypso added. "Wards. People."

Elias's voice was steady, low. "Pandora unravels, I reinforce. Between the two of us, we make magic behave."

It was mesmerizing. Pandora's threads glowed brighter as they wound toward the vial Dom had brought. Elias steadied the bowl beneath her light, and the two magics met in a soft hiss of heat and power.

"I'll weave the detective's blood into the spell's matrix," Pandora said. "Fool the ward into thinking it's Matron Black. With McDara being her nephew their, blood is close enough in relation."

Elias nodded, tightening his binding with another flick of his wrist. "Once it's stable, I'll seal it. You'll have maybe fifteen minutes before it breaks apart."

"Fifteen minutes," Calypso handed them a small crystal phial, her voice calm but tight. "That's all you'll need, Sonia. You get in, grab the key, and get out."

I nodded, my throat dry.

"You must be out before those fifteen minutes is up," Calypso insisted. "After that, Matron Black will know what happened."

But as the twin's magic pulsed through the room, Pandora's head tilted, her expression shifting. Her eyes—deep emerald, almost luminescent—lifted to me. "There's something else."

Elias glanced up from his work, brow furrowing. "Pan—"

"Quiet," she murmured. Her gaze stayed fixed on me. "There's a tether on you. Old, dark. Not from the curse. This one's...alive."

The words froze the air between us.

My pulse tripped. "You can *see* that?"

Pandora's lips curved, but it wasn't a smile. "Tethering magic is my specialty. I see connections, bonds, the threads that tie souls together. And yours..." She trailed off, her eyes narrowing. "It's threaded with something ancient. Something that doesn't belong in this realm."

She didn't need to say his name. I felt Death's attention sharpen beside me, the temperature around us plummeting a few degrees.

Calypso gave a low whistle. "You're seeing Death, aren't you?"

Pandora's gaze flicked to her, then back to me. "Let's just say I see the outline of a shadow wrapped tight around her."

Elias, ever the steady one, touched Pandora's arm. "Focus. The potion."

She inhaled sharply and nodded. "Right. The potion."

Still, when she turned back to the table, I could feel her thoughts lingering on me—and the darkness tethered to my soul.

The potion pulsed faintly inside its crystal phial—silver-gold and crimson light curling together like smoke. The air in the archives still smelled of burned sage and iron.

"It's ready," Elias said, sealing the rim with a shimmer of binding light.

Dom straightened from the table, already shifting back into his role as field muscle. "Then I'd better get back to McDara before Matron Black starts asking where her favorite headache went."

Calypso shot him a look. "Be careful."

"Always am," he said with that lion-grin, though the tension in his shoulders betrayed him. He tucked his comm into his belt and disappeared up the stairs, tail flicking once before vanishing into the dark.

That left the rest of us surrounded by the low hum of wardlight and the twins' unsettling focus.

"Keyleth, you should head out as well," Calypso said, not unkindly. "The less non-members in the House, the less suspicion Matron Black will have when the key is taken."

Keyleth folded her arms. "So that's it? I'm supposed to leave while you all stay here and play with blood wards?"

Pandora glanced up, her expression cool and curious. "You'd be safer outside the House. You're not a House member. You don't have a tether to the wards."

"I'm not leaving her." Keyleth's voice softened, but the resolve in it was steel. "I'll go with Sonia—as a soul-echo. If something happens, I can pull back to my body and tell you."

The reaction was immediate. Pandora's eyes lit with fascination, and Elias's hand twitched like he wanted to take notes he didn't have. Their attention was too sharp, too clinical.

"That's...extraordinary," Pandora breathed. "You can actually project your essence without an anchor?"

Keyleth's golden eyes narrowed. "Don't look at me like I'm a specimen in one of your jars."

Before it could sharpen further, I stepped between them. "She's coming with me," I said firmly. "We'll get the key. You three just—be ready."

Elias and Pandora exchanged a glance—something unreadable—but they both nodded.

"Just be careful," Calypso said, stepping over to Pandora and Elias' station and plucking the phial out of his hand. She then gave it to me. "Both of you."

Keyleth's projection shimmered free of her body, gold light unfurling like spun sunlight, as her echo formed beside me. "Let's go before anyone changes their mind," she murmured.

Death followed silently, a shadow that glided instead of stepped, still invisible to everyone but me.

We slipped out of the archives, moving fast and low through the narrow, glass-walled corridors. The Black House was quieter than it had any right to be, the hum of wards like an invisible heartbeat underfoot.

Keyleth's soul-echo drifted just ahead of me, faintly glowing, her voice a soft thread. "Is he still with us?"

"Death?" I whispered.

"Mm-hmm."

I nodded. "He hasn't left since we started."

"Good." Her tone was thoughtful. "There's something about those twins—and Elias." She glanced back at me. "They might be your allies, but gods, Sonia, Pandora gives me the creeps."

A shiver traced down my spine. "You're not wrong."

We reached the grand landing, the staircase spilling open like a ribcage into the upper hall. Far below, voices carried—raised and sharp. McDara and Matron Black. Even from here, I could feel the tension in his words, the coiled fury in hers.

Keyleth met my gaze, her echo shimmering with determination.

Now or never.

We slipped into Matron Black's office.

The door clicked shut behind us, the echo of the argument still rumbling through the halls like distant thunder.

Matron Black's office looked more like a sanctum than a workspace—massive and unnervingly alive. The walls were lined in tall glass panels veined with slow-moving shadow, faint light pulsing behind them like the heartbeats of something caged. And at the center of it all sat her desk.

It wasn't just furniture.

It was *breathing*.

A beast carved from ancient, enchanted wood—its surface rippling with veins of dark amber as though a living essence slumbered beneath. When Keyleth and I stepped closer, faint glyphs flared and faded across the grain, curling into the shape of claws and antlers before disappearing again.

Those were not Mage sigils. They looked too old. Ancient and harsh. Whatever they said, they were keeping the essence that resided in the desk bound.

I whispered, "It's like it remembers being alive."

Keyleth grimaced but crouched near the base, her fingers brushing the air an inch above the floor. Gold light flared from her palms, seeping outward in delicate ribbons as her magic searched the room. The scent of ozone and crushed lilac filled the air; somewhere in the walls, the wards hummed in answer.

"Come on," she murmured. "Show me where you're hiding it."

The golden threads rippled across the floor, climbing the desk's carved flank, then veering toward the far wall where a towering shelf of ledgers stood. The light stopped on a single panel of glass framed by black steel.

Keyleth blinked. "There."

I hurried over. "Behind the shelf?"

Keyleth nodded. "There's a concealment charm—but it's faint. I can feel raw magic bleeding through it."

Death, still a dark blur near the corner, moved closer, his presence pressing against my senses like the air before a storm. With one flick of his hand, the illusion melted away. I started at his use of magic. Small as it was, the fact that he was able to use even a drop of it in the Living Lands meant our bond was still growing into something I did not understand.

The hidden recess gleamed faintly behind the dissolving glass, carved into the wall like a wound.

Three objects rested inside, laid out with the reverence of an altar.

The first was a metal ring that looked like it had stars captured in the flat face at its peak, no bigger than my finger, forged into a narrow, twisting shard that seemed to hum against the air. Its surface was dull iron, but light moved under it like trapped lightning.

The second was a silver locket, oval and smooth, engraved with sigils so old they had almost worn away. A faint trail of smoke seeped from its hinge, disappearing before it reached the ground.

And the third—a crystal sphere attached to a chain, faintly pulsing from within, like a heart sealed in glass. Shadows swam under its surface, dark as ink.

My stomach sank. "Three of them? You've got to be kidding me."

Keyleth's projected form leaned forward, her expression tense. "It's one of these. I can feel the raw magic leaking through."

I ran my fingers just above the opening, not daring to touch. The air pulsed cold around the metal ring and the locket, warmer around a sphere that sparkled. My Ghost Whisperer magic stirred uneasily, whispering across my skin like static.

I swallowed. "Two of them feel...dead. Like the air around them is full of ghosts. But the third..." Hesitation caught my voice. "Judgment. It feels like judgment. Does this one have raw magic in it?"

Death went utterly still. His form wavered, the shadows around him sharpening into jagged edges. His hand reached out to cover mine, the pads of his translucent fingers sinking into my hand. "Don't touch it."

I glanced back, startled by the fear in his voice. "Which one?"

His eyes—silver gone to steel—cut toward me. "The ring. It is of dead things that even Ghost Whisperers should not mess with. It isn't a key. It's a *sentence*."

Keyleth's brow furrowed. "What does that mean?"

"It means," Death said softly, "whoever forged it captured divine retribution inside. Even I would think twice before holding it."

The word *divine* in his mouth sent a chill up my spine.

I turned back to the recess, pulse hammering. "So that leaves…"

Keyleth pointed, golden threads gathering around the crystal sphere with the odd sparkles at its peak. "That one. It's soaked in raw magic. I can feel it humming through every inch of the room."

I stared at it—the key that looked more like a relic than a tool—and drew in a slow breath. "Then that's the one."

Death didn't speak, but the tension radiating off him was palpable, his shadow flaring like a heartbeat behind me.

The phial trembled in my hand, the potion inside swirling gold and crimson like living fire. I crouched before the recess, the crystal sphere glinting faintly within.

"Here goes nothing," I whispered.

When I poured the potion over the carved edge of the opening, it hissed on contact. The sound was alive—wet and hungry. For a moment, bloodred veins spread across the stone, pulsing like they'd been waiting for a heartbeat to answer. The air burned cold.

Then, as quickly as it flared, the ward shuddered and went still.

"Did it work?" Keyleth's voice was quiet, shimmering from her projection.

Only one way to know.

I reached for the crystal sphere.

The moment my fingers brushed the metal of the chain, my gold bracelet exploded with light. Pain ripped through me—bright, blinding. The brand on my throat burned until it felt like my airway was cut off. My muscles locked, my lungs seizing. It felt like lightning coursing through every nerve.

"Sonia!" Keyleth's projection flickered toward me, hands outstretched but useless.

Death appeared at my side in an instant, his voice a dark snarl of alarm. "Let go."

"I—can't—"

The pain broke in a violent wave, slamming me forward. I gasped, the crystal digging into my palm, its pulse thrumming like a second heartbeat. My bracelet dimmed, and the magic went still.

For a moment, the room smelled of ozone and burnt metal.

"I'm fine," I lied, my voice rough.

Death's hand hovered near my shoulder. "You are *not* fine."

But I ignored him, shoved the crystal deep into my pocket, and forced myself upright. "We got what we came for and only have fifteen minutes to get out of the House before the blood-ward reacts."

Keyleth didn't look convinced. "Sonia—"

"Go," I cut her off, breathless. "Someone might see you. Go back to your body. I'll meet you in the archives."

Her projection flickered, the gold fading from her eyes. "Be careful," she whispered before vanishing like candlelight snuffed out.

Now it was just me and Death.

The silence in Matron Black's office was a living thing—sharp and aware. Every pulse of my heart felt too loud.

I turned, cracked the door open, and slipped into the hall.

The Black House was still unnervingly quiet, the walls gleaming with mirrored glass that reflected fragments of my movement—a flash of my hair, my hand, the shadow that wasn't mine trailing behind me.

"Ten minutes now. You lost time when the key reacted to you." Death murmured, his voice low and cold. "That's how long you have before the blood-ward alerts her to the theft."

"Plenty of time," I whispered, even though my pulse was hammering in my throat.

I hurried down the hallway, boots silent against the polished floor. At the end, I turned the corner—and collided with someone solid.

The air punched out of my lungs.

Matron Black stood there, draped in silver silk and frost, eyes the color of molten onyx. Her smile was small, sharp, *knowing.*

And right behind her—fuming, jaw tight enough to crack—was McDara.

"Sonia," Matron Black purred, "how...unexpected."

My stomach dropped. Ten minutes.

If I didn't get out of this House *now*, there'd be nowhere left to run when the alarm screamed through its bones.

34

Matron Black's gaze pinned me in place, the kind of look that could peel secrets from bone.

"Miss Byrd, it is quite late for you to be visiting the House." she said smoothly, "I think you and I should have a word."

Every instinct screamed *no*. I opened my mouth, but McDara stepped forward, voice a low growl.

"Our business isn't finished, Everiss."

Her head turned toward him with serpentine grace. The air around her shimmered—heat or power, I couldn't tell. "Ah, Cillian," she murmured, her tone like silk drawn over a blade. "I know you wish for your sister's remains."

McDara's jaw clenched, but he nodded once.

Matron Black studied him for a long, unbearable heartbeat. Then she sighed, the smallest of creases forming between her eyes, and in that moment, I remembered that Deidre had been her niece. McDara her grieving nephew. "The Mage Council insisted on cremation. They feared the dark magic lingering in her body could not be purged."

McDara's face went stark—like he was gutted and relieved in the same breath.

"I will have Deidre's ashes sent to you," the Matron finished softly. "It is...regrettable the traditional Mage funeral will have to be altered."

Something cracked in him. His shoulders sagged, and for a terrifying second, I thought he might fall. I reached out on instinct, my hand finding his arm. His skin was cold.

"That's...good, right?" My voice came out small, hopeful. "You'll get to put Deidre to rest."

McDara looked down at me—eyes glassy, mouth parting like he wanted to speak but couldn't find the words. He only nodded, barely, and I felt his pain like a physical thing radiating through him.

Behind me, Death's presence flared—cold, razor-edged irritation slicing through the air. I didn't have to look to know his expression; I could *feel* it, like shadows scraping down my spine. But I didn't move my hand from McDara's arm. Not yet.

Matron Black's voice cut through the quiet, each word deliberate. "Detective McDara, you and your Shifter may leave now." The way she said *Shifter* dripped disdain, like a slur dressed up in civility. She couldn't even bother herself with using Dom's name.

McDara stiffened, but he didn't take the bait. He gave a shallow nod. "Fine."

"I'll walk you out," I said quickly, already needing to move, to *breathe.*

Matron Black's gaze slid back to me, her painted mouth curving into something that wasn't a smile. "No. You'll stay. I wish to speak with you alone."

Every drop of blood in my body went cold.

I forced a nod, watching as McDara hesitated—his eyes flicking from me to the Matron, reading the tension that laced every inch of the air between us.

"Go," I whispered. "Tell everyone I'll see them soon." *Tell them I'm freaking screwed.*

After a beat, he turned and walked away, the tangle of glass hallways swallowing him up like the House was feasting.

The silence that followed pressed on my ribs.

Matron Black turned toward me fully now, the faintest smile ghosting across her lips. "Now then, Miss Byrd," she said, voice soft as poison, "we have a very important matter to discuss."

My heart pounded so loud I could barely hear myself think.

And somewhere behind me, unseen by her but very much *there*, Death's shadow moved—sharp, coiled, and ready to strike.

Gods, please let me get out of this House before the alarm goes off.

The Matron's stare felt like a blade pressed to my throat—light enough not to cut, sharp enough to promise it could.

I tried to breathe past the pressure in my chest. "Could we...maybe talk downstairs?" I managed. "One of the reading nooks, maybe? You can actually see the stars this far from Old Town. We can watch them through the glass."

For a heartbeat, I thought she might refuse. Her expression didn't shift, but I felt the weight of her gaze strip me bare—my nerves, my pulse, every half-formed lie. Finally, she inclined her head. "Very well."

I followed her down the corridor, Death's shadow sliding at my back like smoke. And I'd never been more grateful for his presence. The House's glass walls caught the dimming light, refracting it in shards of gold and crimson. The whole place glowed like the inside of a throat—beautiful, suffocating.

We stepped into one of the lower-level alcoves. The furniture gleamed white, sculptural, cold. Oval couches circled a low table of black stone; everything looked pristine, untouched. A room meant to be admired, not lived in.

Matron Black sat with effortless poise, folding one leg over the other. "You've been absent from the House," she said. No warmth, no accusation—just fact sharpened into a weapon. "Your training has suffered. My excusal was only for the day after your magical fatigue. Your instructors report you haven't attended sessions in a week. If you were well enough to leave this House then there is no reason you could not attend your lessons."

My mouth went dry. "I...drained too much of my magic," I said, forcing steadiness into my voice. "You remember Dr. Fenwick tending to me in the med lab. He said that I had drained my magic down to my soul and it scared me, and then—" I stopped. The words knotted in my throat. "Then he died."

Silence settled between us like ash.

Her eyes softened, but it was the kind of softness that wasn't human. It was practiced. "A tragedy," she murmured. "Such a gifted man. The report says it was a stabbing, not magic. Very odd."

I could only nod.

She watched me for a long time, the way a spider might study a trembling web. When she finally spoke again, her voice dropped to a near-whisper—intimate, conspiratorial. "I had Dr. Fenwick researching how to cure you of the bloodline curse."

The air left my lungs. "What?"

Her painted mouth curved faintly. "Yes, Sonia. He wasn't simply treating your exhaustion. He was working on something much more...significant. I do not want my only Ghost Whisperer to perish."

The world seemed to tilt, the sunset's reflection rippling across the glass walls.

I stared at her, pulse hammering in my ears, as Death's shadow tightened protectively around my shoulders.

Matron Black had tasked Dr. Fenwick to find a cure to my family's curse, and someone had killed him to stop him from helping me. Why?

Why was it so important that I die?

Matron Black leaned back in her seat, the dying sunlight catching in her rings so they glinted like tiny mirrors of blood. "Your time for consideration," she said smoothly, "has ended."

My pulse stuttered.

Her gaze never wavered. "I will have your answer, Miss Byrd. Will you join the Black House? Here you would have everything you desire—Ghost Whisper training, resources beyond your comprehension, and an entire House of Mages working to cure you of that wretched curse."

The words were honeyed, meant to sound like salvation, but they slid down my spine like oil and poison.

A whole House of Mages hadn't saved Grace. It hadn't saved *any* of the Ghost Whisperers in my family tree.

And yet...if I said no, that refusal would be a noose. The Matron didn't take rejection lightly. Refusing her was as good as writing my own epitaph.

Sonia.

His voice slid through my thoughts, low and cold as a storm beneath ice.

Don't do it.

My breath caught. I could feel him—Death—standing just behind me, unseen by the Matron, his power curling through the air like smoke. It had been so long since he'd spoken into my mind I'd thought, with his control on his magic in the Living Lands growing, he had lost that ability.

Don't you dare tether yourself to her, he hissed.

I pressed my trembling hands to my knees, trying to anchor myself in the now. The Matron waited, expression serene, like she already knew my answer.

And the clock was ticking down from ten minutes faster than I could think.

I forced myself to meet her eyes. "I'll join," I said, the words tasting like iron.

A smile unfurled across her face—slow, triumphant, venomous. "Excellent."

Foolish girl.

Death's voice was no longer calm. It was thunder cracking inside my head.

If she so much as lays her magic on you—if she marks you, binds you, touches you—I will drag you into the Deathscape myself, and you will not leave it.

The raw fury in his tone made me shudder.

Matron Black's smile deepened, the corners of her painted mouth curving like a blade. "Welcome home, my dear."

A chill spread through me, a prickle of shadow and warning. Death's power coiled tight around my shoulders, looping around my neck, protective and possessive, while the Matron's magic pressed against my skin in a slow, suffocating bloom.

Two opposing forces—darkness and decay, both wanting me. Both claiming me.

And I stood between them, every breath tasting like fear and inevitability.

"Follow me," Matron Black said.

Her tone was velvet-soft, but there was no mistaking the command threaded through it.

I rose on shaky legs, pulse thudding in my throat. She didn't say where we were going, and I didn't dare ask. Maybe she meant to escort me out—hand me off to Calypso until the initiation. Or maybe, the Woods forbid, she intended to *start it now.*

The thought turned my stomach.

The Matron moved with slow, regal precision through the glass corridors, the sunset bleeding to indigo beyond the enchanted walls. Every reflection caught our shapes like ghosts—her tall, silver-silhouetted form and my smaller one, trailing behind.

As we descended the main staircase, I spotted movement below.

McDara.

He stood near the entryway, jaw tight, Dom at his shoulder. Keyleth was with them, her hands raised in a placating gesture, as if trying to calm the guards flanking them.

Escorted out.

That was the polite term for it.

McDara caught sight of me just as they were ushered toward the doors. His eyes locked on mine—dark, warning, frantic. I wanted to run to him, to tell him I was fine, to tell him to *go,* but the Matron's hand ghosted to my shoulder, a light, proprietary touch. My breath snagged.

We passed them. The great doors shut behind their figures with a sound like the sealing of a tomb.

The hallways ahead grew dimmer, narrower. The air thickened—heavier with magic the deeper we went. I could feel Death close behind me, silent and furious, though he said nothing. His presence trembled like a drawn blade, waiting to strike.

"This way," the Matron murmured, and the polished glass gave way to stone. The floor hummed faintly underfoot.

She stopped at a door of black iron veined with faint, silver sigils. My heartbeat stumbled.

"I thought—" I started, but she pushed the door open.

"Inside," she said.

No. Telling her I would join was supposed to buy me time. The ability to leave this House without Matron Black snapping and doing something exactly like this.

The room was small, windowless, the air thick with old incense and dust. A faint shimmer of wards lined the walls. It smelled like stone and something darker—like the ghost of fire.

I didn't move forward. "Matron—"

Magic jammed against my knees and torso, propelling me forward and into the room. The door slammed.

I spun, grabbing the handle, yanking hard. It didn't budge.

Sigils flared along the frame, locking in a lattice of light that burned cold.

"Matron Black?" I called, forcing calm into my voice. "What is this?"

Her voice drifted through the door, smooth and almost fond. "Precaution, my dear. Until your initiation. You understand."

No. No, I didn't.

I slammed my palm against the iron door, heart hammering. "You can't just—"

But she was already gone.

The silence that followed pressed on my ribs until it hurt. No windows. No sound. Just my reflection trembling faintly in the glossy wall opposite me.

Panic clawed at my ribs. The room felt smaller by the second—each breath dragging tighter, shallower. I tried the door again, palms slick against the cold iron, but the sigils only pulsed brighter, mocking me.

"Damn it," I hissed. "How am I supposed to get out of here?"

Death's voice filled the room like a storm breaking. "What did you expect when you told that Mage you would join her House?"

I sighed.

He stepped out of the shadow in the corner, tall and terrible, silver eyes burning through the dim. "Of course she would lock you up. Don't be foolish. Did you think she'd offer tea and congratulations?"

"Don't—" I spun to face him, fists clenched. "Don't call me foolish or dumb."

He moved before I could blink—sudden, silent, right in front of me. The air between us vibrated with his fury.

"I am *not* calling you dumb," he said, voice low and dangerous. "But your decision? That was the stupidest thing I've seen you do since you fell into my realm and let me bind you to me."

The words hit like a slap. My pulse jumped, half rage, half shame. "I didn't have a choice!" I snapped. "If I said no, she would've locked me up!"

"Which is exactly what has happened."

I wanted yell at him, scream, maybe shove his ridiculously broad chest, but I knew I'd only go careening through his incorporeal form...and look more like an idiot than I already did.

He raised a hand sharply, cutting through my words. "Enough." His shadows curled and snapped around us. "Come to the Deathscape. Now. Then we'll return to your little non-Mage friends' house before this place swallows you whole."

I wanted to scream at him, tell him he didn't get to order me around—but fear and fury twisted together until all I could do was obey.

Fine. I'd go. I'd get out of this damn room.

I reached for the tether that always lived beneath my ribs—the one that linked me to the Deathscape—and *pulled.*

The breath tore out of my lungs. My knees buckled, the world tilting sideways. I hit the ground hard, choking on a scream that wouldn't come.

Death dropped beside me, hands hovering but not touching. His face went grim, almost ashen. "This room is warded against Ghost Whisperer magic," he said tightly. "A thousand times over. Layered to keep you from crossing realms. To keep you from reaching me, like she knew you could."

My bones pulsed with a raw, searing ache. I could *feel* the magic humming in the walls—old, heavy, cruel.

A shiver slid down my spine. "How—how could she know how to do that?"

He didn't answer.

Only the low flicker of the sigils answered me—like laughter in the dark.

I was still on my knees, the burn on my wrist throbbing like a heartbeat that wasn't mine, when a faint sound shimmered through the air—like glass windchimes caught in a whisper of wind.

Then a flash of purple light.

"Phontine?"

My tiny friend hovered near the ceiling, her violet wings beating slow and soft, scattering motes of ghostlight that drifted like falling ash.

How could she get into this room?

"The sweet Woods, Sonia," she breathed, pressing a tiny hand to her chest. "You look like death."

I laughed once, a brittle, humorless sound. "Present company must be rubbing off on me."

Death didn't move, but I felt his shadows coil tighter. He didn't like her here.

"How did you even get in?" I asked. "This room's warded six ways to hell. I can't even *breathe* properly, and yet—"

Phontine's expression flickered—just for a second, something unreadable passing through those wide, lilac eyes. Then she smiled too wide. "Pixies don't really follow the same rules. You know that. I'm tied to you, Sonia. Wherever you are, I can be."

My stomach twisted. That wasn't...entirely true.

"But you can't reach me in the Deathscape," I said slowly.

The silence that followed stretched, long enough for my nerves to start screaming.

Phontine fluttered down and landed on my knee, her wings dimming. "That's different," she said softly. "That's not even on the same plane of existence."

That was true. *Of course* it was true, made sense.

Death leaned close behind me, his breath a ghost against my ear. "You might want to look into the nature of Pixies," he murmured, so quiet it was barely sound. "Particularly the ones who attach themselves to mortals."

I stiffened, glancing at him over my shoulder—but he was already fading back into the shadows like remaining here in a room meant to strangle anything that was not Mage-born cost him.

I mentally shook myself. I was not about to doubt my oldest friend. My best friend. This fucking city was making me see betrayal everywhere.

Phontine looked at me expectantly, her small face earnest. "I'm guessing the lovely Matron Black trapped you in here and we need to get you out before she comes back?"

"Yeah," I whispered, scanning the room. Bare walls. Bare floor. Not even a chair to break or a hinge to pry. Just smooth stone and the faint hum of magic pressing against my skin.

No window. No weakness.

My pulse quickened. "There's nothing here," I said. "No way out—"

The rest of my words died in my throat.

A sound.

Soft at first, then scraping.

Metal against stone. From the *other side* of the door.

Phontine froze, her wings going still. Death materialized fully now, eyes burning silver, every inch of him taut.

The scraping came again—slow, deliberate, closer.

My breath caught.

Someone—or *something*—was trying to get in.

35

The scraping stopped.

Then—click.

The lock released with a sharp hiss, and the heavy door swung open.

I stumbled back, ready to call up what little magic I could still reach.

It wasn't Matron Black.

Elias stood in the doorway, framed by the faint, green glow of the wards. His dark brown hair looked artfully messy, like he'd run a hand through it just to make it fall perfectly wrong. The golden light from the corridor caught in his eyes—bright, sharp, assessing.

"Relax," he said. His voice always carried that effortless arrogance the Mages of Blakewell seemed to breed. "Pandora sent me. She saw your little Old Town friends getting thrown out. One was colorful about what the Matron was doing to you."

Relief washed through me, chased quickly by suspicion. "How did you—"

He cut me off with a small, impatient motion of his hand. "The twins are covering for me. I only have a few minutes before someone notices I'm not where I'm supposed to be."

Behind me, Death hovered like a storm barely leashed, his silver gaze tracking every move Elias made.

Elias looked at me again, and a faint smirk touched his mouth. "I can't help you get out. You'll have to manage that part on your own. I've already risked enough opening the door."

"Right," I said, throat tight. "Thank you."

He tilted his head, watching me for a heartbeat too long, his gaze a little too interested. "Be quick, Sonia." Then he was gone, the sound of his boots fading down the hall.

For a second, the silence after him felt heavier than the room had.

Phontine fluttered out from behind my shoulder, her wings sparking faint, lavender light. "Well," she said, voice bright with mock cheer, "isn't *he* a delight. Do you think he practices that smug face in a mirror, or is it natural Mage superiority?"

A laugh sputtered out of me—half nerves, half genuine amusement. "Definitely natural."

"Figures." Phontine wrinkled her tiny nose, settling on my shoulder. "All that power and not an ounce of charm."

Death made a low sound that might have been approval—or agreement.

I slipped into the hall, my pulse thudding, scanning for movement. I shut the door behind me as best I could with a slab of magicked metal that didn't have a handle, but it was better than leaving it gaping wide open.

The upper corridors were too exposed, too close to the Matron's wing.

So, I turned left, toward the narrow, back stairwell that led down to the basement—to the archives.

Stone walls closed in around me, cold air brushing my skin like ghost fingers. Phontine's light shimmered softly ahead, and Death's presence loomed at my back—silent, protective, furious.

One wrong step and I'd never leave the Black House again.

But for now, the door was open.

And that had to be enough.

The corridors of the Black House blurred as I moved—shadows swallowing one hallway after another. Twice, I flattened myself against the glass wall as figures passed, their magic whispering faintly through the air like static. My heart hammered, every beat a countdown.

"Left," Phontine whispered from my shoulder, her violet glow dimmed to a faint shimmer. "That one's empty."

I followed her lead, slipping into the spiral stairwell that cut down toward the archives. The air grew colder with every step, heavier. The scent of dust and candle soot filled my lungs.

"There's barely three minutes left before the blood-ward sounds," Death whispered on a cold breath, chilling the back of my neck and making my feet hurry.

When I reached the archives' door, I pressed my hand to the handle—just a breath—and then eased it open.

Silence. Rows of shelves stretched into darkness, each carved with protective sigils that looked older than the House itself.

Death appeared at my side, silver eyes gleaming faintly in the gloom. "You've done this before," he murmured.

I nodded once. "Last time, I followed a faceless ghost down here."

He arched a dark brow. "Ah. The night you were covered in soot and pretending you weren't shaking." A faint smirk ghosted across his mouth. "Now the mystery is solved."

Phontine made a soft huffing sound. "Less flirting, more escaping, please."

I rolled my eyes but smiled despite the nerves tightening my chest.

We moved deeper until we reached the back wall—the same wall that wasn't a wall at all. My fingers found the crack in the stone, the faint give beneath the edges. I pushed, and the hidden panel shifted open with a slow groan.

The crawlspace yawned beyond—low and narrow, smelling faintly of earth and old bones.

Phontine fluttered ahead, her glow painting the walls with flickering, lavender light. "All horror movies start with a beautiful girl going into dark places, you know."

I crouched and crawled after her, the rough stone scraping my palms. Death's presence followed like a cool wind, though his form wavered in the confined space.

The tunnel curved and dipped, opening finally into a larger chamber—one of many. Old, hollow crypts lined the walls, their inscriptions faded. The ceiling was so low in places I had to duck.

"This isn't just beneath the House," I said quietly. "It's a catacomb."

"Older than Blakewell itself," Death replied, his form hardening around the edges and becoming visible now that we were away from the House wards. "You tread through the city's bones."

Phontine's wings gave off a brighter pulse. "Okay, creepy dead-guy poetry aside, we need to keep moving before anyone notices you're missing."

I bit back a retort, mostly because she was right. We turned toward the one tunnel not blocked by collapse, our footsteps whispering over damp stone. The walls seemed to breathe around us, the air thick with old magic and moisture.

Then—*it hit.*

A sharp crack split the air behind us, followed by a low, thrumming pulse that rolled through the ground.

"The blood-ward," Death said darkly. "She knows something was taken."

Phontine whirled midair, wings flaring violet. "What did you steal? Never mind, *run!*"

The floor trembled as magic surged through the tunnels—alive, hunting, furious. Every sigil we passed flickered red, the light chasing us like veins of fire spreading through the walls.

"Go," Death barked, his voice echoing everywhere at once. "That tunnel—there, the only one still open!"

I didn't think. I ran.

The air pressed tighter with every step, heavy with the taste of iron and smoke. Phontine darted ahead, her glow bobbing wildly. "Left! No, right—*that* right!"

My lungs burned, my pulse a drum in my ears. Behind us, I could feel the ward's power racing closer—like claws scraping stone.

Death's form flickered beside me, his shadows pulling me forward even though he couldn't touch me. "You're nearly past the wards," he said, his voice taut. "Another fifty paces—"

"I don't *do* paces!" Phontine shrieked. "I have wings, remember?"

"Then flap faster," I gasped.

The tunnel dipped sharply. My boots skidded on damp rock, hands scraping the walls for balance as the air grew colder—sharper.

And then the pulse changed. The oppressive weight of the Black House's magic thinned, replaced by something freer, wilder.

Death's tone softened, threaded with relief. "There. You're clear of the House's reach."

I stumbled to a halt, chest heaving, leaning against the rough wall as the ringing in my ears faded.

The blood-ward was still screaming behind us, echoing through the stone—but we were past it.

Barely.

Claustrophobia clawed at me—the weight of earth pressing down from above. I forced myself to breathe evenly.

"I do not sense danger," Death said softly, and his tone gentled like velvet. "You are safe, Sonia."

It shouldn't have helped. But it did.

He stayed close, his shadow brushing against my peripheral vision like a steadying hand I couldn't feel. "You can come to the Deathscape. The Pixie can return to the non-Mage's dwelling."

"Her name's Phontine," I muttered.

He gave a low, amused hum. "Yes. That one."

Phontine looked back over her shoulder, wrinkling her tiny nose. "Nice to know I rank just above household furniture."

Despite everything, a quiet laugh escaped me. "Both of you, stop."

We caught our breath for a moment more until a faint sound rolled through the air—distant but sharp.

A scrape.

Then another.

I froze.

Death's tone changed instantly, all warmth gone, every syllable a command. "Do not move," he whispered. "Do not even breathe."

The tunnel went still.

Even the air seemed to hold its breath.

And somewhere ahead—something dragged itself closer.

Before I could ask why, his shadows unfurled. They poured from him in waves, cold and dark, curling around me and Phontine until we were swallowed whole. The world muted—colors bled away, sound muffled, my own breath barely audible.

It wasn't just darkness.

It was *his* darkness.

It wrapped around me like silk and smoke, alive and curious. I could feel it—the awareness within it—brushing against my skin as if it knew me, remembered me. One tendril slid along my cheek, a cold caress that made my breath hitch. Another twined through my fingers, featherlight, stroking once before dissolving back into the air.

They weren't trying to restrain me. They were soothing me.

Comforting me.

It was terrifying how intimate it felt, how easy it was to forget that the shadows belonged to something ancient and dangerous. In their embrace, my heartbeat slowed. For one impossible moment, it felt like being *held*.

Through the veil of shadows, I heard boots scraping stone...

Then came the low murmur of voices—four men, their words slurred by exhaustion and the weight of what they carried.

Two sacks dragged behind them. The shapes inside were unmistakably human.

I pressed a trembling hand to my mouth. *Bodies.*

The lead Mage's coat brushed the tunnel wall as they passed, his hands glowing faintly blue with containment magic. "Hurry," he hissed. "The sacrifices must reach the mist before it stabilizes again."

Sacrifices.

To the *mist.*

Every nerve in my body screamed to move, to stop them, but Death's shadows coiled tighter around me—a cold hand over my instincts.

One of the other Mages grunted, voice low and grim. "Chief wants them breathing. Says the obelisk feeds better that way."

The group's footsteps faded, the dragging sound growing fainter until there was nothing but the echo of their words hanging in the dark.

Death didn't release the shadows. Not yet. His form flickered, the strain carved into the sharp lines of his face. I could feel it—how much it cost him to hold this cloak here, in the Living Lands.

"Death," I whispered. "You're burning yourself out."

His gaze, pale and blinding, cut to me. "You forget what I am, Little Bird." But even his voice was thinner, fraying around the edges.

I hadn't. I just wasn't sure what he was *becoming*. Every time he used magic here, he lasted longer. Moved easier. Looked more solid.

"What about our bond is letting you do this?" I murmured, almost to myself.

Something flickered in his eyes, something like fear, quickly buried beneath that usual, cold control. "Later."

Phontine's tiny voice trembled beside my ear. "I don't like this. Those Mages felt wrong. Like rot under the skin."

Death's gaze snapped to her, the temperature in the tunnel dropping several degrees. "Pixie," he said, and even in a whisper it was a command. "Go. Now. Your light will be a beacon if you stay until I drop the shadows."

Phontine hovered midair, torn between obedience and concern. Her wings trembled, catching the faint gleam of his magic. "But—Sonia—"

"Go," I said softly. "I'll meet you at Keyleth's."

Her little shoulders slumped, but she nodded once. Then she was gone—vanishing in a streak of violet light.

The silence that followed was heavy. Intimate.

Death was still cloaking us, though the effort had drained the color from his face. I reached up without thinking, my fingers brushing his cheek—cold, unreal, and yet *there*.

"I'll come to the Deathscape," I whispered. "You don't have to keep holding this."

His shadows pulsed at my words, curling tighter for a heartbeat like he didn't want to let me go. Then they slowly receded, leaving the tunnel dim and bare.

"Then come to me," he said softly.

And I did.

The Deathscape welcomed me like a wound reopening.

Heat shimmered off the red sand, the air heavy with silver haze that clung to my skin like frost. My pulse stumbled. Every time I used my magic to come here, it took more from me—my strength, my breath, my bones—but I couldn't let him see that. Not now. Not when the air itself vibrated with his fury.

The moment I solidified, Death's hands found me. Rough, desperate. Shadows coiled around his fingers, alive and restless.

He gripped my face, forcing me to meet his gaze.

"Do you have a death wish, Little Bird?" His voice scraped low. The silver of his eyes burned like molten moons.

My heart lurched, but I refused to look away. "There was no good way out from that conversation with Matron Black."

His mouth curved—a shape that wasn't quite a smile. "You seem determined to throw yourself at everyone's mercy but mine."

"What?" I tried to pull back from him, but his fingers had fisted in my hair, holding me close. "I bargained with you to learn how to use my magic. I'm at your mercy *right now*."

"You should *only* be at my mercy." Death seethed. "None of them cares for your best interest."

The sand around us darkened, the horizon rippling as his shadows surged. Before I could blink, the world bled away. The air twisted—and we were in his study.

Books lined the walls in uneven stacks, relics and bones and glass jars glinting faintly in the dim light. The scent of dust and something electric—ozone and storm—filled my lungs. His home always felt like a cathedral to endings.

Death paced in front of me, a thunderstorm given form. The faint edges of his beast—the thing beneath his skin—kept flickering through him, muscle and bone turning to shadow and claw before solidifying again.

"Do you think I haven't seen what you're doing?" he bit out. "Throwing yourself into danger. Bargaining with Mages who would carve your soul apart. Planning to walk into cursed towns like you were born for slaughter."

I swallowed, fighting the sway of dizziness that clawed at my vision. My magic still burned low, too low, but I forced my chin up. "We have a plan. Keyleth and McDara think—"

"I don't care what they think." His voice cracked like a whip, and the candles guttered out. Shadows spilled across the room, writhing, alive. "You speak of plans and keys and ledgers, but none of that will matter if you're *dead*. Or your soul is bound to that Matron."

"Then what?" I demanded. "You want to lock me away here?"

He stilled.

When his eyes found mine again, there was no silver—only black. Endless, suffocating black.

The answer slid out of him in a low growl. "Yes."

The shadows around us shifted, rising like smoke, curling against my arms, my throat. They felt like breath—cool, intimate—sliding over my skin. One tendril brushed my cheek, almost tender. Another threaded through my fingers, curling as if it didn't want to let go.

I could feel him in all of it. The ache of his restraint. The hunger beneath it.

"Death...I was just being sarcastic." My voice trembled, and I hated that it did. "You can't keep me here."

"I can." The beast beneath his words rumbled like thunder in a cave. He stepped closer, and the air thickened. His form flickered again—half man, half shadow creature, black fire crawling beneath his skin. "Here, you are mine. Here, the curse might never touch you. Tell me why I shouldn't chain you to this place and be done with it."

Because I would die without the living world, I wanted to say.

Because if he kept me, he'd become the monster I feared he was.

But all that came out was a whisper. "Because you promised to protect me, not cage me."

His expression fractured. For a heartbeat, the fury broke—and I saw the loneliness beneath it. The centuries of it. Then it was gone, buried under shadow.

"I protect what's mine," he said softly. Dangerous. Intimate. "And I decide what that means."

The shadows surged, closing around me like a lover's embrace—velvet and suffocating. They pulsed with his heartbeat, his power, his warning. And for the first time, I felt the truth of him.

He wasn't the reaper who flirted in riddles.

He wasn't the teacher who teased me into control.

He was the end of all things.

And he was *so close* to forgetting mercy.

I could *feel* it—how close he was to breaking.

The Deathscape trembled with it, the air thick with power too vast, too old. Shadows clung to him like a second skin, restless, hungry, whispering of the abyss that lived beneath his ribs.

If he caged me here, I wouldn't last. My soul would wither, piece by piece, until I became one more echo in his endless collection.

But beneath all that terror and wrath, something else pulsed—fear.

Real, human fear.

And the knowledge of it shattered something in me.

Death. The being who had collected kings and gods alike.

He was *afraid.*

And it was me he was afraid of losing.

I stepped closer. Slowly, deliberately.

My boots scuffed against the smooth stone floor, the air trembling as if unsure whether to flee or bow.

"Death," I whispered.

His eyes snapped to me—flaring from molten silver to hollow black, monstrous and bright all at once. The beast and the man warred behind that stare.

Every instinct screamed at me to stay away.

I didn't listen.

I raised my hands, pressing them to his chest. His skin burned cold beneath my palms, shadows rippling under it like a pulse out of sync with the world.

He didn't move. Didn't breathe.

I slid my hands higher, over the hard plane of his chest, to his shoulders. The shadows recoiled, then slithered back, hesitant.

"Stop fighting me," I murmured.

A muscle in his jaw twitched. "You don't understand what I could become."

"I think I do." My voice barely carried. "Do not let the beast come out because of fear."

His form flickered—half shadow, half man—and I saw the creature he fought to cage: wings of smoke, claws tipped in night itself. The sheer *power* of him made my knees weaken. But I stayed. The Wood damn me, I stayed.

Then, before he could turn away, I rose on my toes and kissed him.

Softly. Just a brush of lips.

It was the first time I initiated an intimate moment between us. I had agreed to the bargain, had responded eagerly to him, but had never sought him out first.

His breath caught—sharp, startled. The shadows hissed, swirling in agitation, but I didn't move. I kissed him again, slower this time, until the silver began to win against the black in his eyes.

Until the air shifted—less storm, more silence.

His hands, trembling with restraint, came up to cradle my jaw. When he kissed me back, it wasn't gentle. It was *devastated*.

The taste of him was cold lightning, salt, and grief. Shadows wrapped around us both, but this time they didn't bind. They trembled—like creatures unsure whether to protect or pray.

When he finally tore his mouth from mine, his forehead rested against me. His voice was barely a breath.

"I would burn the realms to keep you safe."

I touched his cheek, my thumb grazing the edge of darkness that still clung there.

"We will find a way to break this curse." I could only whisper the words against his skin. "It will be dangerous, but you don't have to leave me through any of it."

I pulled back enough to look up into his once again silver eyes.

"I…" A hard swallow. "I don't want you to leave through any of it." Death gathered me against his chest, holding me so tight my feet left the floor, and I was reminded just how much taller he was than me. "I feel safer when I know you're with me."

After that, the fury drained from him like ink seeping from a broken pen.

We didn't speak. Didn't need to.

He drew me down with him onto the velvet-dark chair near the shelves behind his ornate desk, his arms still trembling faintly as the last traces of shadow melted from his skin. For a long while we simply sat there—his power humming low and steady, my heartbeat finding its rhythm again against his chest. The Deathscape stilled around us, a rare peace settling where rage had been.

By the time he finally exhaled, I could tell the storm inside him had quieted.

"I'm going to stay with Keyleth," I said softly, fingers tracing the seam of his sleeve. "It isn't safe at the twins' apartment anymore with Matron Black being able to have such easy access. Especially, if she starts suspecting that I took the key."

His gaze flicked to mine—silver again but dimmed by how much magic he had forced into the Living Lands. "The non-Mage," he murmured, and the faint curl of resignation in his tone almost made me smile. "I spent more energy than I'd like being visible in the Black House today. I'll recover, but until you're settled, I'll be watching even if you cannot see me."

I tilted my head. "You know that sounds a lot like being *overprotective*?"

"An accurate description," he said without apology.

I leaned in, brushed my lips against his cheek—a light, fleeting thing. "Try not to terrify any mortals while you're watching, alright?"

His smile was faint but real, shadowed and tired. "No promises."

"Actually," I dug into my pocket and pulled out the crystal sphere, pinching its delicate chain through my fingers. "Can I keep this here? I don't know where else it would be safe, and if Matron Black is actively hunting it, she can probably track its raw-magic signature."

"Of course." Death gracefully plucked it from my hand and set it on the shelf behind his desk. It fit there, blending seamlessly with the other, random artifacts.

"Thanks," I stepped back, feeling the pull of my own magic coil tight in my veins. The air shimmered, silver bleeding into red, then everything folded.

The world lurched.

I stumbled out onto a quiet street in New Town, the faint glow of the streetlamps catching on the low cloud coverage. I'd aimed for the twins' apartment, but my magic clearly had other ideas. The ground swayed beneath me; the edges of my vision sparkled darkly.

Too much.

I'd used too much.

The ache in my body wasn't the pleasant thrum of spent magic—it was deeper, hollower, tugging at the fragile thread that anchored me to the Living Lands. My soul felt thin, stretched.

Not again, I thought. *Not that close.*

I forced a breath, straightened my shoulders, and pulled my phone from my pocket. The screen's glow stung my eyes.

"Hey," I said when Keyleth picked up, trying to sound steadier than I felt. "Can you meet me at the twins'? I, uh...yeah I'm alright. I'll explain, but...after everything with Matron Black, I don't think I can stay there anymore."

Her voice crackled through the line, warm and normal, grounding. "On my way."

I smiled faintly, though my hands shook as I hung up. The night air felt colder than usual, but I told myself it was nothing—just fatigue. Just magic.

And as I started toward the apartment lights in the distance, I ignored the whisper at the back of my mind that said something inside me was beginning to unravel.

By the time I reached the twins' apartment building, the night felt...wrong.

Not dangerous, exactly. Just *off.*

The lights in the stairwell buzzed faintly, shadows pooling too thick at the corners. I could sense the wards of the Black House even here, like invisible threads tugging at my magic, reminding me that the Matron's reach was longer than I liked to admit.

I lifted my hand to the door keypad—and froze.

Something in me whispered, *wait.*

It wasn't fear. Not exactly. More like an ache at the base of my ribs, the kind that came before a haunting.

Phontine materialized beside my shoulder, her violet glow dim under the hall light. "Finally you're back!" I could feel her gaze flitting all around my face, the tightening in my jaw, the pinched set of my lips. "You feel like something's off too?" she asked quietly.

"Yeah." My throat felt tight. "We'll wait for Keyleth."

The Pixie nodded, wings flickering once in agreement. "Probably smart. I don't like how the air tastes here."

So, we waited.

The hallway clock ticked too loud, each minute stretching. When Keyleth's car finally pulled up outside, the sight of her blonde curls in the reflection of the glass door made my shoulders ease. She jogged up the steps, cheeks flushed from the cold.

"Sorry," she said, smiling. "Traffic was awful. You okay?"

"Better now," I admitted, unlocking the door.

We went up together.

The apartment was too quiet when we stepped inside.

Calypso sat curled on the couch, legs tucked under her, a blanket draped across her knees. Pandora stood near the window, arms folded, her expression unreadable. Elias leaned against the wall, dark eyes flicking between them like he'd been part of a conversation that had stopped the moment I walked in.

"Hey," Calypso said, smiling faintly. "You made it back."

"Yeah." My voice came out steadier than I felt.

She gave a small wave to Keyleth who returned it. I glanced over my shoulder at her, but Keyleth stayed by the door. It was like she was afraid of closing us in with them.

Phontine hovered close to my ear. "I'll go pack," she whispered, and zipped off down the hall before anyone noticed.

I took a breath, glancing at Calypso—the friend who had opened her home, shared her coffee, laughed with me when the world felt too heavy. It shouldn't feel strange to be here. It shouldn't feel like standing on the edge of a ledge.

"I need to talk to you," I said. My fingers twisted around the strap of my bag. "All of you."

Calypso straightened, alarm flickering across her face. "What's wrong?"

"The Matron," I said. "She—she trapped me in the House earlier when I said I'd join the House. I don't think it's safe for me to stay here anymore."

The words hung in the air like frost.

Calypso's eyes widened. "She *what?*"

Pandora looked at Elias, unblinking.

"Matron Black used the House wards to keep me there, like she wants. If she can do that, then she can probably reach me through here too. Through you." I swallowed hard, not sure how to take their surprise. "I can't risk it."

Calypso was already shaking her head. "Then you shouldn't stay. I don't want you in danger because of us."

Her answer came so quickly it almost startled me. Relief loosened something in my chest.

But when I looked to Pandora, she didn't nod. Didn't say anything. Neither did Elias. They just *watched* me, silent and still, like they were listening to something I couldn't hear.

The unease returned, sharp and cold.

Calypso turned to them. "Did you hear me? She can't stay here if the Matron can reach her."

Pandora's gaze shifted to her sister then back to me—her eyes too dark in the lamplight. "Where she's staying won't stop the Matron."

I didn't answer. Couldn't.

The discomfort in my chest solidified into something else entirely—instinct.

Something was wrong here. Very wrong.

The silence stretched too long. Pandora's words still hung between us, sour and heavy, so I forced a breath and shifted the conversation before it could curdle further.

"Look, that's not the only reason I came back here," I said. "You need to know what happened after I got out of the House."

Elias's head lifted slightly, curiosity flickering in his eyes. Calypso turned toward me, still frowning.

"I'm actually shocked you're here. After the blood-ward went off, Sonia, if you hadn't gotten out with Matron Black's item..." She swallowed hard, like the memory of Matron Black's reaction was enough to fuel nightmares for a lifetime.

"They did trap me," I cut in. "At least until Elias helped."

Calypso's brows knit. "Elias helped you?"

Her tone held that edge of confusion—like she was hearing it for the first time.

Elias's expression didn't change, but the muscle along his jaw ticked once.

"Yeah," I said, glancing between them. "He got me out of the warded room."

The air thickened a little, tension rippling through the space. Pandora's gaze slid toward Elias, unreadable, and Calypso looked between them both like she was suddenly on the outside of a secret.

I pushed on. "Once I was free, I went to the archives. There's a section below the House most people don't know about. Old, half-buried tunnels that connect under Blakewell."

"That's impossible," Pandora said, voice flat. "The House sits on solid bedrock."

"Apparently not." I met her eyes, holding steady. "I found a way through. And I wasn't alone down there."

Elias's posture shifted—small, but telling.

"What do you mean?" Calypso asked.

"I saw Mages," I said quietly. "Four of them. They were dragging two sacks that looked like..." I hesitated, the image flashing behind my eyelids—those heavy shapes, the muffled sound of something alive inside. "...people. They kept talking about sacrifices to the mist."

Pandora's face didn't move, but Elias's eyes narrowed.

"I think they're connected to whatever's corrupting the mist," I continued. "Maybe even the same ones you two were assigned to investigate."

That got their attention. Both turned to me fully now, their silence sharper than questions.

"I thought you should know," I said, voice low. "Whatever they're doing, it's happening right under the city."

For a long moment, no one spoke. The air pulsed with quiet, electric tension.

Then Elias asked, too calm, "You're certain it was a rogue group?"

"Yes," I said. "No House markings, no identifying sigils. But their magic...it felt old. Wrong."

Pandora finally moved, brushing a hand through her hair. "We'll report it," she said, but her tone was mechanical—an echo, not a promise.

"I should go grab my things," I said, needing an excuse to move, to breathe.

Before I could take a step, Phontine zipped up from the hall, a tiny blur of violet light. "Already done!" she announced proudly, her arms crossed over her chest. "Didn't trust the vibe in there."

A shaky laugh escaped me. "Thanks Phon."

Keyleth was already reaching for one of the rolling suitcases by the door. "Then let's go before that vibe gets worse," she said, tugging the handle up with a snap.

I slung my travel backpack over my shoulder and turned to Calypso. "I'll talk to you soon," I told her softly. "And…thank you. For letting me stay."

Calypso's eyes shone, but her voice was steady. "You always have a place here, Sonia."

I wished I could believe that as easily as she'd said it.

36

I woke to the scent of clay dust and jasmine paint thinner.

Keyleth's spare bedroom was a riot of color and chaos—half art studio, half closet, and somehow still the most welcoming place I'd been in weeks. One wall was completely overtaken by shelves of pottery in various stages of creation—bowls that sagged charmingly to one side, mugs painted with galaxies, and a sculpted cat whose tail had fallen off and had been glued back on with glitter. Sunlight spilled through gauzy curtains the color of honey, turning the air gold.

The narrow twin bed I'd slept in was wedged between a stack of canvases and a dresser splattered in teal and lilac paint. A beaded mobile tinkled softly above my head every time I moved. It was very *Keyleth*—chaotic, enchanting, a little too bright—and I couldn't help but smile.

Still, a quiet ache pulled at my chest.

I missed home.

The creak of my old brownstone's floorboards. The smell of rain on concrete. Even the way my mom's coffee pot wheezed like it was dying every morning.

Gods, I hadn't called her in two weeks. Or was it three?

I sat up fast, tangled in the sheets, and grabbed my phone from the nightstand. My thumbs flew over the screen as I stood and tried to find something that vaguely passed for clean jeans.

> **Me:** *Hey Mom, I'm so sorry I haven't called. Things have been crazy lately, but I'm okay. I promise. Love you.*

I hesitated, added a heart emoji, and hit send.

The silence after felt heavier than it should have.

With a sigh, I pulled on my sweater—an old one for my culinary school days that said *I Came. I Saw. I Sautéed.*—and shoved a black headband onto my head to keep the bangs from my bob out of my eyes. My limbs still ached from the magic I'd burned through yesterday, but I ignored it. I wasn't ready to think about what that meant.

When I stepped out into the hallway, the apartment was quiet. A faint trail of cinnamon and espresso lingered in the air, the telltale signs that Keyleth had already left for her morning shift at The Obsidian Quill.

Typical Keyleth—up with the dawn, probably humming to her plants as she went.

The silence she left behind felt strange, but safe. For now.

The enchanted staircase creaked and hummed under my feet as I descended. Each step shimmered faintly, the air pulsing with soft, blue light that carried me down through the center of Keyleth's old-fashioned clock. The glass face above glowed faintly amber from the morning sun, gears clicking softly as I passed.

The scent hit me first—espresso, cinnamon, and the faintest trace of vanilla sugar. The familiar symphony of The Obsidian Quill.

The coffee shop was alive with the morning rush: chatter, clinking mugs, milk steam hissing behind the counter. The air was a whirl of energy and warmth, sunlight bouncing off mismatched teacups and greenery that crept up the brick walls.

And right in the middle of it—Phontine.

She was lounging in a wide, ceramic mug on a two-seater table by the window, wings half-submerged in a pool of black coffee that steamed gently around her. Her hair was damp, her skin gleaming faintly gold in the light.

"Well, look who finally woke up," she said, stretching like a cat. "I was about to send a search party. Or at least another cup."

I laughed despite myself. "You know that's not sanitary, right?"

She sipped a droplet off her arm and smirked. "For you mortals, maybe, and it's not like I'm sharing this glorious elixir."

Rolling my eyes, I scanned the counter until I spotted Keyleth—her hair piled in a messy bun, apron streaked with flour, moving like organized chaos between the espresso machine and pastry case.

I waited for a lull in the crowd before stepping up. "Hey," I said, "do you...maybe need any help around here?"

She blinked at me, mid-pour. "Help?"

"Yeah. I mean—if you have any open shifts or something. I could use the work, especially since I'm living here now."

Keyleth's expression softened instantly, though there was a flicker of hesitation. "I do have a couple part-time slots open. Nothing steady, though. A few mornings a week."

"That's perfect," I said too quickly.

She smiled, though her eyes searched mine for the real reason. "You sure?"

"Yeah. Anything's good."

I didn't tell her that my bank account was empty. That I'd spent my last twenty on groceries before everything went to hell with the Black House. That the thought of calling my mom for money made my stomach twist with guilt.

Keyleth reached across the counter and squeezed my hand. "Then welcome to the Quill, apprentice barista extraordinaire."

Phontine raised her coffee-soaked hand from across the room in salute, a little ring of coffee sloshing over the rim.

I smiled, but my chest still ached.

At least for now, I had somewhere to belong.

"Hey," Keyleth's tinkling voice had me turning around. "Here, on the house."

"Oh, no." I was already shaking my head. "Key—"

"It's a thank you." Keyleth practically shoved the lavender-scented, foam latte into my hands.

"For what?"

"I've wanted a roomie ever since I came to Blakewell." Keyleth winked at me, steam from the espresso maker puffing around her. "You made my dream come true."

A little stunned, with a small smile pulling at my lips, I carried my coffee over to the little, two-seater table by the window and sank into the chair across from Phontine. She was still luxuriating in her oversized mug, wings spread lazily over the rim, steam curling around her like a halo.

"Comfortable?" I asked, raising a brow.

Phontine sighed dramatically, dunking herself until only her head and the tips of her wings were visible. "Darling, if I could live in coffee, I would. It's the only form of mortal alchemy worth respecting."

I laughed softly and took a sip of my own cup. The morning hum of the Quill swirled around us—laughter, clinking spoons, the smell of cinnamon and chocolate. For a moment, it almost felt like normal life.

Phontine tilted her head, eyeing me over the edge of her makeshift bath. "You realize we've been in Blakewell all of, what, two and a half months? And somehow, we've lived in half the city already. House hopping, curse dodging, ghost whispering—really getting the full tour."

I smiled, shaking my head. "Yeah. But out of everywhere we've stayed, I think crashing with Keyleth is my favorite. There's something about the chaos that feels...safe."

Phontine flicked a tiny droplet of coffee in my direction. "You're just saying that because she keeps feeding us pastries."

"Maybe," I said, grinning.

We let the quiet settle between us for a while, the noise of the café fading into background warmth. I watched the light shift through the window, tracing gold across the steam of her cup.

Then I said it before I could talk myself out of it. "You've been gone longer lately."

Phontine froze mid-stretch, one wing still half-unfurled.

I pushed on, softer. "During your recharging. You're gone longer than you've ever been, and I..." I swallowed. "I worry about you."

She tried for a smirk, the usual mischief flickering back to life. "Worried I've found a more glamorous Whisperer to haunt?"

"Phon," I said quietly. "I can't lose you too."

Her expression softened instantly. I stared down at my coffee, words tumbling out before I could stop them. "Everything keeps changing. The House, the curse, Mc-Dara...Death...I don't even know what's happening between us anymore. I just—" My voice broke a little. "I need to know you're okay."

The Pixie's teasing melted away. She fluttered up out of the mug and landed on the table beside my cup, her tiny hands resting on the rim.

"Hey," she said gently. "Look at me."

I did.

"I'm okay," she said firmly. "Really. I've just been taking longer breaks because the mist's been draining my magic faster than usual. It's like the air itself is heavier lately. But it's nothing you need to worry about, got it?"

"Phon—"

"I mean it," she said, touching my finger with her tiny hand. "You keep worrying about the curse or your very strange love life. Let me handle me."

I nodded slowly, though something in her tone lingered—like she was trying to convince herself, too.

Still, I let the warmth of her reassurance settle in. For the first time in days, I almost believed that maybe—just maybe—we'd be okay.

Phontine was in the middle of explaining how bean-water enlightenment could cure all mortal ailments, when the bell over the Quill's door jingled—and my breath caught before I even looked up.

McDara and Dom.

They cut through the morning crowd like they didn't belong to it—McDara in his usual dark coat, collar turned up against the cold, hair slightly mussed as if he hadn't bothered with sleep, Dom beside him, all warmth and swagger, flashing smiles that could melt glaciers and probably did.

They ordered at the counter, Dom leaning far too casually against it, and for one wild moment, I thought maybe—maybe—they wouldn't see me.

But then Dom's gaze swept the room. And landed right on me.

"Ah, there she is!" he said, grinning wide enough to draw half the café's attention. "Our favorite trouble magnet and her sparkly sidekick!"

Phontine groaned into her cup. "Oh, wonderful. The muscles and the brooding one."

McDara followed Dom's lead, his eyes finding mine. That familiar heaviness settled in my chest—the way he looked at me, like he'd been trying not to.

They dragged another two-seater table across the floor and shoved it next to ours, ignoring the barista's withering glare. The screech of metal legs on tile made Phontine wince.

"Morning, Sonia," McDara said. His voice was softer than I remembered, rough at the edges. "Glad to see you made it out of the Black House."

"I did," I said carefully, setting my cup down. "Eventually."

He nodded, eyes flicking down, then back up to me. "I tried to get the Matron to let you leave with me. She wasn't having it."

Something in my chest twisted. "That sounds about right."

Dom whistled low, settling into his chair like he owned the place. "Honestly, it's a miracle you *did* get out. You've got to tell us—how the hell did you pull that off?"

I glanced between them—Dom's eager curiosity, McDara's quiet, watchful intensity—and decided on the short version.

"Elias opened the warded door," I said. "Got me out before anyone noticed. I made it to the archives and found a tunnel that led under the House. It goes deeper than I thought—under half of Blakewell, maybe more."

Dom's brows rose. "And you just...followed it?"

"Yeah," I said. "And I wasn't alone down there."

McDara leaned forward. "What do you mean?"

"I think I saw them," I said quietly. "The rogue Mages. The ones behind the mist corruption. They were dragging two sacks—heavy ones. Talking about sacrifices."

For a heartbeat, the noise of the café faded. Dom's easy grin faltered. McDara's eyes darkened.

"Bloody hell," Dom muttered. "You're sure?"

"As sure as I can be," I said. "Their magic didn't feel right. Twisted. Wrong."

McDara sat back slowly, his gaze distant now, calculating. "We should check the tunnels. See if they're still there."

Phontine dipped a wing in her cup, muttering, "You mortals really know how to ruin a good coffee."

That pulled a small laugh from me—thin, but real. McDara's mouth curved, almost smiling, and for one flicker of a heartbeat, it felt like old times again.

McDara's gaze lingered on me a little too long, the world narrowing until it was just his eyes and the low hum of the Quill around us.

"I'm glad you made it out of those tunnels," he said quietly, the sincerity in his voice catching me off guard. "Before anyone saw you."

The weight behind his words made my pulse hitch.

Then his tone sharpened, quiet but cutting. "You're sure no one saw you, Sonia?"

That intensity—fierce, protective, almost desperate—made it hard to breathe.

I nodded. "I'm sure. Death cloaked me in shadows. They couldn't have seen a thing."

I didn't miss the flash of something sharp and twisted behind McDara's eyes at me mentioning Death.

Dom leaned back in his chair, breaking the tension with an easy grin. "Then that's something. The tunnels are a good lead. Word is some of the other units might already be checking them out."

I frowned. "Other units?"

McDara sighed, rubbing the back of his neck. "After the big incident with the mist—when it failed over half the city—the chief reassigned nearly every available officer and detective to root out what's causing it. What's behind the failures, the mist itself. All of it."

My stomach tightened. "But...we *know* what's causing it. The mist isn't failing—it's being controlled. Orchestrated by the Mage Council and powered through the Black House. We've seen the evidence."

His expression hardened. "The chief doesn't know that. And if I said anything, it'd be my word against the Mage Council's. Against a House like the Black House."

Dom gave a low whistle. "Not exactly a career-saving move."

McDara's eyes flicked to mine again. "It's better to find the group that's tampering with the mist. Expose *them*, and we might finally have something the Council can't bury."

I wanted to argue—wanted to scream that the rot started at the top—but all that came out was a slow nod. "I get it."

The table fell quiet.

Phontine dipped her wings into the cooling coffee, pretending not to be bothered, though her glow dimmed in sympathy.

McDara cleared his throat after a moment, his fingers drumming once against the table. "There's...something else."

That tone. Careful. Hesitant.

I knew I wasn't going to like whatever came next.

He exhaled, eyes darting briefly to Dom before returning to me. "With the reassignment orders, Dr. Fenwick's case is being closed."

The words hit like a punch to the ribs.

"What?"

"The chief signed off this morning. Official reason: insufficient evidence."

My pulse roared in my ears. "That's impossible. You *know* it wasn't a random mugging or whatever bullshit they've labeled it as. He was murdered."

"I know," McDara said softly. "But it's out of my hands now."

Dom shifted uncomfortably, gaze sliding toward the window. Even he didn't have a joke for this.

I sat back, staring at the steam curling from my forgotten cup, the bitterness settling deep in my chest. Dr. Fenwick's face flickered behind my eyes—the gentle patience, the quiet warnings, the way his blood had soaked the university's steps.

Out of his hands.

Maybe.

But it sure as hell wasn't out of mine.

The words barely settled before I was already leaning forward. "You don't get it—Dr. Fenwick might've been killed because of me."

Both men froze. Even Phontine stopped her lazy floating and looked at me sharply.

"What are you talking about?" McDara asked. "I know that he wanted to tell you about Grace—"

"Last night," I interrupted, my voice trembling despite my best effort to steady it, "Matron Black told me that she'd had him working on finding a cure to my bloodline curse. If that's true, then—"

"Then someone didn't want him to find it," Dom finished quietly, all the humor gone from his tone. He sat back in his chair, the usual grin replaced with something grim. "Damn. That actually tracks."

McDara's jaw flexed. "It does," he admitted. "If he was close to something—if he was close to finding a way to break it—someone might've wanted him silenced."

The table went still, the sound of the café fading beneath the pounding in my ears.

"He didn't die from magic," McDara added after a moment. "He was stabbed. Multiple wounds. Brutal, deliberate." His gaze met mine, steady but heavy. "There's nothing that ties it directly to the Black House. No witnesses. No evidence."

"So that's it?" My voice cracked. "He dies trying to help me, and the House gets to pretend it was random violence?"

McDara looked away first. Dom stared into his coffee like it might offer an answer. Neither of them looked convinced, but neither could say what we were all thinking aloud.

I pressed a hand to my chest, trying to ease the tightness there. "Why would anyone go that far just to make sure I die at twenty-five? Why is it so important that I do?"

No one had an answer.

The question hung between us like smoke, bitter and suffocating, until even the warmth of the Quill couldn't touch me anymore.

The silence stretched, heavy and bitter, until Dom finally leaned forward, elbows on the table. "Hey," he said, his tone gentler than usual. "For what it's worth…when we talked to Dr. Fenwick's ghost, he told us what he probably would've told you that night. Any information he had you got."

I blinked, lifting my head and managing a nod. "Yeah, you're probably right."

Across the table, Phontine gasped, wings fluttering so fast she sent a ripple through her coffee. "Wow, you *summoned* the doc? Like, intentionally? What have I missed while I was recharging?"

"Apparently everything," I muttered, rubbing my forehead. A dull ache had started behind my eyes—the kind that came from too many emotions crashing at once.

McDara's voice cut through, calm but firm. "Sonia. We're still following the plan. Fenwick's message, Grace's ledger—they line up. We have the key now. The next step is Larkend."

I lowered my hand, meeting his gaze. That quiet certainty in his tone was comforting to hear, even as exhaustion pressed down like a weight.

"We'll find what Grace was after," he said. "We'll finish what she started."

Phontine straightened in her cup, her glow dim but determined. "Guess that means we're going ghost hunting in the cursed town over."

Despite everything, a faint smile tugged at my lips. "Guess it does."

But beneath the flicker of hope, the ache in my head pulsed harder, whispering a truth I couldn't shake—

Something about this plan felt like walking straight into the dark.

Dom's phone buzzed against the table, the sound cutting through the lull in conversation. He grimaced when he glanced at the screen.

"Sorry," he muttered, already standing. "It's from the Pride. We've been having a rough go since the mist incident—territorial disputes, half our patrols grounded. If I don't answer, they'll think I'm dead."

"Wouldn't want that," Phontine mumbled from her cup, her voice thick with sleep.

Dom gave her a lazy salute, then looked at me. "Don't go planning world-damning missions without me."

I forced a small smile. "No promises."

He winked and disappeared through the door, the little bell chiming behind him.

The quiet that followed felt different—denser somehow. The air between McDara and me carried a kind of fragile gravity.

Phontine was half-submerged in her coffee, eyes closed, wings twitching softly like she was dreaming.

McDara leaned forward, elbows on the table, studying me with that steady, measured look that always seemed to see too much. "If I showed you a map of the tunnels," he said slowly, "do you think you could mark where you saw the rogue Mages?"

I blinked, thrown off by the sudden shift back to work. "Maybe? But...I'm kind of directionally challenged," I admitted, a faint laugh escaping me. "I can't give directions to save my life. But if we were down there, I could find the spot again. Sort of a muscle-memory thing."

He nodded thoughtfully, rubbing the edge of his thumb over his knuckle—a habit I'd seen a thousand times when he was thinking something through that he probably shouldn't.

"This is probably one of my worst ideas," he said finally, looking up. "But would you be willing to go back into the tunnels with me? Just to scout the location. Nothing more."

The request hit me like a soft punch to the chest.

I hesitated, glancing toward the window where sunlight fractured through the glass. The thought of those tunnels—cold, humming with old magic—made my stomach twist.

And then another thought hit me.

I'd be alone with McDara. For hours, probably. Tight spaces. His magic brushing mine. His voice echoing through the dark.

Once, that would've made my pulse quicken in ways I'd try not to think about.

A part of me still thrilled at the idea—some stubborn muscle memory of wanting him, of craving the steadiness he brought into the chaos.

But most of me didn't.

That was the strangest part.

The feelings that used to burn so bright now felt like ghosts themselves—familiar shapes without warmth. This not-falling-for-McDara-anymore thing still felt foreign, like I was wearing someone else's skin.

I looked down at my hands, trying to ground myself in the present. The ache in my chest spread—grief for Fenwick, anger for the lies, exhaustion that ran bone-deep. And beneath it all, something else: the faint brush of energy across my neck, like a fingertip tracing my skin.

I froze.

That feeling. Familiar. Ancient.

Death.

He was watching—just as he'd promised.

The thought steadied me somehow, even as it sent a chill through my veins.

But then McDara added quietly, "If the mist fails again, we won't just be dealing with injuries. People will die. Maybe a lot of them."

That broke through my hesitation. Being alone with McDara in the tunnels wouldn't mean the same thing that it would have a month ago. We were friends now. Just friends.

I lifted my gaze to McDara's. "Alright," I said. "We'll go. But only to scout."

His jaw flexed once in what might have been relief, though his eyes told another story—something heavier, something that hurt to look at.

"Only to scout," he agreed.

Phontine snorted softly, one wing twitching out of her cup. "Famous last words," she murmured.

Neither of us corrected her.

Dom returned with his phone pressed to his ear, his expression hard. "We've gotta go," he said, cutting off whatever McDara was about to say. "The mist's failed in Lion Pact territory—it's not coming back up."

McDara's chair scraped across the floor. "How bad?"

"Bad enough that the Pride's losing control of their borders. Chief's sending containment teams, but..." Dom's jaw flexed. "You know how that goes."

McDara was already on his feet, coffee forgotten. "Let's move."

They both turned to me, Dom offering a quick, strained grin. "Bye, Sonia."

"Be safe," I said softly.

And then they were gone—two shadows swallowed by the morning light.

The quiet that followed hummed through my ribs.

I didn't stay long after that. The ache of doing nothing was worse than exhaustion itself, and the weight of Grace's ledger in my bag was a constant pulse at my side. I couldn't avoid the university forever. It was the best place to research something from Grace's ledger. That is, if I found anything new to research.

Phontine fluttered alongside me as we made our way through Blakewell's city center. The air smelled of roasted chestnuts and morning fog still clinging to the streetlamps.

And then the lights dimmed.

The air changed—thicker, colder.

He was there.

He appeared beside the fountain—like the shadows themselves decided to remember what form they once wore.

My heart lifted before I could stop it. "Hey," I said softly. "You keeping your promise?"

For a moment, he said nothing. His presence should have been comforting—like it was lately—but the magic rolling off him was jagged, volatile. His eyes burned silver-bright, and the shadows around him writhed like living smoke.

Then I realized: this wasn't calm. This was *anger*.

"Why are you upset?" I asked carefully.

That was all it took.

His temper *snapped*.

"Why?" His voice was thunder cracking in an empty hall. "Because you parade through the city with your Mage again. Because you think you can toy with me while keeping your options open."

The words hit low, cruel.

His temper hit like a stormfront, shadows clawing into the cobblestones, black veins of magic spreading beneath our feet. The outline of his shadow-beast flared—a skeletal thing of wings and talons overlaying his form.

Phontine darted behind my shoulder, whispering, "Oh, this is not good—"

I took a breath, fighting the pulse of my own magic rising in defense. "Stop it. You think this is about keeping my options open? I'm working with McDara because I saw what happened when the mist failed!"

The shadows hesitated, twisting in place as if listening.

"I was there," I went on, voice shaking. "I saw the panic. The screaming. I was almost trampled. I saw Magicals getting beaten in the streets because humans were terrified. You don't get to accuse me of *playing* when I'm trying to stop that from happening again!"

His form flickered—skin shifting between the silvery pale I knew and the dark translucence of the beast beneath. He towered over me, a living eclipse, but I refused to step back.

I got right in his face, voice trembling. "The fact that I've fallen asleep in your arms more times than I can count this week should be proof enough that I'm not trying to get McDara—who *doesn't want me*—back!"

The air went still.

His eyes widened, the fury faltering into something raw and unguarded. The shock on his face was startling. Like the thought that I wouldn't betray him was a foreign concept, and maybe in a place like the Deathscape it was.

The shadows recoiled, sinking back into the cracks they'd carved.

For the first time since I'd met him, Death had no words.

My throat ached. "Leave me alone," I whispered.

He watched me walk away. The feeling of his eyes pinned on my back following me until the city swallowed me whole.

37

The rest of the day blurred.

Veritas University loomed gray and solemn under the autumn sky, its clock tower striking noon as Phontine and I climbed the marble steps. My chest felt tight the whole way up. The library steps—steeped and gilded with wards—were completely clean where Dr. Fenwick had died. Like it had never happened. Like it was just a bad dream I was still waiting to wake from.

I stopped there for a long time. Just breathing.

Then I pushed through.

Phontine and I spent hours buried in Grace's ledger—page after page of messy scrawl, half-translated notes, experiments written in a shorthand even the archivists would've struggled with. Margins filled with odd phrases that sounded more like prayers than notes: *the root remembers, the blood answers, the gate must drink to open.*

Somewhere between the alchemical diagrams and the erratic sketches of sigils, I found something different—two pages that had been glued together and half-torn apart. Inside, a map. Rough, but unmistakable.

Larkend.

And beneath it...fissures. Like veins spider-webbing through the page.

Grace and David had written that Larkend wasn't just built on a wellspring of raw magic—it *was* the heart of it. The place where the old magic first broke through the crust of the world. That it was here before the Three Great Woods appeared. From there, it spread out in lines—ley lines—radiating like fractures in glass. And one of those lines cut straight through Blakewell.

Phontine hovered over my shoulder, frowning. "So, Blakewell's sitting on one of the cracks?"

"Not just sitting on it," I murmured, tracing the ink-stained line with my finger. "It's connected. Maybe even feeding off it."

It made sense in a way that terrified me. The constant hum of magic in the city, the strange pull the Black House had always exerted. If the same current that pulsed beneath Larkend flowed under Blakewell...then everything Grace was researching—the curse, the experiments, the deaths—it all circled back to this.

None of it made sense yet. Not fully. But it was starting to form a pattern, and I wasn't sure I wanted to see what the shape would be.

By the time we left, my head was pounding and my heart felt like it had been wrung out.

That night, the three of us—me, Phontine, and Keyleth—curled up in her living room. The scent of popcorn and jasmine candles filled the air, a movie flickering across the wall. Keyleth had passed out twenty minutes in, blanket tangled around her, hair up on top of her head in a protective styler for her curls that she called The Pineapple. Phontine was snoring softly from her tiny nest in an empty teacup.

I was the only one awake.

And angry.

Still angry.

My eyes stayed on the movie, but I wasn't seeing it. All I could think about was *him.*

That he'd think so little of me. That he'd believe I'd play with him and McDara like they were pieces on some emotional chessboard.

The words had been sharp because they were meant to wound—and gods, they had.

Because if I looked too closely, the worst part was that a tiny, ugly voice inside me whispered, *maybe he's not wrong.*

Maybe I was stringing them along. Because I *did* care about them both.

No.

I shut that thought down fast, dragging a shaky hand through my hair. I wasn't stringing McDara along because he made it very clear that while I was cursed, we could only be friends, and I...was becoming okay with that. And Death—that stupid, territorial reaper—shouldn't be jealous! I had kissed him more times than McDara. Had let him touch me in ways no one had in a long while, but yet here he was getting all pissy and going beast mode on me.

The ache in my chest flared as I stood, going into my room and gathering clothes and my toiletries for a shower.

That was when the shadows stirred.

He appeared near the doorway, half-formed, like the air itself was trying to block him out of my space.

"Come to me," Death said softly.

I lifted my chin. "Not now."

His head tilted. "Sonia." The way he said my name—low, rough, like it cost him something—scraped across my nerves. "Come to me."

I ignored him, clutching my clothes tighter, and headed for the bathroom.

Then the air *folded.*

A heartbeat later, the world shifted—cold wind, red horizon, and the sound of whispering sand.

The Deathscape.

His study. Huge desk with its shelves climbing to arched stone walls into shadows, laden down with odd trinkets and relics of forgotten lives. Before me was the wide expanse of the room. It's center clear of everything but a pedestal that held a small glass sphere and Death. My eyes halted as they caught sight of him, the tomes lining the rest of the walls in this room forgotten at one look at him.

I stumbled, breath catching, and his arms caught me before I could fall. His touch was ice and heat all at once. My clothes and toiletries tumbling to the floor.

"Death," I snapped, shoving at his chest. "You can't just—"

But he was already moving, lifting me with an ease that made protest useless.

With one step we were by a stone wall that held something reflective, but my attention couldn't stray for even a half second from him. He steadied me on my feet but kept me caged between his arms.

"Let me go," I hissed, trying to twist free.

"Not yet." His voice was low, frayed around the edges but his hands left me at once. He still stood close enough for me to smell the night-dark scent of his shadows. "Not until I say what I should've said earlier."

I went still.

The red sands of the Deathscape bled in a red shine from what must have been a sizable mirror behind him. I was still angry, still shaken—but the moment he leaned closer, the world seemed to contract to the span of his reach.

He didn't speak right away. He only looked at me, eyes bright silver and full of that dark hunger that made my pulse stumble. Shadows rolled off him like smoke, curling around his body, curling around *me*.

When he finally spoke, his voice was low enough to scrape across my nerves.

"I hate that I upset you."

It wasn't an apology. Not really. But there was something raw in the words, something that sounded like confession.

He moved closer, slow, predatory. "I hate that you looked at me like you wanted to disappear. I don't ever want to see that again."

"Then maybe don't say things meant to hurt," I managed, though my voice barely carried.

His smile was faint, dangerous. "That's the thing, Little Bird. I don't always know how not to. It is... I will learn what upsets you. And until I do, I know how to make you forget the hurt."

My breath caught as he leaned down, bracing his hands on either side of me, trapping me in the scent of cold endless magic and storm. "I plan to be very good to you. That you'll forgive me before you realize you have."

"Death..." My warning came out soft, unsteady.

He tilted his head, eyes glinting. "You don't believe me?"

The air between us buzzed—magic, tension, want, all tangled together. The threat of his touch was everywhere: in the way his shadows brushed my wrists, in the way his gaze traced my mouth like a promise.

"I don't want your games," I whispered.

"I'm not playing," he said, his tone darkly tender. "Everything I do to you is real."

My pulse stuttered. The Deathscape itself seemed to hold its breath.

And even as I glared at him, furious at his arrogance, a part of me—the foolish, aching part that still needed him—leaned toward the danger anyway.

His next breath touched my cheek—cool and endless, like the exhale of the Deathscape itself. "You shouldn't look at me like that," he murmured.

"Like what?"

"Like you want to be ruined."

Before I could speak, his mouth crashed into mine.

It wasn't gentle. It was a clash of want and fury and need so sharp it stole the air from my lungs. His hands framed my face, fingers sliding into my hair, holding me there as though he feared I might vanish if he let go. Shadows poured over my skin, cool and alive, dragging shivers down my spine until I was trembling against him.

I should have pushed him away. I *meant* to. But the moment his tongue brushed mine, every thought dissolved into the taste of storm and starlight.

"Death—"

He swallowed the sound, kissing me harder, rougher. His teeth grazed my lower lip, a dark promise behind the pain. The ache in my chest twisted into something molten, something reckless.

My palms slammed against his chest to shove him back—but instead, they fisted in his shirt.

He made a low sound, something between a growl and a groan, and deepened the kiss until the Deathscape itself seemed to sway with us. The world narrowed to the heat of his mouth, the pull of his shadows coiling around my waist, the pulse of my own betraying heartbeat hammering, *yes, yes, yes.*

When I finally tore my mouth from his, my breath came ragged. His forehead rested against mine, his voice a whisper that scraped against my bones.

"Still angry?"

"Yes," I breathed, though it came out closer to a sigh than defiance.

He leaned in until his lips brushed mine again, that dark, velvet tone threading through every word. "Then I suppose I'll have to try harder to earn your forgiveness."

The promise in his voice wasn't sweet—it was dangerous. A vow wrapped in sin. His shadows stirred at his feet like smoke answering a command, slipping up my thighs, my waist, until I could hardly breathe from how close he was.

"Death—"

He silenced me with another kiss, deeper this time—slower, devastating. Every movement deliberate, coaxing, undoing. His hands gripped my hips, dragging me closer, as if proximity alone might burn away the anger between us.

And maybe it did.

Because when his mouth left mine and found the hollow of my throat, whispering, *"You'll forgive me and you'll be begging me to accept it when I'm through, Little Bird,"* against my pulse, all I could do was tremble and surrender to the beautiful, impossible ruin of him.

His hands slid to my waist, fingers biting in hard, and he spun me around, his front pressed to my back, and I could feel every hard, delicious line of him.

"Look at the mirror," he said, voice low. Command threaded with reverence.

I obeyed—because gods help me, I wanted to.

The mirror loomed in front of me, gilded in a red tint from the desert beyond this mountain palace. It was angled to the mountains, but before I could see what it was used to watch for, a tendril of shadows titled it. My own reflection stared back, flushed and trembling. Lips parted. Eyes wide.

"Do you see her?" he whispered, heat ghosting across my spine. "That girl in the glass?"

I swallowed. Nodded.

"She's mine," he growled. "And I want you to watch what that means."

His hands slid over my waist, dragging me back against him. My gasp fogged the mirror—just before his mouth found my neck, his hips grinding into me with slow, devastating promise.

I watched it all.

Watched his hands roam like they'd been starved. Large hands tugging at the thin straps of my tank top until they were pulled off my shoulders. My breasts bared for him and the chilled air of this realm, nipples pebbling instantly. And then I felt the warmth of his palms as he slid those hands over me. A kneading, long, graceful finger pinched the tight peaks until I shuddered against him, then tugged with a sharp motion, and I had to bite my lip to keep the whimper from escaping. He smiled against my hair like he knew I was trying my damnedest to have no response to him and failing. I watched my own body arch into the contact, shameless and begging.

"Look," he breathed. "Look at what you do to me."

His eyes met mine in the mirror—silver, ruined, *hungry.*

Then he pressed his hip against my backside again, and the steel curve of his desire dug into me, and I couldn't keep the whimpering want from leaving my lips.

"Let yourself enjoy this, my Sonia," he all but growled into my ear, breath hot and teeth sharp on my neck. "Let me please you."

I couldn't tear my gaze away.

"You think you're the one unraveling?" His voice was frayed now. "I've been breaking for you since the moment you let me touch you."

He spun me, lifting me onto the desk behind us—directly across from the mirror.

Then he dropped to his knees.

My breath caught. My legs opened. And he—

"Oh." The soft, breathless word fell from me as he placed a kiss over my panties through my thin lounge shorts, right where my throbbing clit was.

His eyes lifted and pinned my hazy gaze as he slid those shorts down and off me.

"Look at the mirror, Sonia." I did, and he lifted one of my legs, bending it and stretching far enough to drape over the corner of his desk. I was opened wide at the perfect angle to watch as he lowered his head, his fingers digging into my leg, and kissed the inside of my thigh. "I've been wanting to try something. To see what you taste like. What sweet sounds you'll give me like this."

He skimmed up my thigh with searing kisses and little nipping bites from teeth that were sharper than any humans. The sensation had me trembling.

As his searching mouth got to the juncture of my leg, he ran his tongue against the seam of my panties, barely an inch from where I needed him to be.

I felt my breathing speed up; my hands were gripping the onyx stone of his desk hard enough to make my nails ache.

"Still angry, Little Bird?"

"Just—" I huffed out a sigh that was more growl than anything. "Please, I need…"

He lifted his head, watching me, waiting for me to finish my sentence as his hand replaced his mouth. He traced my mound and slipped ever closer to my opening without touching it.

"If you're trying to make me like you, this teasing isn't working." I growled, feeling my nostrils flare.

A wicked, amused grin graced his lips, and I wanted to kick him. Or pull his face closer to where I wanted it.

"Would this"—his finger pressed down hard on my clit—"make you forgive me?"

I shuddered, head nodding and hips canting as he began to rub me in agonizingly slow circles.

My gaze flicked back to the mirror to see the god of death kneeling before me, all but demanding I forgive him because the thought of me being mad at him was something he couldn't stand.

I looked back down at him, at how his pupils had blown so wide there wasn't any silver left.

"Please," I whimpered, pouring all of my need into the way I watched him. "Please I need it."

"Need what, my Sonia?" Death's breathing was becoming as ragged as mine. "Tell me and you can have it." Another kiss to my inner thigh, and the pressure of his finger increased, pulling a low moan from me. "Anything you want. Ask for it and it's yours."

"I want," I swallowed on the words, but any embarrassment I might have had was leaking out of me with the dampness soaking my panties. "I need your mouth on me."

Death's finger pulled away, and I wanted to scream at the lack of friction, and then the heat of his mouth replaced the teasing circles.

"Here?"

"Yes."

"And what would you want me to do with this delicious little—"

I reached my hand down, fingers threaded roughly into his hair, and smashed his mouth onto my panties.

A deep chuckle was his first response, the second was to hook his finger into the sides of my panties and rip them off me.

I nearly sighed with relief and melted off his desk as the heat of his mouth met my skin.

"Watch," he growled between breaths. "Watch what you taste like on my tongue."

I moaned—body writhing, thighs trembling, unable to look away.

He sucked on my clit hard, once, twice, three times before moving away to slick every inch of my core that he could reach. It was like he was memorizing me, tasting every bit of skin he could find, and I was shaking above him.

He smiled against my skin. "That's it. Break for me."

When he returned to my clit and sucked again, my legs snapped closed around his head.

His muffled groan told me how much he liked that, but I didn't care. I didn't think I could have forced my legs apart if I wanted to, and as I felt the tip of one long, thick finger circling my entrance, all thought turned to putty in my mind.

He pressed into me and the sounds that left me were erotic, foreign, but I couldn't dwell on it as he curled that finger, just like he did the last time his hands were on me.

Death might not have touched anyone in this millennia, but he learned fast, and he knew just the spot inside of me that made my vision blur and my breath turn to near screams.

He released the suction on my clit, and I felt the pad of his tongue flatten against me and drag up, flicking my clit with each pass.

"*Yes, yes.*" It was a chant that filled his study, my hands fisted his hair to keep from falling back onto his desk. I didn't want anything to keep the delicious pressure from building inside of me, and it felt like I was going to explode there was so much sensation. My spine was tingling with a white-hot need that curled from my belly and sent shocks through my body to my fingers clutching Death to me.

"Yes, please, don't stop."

Death inserted another finger, and the feeling of fullness had my core clutching around him. His delighted moans vibrated my clit, and soon he was sucking on it again, the sharp points of his teeth adding just a spark of danger that I couldn't stop myself from falling over the edge. Pressure exploded into my core and shot through my body. Completely encasing me in bliss.

I barely felt Death pull away and gently slide his fingers from me. My body was shaking from blissful aftershocks, and the cool substance of his shadows was the only thing holding me upright on the desk.

My eyes opened, blurry and disoriented. I had never come that hard in my life, but leave it to Death to wring that much pleasure out of me.

He kissed my thigh like it was sacred.

Only then did he rise.

He stood between my legs, flushed and *wild*. His cock strained against his pants in a hard, long line, but he made no move to free himself.

I blinked, my hazy mind shocked at the lack of...expectation from him. Twice now he had touched me with no demand that I return the action.

As my body went limp and sagged on his desk, he slipped his arm around me, and I nearly cooed at the contact.

Then his fingers, the ones that had been inside of me and still held my scent, pinched my chin and lifted my head until I met his gaze.

"Are you still angry?"

A breathless laugh sparked in my chest and floated around us.

"If that is how you apologize, then I should be mad at you more often."

The wolfish grin that looked down at me was edged, still hungry and waiting.

"No," I smoothed my hands up his chest and lend forward. "I'm not angry at you anymore." Then I caught his lips in a kiss.

His kiss still held yearning, need, and I remembered that the first time he had touched me like this he had bundled me up immediately and cuddled me off to sleep. As his arms began lifting me, cradling me to his chest, I knew that I wouldn't be satisfied until I got to touch him. Make him feel an ounce of the pleasure he had just wrung from me.

Death made quick work of walking down the dark hallways to his room, and as I predicted, began tucking me under the shadow-soft covers, laying out his body on top and pulling me to his chest.

The quiet between us felt alive—restless, charged. Death's arm was wrapped around me, holding me close, but his magic wouldn't still. It rippled beneath his skin, pulsing against me like a heartbeat that didn't belong to the living. Every rise of his chest came slower than the last, heavier, as though he were fighting something inside himself.

Beneath my cheek, I could feel it—the faint thrum of power in his veins, quickening. His blood was pounding, his magic straining like a storm begging to be unleashed. And yet...he didn't move. Didn't reach for me.

He just held me.

Even with all that dark energy trembling through him, Death stayed utterly still, his control absolute. He hadn't brought me here to take anything from me. He only meant to hold me—steady, protective, and achingly human in the one way he would never admit.

And gods help me, that restraint was somehow more intoxicating than anything else.

My fingers drifted without thinking, tracing idle patterns over the dark fabric of his shirt. Each breath drew the scent of him deeper—storm, shadow, the faint metallic sweetness of magic.

When I began to slip the first button free, his body went rigid.

The air changed—sharper, quieter.

I looked up, catching the flash of silver in his eyes. "Can I not touch you?" I asked softly.

For a moment he only stared at me, as if the question didn't translate into a language he understood. "You...want to touch me?"

The words came out rough, almost disbelieving.

I nodded, my hand still resting against the solid warmth of his chest. "I do. You're always the one holding me, shielding me, giving—" I swallowed. "I just want you to know what it feels like when someone reaches back."

The shadows around us trembled, tightening, and his eyes were pinned on me. His body unmoving but for the sharp racing of his magic across his skin.

He drew in a breath that sounded like the first he'd taken in centuries, his voice a low murmur against my hair. "You would do that...for me?"

"Yes," I whispered. "Because I...I want you to feel pleasure too."

He closed his eyes, the faintest shiver running through him, and for once there was no darkness in it—only wonder. When he looked down at me again, his expression was raw, reverent.

"Then," he said quietly, "touch me."

And when I did, his breath hitched—not from hunger this time, but from something far rarer for Death himself.

Awe.

I nodded, my hand still resting against the solid warmth of his chest.

His skin was pale—too pale, as if it remembered moonlight better than blood. Beneath it, lean muscle shifted, all controlled power and impossible grace. When I brushed my fingers over him, his breath caught—soft, sharp, almost human.

It was like touching the edge of a storm.

His magic lived under his skin, alive and aware, drawn to the contact as if it recognized me. It moved with heat and chill all at once, curling around my fingertips in silver currents that shimmered faintly in the dim light.

I could *feel* him—his pulse, his restraint, the quiet thunder of energy barely contained. Every line of him was honed, carved by centuries of power, but under my touch he trembled, the faintest shiver that betrayed how much this moment costed him.

He looked down at me then, and for a heartbeat, Death didn't look immortal. His eyes, usually so sharp and distant, had gone soft—silver turned liquid, threaded with wonder.

When I traced the hollow of his collarbone, the movement slow, reverent, his lips parted like he'd forgotten how to breathe. His magic flared against my skin, bright and tender and utterly undone.

For the first time, I realized he wasn't made of cold and shadow.

He was alive in his own way—burning, restless, aching to be *known*.

And I was the only one who ever had.

I let my fingertips trail down to his abs, stacks of well-defined muscle that had my mouth watering. I painted each one with my fingerprint, ghosting a circle around his belly button, watching his muscles constrict and flex at my passing touch.

Then I slid my hand down to the waistband of his night-dark pants. I didn't see a button or a zipper, so in a quiet voice, throatier than I realized from my own screaming earlier, I asked him to take them off.

Death looked at me, my request sitting in the air between us. His chest rose and fell in quick succession, but I didn't see panic in his face, only the dulled, glazed look of someone enjoying being touched for the first time in too long.

I didn't want him to wait a second longer to have my touch on him, and I selfishly wanted to feel the heavy weight of him in my hand, not just pressed against my body between layers of clothes.

Death swallowed. The literal embodiment of the end gulped before his pants dissolved like shadows.

My mouth went dry at the sight of him. Thick and long and curving back toward his stomach like it was seeking my hand. So, I reached out and fitted it around him. Fuck, it was so satisfying holding him like this. He was heavy and throbbing and so gorgeous, I didn't think I'd ever seen a cock look so good before. I wanted to devour it.

Death let out a strangled breath, his arm tightening around me like he was worried I would disappear at any moment.

I was literally pinned in place, but I didn't mind as I snuggled deeper into his side and began explore his wonderful cock.

My fingers stroked down the length softly, featherlight, and I peeked up at Death. His eyes were pinned to my hand, jaw clenched. I gave him a few more soft strokes, and when it sounded like he would never take a full breath again, I slid my hand down to his base and squeezed just hard enough to have him gasping. I kept that same pressure, and I stroked up to his head but stopped before touching it and back down again. Over and over until I had him panting. On another upward stroke, I slid my thumb over the blunted head and gathered the moisture there, spreading it around. The moan that tore from his lips was the best gratification I could have asked for.

I slid back down his shaft. He was throbbing more now, the blunted head becoming engorged and red. I tightened my grip, and as I slid up and down, I added a twisting motion at the tip, jerking the head just so, and watched as Death lost his mind.

He turned his head and buried his face into my hair, panting and growling words that I didn't think were in English.

I continued relentlessly until his hips jerked.

"Yes," he panted, "Like that, tighter."

I slowed down, loosening my grip just a little.

The arm that was around me became uncomfortably tight as he groaned.

"*Sonia*," he whispered, half breathless, half caught in another moan, as I jerked the tip in just the right way that I had found took his breath away.

"I like you saying my name like that," I murmured into the hollow of his throat.

"I'll scream it across the Deathscape if you will just—"

I fisted his cock and returned to my fast-paced pleasure of him.

The next sound from his mouth might have been my name, or a curse, or a plea, but whatever it was, it had me grinning, and Death stiffened right before pouring out his pleasure all over my hand and his stomach.

His body, still trembling, and my hand, still curled around him, were both drenched.

For a moment we just lay there, Death gasping into my hair. Then a cool tendril of shadows slipped over the bed, tangling up his legs and finding my hand first, somehow cleaning away the mess before moving on to Death's skin.

Death's body shivered faintly, every muscle drawn taut as if he couldn't quite remember how to *be* still. Shadows, once wild and restless, softened around us, curling protectively over the sheets like a living exhale.

He pressed his forehead to mine first, then buried his face against the curve of my neck. His breath came uneven—half pant, half sigh—as though the act of breathing itself was a forgotten language relearned in my arms.

"Thank you," he murmured, voice rough and low. The words vibrated against my skin. "It's been...so long."

I felt it then—the weight of centuries behind those few syllables. The loneliness. The ache of a being who'd watched everything die and had never once been touched simply for the sake of comfort.

His hands flexed at my back, possessive, anchoring me to him.

I stroked my fingers through his silver hair, feeling the faint pulse of magic under his skin, still thrumming, still alive. His heart—or whatever echoed as one—beat against my palm, a quiet, uncertain rhythm.

When he finally lifted his head, his silver eyes looked unguarded, almost boyish. "You shouldn't have given that to me," he said softly, wonder tangled with guilt. "There's no way I could let you go now."

I chuckled, pressing my face into the crook between his neck and shoulder, thinking that didn't sound so bad.

38

Crossing back into the Living Lands always felt like falling.

One heartbeat I was wrapped in the cool stillness of the Deathscape—the faint trace of his magic still clinging to my skin from a night of sleeping next to him—and the next, I was gasping in the warm, sunlit air of Keyleth's kitchen.

The world tilted. My vision blurred. Stars burst white-hot behind my eyes.

I gripped the counter, willing my knees to lock. The drain came fast this time, like the curse was waiting just under my skin, greedy for the magic I'd spent crossing realms.

It's fine, I told myself. *Just fatigue. Just the usual pull.*

But the pounding in my head said otherwise.

"Byrd."

I startled.

McDara sat at Keyleth's tiny kitchen table, mug in hand, sleeves rolled to his elbows. The sunlight cut across his face, catching the faint stubble on his jaw. He looked like he'd been waiting for a while—like maybe he'd been waiting for *me*.

His eyes swept over me, sharp and assessing. With mortification I realized I had no underwear on. Death had destroyed them, and my sleep shorts were...gods I hoped he couldn't tell.

"You just came from the Deathscape, didn't you?"

"What?" I squeaked, trying to act casual even as the floor felt like it might slide out from under me. "Morning to you, too."

"Were you there all night?" His tone wasn't angry—just tight, controlled in that way that meant he was anything *but* calm. His gaze dropped to my clothes. "You're wearing pajamas."

Embarrassment hit me in full force—heat painting my cheeks and throat. The memories from last night tangled with the lie I was about to tell.

"I was training," I said quickly. "Guess I fell asleep. You know how it gets."

The lie came too easily. It even sounded believable. You know, if I trained in my pj's...

Before he could say anything else—before he could *look* at me like that again—I brushed past him. "I need to change."

"Sonia—"

"I'm fine," I said, too sharp.

His silence followed me down the hall, heavy as a hand on my back.

I closed the door behind me, leaned against it, and exhaled hard. My pulse still hadn't steadied. I could feel the echo of the Deathscape in my veins—his magic and mine still intertwined.

And under all of it, a whisper of what I'd felt waking up in Death's arms. He hadn't been gone when I woke this time and it was...

The quiet. The warmth. The safety I shouldn't have wanted.

I leaned against the door, willing my pulse to stop trying to outrun my thoughts.

Clothes. Focus on clothes.

I dug through my bag until I found something that felt like *me*: dark ripped jeans, my favorite velvet, sapphire top, and a vintage leather jacket that still smelled faintly of bergamot and old paper. Classic Sonia Byrd—functional, comfortable, a little goth. The girl who dealt with ghosts and coffee orders, not gods and monsters.

I pulled the top over my head and stared at my reflection in the mirror above the dresser. My face looked the same—maybe a little paler, eyes a little too bright—but something *felt* different.

A laugh escaped me—soft, incredulous. "Bless the Woods, I'm losing it."

But the thought wouldn't leave.

He hadn't had a friend since the 1300s. The *1300s*. Centuries of silence. Centuries without anyone daring to reach for him, to talk back, to tease him. And now...me.

I buttoned my jeans, trying to ignore the warmth blooming in my chest.

He had me because of our bargain, but that needed to be it. I couldn't actually...like him.

But most of our kisses weren't because of the bargain. The two times he made me come surely weren't...

I wasn't supposed to even *like* him. Trusting Death was insane. Yearning for him was worse. He was ancient, dangerous, unpredictable—and yet I kept leaning toward him like he was gravity itself.

It was crazy that I felt safe in his arms.

Crazier that I missed his touch the second I stepped away.

And absolutely deranged that I wanted to see that rare, real smile again—the one that softened everything sharp about him.

I still didn't know completely what he got out of our bond...

I brushed my hair back, staring at myself in the mirror.

This wasn't supposed to happen.

I wasn't supposed to pick at him, tease him, crave the way he teased me back.

But maybe it was too late for *supposed to.*

Because if I was being honest—really, brutally honest—Death was already well on his way to getting my heart.

When I finally stepped out of my room, the apartment smelled like cinnamon and rain—Keyleth's wards always carried the faint scent of whatever the weather was outside.

McDara was standing in the living room, framed by the window that overlooked the street in front of The Obsidian Quill. Morning light poured across his shoulders, catching in the dark strands of his hair. He looked carved from quiet worry and too many sleepless nights.

For a heartbeat, I just watched him. The steady rise and fall of his chest. The way his hands were braced on the windowsill, knuckles pale.

He turned when he heard me. "Hey."

"Hey," I said softly, still trying to shake the last of my nerves from earlier. "Where's Keyleth?"

"She had to open the Quill," he said, nodding toward the street. "She let me up before she left."

"Oh." I hesitated, unsure why he was here, but not wanting to ruin the fragile rhythm we'd managed to find these past weeks—the kind that almost felt like friendship, even if it was built over too many things unsaid.

I opened my mouth, fumbling for something casual to say, but McDara spared me the effort.

"I came to pick you up," he said.

My brow lifted. "Pick me up?"

He straightened from the window, crossing his arms loosely. "You said you could find the spot in the tunnels where you saw the rogue Mages. I pulled the maps, but we'll need to overlay them with your memory. Thought we'd start there before the next mist shift."

Relief unwound in my chest. "Yeah. Yeah, I can do that."

"Good." His mouth twitched, the hint of a smile barely there. "Grab whatever you need. I'll drive."

Before I could answer, a groggy voice drifted from the top of Keyleth's bookshelf.

"If you're going spelunking again," Phontine mumbled, hair sticking out in violet tufts, "we're getting coffee first."

I laughed, the sound breaking some of the morning heaviness. "That's fair."

McDara glanced up at the tiny Pixie sprawled across a stack of Keyleth's novels, one brow arched. "Do I even want to know how much caffeine she can handle?"

Phontine yawned. "All of it."

I smiled and grabbed my bag. "Coffee to go, then tunnels. Deal?"

McDara nodded, his eyes softening. "Deal."

I expected him to turn toward the outskirts of Old Town—the entrance to the tunnels—but instead McDara veered right, heading deeper into Old Town.

"Uh," I said after a few blocks, watching the familiar spire of the precinct come into view. "You do know the tunnels aren't under the police station, right?"

He shot me a look that was almost a smile. "Calypso reached out early this morning. Said she has information about the rogue Mages. I figured we should hear what she has to say before we go crawling around blind."

Calypso.

I hadn't heard from her since I left the twins' apartment. The mention of her name stirred a mix of warmth and unease in my chest.

The closer we got to the station, the louder the city became. Sirens wailed in the distance, a pulse that never stopped. Outside the precinct, Mages and human officers alike were shouting orders, phones ringing, the air thick with the sharp bite of ozone and tension.

Inside was worse.

The lobby buzzed with movement—dispatchers, detectives, Enforcers in spell-resistant gear. The walls hummed faintly with protective wards, and even they seemed strained, the sigils flickering. The whole building vibrated with the sense that Blakewell was hanging on by a thread.

For the first time, I realized how little of the mist's collapse I'd actually seen. The chaos, the fear—it wasn't confined to one corner of the city. It was everywhere. And if it didn't stabilize soon, Blakewell might not survive it.

McDara moved fast through the noise, cutting down the hall that led to the lower offices. I followed, my boots echoing against the tile.

He opened the door to his and Dom's shared office without knocking.

Dom was already there, sitting at his desk, a stack of case files spread in front of him. Calypso occupied the guest chair across from him, her hands wrapped around a steaming mug that smelled faintly of over-boiled coffee.

She looked up immediately, and her face lit up when she saw me. "Sonia!"

I blinked, taken aback by how genuine her smile was. "Hey."

"It's so good to see you." She set the mug down and stood, brushing her skirt smooth. "I've missed having you as a roomie. It was nice having someone around who wasn't Pandora and her dramatic monologues about the downfall of modern Mage society."

Dom snorted into his coffee.

Despite myself, I laughed. "Yeah, I can imagine."

Calypso grinned, her gold eyes bright. "I mean, I love her, but she could make a comedy sound like a funeral."

McDara shut the office door behind us, the sound muffling the noise from the hall. He crossed his arms and gave Calypso that steady, patient look that meant he was about to steer us back to business.

"Alright," he said. "You said you had information about the rogue group?"

Calypso's smile faded, and she nodded. "I do. And you're not going to like it."

Calypso reached into her satchel, pulling out a thin stack of papers bound with string. The edges were smudged with ink and dust, faint scorch marks running across one corner.

"I took these from Elias's field journal," she said, glancing up at McDara. "He's been working on who's behind the mist longer than anyone, and Pandora's just started helping him and his team."

Dom let out a low whistle. "You stole a Mage investigator's notes?"

Calypso's lips curved faintly. "Borrowed. He won't know they're missing until I tell him I took the notes to help his investigation."

McDara crossed his arms. "You realize that by sharing this, you're going directly against what Matron Black would want. And against your own House members."

Calypso met his gaze steadily. "I know. But I also know Sonia." Her voice softened when she looked at me. "The moment she told us about seeing those rogue Mages in the tunnels, I could tell she wouldn't let it go. She's going to look into this—with or without anyone's blessing. And I don't want my friend getting herself killed."

Her words hit somewhere deep in my chest. I could see genuine concern in the way her hands trembled slightly as she passed me the pages.

McDara, though, stayed quiet. I could feel the suspicion radiating off him. He didn't say it aloud—he wouldn't, not until we got all the information we needed—but I knew what he was thinking. That this was too neat. Too convenient. That maybe Matron Black was using Calypso as her pretty, kind-eyed mouthpiece.

I met his glance briefly and gave a small shake of my head. *Let me read first.*

The papers smelled faintly of dust and ozone. I spread them across the desk, my eyes scanning the scrawled handwriting. The deeper I read, the colder my stomach became.

"Blakewell," I murmured, "is built on a raw magic rupture."

That tracked eerily well with Grace's note that veins of raw magic, ley lines, sprouted out from Larkend.

Calypso nodded. "A pre-Wood ley line that comes from the raw-magic source Larkend is built on top of. There are several of these ley lines that sprout out from the original source. These raw-magic sources and ley lines are older than recorded magic itself. Older than the Woods that appeared in 1872."

McDara leaned closer, brow furrowing. "And the Council?"

"Besides ignoring any mention of magic existing pre-Wood era? They installed a siphon node here in 1999"—she said, tapping one of the diagrams—"to power the mist. It's not just a barrier—it's a siphon field. Draws on the raw energy bleeding through the rupture."

Dom cursed under his breath. "So the mist isn't protecting the city—it's draining it."

"Not exactly," Calypso said carefully. "The mist uses the energy to power an illusion field. It keeps humans from panicking when they see Magicals. A glamour, of sorts. But…"

She hesitated, glancing at me before finishing. "The rupture's unstable. Too much energy is leaking out now. The siphon can't handle it anymore. That's why the mist is failing."

"So, someone has started siphoning off more raw magic alongside what the mist is taking, and now we're seeing the effects?" Dom asked.

The words hit like a thunderclap.

My heart kicked hard against my ribs. "If it collapses completely—"

"Blakewell will tear itself apart," McDara finished quietly. "It will be another Larkend."

For a long moment, none of us spoke. The noise of the precinct outside the door felt far away, muffled, unreal.

The city wasn't just in danger.

It was dying.

And somehow, I couldn't shake the feeling that my curse, Grace's research, and this rupture under Blakewell were all threads of the same knot tightening around us. And it all led to Larkend.

By the time we left the precinct, resolve had sharpened every edge of the morning.

Dom had the car running before McDara even reached the curb, the engine growling like it shared his mood.

"They're bleeding magic from the node," McDara said as we sped through the narrow streets. "If they keep it up, the rupture will widen. We find them, we stop them. No more waiting for the Council to clean up its own mess."

Dom gave a short nod. "I'll take the west access. Sonia, you and McDara hit the southern tunnels—the place you saw them last. Calypso, you're with us until you link up with Elias and Pandora's team."

Calypso's emerald eyes glimmered in the rearview mirror. "If we cross paths, I can vouch for you. Elias and Pandora are technically supposed to arrest outsiders poking around down there. I'd rather avoid that paperwork."

Her attempt at humor didn't quite land. The car was too quiet, the air too heavy.

When we reached the old service streets of Blakewell's abandoned tram station, Dom took the lead and steered us away from the midday traffic lull, his voice low but steady as he outlined the plan. "Easiest way down is the old drainage access—the one with the broken grate. Big tunnel, runs under the tram line. Been open for years."

Phontine clung to my jacket collar, wings quivering. "I swear, every time we do something like this, my lifespan shortens by a decade."

"Do Pixies have decades or are you all immortal?" I whispered back.

"If I die of stress tonight, you'll have your answer."

Calypso adjusted the small satchel at her side, wards gleaming faintly along its strap. "Before we go in," she said quietly, "there's something you should know."

McDara stilled. "Now's not the best time for surprises."

"This one is," she replied. Her gaze met mine. "Matron Black's issued a Mage-wide alert. If any House member sees you, Sonia, they're to detain you and bring you to her immediately."

The words hit like a slap of cold air.

"What?"

"She's suspicious of everyone after you stole the key, and she's on the war path," Calypso said. "I'm guessing it's also connected to your little escape from the House. Whatever she's planning, she doesn't want you anywhere near it. So keep your hood up, eyes open, and stay close to them."

Phontine hissed, tiny sparks flaring off her wings. "That bitch."

McDara's jaw tightened. "She won't touch her."

Dom's voice carried from the shadows ahead. "Let's move, before someone else decides to check this place out."

We slipped into the tunnel.

The air was cooler here, thick with damp earth and the faint metallic taste of old magic. Our boots echoed softly against stone; Calypso whispered a light dampening spell that swallowed the sound a few feet away. Ahead, McDara's wardlight flared and dimmed in rhythm with his breathing.

I matched his pace, the adrenaline singing in my veins. Beneath the fear, a strange excitement built—like standing on the edge of something vast and dangerous and knowing I'd already chosen to jump.

If the rogue Mages were still down here, we'd find them.

And if Matron Black's people were looking for me—

They'd have to catch me first.

39

We walked through the darkened tunnel, McDara's light behind us a soft slow that barely gave me enough light to see by. I was grateful that Dom had taken lead. With his lion shifter eyes the darkened tunnel was no issue for him.

Phontine peeked from my collar, long, pointed ears twitching. "These are the tunnels that every kid in Blakewell dares each other to go near, right? The one supposedly haunted by headless Enforcers?"

Dom grinned over his shoulder. "That's the one."

"How do you know that, Phon?" I asked.

"While you're busy being haunted and touring the Deathscape," she huffed, "I might have been people watching."

"We can take on headless Enforcers." Dom shrugged.

Calypso rolled her eyes. "Real confidence-inspiring, Dom."

He checked his belt for weapons, still smiling. "Hey, nothing wrong with a little nostalgia."

But the smile faded when I spoke again. "The group I saw wasn't near Old Town. It was close to the Black House."

McDara turned from the passenger seat to look at me. "You're sure?"

"Positive. If we go through the Old Town entrance, we'll be walking halfway across Blakewell underground. It'll take hours."

The thought made my stomach tighten. Just imagining the weight of all that earth above us—miles of it—made it hard to breathe. The tunnels weren't just dark; they *pressed in.*

"Then we don't go that way," McDara said firmly. "We need an entrance closer to New Town."

Dom nodded. "The only other one I know is in the monument at the city center. The Council built over an old access shaft when they raised it. Still connects to the network."

Calypso blinked. "You're telling me there's a secret passage under the city's most famous landmark?"

Dom's grin came back, a flash of mischief. "It was a shock for me to learn about too while I was diving into city mapping plans for housing and the like. You know, it's not all that surprising seeing that they fence the monument off after dark."

McDara's gaze flicked to me. "That'll get us closest to the Black House. We'll go there."

The drive through Blakewell was strange that morning. The air itself felt charged, restless—magic flickering and pulling at the edges of things, like static before a storm. The invisible current of the mist was faltering; I could *feel* it, that faint hum that always lingered under my skin when the mist was steady, now rising and falling in uneven waves.

Outside, Old Town blurred past in shades of gray and bronze. Narrow, brick buildings leaned into the wind, their iron balconies heavy with dying ivy. Streetlamps still burned though it was full daylight, halos of gold diffused through the cold drizzle that hadn't quite become rain.

As we crossed into the city center, the air shifted. The streets widened into cobblestone plazas, lined with Gothic spires and slate rooftops blackened by centuries of smoke. The scent of roasted chestnuts and wet stone drifted through the cracked car window, mingling with the faint, metallic taste of magic bleeding into the atmosphere.

December had wrapped Blakewell in its gray coat—cold wind off the lake through the forest's edge, skies the color of old pewter, a city that looked beautiful even as it frayed at the edges.

Bless the Wood, November had passed in a blur of weeks. More time gone.

Dom parked at the curb, cutting the engine. The moment the car stilled, the hum of magic became audible; a low vibration rising from beneath the monument's base.

"Guess it's still active," Calypso murmured.

McDara stepped out, rolling his shoulders as if shaking off invisible weight. His magic stirred the air—quiet, contained, but powerful. I followed, boots crunching against the cobblestone, the monument's reflection stretching across the wet street like a black blade.

He approached the base, kneeling near a small circle of sigils half-buried under grime. "Council locked it down with sigils," he said, brushing his fingers over the markings. "But they never accounted for a group of rogues to hack the spellwork to get into the tunnels. The sigils are weakened from the rogues manipulating them over and over. This should be easy."

A faint smirk tugged at his mouth.

He pressed his palm to the stone. The sigils flared to life—pale blue light spilling across the marble like liquid. The monument shuddered. Then, with a deep grinding sound, a section of the base split open, revealing a spiral of iron steps descending into darkness.

Calypso whistled softly. "You know, I always wondered why the pigeons avoided this thing."

Dom peered into the opening. "Now we know. Into the abyss we go."

I swallowed hard, staring into the tunnel yawning beneath the monument. The air rising from it was cold and damp, tasting faintly of copper and ozone.

Phontine's tiny hand tightened in the fabric at my collar. "Still think this is a good idea?"

"No," I whispered. "But it's the only one we've got."

McDara looked back at me, offering a magic-warmed hand. "Stay close."

I took it, steadying myself as we stepped into the dark together.

The stone closed above us with a hiss of old magic, sealing out the daylight.

And Blakewell's heartbeat pulsed all around.

The air changed the moment the monument sealed above us.

Gone was the faint hum of the city, replaced by a silence so deep it pressed against the skin.

McDara conjured three small orbs of light—blue-white wardlight that floated above our heads, casting the tunnels in an uneven glow. Phontine added her own faint shimmer, her violet wings trailing luminescence that glinted off the damp stone.

The air smelled of iron and wet earth, old water and forgotten magic.

Our footsteps echoed.

Too loud. Too human.

The tunnels wound on and on, carved through the bedrock like veins. The walls were slick with condensation, sigils half-faded by time etched between layers of crumbling brick. Every turn looked the same. Every shadow seemed to breathe.

I hated it down here.

The weight of the city above felt heavy—like all of Blakewell's history was sitting on our shoulders. The darkness pressed close, thick as water. My pulse wouldn't settle, my breaths coming shallow, uneven.

Dom led the way, his flashlight bobbing ahead. Calypso followed close behind, fingers tracing sigils of protection along the walls as she walked. McDara stayed beside me, watchful, silent. The air between us hummed with shared tension in the wardlight.

When we finally reached a junction where five tunnels branched off, I felt the dread bloom low in my gut. One of the passageways had caved in, rubble piled high beneath a spray-painted sigil—crude, jagged, demonic in shape. The paint was dark and glossy, like something that had never fully dried.

I froze. "Here," I whispered. "This is it."

Everyone stopped.

Calypso tilted her head. "You're sure?"

"Positive." My throat felt tight. "I saw them here. Four Mages, dragging two sacks. They looked...heavy. Like bodies."

The silence that followed was absolute.

McDara's eyes flicked toward the open tunnels. "Which way did they go?"

I swallowed hard and pointed to the far-left passage, where the air seemed colder somehow. "That way."

He nodded once, jaw set. "Alright. Dom, Calypso, you each take a tunnel, and I'll take the one Sonia said she saw them go down. Only search deep enough to either confirm signs of the rogue Mages being there or not and then come right back here. Sonia, don't move from this spot."

I nodded. That was all I could manage.

Their lights drifted down the left corridor, growing smaller, smaller—until only faint glows marked their shapes in the dark. Then those, too, vanished.

The silence came rushing back.

My pulse was a drumbeat in my ears. The walls felt closer than before, the air thicker, harder to breathe.

Phontine landed on my shoulder, her glow dimming. "Sonia, you're okay. You need to breathe. In and out, okay?"

But I couldn't.

Not here. Not with the darkness pressing in like it wanted to crawl beneath my skin.

My hands shook. The sigil above the collapsed tunnel seemed to twist when I looked at it too long.

All I could think—*all I wanted*—was him.

"Death," I whispered. "Please."

The shadows stirred like a held breath exhaling. Then he was there—rising from the darkness like it had missed him.

I didn't even hesitate. I went straight to him, heart pounding, reaching for his chest. My arms passed through him.

Of course they did.

A broken sound left my throat, half laugh, half sob. "You're not...I can't—"

Amusement flickered across his face—soft, dangerous, beautiful. "It's alright, my Sonia."

He closed his eyes. The air pulsed. The shadows thickened, solidified, drew inward.

When he opened them again, the silver light there was blinding.

This time, when he reached for me, I felt him. Not completely—like touching someone through a thick sheet—but *enough*. Enough to feel the weight of his hand at my waist, the faint press of his thumb against my back.

The relief was instant and overwhelming. I leaned into him, inhaling that strange, cold scent that was his alone—like the darkness between stars, like the breath before a storm.

For the first time since we entered the tunnels, I could breathe again. And I didn't even let myself dwell on that fact that Death was gaining enough magic in the Living Lands to be almost solid.

For a long moment, I just breathed him in—cool air, the faint scent of storm and stone, that strange sense of stillness that always came with him. His presence quieted everything. Even my fear.

Then I forced myself to straighten, pressing a shaky hand through my hair. "I, uh...apparently have a thing about being buried alive," I said, aiming for humor and missing by a mile. "Who knew?"

Death's mouth curved, faintly amused. "Claustrophobia," he said softly, tasting the word like it was new to him. "Curious thing for someone who walks between worlds."

"Yeah, well," I muttered. "The in-between doesn't have ceilings."

His gaze flicked over the branching tunnels, silver eyes cutting through the dark. "What are you doing down here, Little Bird? Searching for those Mages you told me about?"

I nodded. "We think they're siphoning magic from the node of raw magic under Blakewell. We have to stop them before the rupture gets worse."

Death's expression darkened. "And in the process, you risk drawing the attention of the Matron who wants you caged—or worse." His shadows coiled around his wrists, restless. "Your priority should be getting to Larkend. Saving yourself. This city isn't worth your ruin."

"That's not your decision," I said quietly. "If the mist fails completely, it'll be chaos. The humans will panic. And if the world learns about the Mage Council experimenting on an entire city? If that comes out because Blakewell gets destroyed?" I shuttered. "Magicals will be hunted and Blakewell will be gone."

He stared at me for a beat too long, something unreadable flickering across his face. "You care too much for a world that will never understand you."

"Maybe," I whispered. "But it's still my world."

Before he could answer, footsteps echoed down the corridor.

The glow of wardlight returned—two orbs, moving fast Calypso, and Dom.

Calypso's light hit Death first, illuminating him in stark relief—dark coat, silver eyes, the faint shimmer of his not-quite-corporeal form. Her face drained of color.

"Get away from her!" she snapped, magic crackling across her palms. "Release her, you traitor—"

"Calypso, wait!" I held up a hand, stepping slightly in front of him. "It's okay! He's not—he's not a rogue Mage. This is Death."

The silence that followed was instant and absolute.

Dom blinked, looking from me to Death and back again. "Yeah," he said finally, a slow grin spreading across his face. "You'll get used to the god of Death hanging around eventually."

Calypso, however, wasn't smiling. She looked at me like I'd just said I was best friends with the plague. "You—*what*?"

"Long story," I said weakly. "Very long. But he's not here to hurt anyone."

Her gaze darted between us, wide-eyed, disbelief plain in every line of her usually polished composure. The golden glow of her magic faltered, flickering out.

I'd never seen Calypso look rattled before—not even when Deidre was being consumed by dark magic.

When she finally found her voice, it came out low, almost horrified. "You brought *Death* into the Living Lands."

Her words landed like a blow.

My heart sank. "Calypso, I didn't—"

She looked away, the movement sharp, too quick. Trying to reel herself back in, to smooth over what she'd just said. But the damage was done.

I felt the distance settle between us like a new wall in the already crumbling world.

Death's shadows tightened around me, protective—almost smug.

And for the first time, I didn't know which world I truly belonged to anymore.

Boots pounded against stone—fast, uneven. McDara's wardlight swung wildly through the dark as he sprinted up the tunnel toward us, his coat a blur, his magic sparking sharp and blue in the air behind him.

"Cillian?" Dom was already moving forward.

McDara didn't slow. His face came into view—ashen, jaw tight, eyes burning with the kind of urgency that made my blood go cold.

Death shifted instantly, his presence sharpening beside me, the shadows around him coiling tight. It was instinctual—the way he moved closer, like a barrier between me and whatever was racing toward us.

McDara's gaze flicked to him for half a heartbeat, shock flashing across his features. "You've got to be kidding me," he muttered, then snapped back to the others. "I found them."

"Who?" Calypso demanded.

"The rogue Mages," he said, breath coming hard. "And not just them. They were in the middle of a sacrifice when the Black House team intercepted them. It's chaos down there—Magefire, blood spells, everything. They're fighting right now."

Calypso's face drained of color. "Is Pandora with them?"

McDara's jaw flexed once. "Looked like it."

That was all she needed to hear. Calypso broke into a run, magic flaring gold around her like a second heartbeat.

Dom swore under his breath and took off after her.

I was right behind them, the tunnel vibrating under our boots. The air grew heavier with every step, the tang of burnt ozone and blood-magic thickening. The faint sounds of battle echoed ahead—shouts, the sizzle of wards colliding, a low, unnatural hum that raised every hair on my arms.

Death matched my pace without seeming to move, his form a darker shadow amid shadows. His silver eyes were molten now, fixed on the path ahead.

"Sonia," he said quietly, almost to himself, "you shouldn't be here."

"I have to be." My voice shook, but it didn't matter. "They need me."

He looked at me, and I could *feel* the war inside him—between instinct and reason, between the urge to drag me back into the Deathscape where I'd be safe and the impossible realization that I would never forgive him if he did.

"Every second you stay," he murmured, "you tempt fate. You do not have battle magic."

"I can summon ghosts," I said, breathless.

Ahead, Calypso's magic flashed brighter—gold and red colliding in a violent burst that lit the tunnel walls. Screams followed, too close now.

We rounded the bend, and the world erupted.

40

The tunnel widened without warning—stone giving way to a cavern so vast it could have swallowed a cathedral.

Light exploded everywhere.

Wards flared and collided midair, sigils snapping open like burning constellations as Mages hurled spell after spell across the open space. The air itself screamed with power. Threads of magic carved through the dark—emerald, gold, and blood-red, the colors searing afterimages across my vision.

The smell hit next: ozone, iron, scorched stone.

Calypso was already drawing her own sigil, sweeping her arm in a tight arc. The air shimmered gold, and her blast cracked against a rogue Mage's shield. Dom slammed his palm into the floor, stone buckling upward to form a barrier as a curse shot past him, sizzling against the wall. He pulled a long artifact from his belt that looked almost like a sword but glowed with runes that had to be of Fae origin.

McDara moved like water—precise, brutal. He spun a sigil with both hands, light flaring between his fingers before it burst outward in a rush of blue fire. The impact knocked two cloaked figures back, their sigils scattering like glass shards.

And through it all, that *sound.*

A deep, rhythmic pulse.

My gaze lifted—and my breath stopped.

In the center of the cavern, four humans lay on raised slabs of stone, white sheets draped over their still bodies. The skin of their arms and legs shimmered faintly with sigils drawn in something that wasn't ink. They'd been prepared—washed, anointed, *offered.*

Above them hovered the source.

An obelisk of raw magic spun in midair, blinding and dark all at once—light folding inward, devouring itself. It wasn't just magic; it was something older, wrong. My mind rebelled at the sight of it, trying to define what it was and failing. It felt alive, aware, watching.

If it grew—if it became whatever it was trying to become—

It would devour more than the city. It would devour *reality.*

The air rippled, pressing against my lungs. Every pulse of that thing's rotation bled emotion—terror, hunger, delight—and each wave scraped against my magic until it felt like my own power wanted to crawl out of me and join it.

"Sonia!" McDara's shout cut through the chaos. "Stay back!"

Too late. The pull had already hooked into me, invisible fingers dragging at the edges of my soul.

Calypso's shield shattered nearby with a sound like breaking glass. Sparks rained over us as she threw another ward. Dom roared something wordless and charged with inhuman speed, that Fae made sword flashing in his hands.

And then Death's hand closed around my wrist.

His grip burned cold, anchoring me. "Don't look at it," he hissed. "Don't *feel* it."

But I couldn't stop. The raw magic sang inside my bones—terrible, beautiful, endless.

For a heartbeat, I understood why someone would worship it. Why they would offer blood and breath to keep it fed.

Then the world snapped back. Death yanked me behind him just as a curse screamed across the cavern, splintering the rock where I'd been standing. His shadows exploded outward, forming a wall of smoke and bone that deflected the blast.

The sound of battle was deafening now—sigils cracking, magic howling, human screams swallowed by the roar of something that wasn't human at all.

And in the center of it all, that spinning heart of raw creation pulsed again—faster, brighter, hungrier.

Blakewell was bleeding magic.

And if we didn't stop this, it would bleed the world dry.

Everywhere I looked, the fight was splintering.

McDara's wards were flickering under a barrage of red-fire sigils; Dom was bleeding from a cut on his shoulder, his magic sword flaring wild with every strike. Calypso and two Black House Mages were locked in a desperate defense circle, barely holding a shimmering dome against the rogue Mages' relentless cursefire. And all I could make out of Pandora was the tangle of her black curly hair through the masses of bodies.

A lucky shot zinged toward McDara's back and split the fabric of his jacket open, deep enough for a spray of blood to fan out behind him.

"McDara!" The wail tore my throat raw, my body shaking in the clutches of Death's shadows.

They were losing ground.

I could *feel* it—the slow collapse of their shields, the raw magic in the cavern pressing harder, feeding on the chaos like it wanted to swallow it whole.

And something in me broke open.

If the dead could defend the living once, they could do it again. I had used Orlla as a shield against Deidre's Maleficaria magic. I could do it again.

I dropped to my knees, pressed my palms to the stone, and reached inward—past fear, past exhaustion—down through the layers of myself where my magic lived. It felt like diving into an ocean made of light and memory, every heartbeat a ripple through water.

Come to me.

The first thread answered like a whisper brushing my ear. Then another. Then a dozen more.

The air turned cold. The fog of my breath ghosted around me as the veil between worlds thinned.

Figures began to form—translucent shapes rising from the cracks in the floor, faces half remembered. They shimmered, silent but waiting.

"Protect them," I breathed. "All the ones my heart has a tie to."

They moved.

The ghosts surged forward, taking the brunt of the next volley of curses. Spells collided with their forms and diffused into harmless sparks. For one heartbeat, the tide turned—Black House Mages gasped in disbelief as phantom shields rose around them, spectral hands deflecting hexes and blades of energy.

McDara threw me a look that was half awe, half warning. *Be careful.*

But I was already at the edge of what I could hold.

The magic roared inside me—too much, too fast. Every ghost I'd summoned was pulling at me now, a hundred invisible threads anchored in my chest. My bracelet began to glow, the sigils carved into them igniting like molten silver.

"*Sonia!*" Death's voice was somewhere behind me—low, sharp, commanding. But I couldn't stop. The ghosts were protecting them—protecting *us*. I had to hold it.

"Just a little longer," I gasped.

Then the first thread frayed.

Light exploded up my arms. Pain seared through my veins, so white-hot it was soundless. The air screamed, and the connection snapped.

The backlash wasn't just energy—it was like the world turned inside out.

Every ghost I'd called screamed as they were yanked backward, torn from the Living Lands in a flash of blinding light.

And Death—

Death was ripped away with them.

I felt it happen. Felt his presence tear free from mine like skin being flayed from bone. My magic convulsed, fighting to hold him, fighting to *keep him here.*

"*No—!*"

A scream tore from my throat, raw and breaking. My knees hit the stone. The world fractured into shards of light and pain.

The silence that followed was unbearable.

My body convulsed, every nerve raw and burning where the bracelet had fused to my skin. The air stank of charred metal. I could barely see. The cavern twisted, my vision swimming with static.

He was *gone.*

Not just absent—banished. My magic had *forced* him back into the Deathscape.

The bond between us screamed in my chest at the sudden loss of him.

And through the haze of pain, I saw movement.

A figure stepping out of the smoke—one of the rogue Mages, his ceremonial robe torn, mask cracked to reveal eyes glowing with corrupted magic.

He was smiling.

And I had nothing left to fight him with.

Everything was noise and heat and pain. My head rang like it had been struck, and the stone beneath my palms seemed to sway. I tried to crawl backward, but my limbs didn't feel like they belonged to me.

The rogue Mage laughed—a low, gleeful sound that echoed off the cavern walls. "Look at you," he sneered. "A little Mage thinking they can live blindly in the mist."

He lifted his arm, fingers carving the air in a fast, practiced pattern. A freezing sigil burst to life, its edges glowing a cruel blue before it flared toward me.

"No you don't!"

Phontine darted forward, a streak of violet light. Her tiny body flared like a star as she threw up a shield sigil of her own. The freezing spell hit it and rebounded in a blast of shards and ice.

The rogue Mage screamed as frost crawled up his arm and spread over half his body, crystalizing his robes and skin in seconds.

"Serves you right," Phontine spat, wings shaking from the effort. Then she whirled to me, tiny hands gripping my hair, forcing my gaze to meet her glowing eyes.

"Focus, Sonia! Look at me."

"I—I can't," I gasped. The air burned in my lungs, my magic a frayed wire sparking under my skin. "Death—he's gone, I—"

"You'll see him again," she said, voice fierce, trembling. "But not if you die down here. Well, you probably will even if you die but it'll be a quick conversation! Now you're a sitting duck. Go to the Deathscape."

"I can't leave you—"

"I'll go to the Quill," she snapped, her wings flaring in a burst of light. "I'll be fine, you idiot. Just GO!"

The rogue Mage staggered, breaking through the frost inch by inch. His magic flared again, hungry and wild.

My vision blurred, his form splitting and reforming like a bad dream. Phontine's face was the only steady thing left in the world—tiny, furious, and glowing.

I pressed a blood-slick hand to the floor, scraping up what was left of my strength. My magic shuddered inside me, broken and jagged, but it still *answered.*

The Deathscape tugged.

Cold, red light bled into the edges of my vision. The smell of ozone gave way to dust and heat. The sound of fighting fell away like a door slamming shut.

Phontine's voice followed me into the darkness. "You better be alive when I get back, Byrd!"

And then the world fell out from under me—and the Deathscape swallowed me whole.

The fall tore through me like lightning.

One heartbeat I was in the tunnels—screaming, burning, bleeding—and the next, the world cracked open. I hit the red sand hard enough to drive the breath from my lungs.

For a moment, I thought I'd died.

Everything was silent but for the low hum of the wind and the pulse of my own heart. My bracelet still burned, a steady, searing ache against my skin. I tried to move, but my body refused. Every muscle was locked, trembling. I could only lie there as the desert's crimson dust began to drift over me like a burial shroud.

The Deathscape stretched out forever—an ocean of scarlet dunes under a sky the color of tarnished silver. The black mountains on the horizon pulsed faintly, as if they were breathing.

Then the sound came.

A roar.

It was ancient and bone-deep, shaking the sand beneath me. The kind of sound that wasn't meant for mortal ears.

I turned my head, every movement agony.

Something vast was tearing across the horizon—a shape born of nightmare and divinity both. It moved like a storm given form, pounding across the dunes in a blur of red dust and shadow.

The beast was enormous, a hound-shaped silhouette wreathed in living darkness. Its eyes burned white-silver, its body formed of interlocking blades of shadow that shifted like armor. Where fur should have been were shards of night itself—each movement catching edges of light, gleaming like weaponry. The ground died beneath its paws, sand turning black where it touched.

Death's beast.

My breath hitched.

It was hunting.

The roar came again—less fury now, more anguish—and it cut through me like the echo of a broken vow.

Closer.

Closer.

The beast slowed when it saw me. Its massive form skidded to a halt, dunes collapsing in waves around it. For a heartbeat, it stood over me, vast and terrible, every breath a thunderclap. Then its shape began to unravel—shadows sloughing off in sheets until the nightmare dissolved into something nearly human.

Death knelt in the sand where the creature had been, his eyes bright with silver fire, his hands shaking as he reached for me.

I wanted to tell him I was fine. That I'd tried to stay safe. But no sound came out.

He gathered me up as if I weighed nothing, his touch cold and careful. The last thing I saw before the darkness closed in was the storm of shadows curling protectively around us—his fury, his fear, his relief all tangled together.

And then there was nothing but the steady rhythm of his voice, low and ragged, whispering my name into the red wind.

I tried to speak, but my lips barely moved.

The red desert swayed around us in ripples of heat, and my tongue felt like sandpaper. "I didn't mean to—" The words slurred, half-formed. "I don't know why my magic...it pushed you away."

Death didn't answer. His silence was a living thing, pressing against my ribs.

He was all motion instead—his hands, cold and careful, moving over me like he was cataloguing damage. Shoulders. Arms. Hips. The press of his fingers over my ribs—slow, methodical, reverent and frantic at once. His touch sent tremors through the places my nerves still worked.

Then he found my wrist and tore my sleeve upward.

The smell of scorched skin hit first. The bracelet's gold surface had warped and blackened, sigils still burning faintly.

The sound that left him wasn't human. A snarl ripped through the air—low, guttural, and wrong. The kind of sound that made the Deathscape itself recoil.

"Easy," I tried to whisper, but he was already working, long fingers coaxing at the twisted metal.

When the bracelet finally came free, smoke curled from my skin. Death's eyes went incandescent—pure silver fire—and the light from them made the shadows around us tremble.

A thread of light appeared between the broken cuff and my chest, thin as silk but pulsing like a vein.

He hissed through his teeth. "A tether. Straight to your soul."

"What does that mean?" My voice was a rasp.

"It means," he said, voice dropping into something dark enough to chill bone, "that every time you used your magic, this cursed thing drank from it—until there would be nothing left of you but an open door. And the one who forged it could walk through. Puppet your body. Wear your soul like a mask. It's a subset of Maleficaria Enchantment magic that I haven't tasted on many ghosts but the ones who bore it..."

Revulsion turned my stomach. "Who would—"

But the question died as he crushed the bracelet in his hand. The metal shrieked before dissolving into ash. The tether snapped with a flash of pain so sharp I cried out.

Then he caught my chin in his hand, forcing my gaze up to meet his.

"You're drained near to ruin," he said, voice soft now but edged with command. "I can give you a drop of my power—no more. You've already had some. Anymore, and I risk burning what's left of your humanity."

I should have protested. I didn't.

When his mouth met mine, it wasn't gentle. It was a collision of cold and heat, of night pouring into my veins. Power slid through me like a tide—pain first, then pleasure so intense it bordered on agony. My raw magic knit together under the surge, the hollow places filling with light.

I gasped when he finally broke the kiss. The world steadied; color returned to the edges of things.

Death's eyes were still silver, but darker at the rims, dangerous.

"Now," he said, voice no longer quite a whisper—more the echo of a thousand tombs. "Who gave you that bracelet?"

I swallowed hard, the taste of his magic still burning on my tongue. My whole body felt heavy, hollowed out and filled again with something that didn't quite belong to me. The Deathscape wind moaned around us, stirring sand over his boots, whispering through my hair.

"I didn't..." My voice caught. "I didn't know it was cursed."

Death didn't move. His eyes were still molten silver, the faintest tremor of restraint flickering through the glow. "Then tell me," he said quietly, each word precise, "who put it on your wrist?"

I stared down at the faint scorch mark where the bracelet had fused to my skin. The edges of it were still raw, pulsing faintly with leftover heat. My mind tried to work through the fog—back to when I first got it.

"It was a gift," I said slowly. "From the twins. And Elias."

A shadow passed over Death's face, subtle but unmistakable.

"They said it was like a friendship bracelet and that having allies in the House was important. I thought—" I swallowed again, my throat tight. "I thought it was kind. That they wanted to be my friend."

"Who handed it to you?"

"Elias," I said, trying to remember every detail. "But Calypso and Pandora...they both had one just like it. That they were meant to match."

The memory twisted something deep in my chest. Calypso's small smile, and the way she had said it suited me. Pandora's dry teasing. Elias's quiet assurance.

I shook my head, dazed. "I don't know which of them meant harm. Or if they all did. I just—" My voice broke. "Calypso's my friend. I *don't* want to believe—"

Death's hand slid to the back of my neck, fingers curling possessively, grounding me. "You want to think she's innocent," he murmured, the words both understanding and dangerous. "But you've been surrounded by liars for too long, my Sonia."

His tone wasn't cruel, but it carved right through me.

I met his gaze, forcing myself not to look away. "She wouldn't hurt me."

Something flickered across his expression—something that might've been pity or rage, or both. "Perhaps not by intent. But intent doesn't stop poison from killing."

His thumb brushed my pulse point, lingering there like he was memorizing it. His power curled faintly through the air around us—restless, protective, hungry for retribution.

"I'll find out who touched that magic," he said. "And if it was her—if it was *any* of them—"

"Don't," I cut in, my voice small but shaking. "Please, don't go after them."

Death's smile was a shadow. "I'll make no promises I can't keep."

The red wind carried the sound of his low growl away into the endless desert. And even though the warmth of his magic still pulsed in my veins, I couldn't shake the cold that followed.

I could still taste the ashes of the melted bracelet in the air. Death hadn't moved from where he held me close, his power restless, shadows twitching like they wanted to devour something. The silver fire in his eyes hadn't dimmed.

"You're staying here," he said at last, the words cutting through the red wind. "Until your magic has mended."

I blinked, the statement hitting harder than it should have. "You can't be serious. Everyone's still in the tunnels—the rogue Mages—"

"You," he interrupted, voice low and sharp, "barely lasted seconds down there." His tone snapped like a whip, and his shadows flared—those terrible, beautiful things that seemed half alive. "You have no fighter's training, your veins are full of borrowed power, and you nearly tore your soul apart today."

The words stung. I flinched before I could stop myself.

He saw it. The fury drained from his face like the tide pulling back. "Sonia," he said more softly, the sound my name made on his tongue quieter, almost tender. "I did not mean—" He exhaled, long and rough. "You frightened me."

That stopped me cold.

Death didn't get frightened.

He leaned closer, his expression unreadable now—half shadow, half man. "Come," he said, and his voice carried that low note of inevitability. "You need to rest. I will take you home."

I didn't fight him. I couldn't. My body was trembling again, exhaustion chewing through every muscle. I let him carry me to his home.

The desert blurred.

A blink later, we were standing in his livingroom—a fire of red flames and shadow roaring inside the stone mouth of a beast. It smelled of heat, ash, and him.

Death sat me on the couch and all but tucked me into it. He gathered every white fur he owned—half a dozen, soft as clouds—and piled them over me like he was trying to bury me in warmth. Then he stretched out beside me, one arm around my waist, the other tangling absently in my hair.

For a long moment, he just held me. His breathing was steady but too deliberate, like someone relearning the rhythm.

"I haven't felt fear since the Black Plague," he said finally, the words barely above a whisper. "Not when kingdoms fell. Not when the Viel Keepers turned me into this. But when your magic expelled me today..." His voice broke off, a rasp of shadow. "The last thing I saw before I was thrown into the Deathscape was you surrounded by spells that could easily take you from me permanently. I remembered what it was to be powerless."

My throat ached. I wanted to tell him I was sorry, that I hadn't meant to, but the words wouldn't come.

He brushed a strand of hair from my face, his touch cool and lingering. "You carry so much grief inside you," he murmured. "It hums in your soul like a chord I cannot quiet."

I frowned faintly, too tired to understand. "What do you mean?"

His gaze met mine—unflinching, ancient, and full of something that almost looked like sorrow. "I thought you would have mentioned it the closer the date came but you did not. Then I realized, with you fighting your own battle with this bloodline curse, you did not remember that the one year anniversary of your father's death is approaching."

The world went still.

I hadn't realized. The date hadn't even crossed my mind. Between the curse, the tunnels, the danger...I'd forgotten.

Guilt punched through me, sharp and immediate.

Death's arm tightened around me, pulling me closer as if he felt it too. "He has not crossed over yet," he said, voice soft as the falling sand outside. "There is still a small window in which I can let you say your goodbyes."

41

For a heartbeat, I couldn't breathe.

The words didn't make sense at first—like my brain refused to process them. *He has not crossed over yet.*

My father.

My dad.

The man whose voice still haunted my dreams, whose laugh echoed in half-remembered corners of my mind, whose death had cracked the world open and left me bleeding in the ruins.

I could see him again.

The thought slammed into me with the force of a tidal wave—sharp, blinding joy cutting straight through the exhaustion and pain. It was too much, too fast. I gasped, clutching at Death's sleeve as if to anchor myself.

"You mean—he's still—?" My voice came out jagged, trembling between disbelief and hope.

Death nodded once, the movement slow, deliberate. "He lingers on the edge of the Veil. Not many souls do for this long. But his tether has not yet broken."

I shot upright, fur blankets falling away, my pulse hammering in my ears. "Then take me to him. Now. Please, before—"

A dozen fears collided at once. *What if I'm too late? What if the window closes? What if this is my only chance and I waste it by asking questions instead of moving?*

"Please," I said again, the word tearing out of me. "You don't understand—I've wanted—" My voice cracked, a sob clawing up my throat. "I need to see him. I need to tell him—"

Death caught my wrist before I could stand, his cool fingers firm but not unkind. "Sonia."

"I can't lose this," I choked out. "You said there's a window—so we go now, right? Before it closes. We can go right now."

His silver gaze searched my face, unreadable but impossibly gentle beneath the cold. "You would go as you are?" he asked softly. "Broken, half-drained, your magic barely holding your soul together?"

"I don't care." The truth tore from me, raw and trembling. "If it kills me, I *don't care.*"

Something dark flickered in his eyes—fear, maybe, or fury at the thought. His thumb brushed the inside of my wrist, right over the faint mark where the cursed bracelet had burned me.

He sighed, a sound that carried centuries. "Always rushing toward death," he murmured, almost to himself. Then, louder: "You will see him, Sonia. I will make it so. But not until I know you will survive the meeting."

I shook my head, frantic. "You can't make me wait—"

"I can," he said, the echo of eternity in his tone.

"Please."

That one word pulled a sigh from him that was dread and agony and surrender all in one fragile sound.

The Deathscape around us seemed to hold its breath—sand whispering, shadows shifting closer. I pressed my hand to my mouth to keep from crying, every inch of me trembling with need and fury and hope all tangled together.

Somewhere out there, my father's soul was waiting.

And I would burn through every ounce of magic I had left to reach him.

The room dissolved around us.

The air twisted—light bending, shadows folding—and then we were standing somewhere else entirely.

I staggered, breath catching. The ground beneath us wasn't sand anymore but smooth white stone, cold as bone. Pale mist drifted across its surface, curling around my boots and spilling over the edge of what I realized wasn't a floor at all—a bridge of rib-like arches suspended above an abyss. Below, rivers of light moved in slow, spectral currents.

Columns rose on either side, carved from the same pale material, etched with sigils that pulsed faintly, like a heartbeat. Above, the sky was neither dark nor light—just an endless sweep of silvery gray, threaded with veins of shadow. The whole place thrummed, alive and watchful.

It was beautiful. And wrong. Like walking on the bones of something divine that could crush you for daring to exist here.

"Where are we?" I breathed.

"The Veil Garden," Death said beside me, his voice echoing softly through the mist. "The place where my realm meets the others—where the layers of the Bone Veils converge. Souls can move on to their final resting place anywhere in the Deathscape, but some that have wandered too long in my realm find themselves here. Others come here because their souls are damned to another layer of the Bone Veils."

My heart jolted. "Then my father—"

"He is near," Death said. "Close enough that I can reach him from here."

Death stood beside me, silent.

"Then do it." I turned toward him, desperate. "Please, before he crosses. Before—"

But he didn't move.

He was watching me instead, too still, his silver eyes unreadable.

"What?" I demanded. "What is it?"

His gaze flicked briefly away, then back. "Since I began training you," he said slowly, "I have...interfered."

"Interfered?"

"I kept your father from passing on." His words fell like stones into the silence. "I held him here—between worlds—in the hope that you would one day have the strength to summon him yourself. But with the curse and the bracelet draining you, that time never came."

For a moment, I couldn't speak. The mists swirled around us, whispering like distant voices. "You—" My chest tightened. "You've kept him here this whole time?"

"Yes."

"Why?"

He exhaled, shadows curling around his shoulders like smoke. "Because I thought it might give you peace. If you were able to summon him and tell him your goodbyes. Those final words loved ones rarely get to speak."

I didn't know what to do with that—this man, this god, this monster—who could speak so gently about something so impossible.

But the tone of his voice was changing now. He sounded distant again. Controlled.

"What aren't you saying?"

"There is a cost," he said finally.

My stomach dropped. "What kind of cost?"

"The balance of life and death cannot be bent without consequence. By holding his soul here, I have already shifted that balance. If I summon him fully—if I bring him to you for a final goodbye—it will demand something in return."

The air grew colder. Even the sands seemed to still.

"What kind of something?" I whispered, though I already knew the answer wouldn't be one I wanted.

Death didn't answer right away. His eyes softened—just barely—but his expression stayed carved from marble.

I had wanted this moment for so long—*needed* it. To see my father again. To say goodbye. And now it hung in front of me like a blade, glittering with promise and threat in equal measure.

For the first time since coming to the Deathscape, I wasn't sure if I was standing on holy ground—or a trap I'd been walking toward all along.

Death's hands closed around mine.

The contact was cool, steady—almost human. But the way his fingers moved, threading through mine only to slip apart again, felt like he was stalling. Like he was giving himself one more heartbeat before he shattered something neither of us could mend.

When he finally looked at me, the shadows in his eyes deepened. The softness I'd seen in him—the quiet humor, the hesitant warmth—was gone. In its place stood the being I'd first met in the Deathscape: cold, divine, and utterly inhuman. Yet beneath the silver gleam of his gaze, something flickered.

"The price," he said quietly, "is memory."

I frowned. "What do you mean?"

His gaze didn't waver. "To see your father—whom you love—you must willingly give up the memory of loving another man."

For a heartbeat, I thought I'd misheard him. The words didn't fit together, not in any way that made sense.

"Wait...what?"

"You will remember him," Death continued, voice soft but unyielding. "His face. His words. The shape he holds in your life. But not the love. That emotion, that bond—it will be severed from you."

The world seemed to tilt. I pulled my hands from his grip, stumbling back. "That's not fair," I said hoarsely. "Why that price? Who decides something like that?"

He tilted his head slightly, shadows tightening around us. "Death and fate hold the balance between worlds. They decide what must be given to restore what is taken."

"That's not an answer." My voice rose, raw and unsteady. "You said *you* wanted balance—so is this your doing? Or is it *Fate's*?"

For the first time, he looked away. The air between us thickened, his expression unreadable. "I told you," he murmured, "the balance demands it."

The silence between us stretched, trembling.

I opened my mouth to demand more—to argue, to beg—but then he went still. His gaze snapped upward, over my shoulder, toward the Veil itself. The mist there had thickened, roiling with colorless light. The sound beneath it wasn't wind anymore—it was *whispering*. Dozens of voices, overlapping, urgent.

Death's expression hardened. "Your father's soul is weakening," he said, tone all command again. "He has lingered too long between realms. If I do not release him soon, he will decay into something twisted—a wraith bound to hunger instead of peace."

I froze. A flash of what Dr. Fenwick had almost become flooding my mind.

He looked back at me, silver light reflecting off the tears on my cheeks. "There is no more time, Sonia. Either I let him move on now...or you pay the price."

My breath hitched. My pulse was a drum in my ears.

To see my father again—to speak to him, to tell him I loved him, to finally say goodbye—I would have to give up the memory of loving another man.

McDara's face flashed through my mind—his sharp smile, the way he said my name, the way he always, *always* tried to protect me. The ache that had built between us like something living.

And yet, as that ache sharpened, another face flashed through my mind.

Death.

The way his voice could drop into something dark and velvet-soft when he teased me. The warmth that bled through his touch, even when it shouldn't exist. The quiet moments when he almost smiled—when he almost looked human.

It terrified me, how easily he'd become the one constant in a world that kept fracturing. How much I'd come to trust him.

The connection with Death was new. Not like the steady familiarity I felt with Mc-Dara.

But Death was the only one who had *stayed*.

For a heartbeat, I wondered—if I lost the memory of loving McDara, what would that make room for?

Would I still find Death's voice a comfort? Would the bond between us twist into something deeper...or darker?

The thought scared me almost as much as the choice itself.

But the image of my father—his laugh, his warmth—rose again, fierce and desperate. I couldn't lose him, not without saying goodbye. After all this was why I came to Blakewell in the first place.

I wiped my eyes, forcing my voice to steady. "I'll pay it."

Death stared at me for a long moment, his expression unreadable. Then, finally, he nodded once.

"So be it."

The air in the Veil Garden began to hum—soft at first, then louder, like the world itself was drawing breath.

And as the mists started to stir, I felt the weight of what I had just done settle into my bones.

The air around us changed.

The Veil stirred—its mist twisting upward, forming shapes like smoke trying to re-member how to be solid. Death stood beside me, his hand hovering at my back but not touching, his power coiling through the air like a storm held on a leash.

I could feel him watching me, but my focus was fixed on the Veil. On the voice I'd been waiting more than a year to hear.

And then—

"Sweetheart?"

The sound broke me.

My knees buckled. My father's voice—rough, warm, full of that soft laughter he always carried even when life kicked him in the teeth. I looked to the side, and there he was.

The fog thinned into the shape of a man—broad-shouldered, hair going silver at the edges, kind eyes crinkled at the corners just like I remembered. He looked solid and yet not; every outline shimmered faintly, as though the light couldn't quite decide if it should pass through him.

"Dad..." My voice cracked. "Oh gods—Dad."

He smiled that same lopsided smile that had once made every scraped knee and bad day better. "Hey, honey."

I threw myself at him before I could think, and somehow—impossibly—he caught me. His arms felt the way they always had: safe, grounding, real. I pressed my face into his shoulder, breathing in a scent that wasn't really there but still *felt* right.

"I've missed you," I sobbed. "So much. You and Mom—you gave me everything. You didn't have to, and you still did. You made me part of something. You made me belong."

He cupped the back of my head like he used to when I was little. "Oh, sweetheart. You were *always* meant to belong with us. The day we met you, your mom said she felt like she'd been waiting her whole life for you. She was right."

"I should've told you more," I whispered. "How much I loved you. How much you meant to me."

His smile trembled. "You told me every day. Every laugh, every call home, every time you rolled your eyes when I told the same bad joke—you told me."

Tears blurred everything again. "It's just not fair. You were fine that morning. You were fine."

"I know." His voice softened, wrapping around me like sunlight on old wood. "One minute I was driving home, thinking about what kind of cake your mom would make that night for my birthday, and then...it was just light. Quiet."

I clung to him tighter, terrified of letting go. "I can't do this without you. And Mom needs you too."

He pulled back enough to look me in the eyes, his expression tender but firm. "Yes, you can. You've always been stronger than you think. Having you join our family—Sonia, that completed us. I'd always wanted to be a father. When your mom and I couldn't have kids, I thought that dream had died. But the day we met you..." His voice broke on a small laugh. "It was like the world finally made sense. You made me the happiest man alive. And your mom has you, sweetheart. That is no small thing."

A sob tore out of me.

He wiped a tear from my cheek with his thumb. "You gave my life meaning, honey. You and your mom. And when it's your time, I'll be waiting right here—just past the river. For both of you."

The light around him flickered, the edges of his form unraveling like smoke in a breeze.

"Dad—" My voice choked. "I love you. By—bye."

He smiled one last time. "I love you, Sonia. Always will."

And then he was gone.

The fog closed, swallowing him whole, and the silence that followed was unbearable.

I sank to my knees, the ache in my chest hollow and infinite. Death stood a few paces behind me, watching, but for once even he said nothing.

Because there was nothing left to say.

I turned toward him, the fog still glowing faintly where my father had stood. My chest ached, but it was a sweet ache, threaded with something close to peace.

Death was watching me—still, unreadable, his eyes silver as moonlight. When I smiled through the tears, he moved without hesitation, drawing me into his arms. His hand slid to the back of my head, the other wiping the wet from my cheeks with a touch that trembled.

I closed my eyes and let myself breathe.

"He's alright," I whispered. "He's going somewhere good. I can see his thread. The one that has no end."

Death's breath ghosted across my hair. "He is," he murmured. "You gave him what he needed."

Relief unfurled through me—warm, bright, alive. For the first time in forever, the weight on my chest loosened. I opened my eyes to tell him thank you—

—and something shifted.

The warmth slipped. Slowly at first, then all at once. The brightness dulled, the edges of the moment softening, draining away.

I blinked up at him. He was still holding me, still smiling faintly—but the sight of that smile didn't send the same flutter through my chest. It didn't send anything.

"Death?" I asked, voice strange to my own ears.

The world felt distant, muffled. A film laid over reality. I still saw him—the lines of his face, the glint of silver in his eyes—but my heart didn't *react*. No rush of comfort. No quickening pulse. Just...nothing.

The hollow spread. All those moments—his teasing, his impossible gentleness, his hands guiding mine through spells—blurred at the edges, stripped of color and feeling. They became fragments of a story I knew but didn't live.

I swayed.

Death's smile faded. "Sonia?"

"I feel...strange." My voice was barely there. "Like—like I'm forgetting something."

He went rigid. His hands came to my shoulders, gripping tight enough to make me wince. "No," he said, voice low, harsh. "No, no—"

He shook his head, eyes flashing. "It was the Mage. You love the Mage. Not..." His voice cracked apart, the last word lost in the tremor of it.

He released me only to pace backward, hands in his hair, pulling. "I'll fix it," he said, voice rising, ragged. "Do you hear me? I'll *fix this.*"

His magic erupted, shadows spinning out in chaotic swirls that made the air pulse with heat and cold at once. "I won't lose you," he said, almost shouting now. "I'll fix it."

"Death—"

He turned toward me, wild and radiant and terrifying. The silver in his eyes burned white-hot, and for the first time, he looked nothing like a god—only a man who'd finally broken under eternity's weight.

"I will find a way," he swore, every word shaking. "I will tear open the Veil itself if I must."

Before I could speak, the shadows collapsed inward, wrapping him in darkness.

I was alone in the Veil Garden, fog curling at my feet, the memory of warmth fading from my skin.

I knew who he was. I knew what he'd done for me. But my heart...my heart was silent.

And I couldn't remember why that hurt so much.

42

The Veil Garden was silent after he vanished.

Not quiet—silent.

The kind that pressed against your skin until you could hear your own heartbeat thudding in your ears.

The fog around me pulsed once and stilled. My legs felt unsteady beneath me, but I started walking anyway, because the stillness was worse. The Deathscape stretched out beyond the arches, vast and endless, red sand shifting beneath a poisoned silver sky.

Each step sank into the desert like it was swallowing me whole.

The horizon rippled. The black mountains in the distance looked closer than they should have been. The air carried a hum—low and constant—like the sound of a thousand voices murmuring through the dunes.

I didn't know where I was going. I just knew I couldn't stay where he'd left me.

My thoughts blurred—like pages from a book flipped too fast to read. My chest ached with a strange hollow grief, something raw and unnamable that wasn't about saying goodbye to my father. It felt fresh, bleeding. Like losing someone twice without remembering the first time.

I pressed a trembling hand to my sternum. "You can't fall apart now," I whispered.

That was when I saw her.

At first, it didn't register. A figure kneeling in the sand, her raven curls catching what little light there was. For a dizzy moment I thought it was a trick—the way the Deathscape sometimes mirrored things that shouldn't be here.

But then she turned her head.

"Calypso?" My voice broke on her name.

She looked up. And my blood ran cold.

Her eyes—those bright, emerald eyes—were clouded and dim. The entire front of her shirt was soaked dark, torn open. I saw the wound before I could look away—deep, ugly, as if someone had gutted her with spellfire.

"No," I whispered. "No, no—"

Calypso blinked slowly, her expression distant. "I told Pandora we shouldn't follow the rogue leader into the tunnels without wards," she murmured. "But Elias said it was fine. He said we were close."

Her voice was soft, but each word trembled with pain. She didn't seem to see me, not really.

I dropped to my knees beside her, reaching out but stopping short of touching her. "Calypso, it's okay, I've got you. We'll—we'll get you back. You're not supposed to be here. You just died, right? I can take you back to the Living Lands. It'll be like—like resuscitation."

She blinked again, confused, her lips parting like she hadn't heard me. "Pandora screamed first," she said, staring down at the blood pooling beneath her. "The mist wouldn't come. It—" She broke off, her gaze drifting past me toward the horizon. "It burned."

Tears blurred my vision. "Stop. Don't say that. You're fine, okay? You're fine."

The desert wind howled across the dunes, lifting strands of her hair and scattering red dust through the air.

"I can take you back," I repeated, voice breaking. "Please, just—let me."

I reached for her hand, but it was cold. Her hand had lost its substance but I should feel the threads of her soul, *her life*, beneath the hazy skin and I held onto that. My fingers passed through hers like smoke.

"Calypso…"

A sound caught in my throat—a mix of a sob and a scream. I'd just said goodbye to my father. I couldn't lose someone else. I couldn't.

The phantom grief in my chest sharpened, a weight I couldn't name pressing down harder. Something in me whispered that I'd already lost more than I remembered.

I pressed my forehead to my knees, shaking. "Please," I whispered to the air. "No more."

When I looked up again, Calypso was still kneeling there, her eyes fixed on something I couldn't see, whispering over and over, "It burned, it burned, it burned…"

The red desert shifted around us, dunes breathing in the stillness, the silver sky hanging heavy and watchful.

I could feel Calypso's presence flickering—thin, fading—like a candle guttering in wind. Panic clawed at my chest. I wasn't going to lose her. Not again. Not so soon after saying goodbye to my dad.

Closing my eyes, I reached inward—down through the tattered remains of my magic until I found the threads of the Veil itself. Faint lines of light shimmered beneath my skin, trembling like spider silk. And there—among the thousands of whispering voices—I felt it.

Calypso's thread.

It pulsed weakly, frayed and unraveling, but it was *hers*.

"I've got you," I whispered, curling my fingers in the air as if I could grip it physically. The thread vibrated, answering the call of my blood. "You're coming with me."

The Deathscape resisted at first—the sand around us rising like waves, the wind screaming in protest—but I held on, forcing my power through the bond. I pictured the Living Lands: the weight of real air, the smell of coffee, the golden light spilling through Keyleth's windows.

The magic burned through me, bright and brutal.

"Hold on, Calypso."

The world tilted. The desert fractured into light, red dust exploding upward like sparks. The ground vanished beneath us, and the pull of the Veil caught me by the ribs—violent, merciless.

And then everything inverted.

The Deathscape fell away in a rush of color and cold, and I was dragged, gasping, through the veil of worlds—taking Calypso with me.

The world slammed back into me like a fist.

Cold air. Damp stone. The scent of blood and ozone.

I gasped, lungs seizing, my knees hitting the tunnel floor. I was back in the Living Lands—alone. The air hummed with leftover magic, the kind that raised the tiny hairs on your skin.

"Calypso?" I called out, my voice echoing through the dark. "Calypso!"

Nothing.

Panic clawed up my throat. My magic still burned in my veins from the crossing, but I forced it to move—to feel—to *find her.* I stumbled through the tunnels, one hand dragging along the rough walls. Every few steps, my boots splashed through blood or water—I couldn't tell which.

Bodies littered the floor.

Black House insignias. Rogue Mages' masks cracked and broken. The stench of spent spellfire hung heavy in the air.

"Calypso!"

My voice broke on her name. The tunnels curved and split in dizzying directions. I took a left, then another, chasing the faint pulse of magic that felt familiar.

And then—

I saw her.

She was standing in the center of the tunnel, facing the wall, her black curling hair tangled and streaked with soot. Around her lay at least six bodies—some burned, some frozen, some simply...still.

"Calypso?" I whispered, terrified of the answer.

She turned slowly. Her eyes were unfocused, her expression blank, but she was *breathing.*

Alive.

I stumbled toward her, every muscle shaking. "Oh, gods...you're okay."

Her gaze slid over me without recognition, then focused. "Sonia?"

"Yeah. Yeah, it's me." I tried to smile, but my lips trembled. "You—" I cut myself off with a fragile breath that was more sob than anything. It didn't matter. She didn't need to know how close she was to...to loosing everything. "But you're back now."

Calypso blinked, frowning faintly as if trying to remember something. I looked down and saw her shirt—ripped, soaked in blood. The wound on her stomach was closed, the skin sealed but red and angry looking, like it was healing wrong.

My chest tightened.

No one knew she'd died. No one had seen her body fall.

And I—

I had brought her back.

It was like resuscitating someone, right? Like pulling them out of the dark before it was too late. It wasn't wrong. It couldn't be wrong.

"You're okay," I said again, mostly to myself. "You're fine."

The sound of boots and shouting echoed from down the tunnel.

"Sonia!"

I turned just as McDara and Pandora appeared, their clothes streaked with soot and blood. Pandora froze the instant she saw her sister. Her hands flew to her mouth, eyes wide, raw emotion spilling over her usually perfect composure.

"Calypso!"

She ran to her, pulling her into a hug, sobbing into her shoulder.

Calypso hugged her back—slowly, uncertainly—but she hugged her back.

And me? My legs gave out.

McDara caught me before I hit the ground. His arms closed around me, solid and warm, the smell of smoke and his cologne grounding me for the first time in hours.

"It's over," he said, his voice rough but steady. "We stopped them. The rogue Mages are gone. The Black House has control of the raw magic node again—for now."

I nodded numbly against his chest, my body trembling with exhaustion and leftover magic.

He pressed his cheek to the top of my head. "It's okay," he murmured. "You're safe."

But I wasn't sure what that meant anymore.

Because even as I clung to him, feeling the steady beat of his heart against mine, I felt... unmoored. My very blood, my magic was restless. Seeking and searching for something I didn't have a name for.

My body urged me to move but my mind, my heart... they were so quiet. A quietness that permeated through my very marrow and made my heart race even more. It was like my heart was insisting that something was missing. Lost.

I felt so lost.

A tear slipped from the corner of my eye and dripped through my lashes, chasing the path of my skin like it could find what I was missing.

And why that absence felt like grief.

T he study of the Black House was cloaked in shadow.

Candles guttered low in their sconces, their light catching on the ancient carved bone of Matron Black's desk. Before her sat an ornate wooden box, carved with sigils that pulsed faintly when touched. Its lid was open. Inside, silk-lined compartments held two strange relics—one a metal ring, the other a small oval locket.

The third space—its center—was empty.

Matron Black's long, jeweled finger tapped the rim of the box, once, twice, a soft rhythmic click that echoed through the stillness. "So," she said, her tone smooth as oil, "the bracelet failed."

Across the desk, the cloaked figure did not answer. They stood half in shadow, hood drawn low.

Matron Black's lips curved, though it was not a smile. "I had hoped," she continued, "that when the girl's magic finally drained under the strain of training, the tether would have allowed us to take control. To bend her into something useful." Her gaze flicked toward the box again. "But I see now I overestimated both the item's craftsmanship and your...restraint."

The figure shifted slightly, the faintest suggestion of movement beneath the cloak, but still said nothing.

Matron Black leaned back in her chair, studying the empty slot where the missing key had once rested. Her expression softened—not with warmth, but with something colder, more reflective. "Sonia is staying with a new friend," she murmured. "Find out everything you can on her. Any secrets. Anything useful."

The words hung in the air like incense—sweet, poisonous, and heavy with implication.

She let the silence stretch, watching the flicker of the candles reflect in her dark eyes. Then, at last, she closed the box with a quiet snap and steepled her fingers.

"Our first priority however," she said, voice returning to that smooth, dangerous calm, "is Sonia. Her twenty-fifth birthday is mere months away. You know what happens when a Ghost Whisperer reaches that age."

The cloaked figure inclined their head once—a single, slow nod.

With a clipped, elegant motion, Matron Black slid open a desk drawer and placed a dagger on the grey surface. Right over the etched sigils that pulsed in the faint light.

"I need you to destroy this." One tap on its bloodstained blade. "Next time we will have to make sure they don't leave the victim right where she can find them." The first signs of irritation marred her smooth voice, and the cloaked figure stiffened.

"She cannot learn about the curse's true nature." Black eyes narrowed, and the essence in the desk became restless as Matron Black watched the figure. "Do you understand?"

The cloaked figure nodded once, sharp, and reached for the dagger. The firelight caught only the faint gleam of a gold bracelet encircling their wrist, its surface etched with tiny moving sigils—and turned toward the door.

Matron Black watched them go, the faintest trace of satisfaction ghosting across her face.

"Soon," she whispered to the empty room. "The price will be paid, and the House will be safe again."

The candle flames flickered—and went out.

To find out what hunts Sonia next — and what Death is willing to become to keep her — continue reading with Ghost Stalker.

Don't Miss What Comes Next

Join my newsletter for exclusive content, sneak peeks, and book updates:
www.brittanyardenauthor.com
Follow for more Blakewell & behind-the-scenes:
Instagram & TikTok: @_brittanyarden_

Acknowledgements

Writing *Ghost Curse* was just as much of a whirlwind as writing *Ghost Whispers*—only this time, it happened while I was recovering from surgery. Much of this book was written while I was stuck in bed and my mind desperately needed somewhere else to go. I was grateful to have this story—to have Blakewell, Sonia, and all the chaos waiting for me when my body needed stillness.

To my family—thank you for your patience, your love, and for stepping in without question while I disappeared into this world yet again. Your support means more to me than I can ever properly put into words.

To my incredible friends, and to the best beta readers on the planet—Ashley and Sammy—thank you for your enthusiasm, your honesty, and for loving this story as fiercely as I do. Your feedback, excitement, and encouragement made this book stronger in every way, and I'm endlessly grateful for you.

To my editor, Katherine at Oak Moss Editorial—thank you for your insight, your care, and your steady guidance through this book. I'm so glad I was able to work with you on *Ghost Curse*, and I appreciate the time and heart you poured into helping shape this story.

And finally, to *you*—my readers—thank you for continuing this strange, beautiful, and thrilling journey with Sonia. Thank you for trusting me as she makes impossible choices and—most dangerously—falls for Death. I'm so grateful you're here for the ride.

Until the next adventure!

Brittany lives with her husband, two tiny adventurers-in-training, and a caffeine addiction that's probably sentient by now. With a background in literature, history, and a lifelong obsession with fairy tales (the darker the better), she was destined to write magic—and mayhem.

She writes romantasy for readers 18+ who want their magic dangerous, their love interests morally gray, and their romance served with the *right* amount of spice. Expect shadow-laced worlds, fantastical chaos, and at least one murder mystery she swears she *didn't* plan. (The stories have minds of their own, okay?)

When she's not wrangling plot twists or toddlers, you'll find her wandering in nature on her lunch break, daydreaming about curses, closed doors, and enemies who *really* should've kissed sooner.

She hopes her books make you laugh, gasp, ache—and maybe stay up too late whispering *"just one more chapter."*

Books by Brittany Arden: where ghosts whisper, tension smolders, and someone's definitely lying.

www.ingramcontent.com/pod-product-compliance
Lightning Source LLC
Chambersburg PA
CBHW032140050726
47591CB00001B/34